Mental Health in Ireland

About the Author

Brendan Kelly CPsychI FRCPsych FRCPI is Professor of Psychiatry at Trinity College Dublin and Consultant Psychiatrist at Tallaght Hospital. In addition to his medical degree (MB BCh BAO), Professor Kelly holds masters degrees in epidemiology (MSc), healthcare management (MA), Buddhist studies (MA) and an MA (jure officii); and doctorates in medicine (MD), history (PhD), governance (DGov) and law (PhD). He is also UCD Clinical Professor at University College Dublin (UCD) School of Medicine; a fellow of the Royal College of Psychiatrists (London) and Royal College of Physicians of Ireland; and a member of the College of Psychiatrists of Ireland. Professor Kelly has authored or co-authored over 200 peer-reviewed publications and 400 non-peer-reviewed publications. He has written several books including *Hearing Voices: The History of Psychiatry in Ireland* (Irish Academic Press, 2016) and *"He Lost Himself Completely": Shell Shock and Its Treatment at Dublin's Richmond War Hospital, 1916-19* (The Liffey Press, 2014).

MENTAL HEALTH IN IRELAND

The Complete Guide for Patients, Families, Health Care Professionals and Everyone Who Wants To Be Well

Brendan Kelly

The Liffey Press

Published by
The Liffey Press Ltd
'Clareville'
307 Clontarf Road
Dublin D03 PO46, Ireland
www.theliffeypress.com

A catalogue record of this book is
available from the British Library.

ISBN 978-0-9957927-1-5

Printed in Spain by GraphyCems.

CONTENTS

Part One
Specific Mental Illnesses

Contents

Contents

Part Two
Mental Health Care in Ireland

Acknowledgements

I am very grateful to the patients, families and colleagues who have worked with me over many years and contributed substantially to the shape of this book.

I am especially grateful to Dr Muiris Houston for writing the foreword and Dr Larkin Feeney for his support during this and various other projects.

I am also grateful to Professor Veronica O'Keane, Professor Patricia Casey, Cambridge University Press, *The Irish Times*, the *Medical Independent*, Dr Michelle Harley, Dr Louise Sharkey, Dr Faraz Jabbar, Dr John Bruzzi, Dr Caroline Maher, Ms Miriam Silke and the College of Psychiatrists of Ireland. Once again, I am very grateful for the support and assistance of Mr David Givens of The Liffey Press (www.theliffeypress.com), and to Dr Shari McDaid (Director, Mental Health Reform) for information about Mental Health Reform.

Information about specific diagnoses in this book is based on the guidelines provided by the World Health Organisation in its *International Classification of Diseases* (10th Edition) (Geneva: World Health Organisation, 1992).

I owe a long-standing debt of gratitude to my teachers at Scoil Chaitríona, Renmore, Galway; St Joseph's Patrician College, Nun's Island, Galway; and the School of Medicine at NUI Galway.

Finally, and above all else, I deeply appreciate the support of my wife (Regina), children (Eoin and Isabel), parents (Mary and

Desmond), sisters (Sinéad and Niamh) and nieces (Aoife and Aisling). Trixie also deserves a mention.

Permissions

This book contains Irish Public Sector Information licensed under a Creative Commons Attribution 4.0 International (CC BY 4.0) licence.

This book also contains public sector information licensed under the Open Government Licences v1.0, v2.0 and v.3.0 (England), and Scottish Parliamentary information licensed under the Open Scottish Parliament Licence v1.0.

Material from the *Medical Independent* and *The Irish Times* is re-used by the kind permission of each.

Material reproduced and adapted from the Irish Journal of Psychological Medicine is © College of Psychiatrists of Ireland, published by Cambridge University Press. Reprinted with permission.

Material in Chapter 1 is drawn from *Mindfulness and Buddhist-Derived Approaches in Mental Health and Addiction* (edited by Edo Shonin, William Van Gordon and Mark D. Griffiths), chapter titled 'Compassion, cognition and the illusion of self: Buddhist notes towards more skilful engagement with diagnostic classification systems in psychiatry', 2016, pages 9-28, by Brendan D. Kelly, © Springer International Publishing Switzerland 2016. With permission of Springer.

Material in Chapter 13 is drawn from Kelly, B.D. 'Revising, reforming, reframing: Report of the Expert Group on the Review of the Mental Health Act 2001' (2015). *Irish Journal of Psychological Medicine* 2015; 32: 161-6. doi.10.1017/ipm.2015.16. ©, College of Psychiatrists of Ireland 2015, published by Cambridge University Press. Reprinted with permission.

Material in Chapter 14 is drawn from the *Irish Journal of Medical Science*, 'The Assisted Decision-Making (Capacity) Act: What it is and why it matters', Volume 186, 2017, pages 351-356, by B.D.

Kelly, © Royal Academy of Medicine in Ireland 2016. With permission of Springer.

Material in Chapter 17 is drawn from: Kelly, B.D. 'Dignity, human rights and the limits of mental health legislation'. *Irish Journal of Psychological Medicine* 2014; 31: 75-81. doi:10.1017/ipm.2014.22. © College of Psychiatrists of Ireland 2014, published by Cambridge University Press. Reprinted with permission.

I am very grateful to the editors, publishers, authors and copyright-holders of these publications for permitting re-use of material in this book. All reasonable efforts have been made to contact the copyright holders for all texts quoted in this book. If any have been omitted, please contact the publisher.

Disclaimer

FOREWORD

Dr Muiris Houston

'Ultimately, it is the patient who guides diagnosis
and treatment. People matter most. Diagnoses
matter substantially less.'

The words of Professor Brendan Kelly tell you the most important feature of this book: it is written for all of us, who at some
point in our lives, will either experience or be touched by mental
illness. It also gives us a glimpse of the author who, in addition to
his academic prowess and multiplicity of higher degrees, has that
crucial skill of writing in a simple, direct style.

Part 1 of the book is laid out in chapters, each devoted to a
common psychological illness. Each one tackles four key questions: what are the symptoms and signs of the illness; how common is it; what causes the illness; and what are the treatment options for the condition? Case histories and the author's style means
each illness is accessible and reader-friendly.

Brendan and I share a passion for patient stories; every story
is unique and each individual's experience is different and complicated and personalised. Illness stories are not static creatures, but
change with time and circumstance. Many mental illness stories

are life-long journeys of personal challenge but also of growth and understanding.

Part 2 of the book covers a range of topics relevant to mental health in Ireland. A chapter on the Assisted Decision-Making (Capacity) Act 2015 has one of the clearest explanations you will read about this complex multi-level legal structure designed to provide decision-making support for people whose mental capacity is impaired or is about to become impaired. It also discusses the topical issue of advance healthcare directives.

The 'everyone who wants to be well' reference in the book's subtitle is developed in an especially engaging chapter on Happiness and Well-Being in Ireland. With a shift in focus from mental illness to mental well-being, it looks at the sometimes elusive concept of happiness in the context of recent Irish studies, asking, among other questions: Can happiness be measured and studied? Has happiness in Ireland declined or increased over the past decade? As well as answering these questions, the author suggests practical ways for us to increase personal happiness and well-being.

Chapters on stigma and structural violence and dignity in mental illness are sobering and thought provoking. It is clear much remains to be done to level the societal playing field between mental and physical illness, in the author's words. to 'promote wellness, enhance human rights, deepen social inclusion, and enhance autonomy'.

Whether you are interested in specific illnesses or the broader aspects of mental health in Ireland, this book delivers in a most readable way.

Dr Muiris Houston

Medical Journalist and Health Analyst, *The Irish Times*

Narratologist and Lecturer, Trinity College Dublin,

National University of Ireland, Galway, and The Galway Clinic

This book is dedicated to Regina, Eoin and Isabel

Chapter 1

INTRODUCTION

One in four individuals will develop a mental illness at some point in their life. Virtually everyone knows someone with a mental illness or a family affected by suicide.

The annual statistics indicate the extent of these issues: each year, hundreds of thousands of people attend general practitioners (GPs) for mental health problems, and tens of thousands attend community mental health teams. In 2015, there were 17,860 admissions to Irish psychiatric units and hospitals, a small increase since 2014 when there were 17,797 admissions.[1] Roughly equal proportions of those admitted were male (51 per cent) and female (49 per cent), and the 20–24 year age group had the highest admission rate. As in previous years, the most common admission diagnoses in 2015 were depressive disorders (27 per cent) and schizophrenia (20 per cent).

Of course, statistics such as these are essential for service planning, but they tell only one part of the story. Behind each admission and attendance, there is an individual human story, and each story affects not just one person, but a network of family, friends and colleagues, as well as the broader community.

Every story is unique. A person's psychological distress invariably reflects their past history, current situation and future hopes. While national statistical trends are clearly identifiable over the years, each individual's experience is different and complicated and personalised, and each occurs at a specific point in time. This is duly reflected in the many and varied strategies that people pursue when they have psychological problems: they talk with family and friends, try to change their habits, go on holidays, and seek to resolve matters themselves in many other ways.

And, most commonly, these strategies work very well: problems pass or are resolved, difficulties ease, and we move on with our lives. People are strong and resilient and resourceful. For the most part, families, friends and colleagues are generous and understanding. We solve most of our problems within these informal networks without any need to move beyond these resources. We get back on the road. We move forward.

This book takes up the story when these normal responses prove insufficient, when a person's resilience feels exhausted, and when further assistance appears to be needed. This book is intended as a pragmatic guide to mental health problems and their solutions, aimed at anyone who has ever felt overwhelmed by their situation, has looked at mental health services and been entirely confused by them. What do the illness names actually mean, if anything? How can generic descriptions of 'depression' or 'anxiety' apply to me? How do I know if I need to see a psychiatrist and how can I access the services I need?

This book looks at all of these issues, examining questions such as: What is depression? What is schizophrenia? What are the various other mental illnesses and how are they defined? For each condition, four key questions are answered: What are the signs and symptoms? How common is it? What is the cause? What are the treatments?

This book also explores some broader issues, including mental health policy and services in Ireland, and how to access care. Other chapters look at additional issues of importance in mental health services today: Is Ireland's suicide rate rising or falling, and what can be done to improve it? Is involuntary psychiatric admission common, and how are the human rights of the mentally ill protected? What underpins happiness and well-being in Ireland? Is it possible to be happy? If so, how?

We start, however, by looking at the ideas of mental health and mental illness in the first place, and examining the purpose of diagnosing anyone with a 'mental disorder' at all: whose interest does it really serve? And how can we make the process better?

What Are Mental Health and Mental Illness?

In 1948, the constitution of the World Health Organisation (WHO) provided a definition of health:

> Health is a state of complete physical, mental and social well-being and not merely the absence of disease or infirmity. The enjoyment of the highest attainable standard of health is one of the fundamental rights of every human being without distinction of race, religion, political belief, economic or social condition.[2]

This definition is notable for three reasons. First, it neatly encapsulates long-standing ideas about what good health really means to people and so it clearly makes a great deal of sense; the WHO might well have got this one right. Second, it presents a very expansive vision of health, challenging us to not only treat illness but also to promote wellness. And third, this definition places *mental* well-being at the very heart of health, emphasising the centrality of the psychological and social dimensions of human life. This makes sense: most of us seek not only to be healthy but also to be happy.

Mental health is, then, a state of complete mental well-being, and not merely the absence of mental illness or psychological problems. But what is mental illness?

A medical illness is a disease or ailment, and a mental illness is a clinically recognisable group of symptoms or behaviours associated in the majority of cases with interference with personal functions and distress. If personal dysfunction is not present, social deviance or conflict do not constitute mental illness: the person's

3

mood, thoughts, judgement, relationships or personal function must be disturbed.

Throughout history, the concept of 'mental illness' has always been (and continues to be) a highly contested, debated one. Mental illnesses are variously conceptualised as spiritual or religious manifestations, legal conundrums, medical diseases, social issues or all of the above, with the balance between competing definitions varying over time. In recent decades, re-definition and expansion of diagnostic categories have proven especially controversial, even though they form part of a much broader trend across all of medicine, as treatment thresholds continually change. For example, cut-off points for treatment of high blood pressure have changed significantly over time, just as there is now strong public demand for psychological services for all kinds of psychological problems, and not just traditionally-defined 'mental illness'.[3]

There is also continual controversy about the use of language in this field. In this book, I have chosen to use the terms 'mental illness' and 'mental disorder'. Some people prefer the term 'psychological problem' and others use 'mental health illness'. While language always matters, it is important to be pragmatic: any common language is invariably imperfect and will suit some people better than others. I am sure that the terms 'mental illness' and 'mental disorder' will change over time, but for the moment these are the most commonly used terms in professional and public discussions, and are found most commonly in official documents (e.g. the Mental Health Act 2001). That is why I have used 'mental illness' and 'mental disorder' throughout this book.

I also move freely between the terms 'psychiatry' and 'mental health services'. Psychiatry is the branch of medicine concerned with the study and treatment of disorders of mental function. I am a psychiatrist, which is a medical doctor who has done additional training in the treatment of mental illness. This differs from a clinical psychologist, who is a specialist in mental processes and behaviour but is not a medical doctor. Both psychiatrists and clinical psychologists work in mental health services and their roles are similar in certain respects, while different in others (e.g. psychologists cannot prescribe medication in Ireland whereas psychiatrists can). The roles of various members of multi-disciplinary teams – which can appear confusing but all of which are vital – are outlined later in Chapter 12 of this book.

Diagnosing 'Mental Disorder': Why?

Much of this book is structured as chapters dealing with different diagnoses in psychiatry: depression, schizophrenia, etc. It is, perhaps, wise to deal at the outset with one key issue that crops up virtually every time I speak or write in public about these issues: why would anyone seek to 'diagnose' any 'mental disorder' in the first place? Isn't everyone different and unique? Isn't it hugely unlikely that anyone's particular psychological distress will map precisely onto pre-existing, 'one-fits-all' categories made out by committees in different countries, all of whom keep changing the categories every few years anyway? Whose interest is really served by these elaborate diagnostic systems which attract continual controversy in the media?

Of course, these are entirely valid points: diagnostic systems are invariably imperfect and approximate. There are, however, other points to be made too. And ultimately, it is the misuse of diagnostic systems in psychiatry that has led to many of the reported problems with them. But first, let us consider the very concept of diagnosis itself.

The idea of 'diagnosis' has always been a controversial element in psychiatry. There are now two chief diagnostic classification systems in use: the WHO's *International Classification of Diseases* (ICD-10),[4] which is used in Europe (including Ireland, and throughout this book), and the American Psychiatric Association's *Diagnostic and Statistical Manual of Mental Disorders* (DSM-5), which is used in the US and, increasingly, globally.[5] These two systems have much in common; both comprise lists of commonly co-occurring symptoms; both are imperfect but have their specific uses; both have been revised substantially over past decades; and both will continue to be revised in the decades to come.

This is how they work. Both ICD and DSM present lists of symptoms which need to be present to a specified degree of severity for a specified period of time in order for a given diagnosis to be made. For example, a DSM diagnosis of 'major depressive disorder' (Chapter 2) requires the presence of five or more out of nine key symptoms, for more than a fortnight, and this must represent a change from previous functioning. The nine key symptoms are:

- Generally depressed mood
- Reduced pleasure or interest
- Significant weight change (loss or gain)
- Insomnia (poor sleep) or hypersomnia (excessive sleep) almost every day
- Psychomotor agitation or retardation (that is, being physically agitated or slowed down) almost every day
- Loss of energy or fatigue almost every day
- Feelings of guilt or worthlessness
- Reduced concentration or decisiveness
- Recurring thoughts of death, self-harm or suicide, or related acts.

For a DSM diagnosis of major depressive disorder to be made, at least one of the five symptoms must be either generally depressed mood or reduced pleasure or interest; symptoms must cause significant distress or impairment in functioning; symptoms must not be attributable to a substance (for example, alcohol), medical condition or other mental illness; and there must have never been an episode of mania or hypomania, which might indicate a diagnosis of bipolar disorder (Chapter 4) rather than major depressive disorder.

While this list of symptoms appears logical and reasonable, and accords with most people's idea of 'depression', a fundamental question still arises: Why do these psychiatric classification systems exist at all? Do they not reduce complex, changeable human states to lists of symptoms and diagnostic codes, removing the humanity, complexity and beauty of each person, and replacing them with cold, impersonal categorisation? Are ICD and DSM simply tools for the 'invention' of new mental illnesses, marketing of new pharmaceutical products, and generation of revenue for pharmaceutical companies and healthcare providers? Why do we need to 'diagnose' at all?

Diagnosis is important for four key reasons: (1) diagnosis creates a common language for talking about commonly-occurring *general patterns* of psychological distress; (2) diagnosis facilitates studies of treatments for mental disorders; (3) diagnosis facilitates study of the causes of mental disorders; and (4) diagnosis protects human rights.[6]

First: diagnosis creates a common language for sharing experiences of mental disorders. How? Diagnosis of most mental disorders is based primarily on the person's history and symptoms rather than biological tests (blood tests, brain scans, etc.) which are mostly used only to exclude other disorders (for example, brain tumours). Technologies such as brain scans do, of course, play roles in certain circumstances, such as dementia, but for most mental disorders the role of such technologies is limited to excluding known physical causes of psychiatric symptoms. There are no blood tests or scans for most mental disorders.

As a result, it is necessary in psychiatry to identify clusters of symptoms which commonly occur together in order to ensure some consistency in clinical diagnosis. That is, if mental disorders are ever to be understood, it is necessary that when someone in Ireland mentions 'panic disorder', they know they are talking about roughly the same thing as when someone in Denmark or France or Italy mentions 'panic disorder'. That does not mean that that specific case of panic disorder in Ireland is identical to one in Denmark or France or Italy: clearly, it is not. But it means that there are some common features that tend to occur together which indicate that we are all broadly talking about the same thing when we mention 'panic disorder'. And that we therefore share a common language when we talk about mental disorder together. This is vital: much of human experience is shared to a significant degree. We need to be able to talk about it.

Openness about diagnosis is also vital in order to ensure that pharmaceutical companies, healthcare funders or others do not drive the 'creation' of new so-called 'mental illnesses', or manipulate information about the effectiveness of treatments, in order to sell their products. ICD and DSM present the best protections in this regard: robust, open revision processes for these classification systems have the potential to defend against cynical manipulation by vested interests as they create opportunity for open, ethical engagement of all stakeholders, including patients, families, carers, mental health professionals, voluntary agencies, healthcare providers and governmental bodies, in developing classification systems. They help us talk together about mental disorders, and allow us to revise our positions every few years as understandings and knowledge evolve.

Second, diagnosis using tools such as ICD and DSM makes it possible to study new treatments for mental disorders. When people present to psychological or mental health services, it is necessary for mental health professionals to have some guide as to which kinds of treatments will work best to address certain commonly-occurring collections of symptoms. Diagnosis and classification are necessary in order to perform research studies and clinical trials to collect evidence about the best treatments for these various collections of symptoms.

For example, evidence from 41 studies involving a total of 1,806 children and adolescents who fulfilled ICD or DSM criteria for anxiety disorders showed that cognitive behavioural therapy (CBT) is an effective treatment for children and adolescents with this particular collection of symptoms.[7] (The use of CBT for various mental illnesses is discussed in subsequent chapters of this book; for example, Chapters 2, 3, 5 and 6.) In order to discover the usefulness of CBT for anxiety disorders in children and adolescents, it was necessary to test CBT on children and adolescents with defined sets of symptoms, rather than children and adolescents randomly selected from the general population. In other words, diagnosis is necessary in order to identify evidence-based treatments that are proven to help with specific problems, and avoid well-meaning but unproven 'treatments' that might well do more harm than good.

Third: diagnosis facilitates study of the causes of mental disorders. There is strong evidence that individuals are more likely to develop the collection of symptoms that ICD and DSM call 'schizophrenia' if they have a first degree relative with that same constellation of symptoms (Chapter 3). While specific genes have yet to be identified for most mental disorders, the emergence of relatively standardised diagnostic systems such as ICD and DSM have greatly facilitated research into the causes of many of disorders, such as schizophrenia. The same argument applies to other causes of states of psychological distress; for example, establishing the precise role of traumatic life events in triggering depression is only possible if we all agree on some core features of 'depression', so that we can be relatively sure that we are not all talking about entirely different things when we say 'depression'. Again, each case will be different, but there is also significant commonality; often, we suffer in similar ways. Understanding this helps identify patterns and, hopefully, causes.

Fourth: diagnosis protects human rights. Most countries have laws which permit involuntary admission and treatment of people with severe mental disorder under certain, specific circumstances (for example, serious risk to self or others). These laws affect only a very small minority of patients: most people with mental disorder are treated in primary care by GPs and other health professionals (that is, entirely voluntarily). Among the minority referred to secondary care (for example, psychiatry outpatient clinics), most are treated as outpatients (again, entirely voluntarily). Finally, among those admitted to inpatient care, approximately 90 per cent are treated on a voluntary basis and only a tiny minority ever require involuntary admission or treatment.

Nonetheless, for those who become subject to involuntary treatment there is a strong need for as much clarity as possible about diagnosis in order to ensure appropriate intervention, treatment and accountability. In other words, doctors and others need to explain clearly why a given person is being treated against his or her wishes. Diagnosis is a key element in ensuring such accountability. While each case will differ, certain key elements need to be present: a defined mental disorder, a need for treatment, and risk of harm or deterioration in health (Chapter 13). Clear diagnostic criteria are vital in ensuring that these requirements are met and that involuntary care is provided appropriately, is in accordance with the law and principles of medical ethics, and can be externally scrutinised (for example, by a mental health tribunal, as now occurs automatically for all involuntary patients in Ireland).

If such systems had been introduced and implemented in an open, accountable fashion, they had the potential to help protect against the alleged labelling of political dissidents as mentally ill in the former Soviet Union in the 1970s and 1980s. Today, ICD and DSM, once used correctly and with an awareness of their limitations, hold similar potential in parts of the world where psychiatric diagnosis is still used for political rather than therapeutic purposes.

In Ireland, when a person is involuntarily admitted under the Mental Health Act 2001, it is necessary, when they are discharged, to enter their diagnosis (in the form of an ICD code) onto a form. Each year, these forms are closely examined at national level and anonymised statistics are published for inspectors and the public to examine. This process greatly increases openness and accountability, and permits comparison of involuntary admission rates across regions and between countries. As a result, we now know that Ireland's rate of involuntary admission is notably low by international standards, and is less than half the rate in England (Chapter 13). Ireland now has a very non-custodial psychiatric service.

These, then, are four key ways in which diagnostic systems such as ICD and DSM are useful: (1) they create a common language for talking about commonly-occurring *general patterns* of psychological distress (although each case will, inevitably, be unique and different); (2) they facilitate studies of treatments for, and (3) causes of, specific mental disorders; and (4) they help protect human rights. Other potential benefits include reducing stigma (once they are used thoughtfully, in the fashion intended), alleviating blame or guilt that individuals or families may feel, guiding patients and families in choosing the best treatments, and assisting with the creation of networks of individuals and families affected by similar symptoms.

Inevitably, ICD and DSM are imperfect and they change continually, reflecting the facts that the biological basis of most mental disorders is unknown and societal expectations of mental health care continually evolve – chiefly in the direction of seeking more professional care for symptoms which were previously managed within families or communities. Both ICD and DSM contain stern warnings against using them in a 'tick-box' fashion: most people will not fit any category *precisely*, and many will have some elements of one disorder and some elements of another in a unique and changeable combination. This is entirely to be expected and it underlines the advice that these guidelines should always be used in a flexible fashion. The *story* of the individual patient always takes precedence over ICD or DSM. The diagnostic criteria are outline guidelines only and using them rigidly or literally gives them a weight and an importance that is simply inappropriate. ICD and DSM have their specific uses, especially in research and ensuring accountability in services, but they are not the be all and end all.

In the end, someone who receives a diagnosis and looks it up in ICD or DSM should remember that ICD and DSM are just outline guides; most people do not fit precisely into any category; almost everyone in the world will see features of themselves in one or more than one category at any given time; and that ICD or DSM diagnoses should not be accorded an air of ultimate authority or given weight that they do not merit. ICD and DSM are imperfect guides which are always trumped by an individual's own unique circumstances and story. While ICD and DSM can help guide good treatment choices, and can reassure patients that other people have experienced roughly similar problems, we simply should not and cannot use ICD and DSM to put people into boxes. That would be futile, impossible and harmful.

The media commonly describe ICD and DSM as the 'psychiatrists' bible', despite the fact that both volumes clearly state that their descriptions are merely guidelines to be interpreted flexibly and with a broad awareness of the multi-factorial nature of psychological and psychiatric distress. Nonetheless, the description of ICD and DSM as the 'psychiatrists' bible' is not entirely without truth: the majority of individuals in most religious traditions engage with their 'bible' or scripture in a highly nuanced fashion, taking certain sections literally, interpreting other sections metaphorically, and completely ignoring other sections. It is useful, sensible and necessary to look at DSM and ICD in a similar fashion, depending on the specific circumstances that present themselves. The patient comes first.

Finally, in the face of continual controversy and discussion about ICD and DSM, it is important that the core tasks of mental health care do not become obscured: the provision of care and treatment to individuals in states of psychiatric and psychological distress, and the promotion of health and social care systems that promote wellness, enhance human rights, deepen social inclusion, and enhance autonomy. Nuanced, thoughtful use of ICD and DSM can help greatly with these tasks by enhancing diagnostic transparency, facilitating research, protecting rights, and assisting in individual cases, once the guidance in ICD and DSM is tempered by an awareness of their limitations and combined with genuine therapeutic engagement with individual patients and families.

Ultimately, it is the patient, and not ICD or DSM, who guides diagnosis and treatment. People matter most. Diagnoses matter substantially less.

The Structure of This Book

This book is divided into two parts. Part 1 examines specific mental illnesses, starting with depression, a common, disabling and often confusing condition. Most of the chapters in Part 1 address four key questions about each mental illness or set of disorders. In Chapter 1, for example, the key questions are:

◊   What are the symptoms and signs of depression?

◊   How common is depression?

◊   What causes depression?

◊   What are the treatments for depression?

Sample case histories are used to demonstrate the symptoms and effects of depression; treatments are outlined; and useful resources and sources of further information are provided at the end of the chapter.

Chapter 3 is devoted to schizophrenia in a similar fashion. Chapter 4 examines bipolar disorder (manic depression) and Chapter 5 explores anxiety disorders, including phobias, panic disorder, generalised anxiety disorder, obsessive compulsive disorder (OCD), post-traumatic stress disorder (PTSD), as well as other conditions with varying relationships with anxiety (acute stress reaction, adjustment disorder, conversion disorder and somatoform disorder, including somatisation and hypochondriacal disorders).

Chapter 6 moves on to eating disorders (anorexia nervosa, bulimia nervosa, and others); Chapter 7 examines alcohol and drug problems; Chapter 8 looks at dementia; and Chapter 9 discusses various other mental illnesses and conditions such as personality disorders, perinatal mental illness (mental illnesses during and following pregnancy), delusional disorders, and various other conditions (for example, seasonal affective disorder, work stress, gender identity disorders, disorders of sexual preference, etc.). Chapter 10 explores the main mental illnesses and psychological disorders associated with childhood and adolescence.

Chapter 11 is devoted to deliberate self-harm and suicide, and explores the rates of each in Ireland, especially during Ireland's recent economic problems and recovery, and compares these with other European countries. This chapter also includes advice on what to do if someone says they are suicidal, information about predicting suicide, and a discussion of measures to help prevent self-harm and suicide. Homicide and murder-suicide are also discussed.

Part 2 of the book examines various aspects of the provision of mental health care in Ireland. Chapter 12 summarises Ireland's current mental health policy document *A Vision for Change* (2006). On a more practical level, this chapter also provides an account of how to access outpatient and inpatient mental health care and explains how community mental health teams are structured and work. Chapter 13 addresses involuntary mental health care in Ireland and summarises current legislation governing involuntary treatment (the Mental Health Act 2001). This chapter outlines the human rights protections for the mentally ill and provides suggestions for future improvements. It includes a clear, step-by-step guide to the process of involuntary admission to psychiatric care in Ireland.

Chapter 14 explains the Assisted Decision-Making (Capacity) Act 2015, which describes a multi-level legal structure to provide decision-making support for people whose mental capacity is impaired or is about to become impaired. The 2015 Act also describes new measures relating to enduring power of attorneys (that is, giving other people decision-making authority which will endure even when the person has developed impaired mental capacity) and advance healthcare directives (that is, making treatment decisions now that will apply in the future when the person has developed impaired mental capacity)

Chapter 15 examines enduring mental illness in the broader context of society, and addresses issues such as increased rates of imprisonment and homelessness among the mentally ill, and steps that might be taken to improve matters to attain greater social justice for the mentally ill, their families and carers.

Chapter 16 shifts the focus from mental illness to mental well-being, and looks at recent studies of happiness in Ireland, asking: Can happiness be measured and studied? Do the Irish rate ourselves as happy? Has happiness in Ireland declined over the past decade, as our economic problems deepened and then began to resolve? This chapter answers these questions and suggests ways to foster increased happiness and well-being. Ultimately, while one can only do a certain amount *explicitly* to increase happiness, Ireland's long history of high levels of happiness, robust social stability, recent positive economic trends, and proposed measures to increase happiness outlined in this chapter, all combine to make the prospects for continued and increased well-being and happiness in Ireland extremely bright.

Finally, Chapter 17 concludes the book with a consideration of dignity, mental illness and human rights, based on the idea that dignity is central to all human rights and to human well-being. Maintaining and enhancing human dignity should lie at the heart of all mental healthcare and social care provision.

Engagement, Tolerance, Compassion

Engagement, tolerance, and compassion are three key values in delivering mental health care and promoting recovery. These values apply to public discussion about mental healthcare as much as they apply to individual therapy, which is also equally informed by the principles of personal choice, recovery and empowerment, underpinned by evidence-based care.

This book is entering the arena of public discussion about mental health care in Ireland. Public discussion is crucial, and much of it is constructive and essential, reflecting the key values of care provision and recovery. A minority of public exchanges, however, lack these values. Nowhere is this more evident than in certain discussions about specific treatments, such as anti-depressant medication (to select just one example).

Many people benefit from anti-depressant medication; some do not. When the benefits of any medication outweigh the adverse effects, it should be continued for the course of treatment. When, after a proper trial, the adverse effects outweigh the benefits, the medication is not useful and should be carefully stopped. Other strategies or other medications can be considered. Different combinations of treatments suit different people.

Public discussion about antidepressants (and all aspects of mental health care) is absolutely vital for sharing information, challenging vested interests, and progressing understanding. There is, however, a tendency for some debates to become unhelpfully polarised, with very negative effects.

Let me give an example. Last year, a woman came to see me who had suffered from two episodes of severe depression in the past and benefitted greatly from anti-depressant medication, along with psychological therapy. She was still taking the medication, with no side effects. It helped her overcome her symptoms, go back to work and get on with her life. She was happy again. A week earlier, however, she was devastated to read in a newspaper that campaigners were saying that anti-depressants were highly dangerous for everyone and should be banned. She was in tears when she came to see me. I assured her that this was not true, but she was virtually inconsolable.

Public debate is vital, but it needs to be informed by humility. If one person finds anti-depressants helpful, that does not mean everyone will find them helpful. If another person finds anti-depressants unhelpful, that does not mean everyone will find them unhelpful. The same applies to all treatments, be they other medications, CBT, various other psychological therapies, electroconvulsive therapy (ECT) or no treatment at all. Patterns might recur, but everyone is different.

Conventional psychiatry has many powerful tools to help, but does not, of course, have all the answers. As a result, real-life experiences of illness and treatment matter deeply. But *everyone's* experience matters. The fact that one person has a particular experience with a specific treatment, either positive or negative, does not mean that everyone else will share that experience. Even when people come together in groups of hundreds or thousands with similar experiences, either positive or negative (for example, in clinical trials or public campaigns), there are always hundreds or thousands more who have different experiences.

All experiences and *all* lives matter. The vocal minorities matter, and so do the silent majorities.

In this book, I have presented a broad range of treatment options for a variety of different states of mental illness and psychological distress. I have outlined approaches that are commonly used and many of the alternatives that are possible. I have focused for the most part on treatments that are supported by systematic evidence and established guidelines.

There are, however, very many other approaches available and, while often not supported by systematic evidence, many of these can provide help for people in various different circumstances. In Chapter 12, I outline some common sense guidelines about engaging with alternative therapies and private care providers which I hope will prove helpful for many.

Above all, however, I would appreciate if the guidance in this book is taken with a background awareness of the key values of engagement, tolerance and compassion. These values apply to public discussion about mental distress as much as they do to individual therapy, which is equally informed by the principles of personal choice, recovery and empowerment, underpinned by evidence-based care.

Most of all, it is important to remember that one size does not fit all. Patterns might recur, but every person is unique; every story is different. We need to seek out and listen to *all* stories, positive and negative.

Even the quiet, unspoken ones.

Especially the quiet, unspoken ones.

Useful Resources

Useful resources and sources of further information are presented at the end of each chapter throughout this book. In a more general sense, there are many books and websites devoted to the general themes of mental health and mental illness. For an overall assessment of the nature of psychiatry and mental health services, the following books provide a variety of perspectives: *Our Necessary Shadow: The Nature and Meaning of Psychiatry* by Tom Burns (Allen Lane/Penguin, 2013); *American Psychosis: How the Federal Government Destroyed the Mental Illness Treatment System* by E. Fuller Torrey (Oxford University Press, 2014); *Unhinged: The Trouble with Psychiatry – A Doctor's Revelations about a Profession in Crisis* by Daniel J. Carlat (Free Press/Simon & Schuster Inc., 2010); *Hearing Voices: The History of Psychiatry in Ireland* by Brendan Kelly (Irish Academic Press, 2016); *Madness Explained: Psychosis and Human Nature* by Richard P. Bentall (Allen Lane/Penguin, 2003).

Endnotes

1   Daly, A. and Craig, S. HRB Statistics Series 29: Activities of Irish Psychiatric Units and Hospitals 2015. Dublin: Health Research Board, 2016.

2   Preamble to the Constitution of the World Health Organisation as adopted by the International Health Conference, New York, 19-22 June, 1946; signed on 22 July 1946 by the representatives of 61

States (Official Records of the World Health Organisation, no. 2, p. 100) and entered into force on 7 April 1948

3   Douglas, L. and Feeney, L. 'Thirty years of referrals to a community mental health service'. *Irish Journal of Psychological Medicine* 2016; 33: 105-9.

4   World Health Organisation. *International Classification of Diseases* (10th Edition). Geneva: World Health Organisation, 1992.

5   American Psychiatric Association. *Diagnostic and Statistical Manual of Mental Disorders* (5th Edition). Washington DC: American Psychiatric Association, 2013.

6   Material in this chapter is drawn from *Mindfulness and Buddhist-Derived Approaches in Mental Health and Addiction* (edited by Edo Shonin, William Van Gordon and Mark D. Griffiths), chapter titled 'Compassion, cognition and the illusion of self: Buddhist notes towards more skilful engagement with diagnostic classification systems in psychiatry', 2016, pages 9-28, by Brendan D. Kelly, © Springer International Publishing Switzerland 2016. With permission of Springer.

7   James, A.C., James, G., Cowdrey, F.A., Soler, A., Choke, A. 'Cognitive behavioural therapy for anxiety disorders in children and adolescents'. *Cochrane Database of Systematic Reviews 2013*; 6: CD004690.

Chapter 2

DEPRESSION

Depression is a common, disabling mental illness. It is also a confusing condition, occasionally difficult to distinguish from day-to-day unhappiness. The key to managing depression lies in recognising when someone is depressed rather than just sad, and offering them support and help as soon as feasible. It is also vital to remember that unhappiness is not the same as depression and there is no benefit in 'medicalising' unhappiness.

This chapter looks at four key questions about depression:

◊   What are the symptoms and signs of depression?

◊   How common is depression?

◊   What causes depression?

◊   What are the treatments for depression?

Useful resources and sources of further information are provided at the end of the chapter.

What Are the Symptoms and Signs of Depression?

Depression can vary greatly between individuals. The symptoms and signs depend on the person's general character, their life situation, any stresses triggering their depression, and various other factors. Sometimes, the clinical picture is very confusing and can initially appear to make no sense at all.

Over time, however, certain patterns emerge in many individuals with depression, and the World Health Organisation (WHO) outlines a range of symptoms that are especially common features of depression in most people.[1] These symptoms include:

- Low mood, feeling down, or feeling low
- Loss of interest and enjoyment in activities which are usually pleasurable
- Reduced energy, leading to increased fatigability and reduced activity
- Marked tiredness after slight effort
- Reduced concentration and attention, with reduced ability to read or follow programmes on television
- Reduced self-confidence and self-esteem
- Ideas of unworthiness and guilt
- Pessimistic, bleak views of the future
- Hopelessness and feelings of helplessness
- Ideas or acts of self-harm, or ideas or acts of suicide
- Disturbed sleep, especially difficulty falling asleep, fragmented sleep, early morning waking (or, unusually, excessive sleep)
- Reduced appetite, generally resulting in weight loss (or, unusually, increased appetite).

According to the WHO, these symptoms should, for the most part, last for two weeks, but shorter periods are reasonable if the symptoms are of rapid onset or unusually severe. There are three levels of severity in depression:

- *Mild depression* features at least two of the following three symptoms: low mood, loss of enjoyment and interest, and increased fatigability. In addition, two other symptoms from the longer list above should be present, although not to an intense degree. The person with mild depression is distressed but does not stop functioning completely as a result of their depression.

- *Moderate depression* also features at least two of the same three key symptoms: low mood, loss of enjoyment and interest, and increased fatigability. In addition, three or four other symptoms from the longer list above are also present. These are commonly quite marked and cause notable difficulty with normal day-to-day activities.

- *Severe depression* features all three of the key symptoms (low mood, loss of enjoyment and interest, and increased fatigability) and at least four other symptoms from the longer list above. At least some of these symptoms are present to a severe intensity.

There may also be other, more distressing symptoms, such as delusions (believing things that are not true) or hallucinations (hearing, seeing, smelling, tasting or feeling things that are not really there). Hallucinations in depression tend to be unpleasant, for example, accusatory voices or smells of decomposing flesh. The individual with severe depression may also feel very slowed down, with reduced bodily movement and a slowing of bodily functions (for example, loss of interest in sex).

These guidelines from the WHO are intended to *assist* with recognising depression. It is not intended that they be used in a 'tick box' fashion to diagnose depression. They are best seen as a guide to the set of questions which need to be answered when we are deciding whether or not someone has depression. Some people without depression may have some of these symptoms. Some people with depression may have very few of them, but may have other symptoms which are not on the list. But if you suspect someone has depression, and they have many symptoms on the WHO list, then it is highly likely that person will benefit from support or help for depression.

Despite the usefulness of the WHO list of symptoms, there is still considerable diversity in the clinical presentations of depression. Individuals with depression may, for example, present with predominantly biological or bodily symptoms, such as low energy, poor appetite and reduced weight. They may have bodily pains, nausea or vomiting. They may also present with predominantly psychological symptoms such as hopelessness and negative thoughts about themselves, their environment and the future. This psychological picture may be further complicated by poor concentration, poor attention and difficulty with memory. Everyone is different.

Another common presentation is with straightforward low mood, just feeling depressed, 'low' or 'down in the dumps'. This tends to be a more profound and persistent lowering of mood than is present in day-to-day unhappiness. In depression there may also be features of suicidality. At one end of the spectrum, this can be in the form of a 'passive death wish', which is an apparent desire to be dead without intent to take actions to die. For example: 'I would never kill myself, but I wouldn't mind if I never woke up again.' Active suicidality is at the other end of the spectrum and may involve making detailed plans or engaging in actions with the intent of killing one's self (Chapter 11).

Before deciding whether or not someone has depression, a range of other possibilities need to be considered. The first possibility is that the individual is not unwell at all, and is simply experiencing unhappiness as a result of day-to-day life. Going through the WHO list of symptoms should help with this distinction. It is also useful to look at the extent to which the individual's psychological state is affecting their life: Have they stopped going out? Stopped going to work, or school, or social occasions? Are they losing weight? Are they unshakably hopeless about the future? These features point towards depression rather than day-to-day unhappiness.

If 'normal unhappiness' is ruled out, and if a diagnosis of depression appears possible, the following other possibilities need to be borne in mind:

- *Medical illnesses* can cause many of the symptoms of depression. Commonly, these illnesses include thyroid problems, dementia (like Alzheimer's disease or Parkinson's disease) (Chapter 8) or other medical illnesses. Most of these can be quickly ruled out by visiting a family doctor although some may require a blood test.

- *Substance abuse problems* can cause a range of psychological symptoms, including depression. The most common drug of abuse is alcohol, although cannabis and other illegal drugs may need to be considered (Chapter 7).

- *Side effects of a broad range of prescribed medications* can include low mood. These medications include benzodiazepines (used for the treatment of anxiety), barbiturates (epilepsy), phenytoin (epilepsy), phenothiazines (schizophrenia), levodopa (Parkinson's disease), statins (high cholesterol), digoxin (cardiac problems), diltiazem (cardiac problems), corticosteroids (asthma and other disorders) and various others.

- *Other mental illnesses* may appear similar to depression, or include low mood as a symptom. These include anxiety disorders, panic disorder, post-traumatic stress disorder, obsessive-compulsive disorder (Chapter 5), bulimia nervosa, anorexia nervosa (Chapter 6), bipolar disorder (manic-depression) (Chapter 4) and adjustment disorder with depressed mood, following a stressful life event (Chapter 5).

As a result of the diversity of possible presentations of depression and the range of other diagnostic possibilities, depression is often missed or misdiagnosed, even though it may account for up to 10 per cent of all consultations with general practitioners (GPs). There are many reasons why depression might be missed, including tendencies to focus on bodily complaints (for example pain) rather than psychological problems, and the common occurrence of medical and psychological disorders together in the same person, distracting attention from the psychological problem. Finally, the young, the elderly, males, the rich and the unmarried are generally less likely to be diagnosed with psychological problems, so that particular attention needs to be paid to these groups in order to ensure that depression is not missed.

Case History: Maura

Maura, a 48-year-old woman, attended her GP complaining of problems sleeping. When asked about her mood, Maura said her mood was fine. She said she had always been 'a worrier' but never had trouble sleeping before. When Maura's GP probed a little further, Maura revealed that she had difficulty falling asleep for the past three months, and also woke much earlier than usual. She had lost some weight and was no longer interested in her weekly bridge evening. Maura insisted she was not depressed but admitted she was more anxious than usual 'for no reason'. 'I'm just being silly,' she said.

Maura's GP explained that Maura fulfilled some of the criteria for mild depression, and would likely benefit from some form of supportive psychological therapy. The general practitioner took a blood test to check Maura's thyroid function (to rule out an underactive thyroid gland) and asked Maura about her periods (in order to rule out menopause or 'change of life' as a contributory factor in Maura's psychological complaints). These being ruled out, Maura attended a psychotherapist once a week for eight weeks in order to discuss her concerns, the various stressors in her life and to take practical steps to promote a mentally-healthy lifestyle. She recovered fully and never looked back.

How Common is Depression?

Depression is a common mental illness. The WHO estimates that, by 2020, depression will be the second most common cause of disability worldwide, after heart disease. Over the course of a lifetime, the chance of developing depression at some point is between 10 per cent and 17 per cent. Over the course of any given year, the chance of developing depression is between 3 per cent and 7 per cent. Overall, the risk of depression is almost twice as high in women (10 per cent) as in men (6.6 per cent). The reasons for this are not clear.

Depression is especially common among individuals who present to emergency departments at hospitals. Among those who present there with mental health problems, depression is the key issue in one-fifth of cases. Depression is also common amongst *all* individuals who come to emergency departments, even for reasons apparently unrelated to mental health or psychological problems: approximately 30 per cent of *all* individuals attending emergency departments have suffered depression in the previous year regardless of the reason for their current presentation. Depression is especially associated with lower levels of education, smoking, anxiety, chronic fatigue and back problems. Almost one in four individuals who present to emergency departments with acute chest pain have depression and more than one in four elderly individuals who present to emergency departments for any reason have depression.

Depression is very common among hospital inpatients too. In England 8 per cent of inpatients in medical wards have depression; in the US the figure is almost 22 per cent. Rates of depression may be especially high in patients with certain medical disorders: one in five patients with cancer have depression, and one in twenty experiences suicidality. In patients with cancer, depression is associated with female gender, low levels of education, longer duration of disease, and higher levels of pain. Among medical inpatients, depression is especially associated with feelings of pessimism, worthlessness, loss of interest in others, and thoughts of death.

Depression is also common among inpatients on psychiatry wards and in psychiatric hospitals. In England depression and anxiety account for more than a quarter of all psychiatric admissions and in Ireland depression accounts for almost a third of admissions.

Overall, these figures show that depression is a very common condition, associated with substantial psychological suffering and reduced ability to participate in day-to-day activities. Depression reduces individuals' ability to work leading to sick leave and, commonly, under-employment. As a result, depression accounts for a substantial proportion of the economic cost of mental illness in Ireland which, in 2006, exceeded €3 billion including more than €1 billion for direct costs of care and another €1 billion due to under-employment and non-employment.[2] In England, the cost of mental ill health is £105.2 billion per year, with depression accounting for a substantial proportion: £7.5 billion in 2007 and, by 2026, it will have risen to £12.2 billion.[3]

What Causes Depression?

The causes of depression are not fully understood. In any given individual, some causes may be readily apparent. For example, a series of stressful events or a serious medical illness may precipitate depression. For many people, however, depression just seems to appear out of nowhere, and the individual might never identify a specific cause or triggering factor.

But while the causes of depression remain unclear, a great deal of research provides fascinating clues about risk factors for depression. We know, for example, that the risk of depression is almost twice as high in women as in men, although this finding is frustratingly difficult to explain. Mood changes are sometimes associated with the menopause. See also Chapter 9 for a discussion of perinatal mental illness (occurring during or following pregnancy).

Depression is not strongly related to social class or ethnic group, although it is more common amongst individuals who are separated or unmarried. This likely relates to loneliness and lack of social support.

One of the best-established risk factors for depression is having a family history of depression. That is, if your mother, father, brother or sister had depression, your risk of depression is increased, compared to an individual who does not have any relative with depression. This extremely robust finding suggests that the genes we inherit from our parents determine, in part, our risk of depression. Genes are the biological 'blueprint' we inherit when we are conceived. Our genes contain all the information required to build and maintain a human body. Genes can undergo spontaneous changes at certain stages ('mutations') and environmental conditions conspire with genes to determine exactly which parts of the genetic blueprint are expressed at various points in our lives. But, by and large, we inherit the vast bulk of our genes from our two biological parents.

All of this is very relevant to depression. If you have a relative with depression, you have an approximately nine-fold increase in risk of developing depression compared to an individual who has no relative who ever suffered depression. At first glance, such a finding might be attributable to either genes or the environment in which one is brought up. Interestingly, though, studies of children adopted at birth and brought up by foster parents demonstrate clearly that biological children of parents with depression have an eight-fold increase in risk of depression *even when brought up by foster parents*. This suggests that the genes we inherit from our parents play a substantial role in determining our risk of depression.

This does not mean that individuals with depression in their family will necessarily get depression, just that their *risk* of getting depression is increased. The importance of genes is further underlined by studies of twins. There are two kinds of twins: monozygotic twins, who have identical genes (like identical twins), and dizygotic twins, whose genes are similar but not identical (like regular siblings). If one dizygotic twin has depression, there is a 28 per cent chance his or her co-twin will get depression too (the same risk as with regular, non-twin siblings). But if one monozygotic twin has depression, there is a 53 per cent chance his or her co-twin will get depression too. This further supports the importance of genes in depression: the more genes you have in common with an individual with depression, the greater your risk of depression too.

Despite this strong familial pattern, no specific genes have yet been identified as conferring *substantial* risk for depression in the general population. Genetic research is, however, increasingly linked with studies of various brain chemicals (neuro-transmitters) associated with depressive disorder. Anomalies of serotonin (a brain chemical associated with mood), for example, have been associated with depression, and there is evidence that specific genes related to serotonin may predispose to depression *when specific environmental stressors occur.* The roles of other neuro-transmitters, such as noradrenaline and dopamine, are not yet fully clear but will hopefully be elucidated in time.

Overall, these findings clearly demonstrate that the genes we inherit from our parents contribute significantly to risk of depression. But these findings also demonstrate that genes are not the only factor determining our risk of depression: if genes were the only factor, then when one monozygotic twin got depression, there would be a 100 per cent chance his or her co-twin would get depression too (because they have identical genes). But that figure isn't 100 per cent but rather just 53 per cent. This suggests that approximately half of the risk of depression is determined by genes and the other half is determined by non-genetic or 'environmental' factors. It is unclear what these environmental factors might be, but there are some indicators from other areas of research in depression.

Intriguing new research has now identified links between depression and disturbances to a range of chemicals (hormones) right throughout the body (that is, not just in the brain). We have already mentioned that disturbances of the thyroid gland – which secretes thyroid hormone – are linked with depression. There is, in fact, detailed evidence that disturbances of thyroid gland function are associated with not only depression in general, but also specific elements within depression, including anxiety, poor sleep, emotional lability, weight loss and agitation.

Many of the disturbances in other body hormones which have been linked to depression relate to the body's response to stress. A key determinant of the body's levels of physiological (or bodily) stress is a complex hormone system involving the hypothalamus and pituitary glands in the brain. These important glands are deeply involved in the regulation of stress-related hormones and there is strong evidence that this system is not working properly in individuals with depression. In addition, the higher rates of depression in women compared to men appear possibly related to the effects of the *cyclical* release of the female hormone oestrogen on various neurotransmitters in the brain, although this requires further study. If true, this would certainly help explain the strikingly higher risk of depression in women compared to men.

Post-mortem studies of the brains of individuals who had depression also provide some interesting clues about the possible biological origins of depression. The human brain is made up of around 100 million 'neurons', which are small nerve cells that communicate with each other using neuro-transmitter chemicals. Post-mortem studies of the brains of individuals who had depression show that certain parts of the brain have reduced numbers of neurons and reduced numbers of connections between neurons in depression. Brain scans of individuals who are still alive confirm the association between depression and biological changes in the brain: compared to individuals without depression, individuals with depression are more likely to show reductions in the size of certain brain areas such as the hippocampus, a key brain area for memory. And the longer the individual has depression, especially untreated depression, the smaller their hippocampus is likely to be. Brain scans are not, however, sufficiently specific to help with diagnosis.

The relationship between these biological changes in the brain and the psychological symptoms of depression is not entirely clear. In other words, it is not known to what extent such biological changes come before the onset of psychological symptoms of depression, occur at the same time as depression, or are a result of depression. The truth is likely a convoluted combination of all three possibilities, complicated in certain cases by treatment for depression, which may also affect the brain.

What is clear, however, is that something profound occurs to psychological functioning in individuals with depression, and there is compelling evidence that this is linked with biological changes in the brain, although the precise nature of these changes is not understood. At the present state of knowledge about the brain, the changes that occur in an individual with depression can be described in several ways, including using the languages of biology, psychology, sociology, religion and various other approaches. What matters most is that the language used is clear and honest, and that it helps point toward a solution for the individual in distress.

For many, the language of psychology makes a great deal of sense, both in terms of understanding and, ultimately, in terms of treatment. From a psychological perspective, there is strong evidence that depression is linked to difficult life events, with periods of depression commonly associated with stressful circumstances or losses (such as losing a job). Many psychological theories of depression have focused on thinking ('cognition') and ways in which patterns of cognition may contribute to depression. There is now strong evidence linking depression with a range of specific cognitive problems, including a tendency towards focusing on negative emotions, information and memories, that is, habitual thinking patterns that focus on the negative rather than the positive in life. Other cognitive problems common in depression include impaired attention and reduced speed of cognitive processing, that is, a general slowing down of thought.

This cognitive approach, focused on identifying unhelpful thinking and behaviour patterns, was highlighted initially by Aaron Beck, an American psychiatrist, who drew attention to a range of specific and unhelpful thoughts and beliefs in depressed individuals. This extremely sensible and pragmatic technique has led to the introduction of cognitive behavioural therapy (CBT) as a standard treatment for many individuals with depression. This form of therapy and various other treatments for depression are considered next.

What Are the Treatments for Depression?

Individuals with depression commonly require assistance and support in order to deal with their symptoms, enter recovery, and maintain wellness into the future. In the first instance, it is important that the individual with depression is able to talk openly about their symptoms, without fear of criticism or judgment. It is also important that any issues relating to alcohol use or other drug use are identified at the outset and, if possible, resolved. Treatment of depression is rendered extremely difficult in the presence of alcohol or drug misuse (Chapter 7).

Treatment of depression is, for the most part, based on a bio-psycho-social approach to management. In other words, there are biological treatments (such as medication), psychological treatments (such as CBT), and social interventions, all of which can be combined to suit the needs and circumstances of any given individual. Let's consider psychological and social treatments first.

Psychological Treatments for Depression

The most commonly used psychological treatment for depression is CBT, which focuses on the use of cognitive strategies – ones related to thinking patterns and habits – and behavioural strategies – ones related to actions and behavioural habits – in an effort to re-frame depressive thoughts, enhance coping strategies, reduce symptoms and promote recovery. Usually, the psychotherapist will meet the patient once per week and point out unhelpful thinking patterns which may deepen or prolong depression. Together, the patient and psychotherapist identify ways to address these errors and habits, and incrementally improve symptoms of depression. There is strong evidence that CBT is highly effective in the management of depression, generalized anxiety disorder, panic disorder, social phobia and post-traumatic stress disorder (Chapter 5). For some patients with mild or moderate depression, the benefits of CBT can exceed those of antidepressant medication.

Interpersonal psychotherapy is another psychotherapeutic approach to depression which emphasises that the occurrence of depression is not the patient's fault, and that the disorder has occurred in the patient's specific psycho-social context, which is significant in terms of recovery. Interpersonal psychotherapy is a time-limited, manual-based, focused, pragmatic therapy which, like CBT, generally lasts for a few months and is undertaken with a trained psychotherapist. There is now strong evidence that interpersonal psychotherapy is highly effective in the treatment of depression, both on its own and in combination with antidepressant medication.

Therapies based on mindfulness, too, offer very specific benefits for many individuals with depression. Mindfulness means paying attention to the present moment, simply and directly. It involves maintaining a careful awareness of your thoughts, emotions and actions, but not judging them. It involves staying focussed on the present moment as much as possible, and when your mind wanders, gently re-directing it back to *now* – the feeling of the chair you're sitting on, the smell of fresh coffee, the person with whom you are speaking.

The concept of mindfulness is rooted in Buddhist and early Hindu psychology and is an essential element of meditative practice in both traditions. Over the past fifteen years, the concept of mindfulness has penetrated deeply into the public mind in many Western countries. Today, it seems that mindfulness is everywhere: on the Internet, in bookshops and in therapy centres across the country. The popularity of mindfulness is easy to understand. Many people feel distracted much of the time, sending text messages, receiving emails, trying to attend to myriad tasks all at once. The practice of mindfulness is the opposite of these things. In other words: *don't just do something, sit there.*

There are many ways to cultivate mindfulness. One way is simply to provide a verbal label for specific things throughout the day. For example, you could mentally label the position of your body each time it changes (that is, 'standing', 'sitting', 'walking'). This promotes simple bodily awareness rather than criticism or analysis. The same technique can be applied to emotions or thoughts, simply labelling each one as it occurs but not trying to interpret, change or linger on it.

Mindfulness is a powerful way to improve psychological well-being. The benefits can be subtle but profound. You might still feel irritation at the usual day-to-day problems, but are less like to respond impulsively. You may still feel disappointed at minor upsets, but the disappointment is proportionate rather than catastrophic. Most of all, you may feel a new kind of inner stillness, a deepened awareness of the present moment, and a reduction in the black cloud of foreboding that many people report feeling virtually all of the time.

Recent years have seen considerable research in the use of mindfulness, not just to increase well-being but also to treat psychological disorders and mental illness. There is now a strong evidence base for mindfulness-based psychological therapies for mild and moderate depression, anxiety disorders (Chapter 5), self-harming behaviour (Chapter 11) and various other common problems (Chapter 9). There is also emerging evidence for mindfulness-based techniques for certain cases of substance misuse (Chapter 7), obsessive-compulsive disorder (Chapter 5) and eating disorders (Chapter 6). Properly used, mindfulness can help promote holistic health in chronic medical illness and deepen psychological care during cancer treatment and in terminal care settings. Most of all, though, specific courses of mindfulness-based therapies, provided over an eight-week period, are now accepted as effective tools for preventing relapse of depression. Guidance on accessing reliable mindfulness courses is provided at the end of this chapter.

Regarding social interventions for depression, there are well-described relationships between depressive symptoms, stressful life events and deficits in social support. Specific social interventions include provision of social support, measures to increase social engagement (for example, going out) and introduction of befriending services for individuals who are isolated, poorly integrated and experiencing socially disabling symptoms. Elements of national social policy may also be relevant: social welfare arrangements, for example, have significant effects on depressive symptoms, with the receipt of government entitlement benefits by unemployed women showing a significant association with reduced depressive symptoms in the long term.

For all individuals with depression, a consideration of the social environment and graded social re-engagement is an essential step on the road to recovery. Self-help groups and organisations such as Aware (see below) are also very helpful for many.

Antidepressant Medication

Biological treatments for depression include administration of medications and treatment of co-existing medical or substance-related disorders (for example, alcohol abuse) (Chapter 7). Antidepressant medications are the medications most commonly used in the management of depression. Most guidelines now recommend newer medications (selective-serotonin re-uptake inhibitors) as first-line treatments for depression, ahead of older medications (such as tricyclic antidepressants and monoamine oxidase inhibitors). St John's wort, a herb, is another useful treatment (although users should note that it significantly reduces the effectiveness of the contraceptive pill, possibly resulting in pregnancy). Overall, though, newer antidepressant medications have fewer side effects than older ones, and are safer.

The choice of medication will depend on the severity of the depression, the patient's treatment history and patient preference.

It is important that the decision to start an antidepressant medication is made jointly between the patient and the doctor or mental health team, and is carefully reviewed after around six weeks to see if progress is occurring. If progress is not satisfactory, treatment needs to be adjusted or re-considered.

All of these medications have various effects on chemicals in the brain, though that is not to suggest that the cause of depression in any given individual can be simply ascribed to any specific 'chemical imbalance'. The biology of the brain is as yet poorly understood, so any simple biological explanations for depression overstate how much is really known about the brain. What is clear, however, is that anti-depressant medications have *some* effects on brain chemicals, and that a majority of individuals find these effects helpful in terms of depression.

More precisely, approximately two-thirds of patients with moderate or severe depression respond to the first antidepressant prescribed. In these patients, the medication should be continued for six to nine months after recovery from a single depressive episode. For individuals who have experienced multiple depressive episodes, there is evidence to support continuation of treatment for up to two years. If there is no or insufficient response to the first antidepressant prescribed after several weeks, it is recommended to either increase the dose, switch to a different anti-depressant or engage in a broader re-consideration of therapeutic options. In the event of poor response after a second antidepressant, alternative treatment strategies may be required (for example, an antipsychotic medication or lithium, a mood-stabilising medication) (Chapter 4).

Many individuals experience no side effects whatsoever from antidepressant medications. Others experience mild adverse effects, such as transient nausea or sickness in the stomach, but opt to stay on the medication on the basis that the positive effects (improved mood) exceed any side effects. Other side effects may include headache, drowsiness, weight change and various others depending on the specific medication. In all cases, potential side effects should be discussed carefully prior to treatment. Specific side effects vary between different medications and are detailed on the information sheets provided with the medications themselves.

In addition, specific issues have been reported with medications in certain groups; treatment of depression in children and adolescents, for example, is outlined separately in Chapter 10.

There is also occasional controversy about antidepressant medication, and in 2010, the College of Psychiatrists of Ireland noted that 'effective treatment of depression is an important means of reducing suicide rates', and addressed the relationship between antidepressant medication and suicidal thoughts:

> Untreated depression can have a fatal outcome. Those experiencing moderate to severe depression frequently describe having thoughts of self-harm. Antidepressants are effective in the treatment of depression. The effective treatment of depression is an important means of reducing suicide rates. A huge volume of research in recent years has failed to establish a causal link between antidepressant use and suicide. At an individual level, the period early in treatment may be a time of relatively high risk, as treatment tends to start when the person's depression is severe and treatment takes some weeks to work. As treatment takes effect and energy and motivation return, people who have recently commenced antidepressant treatment may be more able to act on suicidal thoughts that are inherent to their condition. That the early recovery period is potentially a period of increased risk for suicidality is something of which all doctors should be aware. The College of Psychiatry of Ireland, in unison with the advice of the Irish Medicines Board, recommends close monitoring of all individuals commenced on antidepressant therapy. There is no evidence of a link between antidepressant use and homicide.

It is important that both patients and their families are aware of these matters and, indeed, aware of *all* of the possible adverse effects of *all* therapies (medications and psychological therapies alike) to ensure that treatment choices are informed, collaborative, sensible, safe and effective. The need for this kind of balanced information and a reasonable approach is especially important in relation to one of psychiatry's best-known and least-understood treatments: electro-convulsive therapy (ECT).

Electro-Convulsive Therapy (ECT)

ECT is an effective treatment for severe, treatment-resistant or life-threatening depression. ECT is often shown in movies and on television as it was administered in the 1950s: in a haphazard fashion, without anaesthetic, and against the patient's wishes. Today, ECT is used less commonly, is given under general anaesthetic, and the vast majority of treatments are entirely voluntary.

Like many treatments across all areas of medicine, it is not understood exactly how ECT works. There is, however, strong evidence that, for a small minority of patients, ECT provides rapid and substantial relief, and can, for some, prove life-saving. The treatment involves the patient receiving a general anaesthetic twice per week for four to six weeks and, while under anaesthetic, an electric current being applied across the brain, producing brain activity similar to that seen in an epileptic seizure or fit.

But does ECT work? The literature on ECT is wide and varied, and much is driven by ideology rather than scientific research. In recent years, however, a very clear picture has emerged. In England, the National Institute of Clinical Excellence (NICE) reviewed the entire evidence base for ECT and now recommends ECT for the treatment of (a) severe depressive illness, (b) a prolonged or severe episode of mania, or (c) catatonia (severe physical manifestations of mental disorder), in order to gain fast and short-term improvement of severe symptoms once all other treatment options have failed, or when the situation is life-threatening.[4]

Predictors of a good response to ECT include severe depression, delusions and prominent biological symptoms (for example, loss of weight, loss of appetite, early morning waking and diurnal mood variation). Potential side effects include headache and memory difficulties, and while these are short-lived in the majority of cases, some people report persistent memory problems. Careful explanation of side effects is essential prior to treatment to allow patients to weigh up the positives against the negatives and make informed choices.

Many critics of the over-use and inappropriate use of ECT in the past choose to apply their arguments to today's practices too, and ignore the fact that the balance of scientific evidence is now clearly in favour of ECT in the very specific, very limited circumstances outlined by NICE. Despite this clear evidence, many contemporary critics tend to focus selectively on parts of the scientific literature that suit their argument, rather than overviews of the entire body of literature.

While it is important that dissenting views are considered with care (Chapter 1), anyone who has experienced the intensely debilitating and life-threatening symptoms of severe depression will appreciate that *no* treatment should be dismissed without clear-eyed, objective evaluation of the evidence. In the case of ECT, the balance of evidence, as presented by NICE, is now very clear: ECT is a potentially life-saving treatment for depression when it is severe, treatment-resistant, and/or life-threatening.

As a doctor and scientist it does not rest easy with me that we do not know how ECT works, and I am deeply disturbed that ECT has been misused throughout the history of psychiatry.[5] Today, however, ECT is highly regulated by the Mental Health Commission and it would be a profound violation of rights to withhold ECT from appropriate patients in the future. ECT is a safe, essential treatment for a minority of patients, some of whom might otherwise die.

Overall Treatment Approaches

It is important that treatment choices for depression take account of all elements of the bio-psycho-social approach to management. Combinations of therapies are likely to be required for many people, that is, both psychological therapy and antidepressant medications. It is imperative that therapeutic choices and plans are communicated clearly to patients and their families, and that care is genuinely holistic and person-centred at all times.

Providing consistent psychological support is a vital element in the management of any mental illness, and can turn a potentially debilitating episode of depression into an episode of illness that is addressed collaboratively and resolved in a fashion that is effective, acceptable and produces sustained wellness for the future.

Outcomes in depression vary from person to person, depending on their circumstances and the severity of the depression, but the vast majority of people with mild or moderate depression recover fully. Overall, 80 per cent of people with depression recover fully, while 20 per cent experience ongoing problems. In severe depression, the lifetime risk of suicide is 10–15 per cent (Chapter 11) but it is much lower in less severe depression. Prognosis is better if the person does not use alcohol or drugs (Chapter 7), adheres to their personal treatment plan, and takes active steps to maintain mental wellness following recovery, that is, has a healthy diet and lifestyle, maintains good physical health, sustains links with family and friends, and addresses any emergent mental health problems early on.

Case History: Paul

Paul, an 18-year-old boy, had been doing well in school until, abruptly, he stopped attending. He pretended to leave home in the morning but spent the day alone sitting in the park. After two weeks of non-attendance, his parents received a phone call from the school. They confronted Paul at home. Paul readily admitted he hadn't been attending school. He said 'there's no point' and 'I might as well be dead'. Paul's parents found a suicide note in Paul's room and a rope stored under his bed.

Paul's parents brought Paul to see their GP who immediately referred Paul to a psychiatrist. It turned out that Paul had been experiencing low mood, suicidal thoughts, and extreme hopelessness for the previous four months. This had started with no apparent trigger, apart from the usual ups-and-downs of teenage life. Paul required careful monitoring, treatment with antidepressant medication and regular sessions with a psychological therapist, focusing on coping skills. After about one month, Paul felt substantially better, and after nine months the antidepressant medication was discontinued. Paul continued to attend the coping skills therapy for over one year, and had no recurrence of his depression.

Useful Resources

It is advisable that anyone who thinks they have any of the conditions discussed in this book sees a health care professional. There are many reasons for this, including a need to rule out any other diagnoses, such as physical illnesses. In addition, some people find it easier to talk with a health care professional, especially if they are too uncertain or embarrassed to talk with friends or family members. Often, a brief talk with a GP will 'normalise' the individual's symptoms by reassuring them that they are not alone in what they are experiencing and that help is available, if needed.

Individuals with any mental disorder or psychological problem, and their families, will find much that is useful on the Internet. As ever though, Internet resources need to be evaluated with care and only trusted when the information comes from a reliable source. Reliable information about mental health can be sourced from the websites of the Health Service Executive (www. hse.ie/eng/health/az), College of Psychiatrists of Ireland (www. irishpsychiatry.ie), Royal College of Psychiatrists in London (www. rcpsych.ac.uk), National Health Service in the UK (www.nhs.uk)

and National Institute of Mental Health in the US (www.nimh.nih. gov).

Evidence-based guidance about specific treatments can be found on the website of the National Institute for Health and Care Excellence (NICE) (www.nice.org.uk). NICE is a UK-based organisation responsible for developing guidance, standards and information on high-quality health and social care, and preventing and treating ill health. In 2009, NICE published *Depression: The Treatment and Management of Depression in Adults* (updated in April 2016) which, like all of their reports, can be downloaded free of charge.

In addition to the above, Aware is an Irish organisation which provides extensive and reliable information on their website (www. aware.ie). The mission of Aware is to help build a society in which individuals with stress (Chapter 9), depression, bipolar disorder (Chapter 4), and other mood disorders, and their families, are supported and understood, do not experience stigma, and can avail of a wide variety of appropriate therapies. Their website is informative, practical and reliable.

Guidance on strategies when anti-depressant medication does not help sufficiently is provided in a book entitled *Still Down: What to Do When Antidepressants Fail* by Dean F. MacKinnon MD (Johns Hopkins Press, 2016).

Reliable mindfulness resources can be accessed through the website of Mindfulness Ireland (www.mindfulnessireland.org).

There are several books which may also be helpful, including: *Coming Through Depression: A Mindful Approach to Recovery* by Tony Bates (Newleaf, 2011); *Flagging the Problem: A New Approach to Mental Health* by Dr Harry Barry (Liberties Press, 2007); *Flagging the Therapy: Pathways Out of Depression and Anxiety* by Dr Harry Barry (Liberties Press, 2009); *Malignant Sadness: The Anatomy of Depression* by Lewis Wolpert (Faber and Faber, 1999); and *Light Mind: Mindfulness for Daily Living* by Padraig O'Morain (Veritas, 2009). Padraig O'Morain is an author and counsellor who also provides an Internet resource focused on mindfulness (www. padraigomorain.com/blog).

Endnotes

1 World Health Organisation. *International Classification of Diseases* (10th Edition). Geneva: World Health Organisation, 1992.

2 O'Shea, E. and Kennelly, B. *The Economics of Mental Health Care in Ireland.* Galway and Dublin: Irish Centre for Social Gerontology and Department of Economics, NUI Galway/Mental Health Commission, 2008.

3 McCrone, P., Dhanasiri, S., Patel, A., Knapp, M. and Lawton-Smith, S. *Paying the Price: The Cost of Mental Health Care in England to 2026.* London: King's Fund, 2008.

4 www.nice.org.uk/guidance/ta59.

5 Kelly, B. *Hearing Voices: The History of Psychiatry in Ireland.* Dublin: Irish Academic Press, 2016 (Chapter 5).

Chapter 3

Schizophrenia

The word 'schizophrenia' often generates significant anxiety and concern, and occasionally panic, but the fact is that schizophrenia is a common, treatable mental disorder. While no cure has been identified, there has been considerable progress with treatment and management over past decades.

Much of the confusion stems from the fact that schizophrenia is a form of 'psychosis'. Psychosis is a state of mind in which a person loses contact with reality in at least one important respect for a period of time, while not intoxicated with alcohol or drugs, and while not affected by an acute physical illness that better accounts for the symptoms (for example, having a high fever). Psychosis can be associated with schizophrenia, severe depression (Chapter 2), severe mania (Chapter 4) and certain other conditions (Chapters 7, 8, 9 and 10).

This chapter looks at four key questions about schizophrenia:

◊ What are the symptoms and signs of schizophrenia?

◊ How common is schizophrenia?

◊ What causes schizophrenia?

◊ What are the treatments for schizophrenia?

Useful resources and sources of further information are provided at the end of the chapter.

What Are the Signs and Symptoms of Schizophrenia?

Schizophrenia tends to first emerge in the late teens or early twenties, and is more common in men than women. Symptoms commence with very subtle changes in childhood thinking and behaviour, but these changes are so vague and non-specific that they are only recognisable when looking back many years later, or in research studies. The vast majority of children with such subtle abnormalities do not develop any psychological or psychiatric problems, and nor is there any known intervention indicated for them at that point. So while these abnormalities cannot be used to diagnose schizophrenia or intervene at that very early stage, they still indicate that, for many people with schizophrenia, brain development takes a different pathway from a very early stage, possibly even before birth, *in utero*.

The first noticeable symptoms of schizophrenia often emerge in the teen years and include anxiety, low mood, social withdrawal or preoccupation with odd beliefs. This description includes most teenagers at some point or other (and many adults too) so, once again, these features do not diagnose schizophrenia, although if they are present to a substantial extent they might identify a young adult at increased risk of psychological or psychiatric problems. Early intervention programmes have been developed in many countries for this group, especially if they also misuse risky substances, such as cannabis (Chapter 7). The shorter the duration of untreated illness, the better the outcome. Early interventions focus on many types of treatment including psychological interventions, social support and, if indicated, medication, as well as family support.

The DETECT service is one such early intervention service in Ireland, funded by the Health Service Executive (HSE) and Hospitaller Order of St John of God (www.detect.ie). More such services are needed in other parts of the country. Early intervention in first episode psychosis was one of the priority areas identified by the HSE's National Clinical Programmes for Mental Health in 2010. The overarching aim of the national programmes is to standardise quality, evidence-based practice across the mental health services, and early psychosis is one of the areas to which particular attention is being directed.

The classic symptoms of schizophrenia, when they emerge, include delusions (unfounded beliefs that persist despite evidence to the contrary) and hallucinations (perceptions without appropriate external stimuli, such as hearing voices). Other features include difficulties with clear thinking and a range of 'negative' symptoms similar to depression (Chapter 2): low mood, loss of interest, depleted energy and persistent social withdrawal.

More specifically, the WHO states that a diagnosis of schizophrenia requires either one major symptom or two minor symptoms to be present for most of the time during an episode of psychotic illness lasting for at least one month, or else at some time during most of the days.[1] The major symptoms described by the WHO are (a) thought echo (hearing one's own thoughts spoken aloud), believing that thoughts are inserted or withdrawn from one's head, or are being broadcast; (b) delusions that one's thoughts, actions, feelings or perceptions are being controlled by someone or something other than one's self; (c) hearing voices giving a running commentary on one's behaviour, voices having discussions about you among themselves, or voices emanating from one's own body; and (d) other kinds of persistent delusions that are culturally inappropriate and completely impossible (for example, having superhuman powers).

Minor symptoms include (a) persistent hallucinations of any sort, occurring every day for some weeks, accompanied by delusions (which may be fleeting) without any apparent explanation; (b) various difficulties with clear thinking, such as sudden interruptions of thoughts, resulting in diminished coherence; (c) changes in muscle tone, such as stiffness or apparent inability to operate one's muscles and/or limbs in the normal fashion, possibly resulting in complete lack of movement ('catatonia'); and (d) 'negative symptoms' such as reduced speech, emotions, energy or interest. There may also be consistent and significant change in other aspects of behavior, such as social withdrawal. For a diagnosis of schizophrenia, these symptoms must not be attributable to alcohol or drugs, or to any known brain disease such as a brain tumour.

In practice, presentations with schizophrenia vary greatly. One person might present with a long history of quiet, paranoid delusions that have finally become problematic for them, possibly after existing for many years. Another might present with a sudden onset of dramatic hallucinations commanding him or her to do certain things or go certain places; such commands might be resisted or ignored, but are usually either distressing or perplexing. Others might present with very vague symptoms, chiefly related to social withdrawal and self-isolation, and it might not be clear if the person is mentally ill, misusing drugs (Chapter 7), or simply choosing to live differently. Sometimes, it is a mix of all three.

Given this enormous diversity of symptoms and clinical presentations, schizophrenia is one of the true enigmas of medicine and, possibly, of the human condition in general. This is partly because 'schizophrenia' is really a term used to denote a cluster of symptoms which tend to co-occur, rather than a biologically defined entity. This places schizophrenia in sharp contrast to conditions such as diabetes, which is biologically defined though measurement of blood glucose, or brain tumours which are diagnosed with brain scans. There are no blood tests or brain scans for diagnosing schizophrenia. Diagnosis is based entirely on symptoms and it is therefore not at all surprising that diagnostic criteria have changed considerably over past centuries, although the essence of the disorder has remained remarkably constant.

Case History: John

John was a 20-year-old university student with no family history of mental illness. While attending college, he began to distance himself from his family and friends. Over a period of around a year, his grades slipped, he stopped phoning home, and he rarely socialised.

One of his friends, Susan, phoned John's parents to say that John was acting strangely. John's parents visited and saw nothing in particular amiss, but felt that John seemed slightly distracted during their visit.

Two months later, John presented to a hospital emergency department in a highly distressed state, saying that there were unusual forces at work on the Internet and he needed to come to hospital. On further questioning, John stated that various common websites had started to send messages specifically to him, warning him that 'dark forces' were at work. John said he did not actually hear voices, but had 'a feeling of voices' coming from outside his head. John added that the relevant websites were now controlling some of his thoughts.

Following a complete history, mental state examination and physical assessment, John allowed his parents to be telephoned and they came to the hospital. It was agreed that John would start taking an antipsychotic medication, link with the multi-disciplinary team, and stay with his parents for the time being. John seemed relieved with the arrangements, although still perplexed.

Follow-up by a community mental health nurse the next day revealed that John's mental state was generally unchanged, although he remained agreeable with the treatment plan. Over the following weeks, John's paranoid delusions began slowly to subside and he became substantially less distressed. Although he did not relinquish his delusional beliefs entirely, he was less vocal about them. His parents contacted the college and John opted to take some weeks off his course. Psycho-education was provided to John and his family, focusing on the nature of John's symptoms, the role of medication and other therapies, the advisability of avoiding cannabis and other drugs, and steps to be taken in the event of any future deterioration in mental health.

Over the following months, John ceased to speak about his paranoid delusions at all. His mood and general inter-activity improved and he was keen to return to college. He spoke with the student support service there and resumed his studies. John con-

tinued to take medication. His return to college was successful and he experienced no further episodes of psychosis while remaining on medication.

How Common is Schizophrenia?

Schizophrenia will affect just under 1 per cent of people at some point in their lives. There are 15 to 20 new cases per 100,000 population per year, an incidence equal to that of Type 1 diabetes in Western Europe. In Ireland, schizophrenia accounted for 20 per cent of all psychiatric admissions in 2015, yielding the second-highest admission rate of any diagnosis (78 admissions per 100,000 population per year), second only to depressive disorders (105 admissions per 100,000 population per year) (Chapter 2).[2]

Schizophrenia also had the highest rate of *involuntary* admission in 2015 (20.2 involuntary admissions per 100,000 population per year), followed by mania (7.7 involuntary admissions per 100,000 population per year) (Chapter 4) and depressive disorders (4.8 involuntary admissions per 100,000 population per year) (Chapters 2 and 13). Patterns are similar in other countries.

Each year approximately 800 people are admitted to Irish psychiatric hospitals and inpatient units with a new diagnosis of schizophrenia or a related mental disorder. Across Europe, up to three million people have a diagnosis of schizophrenia at any one time, but many millions more are affected directly or indirectly owing to the effects of the illness on family, friends and broader communities.

In societal terms, schizophrenia exerts substantial economic costs: in 2000, the annual cost of schizophrenia to the US was $40 billion (€37 billion) – three times as much as the US space programme.[3] In 2002, the estimated cost in the US had risen to $63 billion (€58 billion), including $23 billion (€21 billion) in direct health care costs.

In England, the estimated societal cost of schizophrenia was £7 billion (€10 billion) in 2004/2005, while in Ireland the cost of schizophrenia in 2006 was €460.6 million, comprising direct costs of care amounting to €117.5 million and indirect costs of €343 million, including €43.8 for informal care borne by families.[4] Lost productivity due to unemployment, absence from work and premature mortality came to €277 million.

The true cost of schizophrenia, however, can only be described in human terms, relating to reduced quality of life, limited opportunity for personal development, ongoing symptoms and increased mortality (see below), as well as the suffering and stress experienced by family members and carers. Much of this is attributable to the broad range of symptoms associated with the disorder, and its impairment of social and psychological functioning for many, as well as adverse, stigmatising social arrangements in most countries (Chapter 15).

What Causes Schizophrenia?

The causes of schizophrenia are not fully understood. The disorder probably results from a complex interaction of inherited genes, disruptions to brain development prior to birth (that is, in the womb), and further contributory factors acting in childhood, adolescence and early adulthood.[5]

To begin with, it is now well established that an increased risk of schizophrenia runs in families. While no single gene has been proven to have a large effect for most people with schizophrenia, evidence from family studies is still very compelling. If a person has a first degree relative with schizophrenia (that is, a parent, sibling, child), their lifetime risk is increased from just under 1 per cent up to 15 per cent. Even if the person is reared apart from their family of origin (that is, adopted), their risk is still increased, at 12 per cent. If a monozygotic or identical twin has schizophrenia, then the other twin, who shares all their genetic information, has a 50 per cent chance of developing the disorder.

These studies demonstrate two important facts: (1) there is a strong genetic element in risk of schizophrenia (that is, it runs in families); and (2) other factors are equally important, such as environment, life experiences, and various other unidentified non-genetic influences. From the genetic point of view, there are likely to be multiple genes of moderate or small effect, which affect some but not all people at risk of schizophrenia. It is worth remembering, however, that, despite these findings, most people with schizophrenia do *not* have a family history of the disorder, and most people with a family history do *not* develop schizophrenia. Therefore, while family history and genes certainly increase risk, other, environmental factors are critically important too.

Looking at studies of the human brain, there is strong research evidence that dopamine, a key chemical messenger in the brain, is not regulated correctly in schizophrenia. Given the highly interconnected nature of the brain, other brain chemicals are sure to be involved too. There are also certain abnormalities of brain structure in some people with schizophrenia, but none of these are sufficiently specific to schizophrenia to assist with diagnosing the illness, ruling it out, or even identifying those at high risk.

There are, however, links between schizophrenia and injuries during pregnancy or at birth, the season of birth (winter and early spring), psychological trauma in childhood, cannabis use (Chapter 7), head injury, migration and social adversity (Chapter 15). All of these factors are linked with schizophrenia to varying degrees but none are fully understood. Some of the risks are also very small. For example, being born in winter or early spring seems to explain at most 3 per cent of the risk of schizophrenia, presumably due to infections during pregnancy, but this is a tiny proportion of the risk and even this is still subject to debate.

This situation is most frustrating for people affected by schizophrenia and their families who seek to understand its causes and figure out why they or their family member has been affected. But this is an exceptionally challenging area of research for several reasons, not least of which is the difficulty in linking various risk factors with each other in a long-running attempt to create a coherent picture of how, precisely, the jigsaw fits together. The association identified between living in cities and developing schizophrenia provides a good demonstration of the challenges involved and the difficulties with reaching firm conclusions.[6]

It has been long recognised that there are more people with schizophrenia in urban areas than in rural ones. Studies in the 1960s and 1970s showed that the most obvious explanation for this turns out to be true, at least in part: people with pre-existing schizophrenia tend to drift into urban areas to seek assistance, accommodation and various other supports, leading to a relative concentration of schizophrenia in cities *as a result of the disorder.*

It soon became clear, however, that this 'urban drift' could not fully explain the association between schizophrenia and cities. Further research duly showed that, even after taking 'urban drift' into account, urban birth, urban upbringing, and urban living are *all* associated with increased risk of developing schizophrenia in later life. Like having a family history of schizophrenia, living in cities is neither necessary nor sufficient for developing the disorder, but it does increase the lifetime risk from just under 1 per cent to just under 2 per cent (using best available estimates). This increase in risk is not nearly enough to advise against living in a city, even among those with a family history or other risk factors, but multiple studies have reproduced this finding, and there is a very convincing dose-response effect: the greater the degree of urbanicity at birth (that is, urban versus suburban versus rural), the greater the risk of schizophrenia. Why? And what can this tell us about schizophrenia in general?

There must be some unidentified causal factor at work here, some biological or psychological features of cities that alter brain development or function to increase risk of schizophrenia. Possible explanations include increased exposure to infections or air pollution in cities, or possibly vitamin D deficiency. But these theories, although logical, remain unproven. Another possible explanation centres on what is best termed 'community disorganisation', and its social, psychological and biological effects on the brain. For example, it is known that migrants experience increased rates of many mental disorders, including schizophrenia, and this appears related to the size of the migrant group in the host country: the smaller an ethnic minority group is, the greater its increase in risk of schizophrenia.[7] Why might this be the case, and what can it tell us about schizophrenia?

Many mental illnesses, including schizophrenia, are associated with disturbances of the body's stress responses as reflected in body cortisol, a steroid hormone produced in situations of stress. Chronic production of high levels of cortisol damages all body systems, including the brain. It is highly probable that belonging to a small minority migrant and/or ethnic group is associated with a state of chronic stress, producing increased cortisol and therefore increased risk of schizophrenia. Childhood trauma and abuse might also act in the same way.

This kind of 'stress effect' is likely to be more powerful in urban areas, as city-living affects the brain's response to stress. Baseline levels of crime, social fragmentation, problems with social capital, and urban decay all contribute further to this risk and likely explain, at least in part, why children in cities have an increased risk of developing symptoms of disorders such as schizophrenia.[8]

This 'stress hypothesis' is a compelling theory with much evidence to support it, but it is still a theory. And even if living in a city does increase risk in this fashion, it remains the case that the vast majority of people in cities do not develop schizophrenia and that the attributable risk is small. So even if all of these findings relating to cities, stress and the brain are borne out in further studies, schizophrenia will still remain, in large part, a mystery.

Ultimately, research in this area is greatly hampered by the fact that schizophrenia is defined by symptoms rather than biological tests. 'Schizophrenia', like 'headaches' and 'fever', is almost certainly an umbrella term that covers a family of different but related 'sub-disorders' rather than a single entity. These sub-disorders, despite sharing certain symptoms, might well have somewhat different origins in different individuals. Different combinations of risk factors, with different sequencing and timing, might combine with multiple genes to produce the clinical picture of 'schizophrenia' as a result of different causal pathways in different people. As a result, the undeniable suffering of people diagnosed with schizophrenia might well reflect different combinations of risk factors producing similar (but not identical) collections of symptoms, reflecting both commonality and individual difference in causes, symptoms and therapeutic need. Several proposed risk factors are, however, definitively disproven: parenting styles do *not* cause schizophrenia, and the illness has nothing to do with 'multiple personalities' or weak or bad personalities.

In summary, 'schizophrenia', as presently conceptualised, is probably attributable to a complex combination of developmental alterations resulting from specific genes; early insults to the brain (possibly even prior to birth); childhood adversity (which might affect brain function); social adversity (which might affect psychological processes); subsequent stress (which further affects brain function and psychological processes); and – in a vicious cycle – additional stress resulting from hallucinations and paranoia, eventually resulting in hardwiring of psychotic beliefs in the brain, and perpetuation of the symptoms of schizophrenia.[9]

There might well be myriad individual variations on this kind of model, but it is now clear that complicated, composite models such as this one best integrate current understandings of risk factors for schizophrenia. More research needs to be done to determine precise genetic and environmental causes, which *combinations* of risk factors confer most risk and how these can be modified at various points in human growth and development.

There is much to be done. For now, however, the causes of schizophrenia remain, for the most part, unknown.

What Are the Treatments for Schizophrenia?

Schizophrenia is a treatable mental disorder. As with all mental disorders, treatment is based on a bio-psycho-social approach: biological interventions include administration of medications, treatment of co-existing medical illness or substance misuse problems and, in a small minority of cases, ECT. Psychological and social interventions include specific psychotherapies for patients and families, as well as enhancing personal supports and social participation.

There is now considerable evidence to support the benefits of proactive, early intervention in first episode psychosis, including schizophrenia. Management involves a multi-disciplinary team working together with the patient, family and primary care team to diagnose and treat the first episode of illness, prevent the development of subsequent episodes, and establish an ongoing management plan aimed at optimising social function and minimising the effects of the illness on the patient and family.

Medication for Schizophrenia

The fundamental principles of treatment in acute schizophrenia are similar to those in many other areas of medicine. Medication should be used at a dose that combines optimal effectiveness with a minimum of side effects. The use of multiple medications is to be avoided as much as possible, although it can be necessary in certain circumstances. Medication regimes should be rational and understandable, with an emphasis on once-daily dosing where possible. Measures should be taken to assist with complex treatment regimes, and these may involve pharmacy blister packing, tablet boxes, tablet counters, or supervision by a family member or therapist. Side effects should be identified early and openly discussed with patient and family, as appropriate.

The UK-based National Institute for Health and Care Excellence (NICE) provides specific treatment recommendations in its review of 'psychosis and schizophrenia in adults: prevention and management', published in February 2014 and (like all NICE guidelines) freely available from its website.[10] The NICE advice covers a range of areas relating to schizophrenia, but places especially strong emphasis on early intervention for first episode psychosis, for which NICE recommends medication in conjunction with psychological interventions such as family interventions and individual cognitive behaviour therapy (CBT) (Chapters 2, 5 and 9). NICE also recommends that the choice of medication is made by the patient and healthcare professional (and, if appropriate, carer) together, taking account of likely benefits and possible side effects such as weight gain, movement problems (for example, restlessness), and potential effects on the heart or hormones (for example, raised prolactin).

The first effective medication for schizophrenia, chlorpromazine, was developed in the 1950s and was followed by a number of related medications (in both tablet and injected forms) which made it possible for some long-term patients to leave large institutions and live with greater independence in the community. These medications included fluphenazine, trifluoperazine, flupentixol, haloperidol, zuclopenthixol, sulpiride and pimozide.

It was soon recognised, however, that these medications could have significant adverse effects, including movement disorders (such as restlessness or Parkinsonism), dry mouth, constipation, sedation, effects on the heart (increasing risk of sudden cardiac death), and various other effects such as dizziness and impotence. A range of strategies were introduced to manage adverse effects and research focused on developing newer treatments that would combine good clinical effects with fewer side effects. A new generation of 'atypical' antipsychotics was duly developed and introduced to clinical practice, so there is now a broad range of antipsychotic medications available for schizophrenia, with different combinations of benefits and adverse effects. Atypical antipsychotic medications currently available include risperidone, olanzapine, quetiapine, aripiprazole, amisulpride, ziprasidone and paliperidone.

In practice, first episode schizophrenia is now most often treated with an atypical antipsychotic medication, though conventional antipsychotic agents are still sometimes used. These newer atypical agents appear to be as effective as older agents in the management of delusions and hallucinations, and seem to have fewer adverse effects in the recommended dosage ranges. In particular, they are associated with a reduced incidence of movement disorders and difficulties with clear thinking. Side effects can, however, include weight gain, impaired glucose tolerance, and diabetes mellitus, as well as dry mouth, sedation, possible effects on the heart, dizziness and impotence. And, as with all antipsychotics, neuroleptic malignant syndrome (NMS) can occur; this is a rare adverse effect (very high temperature, confusion) that needs to be managed in hospital and can be fatal if not treated. For all patients, it is recommended that, prior to commencing these medications, the person has a cardiac tracing performed (electro-cardiogram or 'ECG'), weight and height checked, and a set of basic blood tests done, including blood glucose. These should be monitored annually.

In first episode schizophrenia, a six to eight-week trial of an optimal dosage of an atypical medication should be combined with appropriate social and psychological treatment. If this does not produce satisfactory clinical results, therapeutic options should be reviewed and discussed with patient and family. It is important to establish if the patient is not taking the medication for any reason, and to address whatever concerns might be leading to this. Another antipsychotic medication (tablets or injections) can be tried for a further six to eight weeks.

In the unlikely event that these steps do not produce sufficient clinical improvement, clozapine can be considered. Clozapine is an antipsychotic medication which can greatly help persons with difficult-to-treat schizophrenia, but it is reserved for treatment-resistant situations owing to its possible effects on the person's white blood cell count. A low white blood cell count can leave a person at risk of fatal infection, so clozapine is a highly regulated medication and requires a careful programme of blood-testing while the patient is on it. This blood testing programme is highly effective in detecting and addressing this problem. Other potential side effects include weight gain, constipation, seizures, cardiac effects, and problems with saliva secretion. Even so, a great number of people have benefitted hugely from this medication, which has been genuinely transformative in the lives of many people with schizophrenia who had extremely distressing symptoms prior to clozapine.

At all stages of treatment it is essential to discuss the treatment plan with patient and carers; the possible adverse effects of medication (if any); and to provide social and personal support for patient and family. There can, however, be particular challenges if the person presents in a highly agitated psychotic state, in a situation of great distress, and possibly presents a risk to self or others.

In this situation, management centres initially on environmental and psychological measures: talking calmly and clearly to the patient, increasing personal space, and ensuring the availability of a comfortable, non-threatening environment for patient and carers. There are many possible causes of acute agitation so care needs to be taken to ensure that the person is not suffering from something other than schizophrenia or something in addition to schizophrenia, such as intoxication with drugs or delirium (confusion) following an injury or illness.

If the person presents a risk to self or others, or if treatment is urgently needed and cannot be otherwise provided, involuntary procedures can be instigated under the Mental Health Act 2001 (Chapter 13). In very acute circumstances of risk, the gardaí can be called, but this is rare event. The gardaí then have the option of instigating involuntary admission under the Mental Health Act 2001.

Finally with regard to medication, decisions to discontinue medication are taken on an individual basis. To date, insufficient attention has been given to correct protocols for reducing and stopping medication, the adverse effects linked with these decisions and with medication discontinuation, and the management of resultant therapeutic challenges. There is a strong need for further research and consideration of these matters.

ECT for Schizophrenia

ECT is not a common treatment for schizophrenia but has a role in certain situations. NICE guidelines, based on an extensive review of evidence, recommend ECT for severe depressive illness (Chapter 2), prolonged or severe episodes of mania (Chapter 4), or catatonia (which can occur in schizophrenia), once certain conditions are met.[11] According to NICE, ECT should be administered to gain fast, short-term improvement of severe symptoms after all other treatment options have failed, or when the situation is life-threatening. Particular caution is advised in pregnant women and older or younger patients; an individual risk-benefit assessment should be performed balancing adverse effects, such as memory problems, with benefits; and patients should be reassessed regularly during programmes of ECT.

More than one course of ECT should be considered only for patients with severe depressive illness, catatonia or mania who have previously had good responses to ECT. ECT should not be used as a long-term treatment to prevent recurrence of depression or in the general management of schizophrenia, according to NICE.

ECT should, then, be reserved for rare, severe situations in certain persons with schizophrenia. In Ireland, schizophrenia, schizotypal and delusional disorders (Chapter 9) accounted for fewer than 9 per cent of all programmes of ECT administered in 2013, the vast majority being prescribed for depressive disorders (82 per cent).[12] Nonetheless, there remains a small minority of patients with schizophrenia, especially those with catatonia, for whom ECT is indicated, effective and – occasionally – life-saving.

Ongoing Treatment

Even if the response to treatment is good following a first episode of psychosis, there is a high risk of relapse if medication is stopped within one to two years. In addition, ongoing management of schizophrenia involves much more than medication, and requires a multi-disciplinary team working together with the patient, family, GP and primary care team to treat the first episode of illness, prevent the development of subsequent episodes, and establish an ongoing collaborative plan aimed at optimising social function and minimising the effects of the illness on the patient and the family.

Continued treatment with antipsychotic medication is part of a package of therapies that can help prevent relapse. Medication may be administered as tablets, injections or both. It is important to discuss treatment with patient and family, and to seek out evidence of adverse effects of medication or non-concordance with treatment. Treatment for depression may also be needed for some people, and this might involve medication at times, as well as psychological therapy and support (Chapter 2).

Long-term use of antipsychotic medication use may be associated with the development of side effects (see above). Each side effect is addressed in its own way. In general, if a side effect develops, it is wise to consider the possibility of other causes also; for example, weight gain may be due to poor dietary habits rather than medication. Appropriate measures should be instigated to address the underlying cause. Some medication can contribute to the development of diabetes, and this requires fundamental reconsideration of the chosen treatment, as well as management of the diabetes.

If the side effect appears to be due to the medication, it may be a good first step to consider reducing the dose or switching to another medication, if this is clinically appropriate and acceptable. There are also specific strategies for the management of particular unwanted effects, such as movement disorders, and a psychiatrist or GP can advise about these. Additional medication can play a role in managing these problems, although the use of complex combinations of different medications is to be avoided where possible, and social or psychological measures should accompany all interventions. There is particular concern in recent times about the effects of certain antipsychotic medications on the heart, and so some medications require cardiac monitoring under specialist supervision.

It is often the negative symptoms of schizophrenia, such as social withdrawal or impaired motivation, that prove most distressing for family and carers in the long term. Current medications that are effective in the alleviation of symptoms such as hallucinations or delusions tend to have a much weaker effect on negative symptoms. There is a strong need to develop further medications that combine enhanced clinical effectiveness with fewer side effects, as these are likely to also prove more acceptable to patients, enhance adherence to treatment, and improve overall therapeutic outcomes.

In addition to pharmacological management, there is a series of other interventions that are critical in the management of schizophrenia. Psychoeducation for patient and family helps develop understanding of the illness and its treatment, and enhances the therapeutic alliance between family and health care providers. Other psychological approaches of proven benefit include CBT (Chapters 2, 5 and 9), family therapy, art therapy (especially for negative symptoms) and self-help groups and forums (Chapter 12).

Recent years have seen particular interest in CBT for certain patients with schizophrenia, focusing on helping them deal with persistent delusions and hallucinations. NICE now recommends offering structured CBT to assist patients with establishing links between thoughts, feelings, actions and their symptoms and functioning, and re-evaluating others people's perceptions, beliefs or reasoning as they relate to target symptoms.[13] Other aspects of CBT in psychosis include monitoring one's own thoughts, feelings or behaviours with respect to symptoms; promoting alternative coping strategies; diminishing distress; and improving functioning.

Social interventions for schizophrenia include the assessment of social and occupational needs, provision of appropriate information and training, and advice on financial and practical matters relating to housing, occupation and social function. Many people with schizophrenia, especially if it follows a chronic course, experience difficulties obtaining and sustaining accommodation. It is important to ensure that accommodation is appropriate to the needs of the patient and that there are no preventable psychosocial stressors likely to hinder recovery. It is also important to recognise the role of support and encouragement from family and friends during both the illness and the recovery phase.

In the case of long-term mental illness, there may be a need to seek accommodation outside the family home, for a variety of reasons. Finding accommodation can be particularly challenging for patients who were homeless prior to presentation. Boarding houses, halfway houses, hostels, lodging schemes, and many other models of accommodation have been explored, with varying degrees of success. Local authorities bear significant responsibility to work constructively with mental health services, patients and families in fashioning appropriate solutions for individual patients.

The location of accommodation and the degree of support offered need to be tailored to meet the needs of the patients involved. Ongoing liaison with local residents may also be required to optimise the therapeutic opportunities offered by community living. There is a strong need for enhanced public funding for accommodation for people with recurrent and disabling mental illness (Chapter 15).

Occupational engagement is another key area for many people with schizophrenia, especially those with recurring episodes of psychosis. The development of acceptable and gainful occupation for people with schizophrenia is dependent on the abilities and aptitudes of the individual person, and the availability of appropriate financial and human resources. In the case of acute schizophrenia there may well be a return to previous employment or education following an episode of illness.

In the case of chronic schizophrenia, there may be a need for further training or a reformulation of employment or training plans. The provision of specific employment programmes can help with rehabilitation and ongoing treatment for people with persistent symptoms or psychosocial disability associated with mental illness. Day centres may form a further focus for daily activity and also provide an opportunity for detailed clinical assessment and liaison with family and carers.

Some people with schizophrenia, particularly with recurrent episodes or ongoing psychosocial disability, may need assistance or guidance with some of the tasks of daily living, such as arranging finances, budgeting and saving. In many cases, this will be carried out independently by the patient, or with supervision from family or friends. In some cases there may be a need for supervision which cannot be met by family or friends, for a variety of reasons. In these cases, a social worker, occupational therapist, community mental health nurse or other member of the multidisciplinary team may undertake to provide assistance in these often difficult-to-navigate areas.

Carer Stress

Many carers and family members are reluctant to report the psychological stress that can accompany caring. Illness can have a stressful impact on all family members, including parents, children and siblings. The effects of this may include loss of personal time, decreased social relationships, poorer health and diminished finances. It is critical that carers are aware of the possibility of carer stress, and are educated about how to avoid or reduce this in themselves and others. Enhanced support is generally needed to make this possible.

Education about mental illness and its effects is a key element in this process. There is a particular need for broad public education initiatives related to mental illness in general and schizophrenia in particular. There is also increasing recognition of the role of advocacy in mental health care and shaping mental health services. An advocate is someone who represents and defends the views, needs and rights of someone who does not feel able to do this for themselves. Advocates may include members of the patient's family, their friends, mental health team members or others. Effective advocacy is associated with increased agreement about treatment goals, greater control over management plans, and improved outcomes. See the Useful Resources at the end of this chapter and also Chapter 12 for further information.

Communication

Fluent communication is a key component in community treatment of any mental illness, including schizophrenia. Communication with patient and family are crucial. Communication between carers is similarly essential for the development of a cohesive, consistent treatment programme. In the case of schizophrenia, there may be a number of locations in which treatment is provided to any one patient: home, clinic, day hospital, workshop and primary care centre. It is essential that there are clear lines of communication between these agencies, and that all are informed about the treatment plans.

Communication with the primary care team is particularly important. The GP is often the first port of call, not only for the patient but also for the family who may be reporting symptoms of relapse, expressing concern about side effects, or developing symptoms of stress or illness themselves. It is essential, then, that the patient's GP knows the diagnosis, treatment plan, and details of any medication being prescribed. This may include, for example, the name of an injected mediation, the dose, frequency and location of administration, and details of how to contact the team in case of missed doses, confusion over appointments, or the development of troublesome side effects.

It is similarly important that the GP and other care providers are clear about the plans to be followed in the case of acute relapse or the development of a sudden need for inpatient care. Effective communication helps patient, family and carers provide the best possible treatment in a fashion that is coherent, efficient, acceptable and, most of all, effective.

Outcome

Schizophrenia is a relatively common mental disorder which can be disabling but is treatable. Seventy per cent of people who experience a psychotic episode will be well within one year, although many will have a second episode. Discontinuing medication within the first 18 months makes the person five times more likely to experience a relapse.

The lifetime risk of suicide in schizophrenia is approximately 10 per cent, which is higher than the general population risk (which is under 1 per cent) (Chapter 11). Risk is especially high in young males during the first few years of schizophrenia, and if there are persistent delusions or hallucinations, drug misuse or previous attempts at suicide. In practical terms, these statistics mean that (a) the vast majority of people with schizophrenia will *not* die by suicide; (b) suicide *cannot* be predicted in any given individual with schizophrenia (as it is still a rare event); and (c) risk will likely be diminished if the person persists with treatment and does not misuse drugs.

Schizophrenia is associated with reduced rates of social interaction, marriage, reproduction and workforce participation, with the result that two-thirds of people with chronic schizophrenia are unemployed. Tragically, most of this 'secondary disability' is not attributable to the illness itself, but to society's prejudicial responses to it. This is a key issue for patients, families and society in general: equal access to the workforce is a fundamental economic and social right. People with schizophrenia commonly experience violations of this right along with *de facto* violations of the right to liberty, including increased rates of imprisonment, often for minor offences, and various other rights such as the right to appropriate housing. Remedying this persistent discrimination, reducing stigma, and combating social exclusion of the mentally ill (including those with schizophrenia), is a task not just for health professionals, but also for patients and their families, service-user groups, and the policymakers who shape mental health policy and social services in Ireland (Chapter 15).

Finally, one of the other long-term challenges in schizophrenia is the recurring finding that the illness is associated with poor physical health. Life expectancy is considerably reduced in schizophrenia: on average, men with schizophrenia die 15 years earlier, and women 12 years earlier, than the rest of the population.[14] This excess is not accounted for by unnatural deaths; the leading causes are heart disease and cancer. As a result, there is a need for ongoing and enhanced focus on the physical health of persons with schizophrenia, including (but not limited to) support in stopping smoking, promotion of improved diet and lifestyle, and screening for cardiac risk-factors such as high blood pressure and cholesterol. In addition, treatment with antipsychotic medication reduces the likelihood of premature death in schizophrenia – providing yet another reason to persist with treatment in this complex, misunderstood but eminently treatable disorder.

Useful Resources

It is advisable that anyone who thinks they may have any of the conditions discussed in this book sees a health care professional. There are many reasons for this, including a need to rule out any other diagnoses such as physical illnesses. In addition, some people find it easier to talk with a health care professional, especially if they are too uncertain or embarrassed to talk with friends or family members.

Individuals with any mental disorder or psychological problem, and their families, will find much that is useful on the Internet. As ever, Internet resources need to be evaluated with care and only trusted when the information comes from a reliable source (Chapter 2).

In addition, Shine is an organisation that aims to empower people with mental ill health and their families through support, information and education. There is useful information about many conditions, including schizophrenia, on their website (www. shine.ie).

One of the best books for people with schizophrenia and their families is *Surviving Schizophrenia: A Family Manual* (6th Edition)' by Dr E. Fuller Torrey (Harper Perennial, 2013). Torrey is a world expert on the disorder and presents the facts in a direct and honest fashion, explaining about symptoms and treatment clearly and pragmatically.

Other helpful books include *Coping with Schizophrenia: A Guide for Patients, Families and Caregivers* by Steven Jones and Peter Hayward (Oneworld Publications, 2004) and *Schizophrenia: A Very Short Introduction* by Chris Frith and Eve Johnstone (Oxford University Press, 2003).

The novel *Human Traces* by Sebastian Faulks (Hutchinson, 2005) provides an interesting historical perspective, and *I Know This Much is True* by Wally Lamb (HarperCollins, 1998) provides a powerful account of a twin sibling with schizophrenia. *If You Don't Know Me By Now* by Sathnam Sanghera (Viking, 2008), later published as *The Boy with the Topknot: A Memoir of Love, Secrets and Lies in Wolverhampton* (Penguin, 2009), gives a moving account of a father's schizophrenia and its impact on the wider family.

Endnotes

1   World Health Organisation. *International Classification of Diseases* (10th Edition). Geneva: World Health Organisation, 1992.

2   Daly, A. and Craig, S. HRB Statistics Series 29: Activities of Irish Psychiatric Units and Hospitals 2015. Dublin: Health Research Board, 2016.

3   Torrey, E.F. *Surviving Schizophrenia: A Family Manual* (6th Edition). New York: Harper Perennial, 2013.

4   Behan, C., Kennelly, B. and O'Callaghan, E. 'The economic cost of schizophrenia in Ireland: A cost of illness study'. *Irish Journal of Psychological Medicine* 2008; 25: 80-87.

5   Howes, O.D. and Murray, R.M. 'Schizophrenia: An integrated sociodevelopmental-cognitive model'. *Lancet* 2014; 383: 1677-87.

6   Further discussion of this topic, and appropriate references, can be found in Kelly, B.D., O'Callaghan, E., Waddington, J.L., Feeney, L., Browne, S., Scully, P.J., Clarke, M., Quinn, J.F., McTigue, O., Morgan, M.G., Kinsella, A. and Larkin, C. 'Schizophrenia and the city: A review of literature and prospective study of psychosis and urbanicity in Ireland'. *Schizophrenia Research* 2010; 116: 75-89.

7   Boydell, J., van Os, J., McKenzie, K., Allardyce, J., Goel, R., McCreadie, R.G. and Murray, R.M. 'Incidence of schizophrenia in ethnic minorities in London: Ecological study into interactions with environment'. *BMJ* 2001; 323: 1–4.

8   Newbury, J., Arseneault, L., Caspi, A., Moffitt, T.E., Odgers, C.L. and Fisher, H.L. 'Why are children in urban neighborhoods at increased risk for psychotic symptoms? Findings from a UK longitudinal cohort study'. *Schizophrenia Bulletin* 2016; 42: 1372-83.

9   Howes, O.D. and Murray, R.M. 'Schizophrenia: An integrated sociodevelopmental-cognitive model'. *Lancet* 2014; 383: 1677-87.

10 www.nice.org.uk/guidance/cg178

11 National Institute for Health and Care Excellence (NICE). Guidance on the Use of Electroconvulsive Therapy (www.nice.org.uk/guidance/ta59).

12 Mental Health Commission. The Administration of Electro-Convulsive Therapy in Approved Centres: Activity Report 2013. Dublin: Mental Health Commission, 2015.

13 National Institute for Health and Care Excellence (NICE). Psychosis and schizophrenia in adults: prevention and management (www.nice.org.uk/guidance/cg178).

14 Crump, C., Winkleby, M.A., Sundquist, K. and Sundquist, J. 'Comorbidities and mortality in persons with schizophrenia: A Swedish national cohort study'. *American Journal of Psychiatry* 2013; 170: 324-33.

Chapter 4

BIPOLAR DISORDER
(MANIC DEPRESSION)

Bipolar disorder (manic depression) is a well-known but much misunderstood disorder that affects 1 to 2 per cent of the population over the course of their lifetimes. It is a potentially very disruptive illness, but it is also very treatable. This chapter looks at four key questions about bipolar disorder:

◊   What are the symptoms and signs of bipolar disorder?

◊   How common is bipolar disorder?

◊   What causes bipolar disorder?

◊   What are the treatments for bipolar disorder?

Useful resources and sources of further information are provided at the end of the chapter.

What Are the Signs and Symptoms of Bipolar Disorder?

The signs and symptoms of bipolar disorder can vary greatly between individuals, depending on the stage of the disorder at which the person presents. In its ICD-10 classification system, the WHO states that bipolar disorder is characterised by at least two episodes in which the person's mood and activity levels are significantly disturbed, being on some occasions an elevation of mood and increased energy and activity (that is, mania or hypomania, also known as 'elation'), and on other occasions a lowering of mood and decreased energy and activity (depression).[1]

Most commonly recovery is complete between episodes. It is rare for people to experience only repeated episodes of mania (and no episodes of depression) and, since the histories and outlook in the mania-only cases closely resemble those who experience both mania and depression, people who only experience mania are also considered to have bipolar disorder (even though they technically only have 'unipolar' mania).

The first episode of bipolar disorder can occur at any age, with a peak age of first onset in the late teens or early twenties. Episodes of mania usually begin abruptly and last for periods ranging from two weeks to five months (generally around four months). Episodes of depression tend to last slightly longer, around six months if untreated.

The WHO describes three degrees of severity of manic episodes: hypomania, mania without psychotic symptoms, and mania with psychotic symptoms. 'Psychotic' means that the condition involves a significant break from reality in at least one important respect (see below).

The first level of mania is 'hypomania' and is a lesser degree of mania, involving a mild elevation of mood for several days, increased activity and energy, unusually prominent feelings of efficiency and well-being, and increased familiarity, talkativeness, sociability and sexual energy. There is also often a decreased need for sleep and diminished concentration. The increased sociability can be accompanied by irritability and apparent conceitedness. Social refinement is often diminished.

In hypomania, these symptoms are not present to a point at which they cause substantial social problems or work difficulties, and there are no psychotic symptoms, such as delusions (fixed, false beliefs, not amenable to reason) or hallucinations (perceptions without appropriate external stimuli, such as 'hearing voices'). If several of the features of hypomania are present for several days, and they are consistent with increased activity and elevated mood, and the person does not have full mania (see below), then

the person fulfils criteria for hypomania. Possible alternative diagnoses in these situations include depression with agitation, or
severe obsessional rituals resulting in increased activity owing
to obsessional impulses and behaviours rather than hypomania
(Chapter 5).

The next level of severity is mania without psychotic symptoms. At this level, the person's mood is elevated out of keeping
with the person's circumstances, and is accompanied by increased
energy, decreased need for sleep, over-activity, and increased
pressure and flow of speech. The person is commonly distractible,
disinhibited, and grandiose in their thinking and ideas. They may
be over-enthusiastic about relatively mundane matters and may
describe an increased appreciation of perceptual stimuli (for example, enhanced and unrealistic appreciation of specific colours
or sounds).

The most distressing aspect of mania is often a behavioural
tendency to embark on impractical, extravagant and inappropriate projects or schemes, sometimes resulting in inappropriate ro-
mantic or sexual activities, hostile behaviours, or generally reck-
less decision-making. For a diagnosis of mania to be made these
features should be present for at least one week; they should be
sufficiently severe to cause disruption to the person's day-to-day
life; and the elevation of mood should be accompanied by clear
over-activity, often alongside pressure of speech, decreased need
for sleep, grandiose thinking, and grossly excessive optimism. A
severe episode of mania is one of the most disturbing episodes of
mental illness that a person can experience and can be uniquely
disruptive to the person's life and the lives of those around them.

It is worth emphasising that the person with mania is not necessarily, or even commonly, happy. The person is normally irritated and frustrated at the extent to which they find themselves out
of tune with the rest of the world: while the manic person's brain is
moving at high speed, the rest of the world seems slow, boring, and

generally un-understanding. This often leads to irritation, hostility and dysphoric (unhappy) mood.

On occasion, mania is accompanied by psychotic symptoms, such as delusions and hallucinations. This is the third level of severity: mania with psychotic symptoms. In this instance, the person has symptoms of mania to a substantial extent, day-to-day life is severely disrupted as a result, and the person's inflated self-esteem and grandiose ideas can develop into delusions. Feelings of irritability can develop into delusions of persecution (for example, the false belief that people are after you). 'Pressure of thought' (that is, speeded up thinking) and 'flight of ideas' (ideas rushing off in all directions) can also become notably prominent. The extraordinary intensity of symptoms can lead to incomprehensible speech and sustained activity to the point of violence, self-neglect and even dehydration. The person can hear voices which confirm their over-optimistic outlook and general grandiosity.

This psychotic state can occasionally be difficult to distinguish from schizophrenia (Chapter 3), although in mania the psychotic features such as delusions and hallucinations are usually clearly consistent with the mood state (for example, of a grandiose variety) while in schizophrenia the psychotic features are generally not clearly linked with mood, and may even be quite bizarre. Pressure of speech and speeded-up activity are also generally more prominent in mania than in schizophrenia.

Some people may have 'schizo-affective disorder' rather than either mania or schizophrenia. This is a condition in which features of both a mood disorder and schizophrenia are prominent simultaneously, or within a few days of each other, as part of the same episode of illness. The WHO describes 'schizo-affective disorder' as either manic, depressive or mixed, depending on the nature of the mood component in the disorder.

Bipolar disorder may also present in a depressive phase rather than a hypomanic or manic phase (Chapter 2). If someone has only symptoms of depression, and has no history of mania, it is impossible to know if they have 'unipolar' depression alone, or will turn out to have bipolar disorder, although a family history of bipolar disorder or particularly atypical features in depression do raise the possibility of bipolarity. Ultimately, however, only time will tell if episodes of mania are to occur in the future.

For the most part, the features of depression in bipolar disorder are the same as those of depression more generally (Chapter 2), and include:

- Low mood, feeling down, or feeling low
- Loss of interest and enjoyment in activities which are usually pleasurable
- Reduced energy, leading to increased fatigability and reduced activity
- Marked tiredness after slight effort
- Reduced concentration and attention, with reduced ability to read or follow programmes on television
- Reduced self-confidence and self-esteem
- Ideas of unworthiness and guilt
- Pessimistic, bleak views of the future
- Hopelessness and feelings of helplessness
- Ideas or acts of self-harm, or ideas or acts of suicide
- Disturbed sleep, especially difficulty falling asleep, fragmented sleep, early morning waking (or, unusually, excessive sleep)
- Reduced appetite, generally resulting in weight loss (or, unusually, increased appetite).

According to the WHO, these symptoms should, for the most part, last for two weeks, but shorter periods are reasonable if the symptoms are of rapid onset or unusually severe. Before diagnosing an episode of depression, it is important to rule out other possible causes of these and similar symptoms, including medical illnesses (for example, thyroid problems, dementia) (Chapter 8); substance abuse problems such as alcohol, cannabis, other illegal drugs (Chapter 7); side effects of a broad range of prescribed medications such as benzodiazepines, anticonvulsants, antipsychotics, certain cardiac medications, steroids and various others; and other mental illnesses such as anxiety disorders, panic disorder, post-traumatic stress disorder, obsessive-compulsive disorder (Chapter 5), bulimia nervosa, anorexia nervosa (Chapter 6), and adjustment disorder (Chapter 5).

Of course, when considering any person's set of symptoms, and before proceeding to any diagnosis, it is always useful to consider the possibility that the person does not have a mental illness at all and is simply experiencing normal ups and downs of life but has, for whatever reason, recently developed diminished ability to cope. There is sometimes a tendency to over-diagnose bipolar disorder, especially in people who have difficult-to-manage mood swings which prompt them to attend doctors, either at their own suggestion or that of others. A diagnosis of mania is only indicated if the elevation of mood lasts for more than one week and is accompanied by other features of mania (above) which are sufficiently severe to cause substantial disruptions to the person's day-to-day life.

Many people with mania-like symptoms which are distressing but do not reach the threshold for mania might well have 'cyclothymia', which the WHO describes as a persistent instability of mood, characterised by periods of mild elation and mild depression. In other words, the person has mood swings which are significantly more than the norm, but are not sufficiently severe to meet criteria for bipolar disorder. This usually starts early in adult life and follows a chronic course, although there can be long periods of stability. These mood episodes are not sufficiently severe to meet criteria for full manic or depressive episodes, but the instability of mood can prove most distressing for the individual. Treatment approaches for this condition are considered below.

If the person is diagnosed with bipolar disorder, there are various sub-classifications of the condition which might or might not prove relevant or helpful, depending on the individual case. Bipolar disorder as described above, with manic and depressive episodes, is sometimes termed 'Bipolar I Disorder'. This is by way of contrast with 'Bipolar II Disorder' in which the person experiences episodes of depression and *hypo*mania only, without experiencing full mania (unless the mania is caused by antidepressant treatment). Bipolar disorder is described as 'rapid-cycling' if there are four or more mood episodes within a twelve-month period. The usefulness of these sub-categories is not fully established, but some people find they help with understanding or pattern recognition.

Case History: Janet

Janet was a 21-year-old student of law at a university, living away from home with three friends. A few months before their exams, one of her friends noticed that Janet was staying up almost all night studying and using her computer. Her friend initially presumed that Janet was simply studying hard for the exams, but, over the following week it became clear that Janet was not eating, and kept rushing out of the house at odd hours of day and night, speaking very fast and telling everyone she was in a hurry. Janet had no history of using illicit drugs nor had she behaved in this fashion before.

After some days of this most unusual behavior, Janet's friend asked her if she was all right and Janet told her that she was better than all right: she had never felt more positive in her entire life. Janet confided that she had a new idea that would make her and her friends an enormous amount of money; that she had a new boyfriend for whom she had just bought a motorbike on the Internet; and that she would soon be leaving Ireland to do humanitarian medical work abroad.

Janet was annoyed when her friend pointed out that buying motorbikes impulsively over the Internet was generally a bad idea and that perhaps Janet should take her new relationship a little slower, and asked the name of the humanitarian medical organisation with which Janet said she was involved. One of Janet's other housemates recognized that Janet was probably unwell and phoned Janet's parents, who came at once.

Janet's parents recognised the signs of mania in Janet imme-diately because Janet's grandmother and uncle both had bipolar disorder and had suffered from episodes of mania before they were treated (successfully) with lithium, a mood stabilising medication (see below). Janet's parents were therefore quite skilled at handling this difficult situation, and persuaded Janet to come with them to the family GP who arranged an appointment with a community mental health team so that Janet could be assessed and commence treatment for bipolar disorder.

How Common is Bipolar Disorder?

Bipolar disorder affects 1 to 2 per cent of the population over the course of their lifetimes and approximately 0.6 per cent of the pop-ulation over any given twelve-month period. It tends to present in the late teens or early twenties, with an average age of onset of 18 years. Bipolar disorder can, however, also present later in life, with first onsets reported in patients in their forties and fifties. If, how-ever, the onset in mid-life is characterised by mania, there should be an especially thorough assessment for other, physical causes for the symptoms.

Bipolar disorder can also occur in children but it is rare, and every child's symptoms need to be carefully evaluated in the con-text of the child's age, IQ, stage of development and personal cir-cumstances. As with all suspected disorders in children, attention must be paid to the child's home, school and social environments before proceeding to diagnosis and/or treatment (Chapter 10).

In Ireland, mania and depression feature significantly in the psychiatric admission statistics, with mania accounting for 1,917 admissions in 2015 (12.5 per cent of all psychiatric admissions) and depressive disorders accounting for 4,806 admissions (25.4 per cent).[2] In terms of involuntary admissions, schizophrenia had the highest rate of involuntary admission in 2015, at 20.2 involuntary admissions per 100,000 population per year, followed by mania at 7.7 per 100,000 population per year and depressive disorders at 4.8 per 100,000 population per year.

Among children and adolescents, there were 25 admissions of children and adolescents in Ireland with mania in 2015 (including one involuntary admission), which accounts for 5 per cent of all psychiatric admissions of children and adolescents. There were also 159 admissions of children and adolescents with depressive disorders (including 7 involuntary admissions), accounting for 32 per cent of all admissions of children and adolescents.

What Causes Bipolar Disorder?

The causes of bipolar disorder are not fully understood. Like all mental disorders which are defined by symptoms rather than biological tests, it is entirely possible that the disorder has different causes in different people or that different combinations of risk factors produce similar but not quite identical clinical pictures in different people. Broadly, the known risk factors for bipolar disorder can be divided into genetic and environmental risks, all of which can combine in different ways depending on the person's particular circumstances.

Turning to the genetic risks first, it is clear that bipolar disorder runs in families: if you have a first degree relative (parent, sibling, child) with bipolar disorder, your life-time risks rises from 1 to 2 per cent to approximately 8 per cent. Interestingly, first-degree relatives of persons with bipolar disorder also have increased risk of (unipolar) depressive disorder without mania.

Studies of twins confirm the importance of a genetic component in bipolar disorder: if you have a twin who shares all of the same genes as you (a 'monozygotic' twin) and that twin develops bipolar disorder, then your risk of bipolar disorder increases significantly more than it would if your twin did not share all of the same genes as you (a 'dizygotic' twin, or non-identical twin) or was just a regular 'first degree relative'. There is also a proportionate increase in risk of 'unipolar' depressive disorder in people who have a twin affected by bipolar disorder. These familial increases in risk have been shown to apply to biological rather than adoptive relatives, indicating a biological or genetic cause, rather than an environmental one, for this particular element of risk.

That said, it is not entirely clear precisely how bipolar disorder runs in families, that is, it is not known which specific genes are responsible for increasing risk within most affected families. There is much research ongoing in this area (including at Trinity College Dublin) and evidence to date suggests that there are likely to be many different genes involved; that there may be some genetic risks shared between bipolar disorder and schizophrenia; and that the relevant combinations of genes may vary from person to person.

While some possible candidate genes have been suggested, there are still no genetic tests for bipolar disorder and there is no way of knowing if one's children are likely to develop it. Moreover, even if precise genes were identified, it is notable that a person who has a first degree relative affected by bipolar disorder still has just an 8 per cent risk of developing the illness: while this is higher than the general population risk (1 to 2 per cent), there is still a 92 per cent chance that a person with an affected first degree relative will not develop bipolar disorder.

Clearly, then, while there is a genetic component to bipolar disorder, there are also other, powerful, non-genetic, environmental factors that are equally relevant, if not more so, in the development of the illness. It is known, for example, that bipolar disorder is more common in high income countries than low income ones (possibly related to diagnostic practices), and more common among people who are separated, divorced or widowed, compared to those who are married or were never married. It is difficult, however, to determine which is the cause and which is the effect in relation to marital status and bipolar disorder. It is, however, now relatively clear that people with bipolar disorder report more traumatic events (for example, childhood abuse) compared to people without bipolar disorder, and this is likely relevant to the cause of their illness.

In terms of brain chemistry, it also appears likely that there are disturbances to various brain chemicals in bipolar disorder, although these have not been definitively characterised to date. It is also likely that the disorder is associated with abnormalities of the various hormones in the body, especially when the person is exposed to multiple or sustained stressful events, which alter the body's hormonal response to stress and appear to increase risk of mood disorders such as bipolar disorder.

It is, therefore, an error to imagine that proposed explanations based on psychological stresses are somehow separate to explanations based on brain chemistry or the body's hormonal responses. Psychological and physical explanations are complementary to each other, and they likely reflect different ways of describing the same psycho-physical processes that make up the cluster of symptoms currently classified as 'bipolar disorder'. As a result, research studies demonstrating possible alterations in brain structure on brain scans are entirely consistent with studies of different cognitive (or thinking) patterns in persons with bipolar disorder: the mind and body are intimately linked to the point of inseparability.

Overall, then, while the ultimate cause of bipolar disorder is not known, it is clear that there are both genetic and environmental risk factors, and that different combinations of risks likely combine in different ways in different people, producing the clinical picture of bipolar disorder, in all of its infinite variety. Specific episodes of the illness might be precipitated by stressful life events, lack of sleep, physical illness or, in women, childbirth (Chapter 9).

And if you have the disorder yourself, it is worth remembering that while your children and other first degree relatives have somewhat increased risk (see above), there is still an overwhelming likelihood (92 per cent) that they will *not* develop the illness at all: there is *a lot* more to bipolar disorder than genes.

What Are the Treatments for Bipolar Disorder?

Bipolar disorder is a very treatable condition. In February 2016, the UK's National Institute for Health and Care Excellence (NICE) published updated guidance about the treatment of bipolar disorder, titled 'Bipolar disorder: Assessment and management'. Like all NICE guidelines, this is available, free of charge, on their website.[3] At the outset, NICE notes the importance of providing good information about bipolar disorder and support for carers of people with bipolar disorder. NICE also suggests that people presenting to GPs with depression should be asked about possible mania or hypomania in the past, before reaching a definitive diagnosis for the current episode.

If mania or severe depression are suspected, or the person appears to present a danger to themselves or others, they should be referred for urgent specialist mental health assessment, that is, the GP should refer the person to the specialist community mental health team covering the area (Chapter 12). Many other people with bipolar disorder can be treated in primary care with psychological and medication-based treatments, but NICE recommends referral to secondary care for the initial commencement of certain medications, such as lithium or valproate (see below), or if response to treatment is poor.

It is also important to monitor the physical health of people with bipolar disorder: weight, diet, activity, pulse, blood pressure, blood lipids and liver function (and, if taking lithium long term, calcium, kidney and thyroid function). If a person with suspected bipolar disorder is referred to secondary care, it is imperative that a thorough psychiatric and physical assessment is performed, and any risk behavior is identified, with an appropriate plan made.

Medication for Bipolar Disorder

If a person has hypomania or mania, and is already taking an antidepressant medication on its own, consideration should be given to carefully stopping the antidepressant and commencing an 'antipsychotic medication.' Antipsychotic medications are also used in schizophrenia (Chapter 3), and specific antipsychotic medications suggested by NICE for hypomania or mania in bipolar disorder include haloperidol, olanzapine, quetiapine or risperidone. Each of these medications has various possible side effects and inter-actions with other medications, so specialist guidance is needed for their safe and effective use. If the person cannot tolerate the first antipsychotic medication tried, or if it is insufficiently effec-tive after an appropriate trial at an appropriate dose, it should be changed.

If these steps do not prove effective, consideration can be given to adding lithium. Lithium is a medication used in bipolar disorder both for the treatment of mania or depression (Chapter 2) in cer-tain circumstances, and for the longer-term prevention of future episodes of mania or depression, that is, as a 'mood stabiliser' (see below). If a person with mania is already on lithium, it is impor-tant to check their blood level of lithium in order to ensure that they are on the correct dose. If the person with mania is already taking another mood stabiliser, such as valproate (see below), the dose can be increased to the maximum in order to ensure that the person is deriving all possible benefit from the medication they are already on. An antipsychotic can be added with a mood stabiliser if the dose of the mood stabiliser is optimal and response is still inadequate.

Further information on all of these medications is available on the website of the Health Products Regulatory Authority (www.hpra.ie). Licenses and guidelines for these medications commonly change, so it is worth consulting this website for up-to-date details about all of these medications if they are being considered.

If a person presents in the depressed phase of bipolar disorder, it is important to try to ensure that treatment of depression does not produce a 'swing' into hypomania or mania. Evidence-based psychological interventions can help greatly in this situation, in-cluding cognitive-behavioural therapy (CBT), interpersonal therapy or behavioural couples therapy (see Chapter 2 for more on the psychological treatment of depression).

If the person develops moderate or severe depression in the context of bipolar disorder, and is not on medication for bipolar disorder, NICE suggests offering fluoxetine (an antidepressant medication) with olanzapine (an antipsychotic medication), or else quetiapine (an antipsychotic medication sometimes used in depression) on its own. Other possibilities, depending on the person's preferences and particular situation, include olanzapine on its own or lamotrigine (another mood stabiliser; see below).

If the person with depression in the context of bipolar disorder is already taking lithium for bipolar disorder, it is important, again, to check their blood level of lithium and adjust the dose accordingly if necessary. If that is satisfactory, fluoxetine with olanzapine, or quetiapine on its own, can be considered, in addition to the lithium. If the person is already taking valproate (another mood stabiliser; see below), the dose should be optimised, before considering adding fluoxetine with olanzapine, or quetiapine on its own, if the response to the mood stabiliser alone is inadequate.

There are various other medication strategies that can be considered, but these are beyond the scope of the present book, and require specialist guidance that is often quite specific to each person's presenting problems, medication history, and personal preferences. In all cases, it is important that medical strategies are explained with care; psychological interventions are offered (see below); and physical health is monitored, especially with medications that are known potentially to affect physical health (for example, through weight gain).

In terms of longer-term treatment, continued use of any medication that has helped to manage an episode of mania or depression can be discussed with the patient. However, the person should also be offered longer-term treatment with lithium, which NICE recommends as the most effective long-term treatment for bipolar disorder. Like many other medications and treatments, lithium's mechanism of action is unknown, although there are many theories. Lithium's effectiveness, however, has been repeatedly demonstrated over time, especially for reducing the frequency of mood episodes in bipolar disorder in the longer term.

In Ireland, lithium is currently licensed for:

- Management of acute manic or hypomanic episodes
- Management of episodes of recurrent depressive disorders where treatment with other antidepressants has been unsuccessful
- Prevention of mood episodes in bipolar disorder
- Control of aggressive behaviour or intentional self-harm in certain situations.

There is also evidence that lithium might be useful for treating cyclothymia or in reducing suicide, but it is not licensed for these indications, indicating weaker evidence for these uses of the medication. For all medications, up-to-date licensing information should be verified on the website of the Health Products Regulatory Authority (www.hpra.ie).

Before commencing lithium, NICE recommends discussing the proposed treatment with the patient in detail; assessing weight; measuring kidney function, calcium level, thyroid function and full blood count (blood tests); performing a cardiac tracing (electro-cardiogram or 'ECG'), if indicated; providing written information about lithium; and co-ordinating care with the person's GP.

Lithium has a narrow therapeutic range, which means that it is very important to get the dose precisely correct: if the dose is too low, the medication will produce no benefit; if the dose is too high, there can be toxicity. Keeping the dose correct involves taking the medication precisely as prescribed; watching for emerging side effects (see below); and having regular blood tests, to ensure the lithium level remains between approximately 0.6 to 1.0 mmol per litre (the precise range may vary from hospital to hospital) and to ensure that your thyroid gland or kidneys are not being affected by the medication.

NICE recommends performing a lithium blood test one week after commencing the medication; one week after every dose change; and weekly until a stable dose is established. The blood test should then be repeated every three months for the first year, and every six months thereafter. Some people should remain on three-monthly blood tests, including the elderly; people taking other medications that interact with lithium; people at increased risk of kidney or thyroid disease, or raised calcium; people with unstable symptoms; people with poor medication compliance; and people whose lithium level was greater than 0.8 mmol per litre (approximately) when last tested. It is also necessary to test kidney function, calcium, thyroid function and weight at least every six months.

Possible side effects of lithium (even at a therapeutic dose) include nausea, slight tremor (shakes in the hand), weight gain, fluid retention, increased thirst, increased urination, worsening of psoriasis or acne, and altered function of the thyroid gland (necessitating blood test monitoring). Signs of toxicity, when the dose is too high, include vomiting, diarrhoea, severe tremor, slurring of speech, unsteadiness, drowsiness, confusion and – in extreme situations – seizures (fits) or coma. Lithium toxicity can be fatal and requires urgent specialist intervention.

Lithium should be avoided in people with diseases of the kidney, heart or thyroid; people with Addison's disease (a disorder of the adrenal gland); and women who are or may become pregnant: lithium increases the risk of cardiac problems in the baby, especially when taken early in pregnancy (often before the woman even knows she is pregnant). As a result, lithium should not be used during pregnancy, especially during the first trimester, unless it is considered essential. If it is considered essential, however, lithium is sometimes used, following a careful consideration of the risks and benefits, and ongoing specialist supervision. If it is

considered essential, serum lithium levels should be closely monitored during pregnancy and the dose adjusted accordingly. It is
also recommended that lithium be discontinued shortly before
delivery and re-started a few days after the birth. Newborn babies
may show signs of lithium toxicity (for example, lethargy, flaccid
muscle tone), so careful clinical observation of the baby and close
monitoring of lithium levels are recommended (see also Chapter
9). Lithium should not be used when breast-feeding.

Other mood stabilising medications which can be alternatives
to lithium for some people include valproate, lamotrigine and
carbamazepine. There are specific protocols for starting each of
these medications; for example, for valproate, it is important to
monitor weight, full blood count, and liver function tests before
commencing the medication, after six months, and then annually.
NICE recommends valproate if lithium is ineffective or, if lithium
is poorly tolerated or not suitable, NICE recommends either valproate, olanzapine or quetiapine (if it has been useful before). In
Ireland, valproate is licensed for the treatment of manic episode
in bipolar disorder when lithium is contraindicated or not tolerated. If the patient responds well, continuation of valproate can be
considered.

Valproate should, however, be avoided in pregnancy as it can
affect the child's intellectual development and increases the risk
of neural tube defects (for example, spina bifida and anencephaly)
from 6 per 10,000 births to 100 to 200 per 10,000 births. Overall,
valproate-containing medicines should not be prescribed to female children, female adolescents, women of childbearing potential or pregnant women, unless other treatments are ineffective or
not tolerated, due to the risk of serious developmental disorders
and/or congenital malformations. Children exposed in the womb
to valproate are at a high risk of serious developmental disorders
(in up to 30-40 per cent of cases) and/or congenital malformations
(in approximately 10 per cent of cases).

Carbamazepine, another medication sometimes used for the treatment of mania and preventing further mood episodes in bipolar disorder (especially in patients unresponsive to lithium), also increases risk of neural tube defects (to 20-50 per 10,000 births) and other problems if taken in pregnancy.

Mood stabilisers can also have adverse effects on infants who are breast-fed. Broadly, antipsychotics are preferred to mood stabilisers for the treatment of bipolar disorder in pregnancy, although antipsychotics, even at low doses, need to be used only if necessary, with great caution, and under specialist supervision in pregnancy. They also have various possible adverse effects, depending on the specific medication used; for example, olanzapine can cause high blood sugar during pregnancy.

Overall, treatment of bipolar disorder in pregnancy is quite complex but – notwithstanding the risks – there are occasions when many of these medications are used in pregnancy. Making decisions during pregnancy involves weighing up the most recent information about the potential adverse effects of the medications with the very substantial risks presented by episodes of mania or depression in pregnancy. Careful decision-making, specialist supervision, and ongoing review are needed, especially following the birth, which is an especially high-risk period for psychosis and mania in women.

Lamotrigine is another mood stabilising medication licensed in Ireland for prevention of depressive episodes in adults (aged 18 years or over) with bipolar disorder who experience predominantly depressive episodes. It is not licensed for the acute treatment of manic or depressive episodes. NICE recommends that if lamotrigine is being commenced, the person should have a full blood count and blood tests for kidney and liver function. Lamotrigine can interact with valproate and the patient should contact their doctor at once if they develop a rash while the dose of lamotrigine is being increased, or if they are pregnant or planning a pregnancy while undergoing treatment with lamotrigine.

For all of these medications, it is important to monitor physical health and to be aware of the individual side effect profile of each agent. The website of the Health Products Regulatory Authority (www.hpra.ie) should also be consulted as its information will likely be more up-to-date than this (or any) book. Monitoring of weight and other aspects of physical health during antipsychotic treatment is discussed in Chapter 3.

Most treatment for bipolar is generally provided on an out-patient basis, but admission (voluntary or involuntary) may be needed if the illness is severe; if there is significant risk of harm to self or others; or if the circumstances of the particular case suggest that treatment can be delivered more effectively and efficiently in an inpatient setting, and the person's condition would deteriorate further if such admission did not occur.

Prescription of medication for bipolar disorder in children is a very complex matter, with limited research to guide choice of medication or management strategies. As a result, guidelines in this area evolve quickly and specialist, up-to-date advice from child and adolescent psychiatry teams is needed in each individual case. (See also Chapter 10.)

In adults, if long-term medication for bipolar disorder is being stopped, it is important to discuss this decision with the patient; to stop treatment gradually rather than suddenly (NICE provides guidelines); to identify signs of potential relapse immediately, acting promptly if they appear; and to monitor for at least two years after stopping medication to ensure there are no recurrences. In practice, it is very common for people who have had especially disruptive episodes of mania or depression to request to stay on effective medication for quite a sustained period in order to minimise the chances of further episodes which can cause significant problems in their personal, social and working lives.

Psychological Treatments for Bipolar Disorder

Accounts of treatment strategies for bipolar disorder tend commonly to focus on medication alone and often ignore the central role of psychological therapies for many people with bipolar disorder and their families. For cyclothymia, self-help techniques and manuals for mood management can prove very helpful, especially *The Cyclothymia Workbook: Learn How to Manage Your Mood Swings and Lead a Balanced Life* by Prentiss Price. CBT can also prove useful, and there are suggestions that lithium can occasionally help, but currently there is insufficient evidence systematically to recommend use of lithium for cyclothymia.

In the context of bipolar disorder itself, NICE guidelines emphasise the importance of person-centred care and the usefulness of psychological interventions which are supported by evidence and have been developed specifically for use in bipolar disorder. In depression, for example, CBT, interpersonal therapy or behavioural couples therapy can prove extremely useful, once provided in line with established treatment guidelines and in addition to any medications that are indicated (Chapter 2).

Overall, a broad range of psychotherapeutic approaches have been explored for bipolar disorder (in conjunction with mood stabilising medication), including psycho-education, CBT, family therapy, interpersonal therapy and psychoanalysis. Most attention has been paid to cognitive and behavioural approaches including, for example, the use of 'family-focused treatment for adolescents', along with medication, in adolescent bipolar disorder. This approach involves psychoeducation, communication training and problem-solving skills training.[4] Patients receiving the family-focused treatment recover from baseline depressive symptoms faster than those not receiving such treatment, suggesting that family-focused therapy is effective, in conjunction with medication, in stabilising depressive symptoms in adolescents with bipolar disorder. There has also been increased interest in the contribution of psychoanalysis in recent years,[5] and more research is needed in these areas.

Some people with bipolar disorder find 'mood diaries' an effective way of noticing, understanding and monitoring their moods.

They can also prove useful for evaluating the effects of psychological therapies or medications, and alerting the patient and their family to early signs of relapse. Structured psychological interventions can also be helpful during the maintenance phase of treatment in bipolar disorder, with a particular focus on psycho-education of patients and families. Sometimes, a person's behavior while manic can produce substantial problems at home or in the workplace, and it is important that the role of bipolar disorder in this behavior is fully understood by those affected.

Electro-convulsive Therapy (ECT) for Bipolar Disorder

ECT is an effective treatment for severe, treatment-resistant or life-threatening depression, which can occur in bipolar disorder. ECT was discussed at some length in Chapter 2, pointing out that there is now strong evidence that, for a small minority of patients, ECT provides rapid and substantial relief, and can, in some, prove life-saving.

ECT will be indicated in just a tiny minority of people with bipolar disorder. But for that small, much-neglected group, ECT can sometimes prove to be the only treatment that works in a severe and occasionally life-threatening episode of the illness. The use of ECT in Ireland is now highly regulated by the Mental Health Commission and it would be a profound violation of rights to withhold ECT from appropriate patients who desperately need it. ECT is a safe, essential treatment for a minority of patients who could otherwise die as a result of mental illness, including bipolar disorder.

Overall Treatment Approaches

Overall, it is important that treatment choices for bipolar disorder take account of all elements of the bio-psycho-social approach to management. Combinations of therapies are likely to be required for many people. People with chronic or recurring bipolar disorder, for example, can develop social problems which require the support and assistance of social workers, occupational therapists, and various other members of multi-disciplinary mental health teams. These should be provided alongside medication and any psychological therapies that are available and indicated.

The outcome in bipolar disorder can vary considerably depending on the course of the disorder, treatments provided, and various other factors. Broadly speaking, over 90 per cent of people who experience a manic episode go on to have further mood episodes. People with rapid-cycling bipolar disorder sometimes do better with mood stabilisers other than lithium.

In ICD-10, the WHO points out that the frequency of episodes in bipolar disorder, and the pattern of relapses and remissions, are variable. The lifetime risk of suicide is estimated at possibly over 10 per cent (Chapter 11) but there is also significant premature mortality for other reasons including cardiac disease, owing chiefly to relatively high rates of smoking. For some people, remissions tend to become shorter and episodes of depression commoner and longer lasting after middle age. For others, prompt and sustained treatment is very successful in preventing further mood episodes and limiting the impact of the disorder on the person's life.

The key thing to remember is that while bipolar disorder is a serious mental illness, it is very treatable. A combination of medication and psychological or social interventions are effective for many people. Treatment can be a continuous, evolving process, and mood stability is always possible provided there is a good relationship between the patient, the treating team and the patient's family.

Case History: Richard

Richard was a 45-year-old man with bipolar disorder. He was hospitalised twice with episodes of mania in his thirties but then commenced treatment with lithium. He quickly reached a steady dose of lithium and experienced no further mood episodes for several years. He was on no other medication. After five years of stability, Richard asked if his lithium could be reduced and stopped, as he had been very well for quite a long period and would like to see if he really needed to stay on the medication.

Richard's psychiatrist discussed the pros and cons with him, and they reached an agreed understanding of what they would do if symptoms developed as his lithium was reduced and stopped. They then reduced the dose of lithium gradually over a three-month period, consistent with NICE guidelines. Richard monitored his mental health carefully during this period, in collaboration with his wife, and in consultation with his psychiatrist and community mental health nurse. Richard did not develop any symptoms during this time. Richard stayed in contact with his psychiatrist for a further two years, during which period there was no cause for concern.

Five years later, Richard's mood went into decline for no apparent reason. He went to see his GP who re-referred him to his psychiatrist. Given Richard's history of bipolar disorder, they recommenced lithium. Richard's psychiatrist also referred Richard to the clinical psychologist on the mental health team who explored Richard's current symptoms with him, and his initial disappointment at needing to go back on lithium. Richard was not keen on receiving any other medication so he was closely monitored during this period to identify if there was any need for additional medication or any evidence of worsening of mood. Happily, after two months of treatment with lithium and attendance with the clinical psychologist, Richard's mood recovered fully.

Although Richard was now very well, he remained quite alarmed at just how quickly his mood had dipped during that period. Richard asked to remain on lithium for the time being, recognising a need to take all possible measures to prevent a recurrence of a mood episode that might endanger his new-found and generally well-sustained mental health.

Useful Resources

It is advisable that anyone who thinks they have any of the conditions discussed in this book sees a health care professional. There are many reasons for this, including a need to rule out any other diagnoses, such as physical illnesses. In addition, some people find it easier to talk with a health care professional, especially if they are too uncertain or embarrassed to talk with friends or family members. Often, a brief talk with a GP will 'normalise' the individual's symptoms by reassuring them that they are not alone in what they are experiencing and that help is to hand, if any is needed.

Individuals with any mental disorder or psychological problem, and their families, will find much that is useful on the Internet. As ever, Internet resources need to be evaluated with care and only trusted when the information comes from a reliable source. Reliable information about mental health can be sourced from the websites of the Health Service Executive (www.hse.ie/eng/health/az), College of Psychiatrists of Ireland (www.irishpsychiatry.ie), Royal College of Psychiatrists in London (www.rcpsych.ac.uk), National Health Service in the UK (www.nhs.uk) and National Institute of Mental Health in the US (www.nimh.nih.gov).

Evidence-based guidance about specific treatments can be found on the website of the National Institute for Health and Care Excellence (NICE) (www.nice.org.uk). NICE is a UK-based organisation responsible for developing guidance, standards and information on high-quality health and social care, and preventing and treating ill health. In February 2016, NICE published updated guidance on 'Bipolar disorder: Assessment and management' and this, like all their guidance, is freely available on their website: www.nice.org.uk/guidance/cg185?unlid=6421790512016824163512

The HSE's yourmentalhealth.ie website also has very useful information about bipolar disorder (www.yourmentalhealth.ie/About-Mental-Health/Common-problems/Mental-health-problems/Bipolar-disorder), as does the NHS Choices website (www.nhs.uk/conditions/Bipolar-disorder).

In addition to the above, Aware is an Irish organisation which provides extensive and reliable information on their website (www.aware.ie). The mission of Aware is to help build a society in which individuals with stress (Chapter 9), depression (Chapter 2), bipolar disorder, and other mood disorders, and their families, are supported and understood, do not experience stigma, and can avail of a wide variety of appropriate therapies. Their website is informative, practical and reliable, and provides plenty of useful information about bipolar disorder.

There are several books which may also be helpful, including: *Touched With Fire: Manic-Depressive Illness and the Artistic Temperament* by Kay Redfield Jamison (Free Press Paperbacks/Simon and Schuster, 1993); *An Unquiet Mind: A Memoir of Moods and Madness* by Kay Redfield Jamison (Borzoi/Alfred A. Knopf Inc., 1995); *The Cyclothymia Workbook: Learn How to Manage Your Mood Swings and Lead a Balanced Life* by Prentiss Price (New Harbinger Publications, Inc., 2004).

Endnotes

1   World Health Organisation. *International Classification of Diseases* (10th Edition). Geneva: World Health Organisation, 1992.

2   Daly, A. and Craig, S. HRB Statistics Series 29: Activities of Irish Psychiatric Units and Hospitals 2015. Dublin: Health Research Board, 2016 (p. 11 and Tables 2.6b, 5.3 and 5.5).

3   www.nice.org.uk/guidance/cg185?unlid=6421790512016824163512

4   Miklowitz, D.J., Axelson, D.A., Birmaher, B., George, E.L., Taylor, D.O., Schneck, C.D., Beresford, C.A., Dickinson, L.M., Craighead, W.E. and Brent, D.A. 'Family-focused treatment for adolescents with bipolar disorder: Results of a 2-year randomized trial'. *Archives of General Psychiatry* 2008; 65: 1053-61.

5   Kelly, B.D. 'Balance and connection: Bipolar disorder and psychoanalysis in psychiatric practice'. *The Letter: Irish Journal for Lacanian Psychoanalysis* 2011; 46: 13-9.

Chapter 5

ANXIETY DISORDERS

The term 'anxiety disorders' covers a broad range of conditions, including phobias, panic disorder, generalised anxiety disorder and obsessive-compulsive disorder (OCD). These can be quite severe but all are treatable.

This chapter looks at four key questions about anxiety disorders and other conditions variously related to anxiety, including acute stress reaction, adjustment disorder, post-traumatic stress disorder (PTSD), conversion disorder and somatoform disorder (somatization and hypochondriacal disorders):

◊ What are the symptoms and signs of anxiety disorders?

◊ How common are anxiety disorders?

◊ What causes anxiety disorders?

◊ What are the treatments for anxiety disorders?

Useful resources and sources of further information are provided at the end of the chapter.

What Are the Symptoms and Signs of Anxiety Disorders?

The World Health Organisation (WHO), in its ICD-10 classification system, includes anxiety disorders under 'neurotic, stress-related and somatoform disorders'.[1] 'Neurotic' literally means involving nerves, and it is best thought of as referring to anxiety disorders or conditions which were once known as 'having nerves'. 'Somatoform' refers to repeated presentations with physical symp-

94

toms and requests for medical investigations, even when there is no apparent physical problem (despite a reasonable amount of medical investigation) (see below). The present chapter explores phobias, panic disorder, generalised anxiety disorder, OCD, PTSD and other conditions with varying relationships to anxiety (acute stress reaction, adjustment disorder, conversion disorder and somatoform disorder).

Phobias

Phobias are a group of disorders in which anxiety is evoked only, or predominantly, in certain well-defined situations or in connection with certain objects which are not dangerous. This leads to the person either avoiding the situation or object, or enduring it with dread. The anxiety can focus on specific symptoms, such as feeling faint or getting palpitations, or on broader anxieties such as dying or 'going mad'. The fact that other people are not similarly anxious does not provide reassurance. Anticipatory anxiety may develop, which is anxiety at the *prospect* of the relevant situation or object, as well as the actual situation or object itself.

There are specific, recurring patterns of phobia that tend to occur and present particular challenges. 'Agoraphobia' refers to a phobia of open spaces, crowds or other situations in which a person perceives difficulty with immediate escape or difficulty getting to 'safety' (for example home, or back into the car). This can manifest as anxiety about leaving home; about being in crowds, shops or public places; or about travelling alone (for example, on buses, trains or airplanes). There is usually a well-established pattern of avoidance behaviour and some people become completely housebound. The presence of other people can sometimes help in the anxiety-provoking situation, although not always.

For a diagnosis of agoraphobia, the WHO recommends that (a) the person's psychological and arousal symptoms (for example, agitation, sweating) must be linked primarily with anxiety and not obsessions or symptoms of other possible mental illnesses; (b) the anxiety must occur mainly in two of the following situations: public places, crowds, travelling alone, or travelling away from home; and (c) avoidance of the relevant situation must be a feature at some point in the disorder, either now or in the past. It is also important that other symptoms, such as, depression, obsessions, etc., do not dominate the clinical picture.

'Social phobia' is another commonly occurring pattern of phobic anxiety. In this situation, the anxiety is focused on fear of scrutiny by other people in small groups, usually leading to avoidance of specific social situations such as eating in public, chatting informally at parties, and so on. There can also be broader avoidance of all social situations outside the home or family circle. There may be specific, irrational fears, such as a fear of vomiting in public. Often, the anxiety is manifest as blushing, which can make the person even more self-conscious; trembling; or a desire to go to the toilet in given social situations. The resultant pattern of avoidance can become very extensive and lead to virtual social isolation.

For a diagnosis of social phobia, the WHO recommends that (a) again, the person's psychological, behavioural and arousal symptoms must be linked primarily with anxiety and not obsessions or symptoms of other possible mental illnesses); (b) the anxiety must occur mainly in particular social situations; and (c) avoidance of the relevant situations must be a feature at some point in the disorder, either now or in the past. Again, it is important that other symptoms do not dominate the clinical picture.

Finally, people can experience phobias of one or more of a very broad range of other *specific* objects or situations, such as heights, darkness, public toilets, the sight of blood or enclosed spaces (claustrophobia). For a diagnosis of a specific phobia, the WHO recommends the same criteria as for social phobia.

Before diagnosing any kind of phobia, it is important to bear in mind that many people have reasonable or even slightly irrational fears that do not constitute mental illnesses. Not everyone who dislikes crowds has agoraphobia. Many people dislike social situations and do not have social phobia. Very few people are entirely relaxed about public speaking, and most people who dislike elevators do not have claustrophobia. There is only benefit in diagnosing a phobia if the person's anxiety is disproportionate and disabling, and if the person's quality of life is diminished as a result.

Panic Disorder

A 'panic attack' is an episode in which the person experiences a sudden onset of palpitation (sensation of the heart fluttering in the chest), shortness of breath, choking sensation, chest pain, dizziness, and/or feelings of unreality, without an apparent physical cause. In addition to the physical symptoms of panic (sweating, shaking, chest pain, etc.), the person also experiences psychological symptoms such as extreme anxiety and, often, an irrational fear of dying, losing control or 'going mad'.

These intense symptoms tend to last just for a few minutes but can feel much longer to the person affected. Unlike agoraphobia, social phobia or specific phobias, the anxiety in panic disorder is not limited to any one situation or trigger, although a panic attack will often create a desire to leave the current situation in an effort to relieve the intensely unpleasant anxiety. As a result, a pattern of avoidance may develop, but it will not be as focused as that seen in phobic disorders.

For a diagnosis of panic disorder, the WHO states that there must be several severe panic attacks within a month in situations where there is no objective danger; the attacks must not be limited to known or predictable situations; and there must be relatively few anxiety symptoms between attacks, although anticipatory anxiety about possible future panic attacks is relatively common and understandable.

Generalised Anxiety Disorder

Generalised anxiety disorder is characterised by substantial, persistent anxiety which is not restricted to any particular situations or circumstances. Common symptoms include sustained nervousness, shaking, sweating, dizziness, vague stomach pain and broad, brooding worries. It shares many symptoms with the disorders already discussed but, critically, is not limited to any specific triggers or environments, and the anxiety is persistent as opposed to episodic.

For a diagnosis of generalised anxiety disorder, the WHO states that the person must have symptoms of anxiety most days for several weeks or, more commonly, several months. These symptoms should involve a mixture of (a) apprehension (worrying about the future, problems concentrating, etc.); (b) physical tension (trembling, fidgeting, headaches, etc.); and (c) agitated bodily over-activity (sweating, heart pounding, dizziness, panting, dry mouth, etc.).

This can be an extremely distressing disorder, developing slowly and going unrecognised for years in many cases, as people gradually adjust and limit their lifestyles to minimise symptoms in the short term. Anxiety can also coexist with depression (Chapter 2) and there can be mixed anxiety and depressive disorders, in which symptoms of both anxiety and depression occur together. In such cases, attention is required to both sets of symptoms, which can sometimes be so closely related as to be virtually indistinguishable from each other.

Obsessive-compulsive Disorder

Obsessive-compulsive disorder (OCD) is characterised by obsessional thoughts and/or compulsive acts. Obsessional thoughts are ideas, impulses or images that keep entering a person's mind even though they find them distressing, if only because the person does not want them repeatedly entering their mind. Sometimes, in addition, the thoughts themselves are obscene or violent, and are thus distressing for this reason too. While the person recognises that the thoughts are their own, the person tries to resist having them repeatedly enter their mind, generally with limited success (at least in the pre-treatment phase).

Compulsive acts are analogous to obsessional thoughts, but take the form of behaviours rather than thoughts: they are repeated over and over again, are not enjoyable, and – at the extent to which they occur – are not goal-directed. The person sometimes views the acts as preventing some dreadful but unrelated event from occurring, despite knowing, logically, that the repeated act (for example, hand washing) has no connection with the feared event (such as having a car crash). Resisting the compulsive act produces an upsurge in anxiety which the person feels can only be avoided or relieved by performing the compulsive act (despite its inherent illogic).

For a diagnosis of OCD, the WHO states that obsessional symptoms or compulsive acts, or both, must be present on most days for at least two consecutive weeks and cause distress or interference with the person's usual activities. The obsessional symptoms much be recognised as the person's own thoughts or impulses, and there must be at least one act or thought that is resisted, albeit unsuccessfully. In addition, the thought of carrying out the act must not itself be pleasurable, and the thoughts, impulses or images must be unpleasantly repetitive.

It can be difficult to differentiate between OCD and depressive disorder because the two types of symptoms commonly occur together, but in depressive disorder the low mood is usually primary or has developed first (Chapter 2), although symptoms of both disorders commonly coexist. Symptoms also vary within OCD, depending on the nature of the illness, the person's personality and various other factors. Some people with OCD have predominantly obsessional thoughts or ruminations, in the form of mental images, ideas or impulses to act. Others experience predominantly compulsive acts or obsessional rituals, often concerned with cleaning (for example, hand washing), repetitive checking (well beyond what is necessary), or tidiness and orderliness (again, beyond usual or logical parameters).

All of these symptoms in OCD are underpinned by an anxiety that if the obsession or compulsion is not completed something terrible might happen which – illogically – the person feels can be prevented by engaging in the obsession or compulsion. Obsessional slowness may also develop, linked with anxiety about doing something wrongly or incompletely.

Finally, some people develop a condition termed 'body dysmorphic disorder', in which the person becomes preoccupied with an imagined problem with their appearance, or devotes disproportionate attention to a very minor anomaly. This can lead to lengthy periods looking in mirrors, comparing one's self with others, or repeated requests for treatment or surgery. This can also be considered as a form of somatoform disorder (see below).

Post-traumatic Stress Disorder

Post-traumatic stress disorder (PTSD) arises as a protracted and/or delayed response to a stressful event or situation that is exceptionally threatening or catastrophic, and is likely to cause distress in almost anyone. Examples of relevant events include natural disasters, war, serious accidents, man-made disasters such as an air crash, witnessing the violent death of other people, or being the victim of terrorism, rape, torture or other crimes.

Symptoms include 'flashbacks' (repeated reliving of the trauma in the form of intrusive memories) or dreams; emotional detachment and flattening; feeling increased distance from other people; diminished responsiveness to surroundings; loss of enjoyment in activities that were usually enjoyed; and avoiding situations and activities that recall the original trauma. This can lead to a pattern of avoidance and, on occasion, outbursts of panic, fear and aggression following relevant triggers. There is also commonly heightened 'autonomic arousal' which refers to living in a state of heightened alertness, for example, jumping at the slightest sound, having difficulties with sleep, etc.

For a diagnosis of PTSD, the WHO states that symptoms should usually start within six months of the traumatic event or situation. There must also be a repetitive, intrusive recollection or re-enactment of the traumatic event in the person's memories, dreams or daytime imagery. It is also common that the person experiences significant numbing of feeling, emotional detachment, avoidance of triggers that might arouse memories of the trauma, heightened 'autonomic arousal' or agitation, mood problems, and various related behavioural abnormalities, all of which support a diagnosis of PTSD.

Other Conditions with Varying Relationships with Anxiety

In addition to the above, the WHO presents various other disorders under the heading of 'neurotic, stress-related and somatoform disorders', including acute stress reaction, adjustment disorder, conversion disorder and somatoform disorder. These have varying relationships with anxiety.

The WHO describes 'acute stress reaction' as a very transient disorder of significant severity, occurring in response to exceptional mental or physical stress (for example, natural disaster, rape). For this 'diagnosis', there must be an immediate relationship between the exceptional stressor and the onset of symptoms (for example, daze, anxiety, depression, withdrawal), with onset usually within a few minutes, if not immediately following the stressor. Symptoms tend to change rapidly and resolve quickly, within a few hours. If removal from the stressful circumstance is not possible, symptoms usually begin to diminish after 24 to 48 hours and have generally essentially resolved after three days.

Adjustment disorder is another increasingly recognised condition which involves a state of emotional disturbance and subjective distress which usually interferes with the person's social function and occurs during a period of adaptation to a stressful or significant life event. Key symptoms include worry, anxiety, depressed mood and feelings of inability to cope, as well as difficulty with day-to-day routines and tasks. Diagnosis depends on the relationship between the symptoms; the person's pre-existing personality and history; and the stressful event itself. Symptoms are usually apparent within one month of the relevant event and resolve within six months without specific treatment.

The WHO also includes 'conversion disorders' under the heading of 'neurotic, stress-related and somatoform disorders'. Conversion disorders essentially involve a loss of connection between a person's identity, memories and current sensations or bodily movements. Previously known as 'hysteria', and also known as 'dissociative disorders', conversion disorders are often associated with traumatic events, life problems or relationship difficulties. If the disorder is associated with a traumatic event, it can simply resolve after a few weeks or months. In some people, however, chronic states can develop (for example, psychological paralyses or loss of feeling), especially when the onset is linked with persisting difficult life problems or protracted disturbances in relationships.

For a diagnosis of conversion disorder, it is important that there is no physical disorder that explains the symptoms and that there is evidence for a psychological cause (for example, it occurs in the context of stressful events, life problems or disturbed relationships). It is also required that symptoms accord with various individual conversion disorders outlined by the WHO, including 'dissociative amnesia' (memory loss, usually for important recent events), 'dissociative fugue' (memory loss plus an apparently purposeful journey away from work or home, occasionally involving a new identity), 'dissociative stupor' (the person disengages from voluntary movement and responsiveness, just lying there as if in a coma), 'trance and possession disorders' (transient loss of personal identity, with diminished awareness of surroundings and/or a feeling of being 'taken over' by another personality or force), 'dissociative disorders of movement and sensation', and various other, less common patterns of dissociation such as 'dissociative motor disorders'; 'dissociative convulsions' or fits; 'dissociative anaesthesia (loss of feeling) and sensory loss'; 'multiple personality disorder'; and mixed patterns of dissociation.

Somatoform disorders, the final category, are characterised by repeated presentations with physical symptoms and requests for medical investigations, even when there is no apparent physical problem identified despite a reasonable amount of medical investigation. The WHO describes 'somatisation disorder' as a condition characterised by multiple and variable physical symptoms for which no adequate physical explanation has been found, for at least two years; a persistent refusal to accept reassurance or advice from several doctors that there is no adequate physical explanation; and impairment of family and social functioning as a result.

This is a slightly different to what is known as 'hypochondriacal disorder' (hypochondriasis) which is a persistent belief that one has one or more serious physical illnesses, despite reassurance that this is not the case. Fundamentally, the person with hypochondriacal disorder is preoccupied with (the possibility of) *serious physical illness* (despite having none) and seeks *tests*, whereas the person with 'somatisation disorder' is preoccupied with *symptoms* and seeks *treatment*. Clearly, the two disorders can overlap.

Finally, the WHO includes a number of other less common disorders under the heading of 'neurotic, stress-related and somatoform disorders', including 'somatoform pain disorder' (focused on pain), 'neurasthenia' (increased fatigue and other symptoms) and 'depersonalistion-derealisation syndrome' (in which people or the environment feel unpleasantly unreal for a sustained period). These can be seen as various manifestations of anxiety or other 'neurotic' symptoms, distilled through the individual's personality, life circumstances and coping mechanisms.

Overall, many of the anxiety disorders have much in common with each other, and with conditions such as fibromyalgia. Precise distinctions between some of them can be difficult and, at times, of limited relevance given the substantial overlaps in treatment (see below).

How Common Are Anxiety Disorders?

Anxiety can occur in many forms and in many circumstances. A certain amount of anxiety is normal and healthy, especially in situations of stress and expectation. If, however, anxiety becomes disabling, it can reach the diagnostic threshold for any of the disorders mentioned in this chapter, depending on the form that the anxiety symptoms take.

The vast majority of people who experience regular levels of anxiety do not, of course, have an anxiety disorder and do not benefit from either diagnosis or dedicated treatment. For those who have excessive anxiety and require treatment, however, it is important that their anxiety is discussed and understood, and that appropriate treatment is offered in a collaborative and empowering fashion, following diagnosis and careful discussion.

At population level, approximately 1 per cent of people have panic disorder and 2 to 4 per cent have generalised anxiety disorder at any given time. These disorders, along with agoraphobia and specific phobias, are generally more common in women than men, and in younger or middle-aged adults. Agoraphobia affects between 1 and 2 per cent of adults at any given time, and is twice as common in women as in men. Social phobia affects up to 10 per cent of people at some point in life, and is equally common in men and women. OCD, too, is equally common in women and men, and 2 to 3 per cent of people will develop OCD at some point in their life.

Conversion disorders are rare in the general population but are present in between 4 and 30 per cent of people attending neurology outpatient departments, and are more common in women than men. Somatoform disorders, including both somatisation disorder and hypochondriasis, are present in approximately 25 per cent of people attending GPs. Adjustment disorder is present in up to 10 per cent of people attending GPs and the lifetime risk of PTSD is approximately 8 per cent

Rates of other disorders, such as acute stress reactions, are difficult to establish, owing, not least, to problems with definitions. There is, for example, continuing controversy about bereavement and, specifically, how common it is that a person's grieving process constitutes a 'disorder'. Broadly, however, there is no such thing as absolutely 'normal' grieving, as each person is different and every situation of loss is unique in various ways. Nonetheless, patterns sometimes emerge, and 'normal' grieving is said to last up to two years, although it can, in certain circumstances, go on for longer.

In addition to feelings of loneliness, loss and tearfulness, it is not unusual for a bereaved person to hear the deceased person speak or have visions of the deceased person (especially at night), or even to chat away to the deceased person just as they did when the person was alive. None of this is necessarily problematic and it likely reflects a gradual 'letting go'. It is probably important not to disturb this process too much: the bereaved person is subconsciously experiencing the loss in a graded and more manageable fashion, and this re-experiencing will most likely fade away in due course.

The term 'abnormal' grief is sometimes used when grief is delayed or prolonged, when it is associated with suicidality, when the deceased person dominates the bereaved person's life disproportionately or completely, or when bereavement is causing substantial problems with a person's functioning. Grief-related problems are more common when the death was sudden or conflictual; when grieving was obstructed (for example, by practical concerns at the time); or when there was (or is) ambivalence about the death. These circumstances are, of course, common to many situations of loss and, even so, most people do not experience disproportionate or pathological problems with grieving.

Psychological therapy can assist with the grieving process in problematic cases, but each case must be considered on its own terms, rather than using rigid guidelines. Many people benefit greatly from bereavement counselling, but most cannot reasonably be considered to have 'abnormal' grieving; perhaps 'different' grieving is a better term, indicating a need for discussion, support, care, time and – perhaps most of all – patient understanding.

Case Study: Emma

Emma was a 35-year-old woman working as a primary school teacher. She described herself as 'always a bit nervous, just like my mother'. She came to see her GP in a state of considerable anxiety because she had to leave work twice in the past week for reasons that she said she could not understand fully.

Two months earlier, during a busy but otherwise unremarkable day, Emma had been seized by a sudden thought that she needed to go home at once or something dreadful would happen. Standing in the classroom, she suddenly became acutely anxious, felt her heart racing in her chest, and thought she could not breathe. She left her classroom and stood outside for a few minutes to catch her breath.

Over the course of the following ten minutes, Emma's symptoms and dizziness resolved. She was 'a little shaky' for the rest of the day, but she got through it and mentioned the incident to nobody, afraid they would think she was 'going mad' (as she, herself, secretly feared).

A few days later, the same thing happened at the shops, and was accompanied on this occasion by a strange feeling 'as if' things around here were 'not real'. Logically, Emma knew that everything around her was indeed real, but 'the feeling of unreality' was strong, unpleasant and difficult to shake off. The feeling was accompanied by all of Emma's previous symptoms too: a feeling of dread, heart racing, shortness of breath, dizziness and excessive perspiration.

Emma was deeply upset by these episodes, not least because she had never heard of anything similar. She was most alarmed that she had to leave work because of these symptoms on several occasions, and she found it increasingly difficult to explain it to the principal of the school where she worked.

Emma's GP listened carefully to Emma's story and was able to tell Emma that these were panic attacks, and that many other people experienced them. Emma would later learn that her mother had suffered from panic attacks for a time, many years earlier.

Emma's GP was able to reassure Emma that panic attacks are a well recognised phenomenon, that they are treatable, and that a number of different therapeutic approaches can be considered, depending on the precise nature of the problem and the patient's own preferred treatment modality.

What Causes Anxiety Disorders?

The causes of anxiety disorders are not fully understood. In any given individual, there is likely to be a mix of psychological, social and biological factors, although some of these might not be immediately apparent, and some might not appear relevant at all in particular cases.

In terms of biology, the risk of developing an anxiety disorder is increased four-fold if you have a family member with an anxiety disorder. There also appears to be a genetic relationship between depression (Chapter 2) and certain anxiety disorders, such as generalised anxiety disorder and panic attacks. These links might reflect commonality in their biological underpinnings and/or diagnostic overlap between these disorders: in some people, anxiety can be a key manifestation of depression, so it is not at all surprising that both 'disorders' can run in the same families.

It is not entirely clear how anomalies in the biology, structure or function of the brain link with the specific symptoms of anxiety disorders. It appears likely that there is dysregulation of at least one particular brain chemical (gamma-aminobutyric acid or 'GABA'), but it appears unlikely that this dysfunction is anything as straightforward as having too much GABA or too little. It is more likely that complex interactions between different brain chemicals are associated with symptoms of anxiety, and that the precise biology might vary between individuals.

People are, of course, constantly changing their brain chemistry with various foods, drinks and (for some) drugs (including alcohol), and these various substances affect brain chemistry in different ways. It is known, for example, that alcohol and abuse of benzodiazepines increase risk of anxiety and panic disorder, and that stopping them improves mental health. Other factors are also invariably relevant in any given individual, including childhood difficulties, separations, personality traits and life stresses such as financial problems or physical illnesses. There is an especially strong relationship between panic disorder and chronic obstructive airways disease, which is characterised by breathlessness and can thus create, worsen and perpetuate anxiety symptoms.

There is strong evidence of a genetic component in OCD as many people with the condition have a family history of OCD, tics or Tourette's Syndrome (a neurological disorder with involuntary tics and vocalisations; see Chapter 10). Again, there are proposed links with dysfunctions of specific brain chemicals (for example, serotonin) or hormones, resulting in diminished ability to stop repetitive mental or physical actions (for example, counting, checking). From a psychological perspective, the temporary reduction in anxiety following an obsession or compulsion serves to re-enforce the behavior and perpetuate the problem. This creates a potential entry point for treatments such as cognitive-behaviour therapy (CBT), aimed at reducing symptoms and distress caused by OCD (see below).

Acute stress reaction, adjustment disorder and PTSD are all multi-factorial disorders requiring stressful events in order to occur, but also likely linked with personality and functioning prior to the trauma. There can also be perpetuating factors afterwards, which relate to the trauma directly or indirectly, or which can be entirely unrelated to the trauma and simply perpetuate PTSD symptoms opportunistically. The causes are often difficult to unravel in these situations but can be of considerable relevance, especially if there is a court action following the traumatic event.

The origins of conversion and somatoform disorders (somatisation and hypochondriacal disorders) are generally described in psychological terms and can be linked with repressed memories, problems with communication or unresolved psychological issues in the past or present. Regardless of the cause, it is clear that once a cycle of anxiety and reassurance is established in, for example, hypochondriasis, it is exceptionally difficult to break this cycle without causing short-term anxiety to the patient, for example, declining to repeat tests that do not need repeating and offering the (often unwelcome) suggestion that the person might benefit from psychological or psychiatric treatment. This needs to be handled with care, as it can change the dynamic of the person's distress and lead to positive treatment outcomes if managed appropriately.

What Are the Treatments for Anxiety Disorders?

Anxiety disorders are treatable conditions. Treatment can involve combinations of psychological therapies, medication and social inputs. Psychotherapy is usually the mainstay of treatment, augmented by other measures as indicated. For all patients and families, psychoeducation, self-help and support groups can also be extremely important.

The National Institute for Health and Care Excellence (NICE) in the UK has published guidance on assessment and management of anxiety disorders, including generalised anxiety disorder, social anxiety disorder, panic disorder, PTSD, OCD and body dysmorphic disorder.[2] NICE places particular emphasis on careful, thorough assessment prior to reaching a diagnosis or offering treatment.

In terms of psychotherapy, CBT is the most commonly used psychological treatment. CBT focuses on the use of cognitive strategies (that is, strategies related to thinking patterns and habits) and behavioural strategies (that is, strategies related to actions and behavioural habits), in an effort to re-frame thoughts, enhance coping strategies, reduce symptoms and promote recovery and wellness (Chapters 2, 3, 6 and 9).

Usually, the psychotherapist will meet the patient once per week and point out errors or unhelpful thinking patterns which may deepen or prolong symptoms. Together, the patient and psychotherapist identify ways to address these errors and habits to incrementally improve symptoms. There is strong evidence that CBT is highly effective in the management of depression (Chapter 2), generalised anxiety disorder, panic disorder, social phobia, OCD, PTSD and a range of other conditions. Its principles can also be applied in online materials, groups and many other formats.

The precise components of CBT vary between disorders. In generalised anxiety disorder, CBT can focus on identifying and modifying preemptory anxious thoughts and replacing them with more reality-based thoughts and better coping methods. Psycho-education, self-help, relaxation techniques and breathing exercises are also very helpful.

A number of antidepressant medications (Chapter 2) are licensed for use in generalised anxiety disorder and can prove extremely useful elements of the treatment package. Certain anti-anxiety medications such as benzodiazepines, however, should only be used in short-term crises (when symptoms are severe, disabling or causing extreme distress), and for extremely short periods, if at all, owing to their addiction potential and possible paradoxical effects. Pregabalin, a different type of medication, can also be useful in certain cases of generalised anxiety disorder under appropriate supervision.

In panic disorder, too, treatment is generally centred on CBT as well as certain antidepressants licensed for the disorder. For phobias, CBT often involves graded exposure to the feared stimulus and response prevention. In agoraphobia, for example, graded exposure to the anxiety-provoking situation is used, with appropriate distraction and cognitive re-structuring; antidepressants can also play a useful role in certain cases with co-existing panic disorder.

Treatment of social phobia or social anxiety disorder involves CBT, self-help and social skills, as well as certain antidepressant medications, if needed. Further assistance is available from Social Anxiety Ireland, which offers information, support and assistance (www.socialanxietyireland.com).

In OCD, treatment involves psychoeducation and CBT, which often centres on exposure to the relevant triggers and response prevention, and can be delivered in the form of individual or group therapy. Certain antidepressants are also used, especially selective-serotonin reuptake inhibitors. The response rate to CBT and/or medication is around 75 per cent. For a tiny minority of people with OCD, brain surgery can be useful if symptoms are severe enough, but this is very rare, as is the use of deep bran stimulation, a promising, less invasive, relatively new technique.

With regard to stress-related conditions, acute stress reactions and adjustment disorders are, by definition, self-resolving. For PTSD, treatment centres on trauma-focused CBT. Eye movement desensitisation and reprocessing (EMDR) is another technique used in PTSD, and involves making side to-side eye movements while recalling the trauma, under specialist supervision. The aim is to help the person's brain process flashbacks so as to come to terms with the traumatic experience and think more positively. EMDR can duly help reduce distress in some people with PTSD.

Certain antidepressant medications can also be prescribed in PTSD for those who decline CBT, cannot engage in it, do not benefit sufficiently from it, or have depression or hypersensitivity sufficiently severe to affect CBT's effectiveness on its own. In these circumstances, certain antidepressants are recommended by NICE, despite limited evidence.[3] As with all medication, side effect profiles should be considered with care prior to use (see the website of the Health Products Regulatory Authority, www.hpra.ie).

In terms of overall treatment choices, NICE recommends a 'stepped care approach' for adults with generalised anxiety disorder, panic disorder, PTSD, OCD or body dysmorphic disorder.[4]

Step 1 is for known or suspected common mental health disorders and involves assessment, psychoeducation and monitoring, as well as referral in appropriate cases.

Step 2 is for mild to moderate disorders, and NICE recommends individual self-help and psychoeducation for generalised anxiety disorder and panic disorder; individual or group CBT for OCD, as well as self-help groups; and trauma-focused CBT or EMDR for PTSD (see above for explanations of these acronyms). Social support and education and employment support are also suggested, along with appropriate onward referral when indicated.

Step 3 is for more serious or debilitating cases and NICE recommends CBT, relaxation, medication or combined interventions for generalised anxiety disorder; CBT and antidepressants for panic disorder; CBT, antidepressants and combined care with case-management for OCD; and trauma-focused CBT, EMDR or medication treatment for PTSD. Self-help groups are also helpful for many of these disorders.

For somatoform disorders, CBT is also commonly used, along with interventions focused on the social context in which the disorder developed and is sustained. Management of conversion disorders can also be quite complex, as it is necessary first to rule out physical illness and treat any other mental illness the person may have (such as depression) (Chapter 2). It is then important to investigate factors possibly perpetuating or supporting the persistence of the conversion disorder, such as 'secondary gain' through increased sympathy for the patient or being excused from certain roles as a result of the symptoms.

For many of these disorders, there can be a role for psychotherapeutic approaches other than CBT, depending on the situation at hand and the patient's preference. Mindfulness-based techniques, for example, can be very helpful for many people (see Chapter 2 and the 'Useful Resources' at the end of the present chapter).

Psychoanalysis is another therapeutic technique that has been unjustly neglected in recent decades and can be of assistance to many, including those who find that CBT is helpful in reducing anxiety symptoms but feel it does not provide sufficient meaning or growth in personal understanding. It is important that space is made for many different kinds of therapy for anxiety disorders and other conditions, not least because each person has a unique combination of weaknesses and strengths, problems and solutions, and this diversity should be reflected in the treatments available.

The vast majority of people with anxiety disorders are treated in primary care or by psychotherapists in the community, without referral to secondary mental health services (that is, psychiatrists and multi-disciplinary community mental health teams; see Chapter 12). For the minority who require referral to secondary mental health services, the vast majority of these are treated as outpatients by community mental health teams in outpatient clinics, day hospitals or day centres, using the treatments outlined above.

A small proportion are, however, admitted for inpatient psychiatric care, when the disorder is especially severe (for example, life-threatening OCD), previous treatments have failed to produce sufficient improvement, or there is significant risk to self or others. Inpatient care tends to be a more intensive version of the treatments already discussed above.

In 2015, there were 1,683 psychiatric admissions to Irish adult psychiatry units or hospitals with 'neuroses' or anxiety disorders.[5] Just over half (54 per cent) were female, and 54 per cent of admissions with neuroses were readmissions, which is less than the proportion of all readmissions (66 per cent). Overall, neuroses accounted for 9.4 per cent of admissions of adults in 2015, and 2.9 per cent of involuntary adult admissions (Chapter 13). The most common length of inpatient stay with neuroses was 10 days, which is significantly shorter than the most common length of stay for all patients (15 days).

There were also 67 admissions of children and adolescents (under the age of 18 years) with neuroses in 2015, of whom just over half were female (58 per cent). These accounted for 13 per cent of all admissions of children and adolescents, and 22 per cent were readmissions. There was one involuntary admission of a child or adolescent with neurosis in 2015, out of a total of 17 involuntary admissions in that age group in that year.

Overall, the vast majority of people with anxiety disorders are treated in primary care or as outpatients, and the outlook for improvement is very good in the absence of complicating factors, such as alcohol misuse, and provided there is sensible, sustained treatment in the context of a good, steady therapeutic relationship. A wider diversity of psychotherapeutic approaches is needed, however, in order to reflect the variety of anxiety disorders that present, and the even wider diversity of people who experience them.

Case History: Peter

Peter was a 50-year-old man in good physical and mental health who was involved in a car accident. His vehicle was stationary at traffic lights when a drunk driver drove the wrong way up a one-way street, through a junction, and crashed into Peter's car from the side. Peter was not physically injured but was most disturbed by the sudden, random nature of the accident. In the days and weeks following the event, Peter developed difficulty sleeping and began to feel nervous much of the time.

Eight weeks after the accident, Peter went to see his GP because he was having intrusive dreams about the event, and said that sometimes during the day 'it suddenly feels like I'm back there: I can hear the crash and feel the impact again. I jump up suddenly.' Peter also said, since the accident, he was not enjoying the activities he usually enjoyed, was finding work 'impossible', and had little interest in talking with his family or meeting friends. He had neither driven a car nor passed the site of accident since its occurrence. In fact, he was reluctant to go out of the house at all and stayed inside most of the time.

Peter felt that the accident had affected him badly, and further discussion with his GP revealed more symptoms of PTSD: general jumpiness, nervousness and a feeling of emotional detachment from others. *Peter felt that the accident was making him depressed, and his GP agreed that there was a problem, feeling that Peter probably had developed PTSD.*

Together, Peter and his GP discussed possible treatment, and the GP referred Peter to a clinical psychologist for assessment for psychological therapy. Peter received a course of CBT and his improvement was significant but only partial. He returned to his GP who recommended continuing CBT but also added in an antidepressant medication, following careful discussion and consideration of possible benefits and side effects.

Six weeks later, Peter's improvement had resumed: he was back driving his car and was going outside most days. Peter's intrusive dreams had declined and, although they still occurred from time to time, he was substantially better than he had been, and was confident of continued improvement in the months ahead.

Useful Resources

It is advisable that anyone who thinks he or she has any of the conditions discussed in this book sees a health care professional. There are many reasons for this, including a need to rule out any other diagnoses, such as physical illnesses. In addition, some people find it easier to talk with a health care professional, especially if they are too uncertain or embarrassed to talk with friends or family members. Often, a brief talk with a GP will 'normalise' the individual's symptoms by reassuring them that they are not alone in what they are experiencing and that help is to hand, if any is needed.

Individuals with any mental disorder or psychological problem, and their families, will find much that is useful on the Internet. As ever, Internet resources need to be evaluated with care and only trusted when the information comes from a reliable source. Reliable information about mental health can be sourced from the websites of the Health Service Executive (www.hse.ie/

eng/health/az), Royal College of Psychiatrists in London (www. rcpsych.ac.uk), National Health Service in the UK (www.nhs.uk) and National Institute of Mental Health in the US (www.nimh.nih. gov). The College of Psychiatrists of Ireland (www.irishpsychiatry. ie) has especially useful information on anxiety disorders: www. irishpsychiatry.ie/Helpful_Info/mentalhealthproblems/Anxiety-Disorders.aspx

Evidence-based guidance about specific treatments can be found on the website of the National Institute for Health and Care Excellence (NICE) (www.nice.org.uk). NICE is a UK-based organisation responsible for developing guidance, standards and information on high-quality health and social care, and preventing and treating ill health. Details of their guidance on specific anxiety disorders were outlined in the text of this chapter (above).

In addition to the above, information and resources relating to panic attacks, agoraphobia, anxiety and social phobia are available on the website of Oanda Ireland, the Out and About Association (www.oandaireland.ie).

There are also several books which may be helpful, including: *Overcoming Social Anxiety and Shyness: A Self-Help Guide Using Cognitive Behavioral Techniques* (Second Edition) by Dr Gillian Butler (Robinson, 2016); *Living With Fear: Understanding and Coping with Anxiety* (Second Edition) by Isaac M. Marks MD (McGraw-Hill Publishing Company, 2005); *Break Free from OCD: Overcoming Obsessive Compulsive Disorder with CBT* by Dr Fiona Challacombe, Dr Victoria Bream Oldfield and Professor Paul Salkovskis (Vermilion/Ebury Publishing, 2011); *Because We Are Bad: OCD and a Girl Lost in Thought* by Lily Bailey (Canbury Press, 2016); *The Compassionate-Mind Guide to Recovering from Trauma and PTSD: Using Compassion-Focused Therapy to Overcome Flashbacks, Shame, Guilt, and Fear* by Deborah H. Lee and Sophie James (New Harbinger, 2013); *Mindfulness: A Practical Guide to Finding Peace in a Frantic World* by Mark Williams and Danny Penman (Piatkus, 2011); *Mindfulness for Worriers: Over-*

come Everyday Stress and Anxiety by Padraig O'Morain (Yellow Kite/Hodder and Stoughton, 2015). Padraig O'Morain is an author and counsellor who also provides an Internet resource focused on mindfulness (www.padraigomorain.com/blog).

Endnotes

1   World Health Organisation. *International Classification of Diseases* (10ᵗʰ Edition). Geneva: World Health Organisation, 1992.

2   www.nice.org.uk/guidance/qs53

3   www.nice.org.uk/guidance/cg26

4   www.nice.org.uk/guidance/cg123

5   Daly, A. and Craig, S. HRB Statistics Series 29: Activities of Irish Psychiatric Units and Hospitals 2015. Dublin: Health Research Board, 2016 (Tables 2.6a, 2.8, 2.14a, 5.3 and 5.5).

Chapter 6

Eating Disorders

The term 'eating disorders' refers to a range of different conditions, including anorexia nervosa, bulimia nervosa and various others. These disorders are widely discussed in popular media and while much of this coverage centres on relevant issues (for example, media images of thinness), much of the coverage often fails to acknowledge the very complex personal, community *and* social factors associated with disordered eating, the treatments available, and the positive outcomes that are eminently possible with appropriate and sustained treatment.

Against this background, this chapter looks at four key questions about eating disorders:

◊ What are the symptoms and signs of eating disorders?

◊ How common are eating disorders?

◊ What causes eating disorders?

◊ What are the treatments for eating disorders?

Useful resources and sources of further information are provided at the end of the chapter.

What Are the Signs and Symptoms of Eating Disorders?

The World Health Organisation (WHO) outlines a number of eating disorders, including anorexia nervosa, bulimia nervosa, overeating or vomiting associated with other psychological disturbances and others.[1] As is the case in all areas of mental health,

118

many people will demonstrate some but not all of the features of any given disorder, and others will demonstrate features of more than one disorder. While it is important not to obsess over the precise criteria in the case of any given individual with disordered eating and related symptoms, the WHO paradigm is quite effective in mapping out fairly common patterns of distress, and thus provides a useful (although far from definitive) framework for thinking about disordered eating that is severe enough to cause significant distress or physical complications. Anorexia nervosa is, perhaps, the best-known condition in this family of disorders.

Anorexia Nervosa

The WHO defines anorexia nervosa as a disorder characterised by deliberate weight loss that is induced and/or sustained by the patient. It occurs most commonly in adolescent girls and young women, but can occur in anyone. The resultant undernutrition can result in various disturbances of bodily function, often relating to specific hormones (see below). The picture is commonly complicated by very restricted dietary choices, excessive exercise and, consequently, further changes in body composition owing to self-induced vomiting and purging, among other behaviours.

Many of these features are, of course, present in many people from time to time, but to a milder degree than is seen in eating disorders, and they are less sustained. A WHO diagnosis of anorexia nervosa, by contrast, requires that *all* of the following features are present:

- Body weight is maintained at least 15 per cent below expected body weight, or a Quetelet's body-mass index (BMI) is 17.5 kg/m^2 or less (for people aged 16 years or over). A person's BMI is calculated using the person's mass or weight, measured in kilograms (kg), and height, measured in metres (m). The BMI is the body mass divided by the square of the body height (that is, kilograms/metres squared, or kg/m^2). Therefore, a man who weighs 70 kilograms and is 1.8 metres (6 feet) in height has a

BMI of 21.6 kg/m². The WHO regards a BMI between 18.5 kg/m² and 24.9 kg/m² as normal, with values below that indicating underweight and values over than indicating overweight or obese (30 or over). These guidelines are not cast in stone, and many factors need to be taken into account when interpreting them, but values of 17.5 kg/m² or lower are consistent with (although not necessarily diagnostic of) anorexia nervosa. The person's stage of growth is also relevant, because people grow at different rates and growth is often uneven.

- The weight loss is self-induced, chiefly through avoidance of apparently 'fattening foods'. There may also be self-induced vomiting; self-induced purging; excessive exercising; and use of appetite suppressants, diuretics (medication to increase loss of fluid from the body) and/or misuse of various other medications with similar effects.

- There is body-image distortion whereby the person perceives their own body in a distorted way. This is often characterised by a dread of fatness that persists as an intrusive, recurring idea, with the result that the person self-imposes a low weight threshold.

- There is a widespread disturbance of body hormones, often manifest in women as abnormal absence of periods (amenorrhoea) and in men as a loss of sexual interest and potency. Other hormones may also be affected, including increased levels of growth hormone (as the body tries to compensate for lack of food), raised levels of cortisol (owing to increased body stress), and changes in the way the body uses thyroid hormone and insulin (as a result of lack of nutrition).

- If the person has not yet experienced puberty, there may be a disturbance in the usual sequence of events in puberty, such as diminished breast development or delayed periods in girls, or persistence of juvenile genitalia in boys. If treatment is successful, puberty is often completed normally following recovery.

Other features of anorexia nervosa can include intolerance of cold; dry or yellow skin; fine hair ('lanugo hair') on trunk and face; low heart rate and low blood pressure; low blood count; and the physical effects of repeated vomiting which can include low potassium levels, pitting of teeth, swelling of parotid glands at the sides of the mouth and scarring on the back of the hand from self-inducing vomiting (Russell's sign).

As a result, initial assessment of a person with a suspected eating disorder will commonly include not only careful history taking and mental state examination, but also a physical examination and various tests, such as full blood count; tests of kidney, liver and thyroid function; tests of calcium and glucose; pregnancy test; and urine tests. Other tests may also be indicated in specific circumstances such as a heart tracing or electrocardiogram (ECG) or x-rays (of chest or abdomen).

It is important that anorexia nervosa is not diagnosed when symptoms are attributable to other disorders, such as depression (which can also occur in anorexia nervosa) (Chapter 2); obsessional or compulsive symptoms (especially if obsessions relate to food) (Chapter 5); personality disorder (Chapter 9); physical illness (especially chronic illness, cancers or disorders of the intestine, such as Crohn's disease); schizophrenia (with delusions about food) (Chapter 3); alcohol or drug misuse (Chapter 7); or just unexplained loss of appetite.

If a person presents with a generally typical picture of anorexia nervosa but lacks one or more of the key features, they might have atypical anorexia nervosa, as might a person who has less severe symptoms of the disorder but is still substantially troubled and affected by certain symptoms of anorexia nervosa or other eating disorders.

Bulimia Nervosa

According to the WHO, bulimia nervosa is a mental disorder characterised by repeated bouts of overeating and an excessive preoccupation with the control of body weight. This leads the person to engage in extreme measures aimed at reversing the perceived 'fattening' effects of food.

There may be an overlap with anorexia nervosa, or one disorder may precede the other, although the age of presentation with bulimia nervosa tends to be slightly later. A person with anorexia nervosa may improve following weight gain and amelioration of other symptoms, but a pattern of overeating and vomiting may then become established. Sustained vomiting can lead to multiple physical complications such as seizures, heart rhythm problems, muscular weakness and further severe weight loss.

A WHO diagnosis of bulimia nervosa requires all three of the following:

• A persistent preoccupation with eating and a powerful craving for food, and the person must succumb to episodes of overeating, that is, consumption of large quantities of food in short periods of time.

• The person must attempt to counteract the perceived 'fattening' effects of food through self-induced vomiting; abusing purgatives, alternating with periods of starvation; using drugs such as appetite suppressants, thyroid preparations or medicines to promote fluid loss (diuretics).

• The person must have a morbid dread of fatness and set a well-defined weight threshold that is below their optimal weight prior to developing the disorder, and below the person's optimum or healthy weight in the opinion of the physician.

Before making a diagnosis of bulimia nervosa, it is important to ensure that the person's symptoms are not better explained by gastrointestinal disorders that cause repeated vomiting; personality features associated with some of the symptoms of eating disorders; or other mental disorders such as depression (especially as symptoms of depression can co-exist with bulimia nervosa) (Chapter 2).

In addition, some people may present with atypical bulimia nervosa which lacks one or more of the key features of the disorder but otherwise present a fairly typical clinical picture. This can apply to people of normal weight or people who are overweight but who experience periods of overeating followed by vomiting or purging.

Other Eating Disorders

The WHO points out that there can be various other forms of disordered eating which cause symptoms and problems in various different ways. Many people engage in overeating when stressed or in response to distressing events such as arguments, problems at work or bereavements. This is 'reactive overeating' and while it is not a good coping mechanism it will most often resolve following resolution of the stressful event or the simple passage of time.

People may also experience vomiting associated with other psychological disturbances such as dissociation or hypochondriasis (Chapter 5), or psychological problems during pregnancy (Chapter 9). Again, these are not primary eating disorders but find their causes and solutions in other areas of psychological or social functioning, and the remedies need to reflect the causes and circumstances associated with the symptoms in each individual case.

How Common Are Eating Disorders?

At any time, approximately 1 to 2 per cent of young women have anorexia nervosa and approximately 1 to 3 per cent have bulimia nervosa. Both disorders are three times more common in women than men, although anorexia nervosa is almost equally common in male and female children. The most common age of onset is adolescence or early adulthood, with bulimia nervosa generally presenting slightly later (age 15-30 years) than anorexia nervosa (age 13-20 years). Onset in men tends to be later, although diagnosis can also be especially delayed in men.

It is important to identify and treat eating disorders and problematic eating habits early, but it is also important not to overreact to food fads or passing habits, especially in young people. Many children are 'fussy eaters' and while normal, balanced eating habits are to be encouraged, it is worth remembering that many if not most children go through phases such as eating only certain kinds of foods, being reluctant to try anything new, or eating only a restricted range of bland, repetitive foods.

It can be very difficult for parents to strike a balance between encouraging a proper diet and not alienating their child or adolescent in the process. In general, parents can only make a wholesome, balanced diet available, encourage general adherence to it, and tolerate transient idiosyncratic eating habits within reason, without disproportionately antagonising the child, or turning food into a battleground that is then used to air all kinds of discontentments (many of which have nothing to do with food). This is difficult territory for many to navigate. Common sense should prevail and parents should be aware that they can do only so much: self-reproach and self-blame profit nobody.

What Causes Eating Disorders?

The causes of eating disorders are not fully known, but the general understanding of the context in which such disorders commonly develop is gradually improving. The WHO notes that, although the fundamental causes of anorexia nervosa remain unknown, there is growing evidence that both biological and socio-cultural factors contribute to the disorder, along with less well-defined psychological and personality factors.

There is, in the first instance, growing evidence of a genetic component in many eating disorders. First degree relatives (parents, siblings, children) of people with an eating disorder show increased risk of eating disorders and anxiety disorders, such as obsessive-compulsive disorder (OCD) (Chapter 5), as well as depression (Chapter 2). First degree relatives of people with bulimia nervosa also show increased rates of alcohol and substance abuse (Chapter 7). It is not entirely clear what biological brain mechanisms underlie this increased risk or produce symptoms of eating disorders, but it appears likely that serotonin (a chemical transmitter in the brain) is involved, as it has roles in regulating appetite, impulse control and moods. Further research is needed.

People who develop eating disorders tend to have low self-esteem, anxious personality traits and obsessive compulsive traits. There can also be limited emotional expressiveness in anorexia nervosa and altered impulse control in bulimia nervosa. These associations are, however, by no means absolute, and many people with anorexia nervosa or bulimia show none or few of these features, and many people with these characteristics will never develop eating disorders. These are, moreover, only associations and are not necessarily causally linked to the disorders, and they are rather vague at that.

In any given individual, then, the specific factors leading to eating disorders will vary depending not only on their genetic inheritance and physiology, but also their environment as both a child and an adult. Anorexia nervosa, for example, has been associated with abuse in childhood (emotional, sexual, physical); contexts or situations in which there is over-regulation of food, or body shape is over-valued; difficulties in familial or other inter-personal relationships; and various other forms of stress, such as failing exams or changing schools.

It is also commonly stated that cultures in which being thin or underweight are valued or celebrated in media have higher rates of eating disorders. While there is much truth in this position, it would be misleading to suggest that media pressure is solely responsible for increased rates of diagnosis of anorexia nervosa since the 1950s. There are many complex factors at work which can be described using the languages of biology, psychology or sociology, and the powerful and generally negative effects of media on body image are certainly one part of this complex mix.

But these three approaches – biological, psychological and social – do not necessarily reflect separate inputs into the genesis of eating disorders; they are simply different languages that seek to describe the same thing: the complex process that leads to an eating disorder. Limited knowledge of the brain makes the language of biology currently inadequate to describe the situation fully, so many people prefer the languages of psychology or sociology, which ostensibly offer meaning or, at least, construct interpretations that satisfy many people's innate belief that human behavior is understandable and that social context provides a logical framework for understanding it. On this basis, it is unsurprising that psychological therapies are central to the treatment of eating disorders.

Case History: Jacqueline

Jacqueline was a 17-year-old girl attending secondary school. She had always been shy and somewhat anxious, but was a high achiever at her studies and generally applied herself well. Over the course of around three months, Jacqueline's parents noticed that she was rarely eating at home, and was getting steadily thinner. They asked her about this, but she said everything was fine, and that she was eating at school and with her friends on the way home. Some weeks later, however, Jacqueline's mother came upon Jacqueline making herself vomit in the bathroom.

Later, Jacqueline's mother spoke to Jacqueline who broke down in tears and admitted that she had been deliberately starving herself because she was afraid of becoming fat and believed that she currently looked fat. She also said that several of her friends were doing the same thing, and had offered her some tablets which, they said, would make her 'thin'. Jacqueline was, however, too frightened to take them as she had already fainted twice at school in the past week. She did, however, continue making herself vomit, up to four times per day.

Following a lengthy, emotional discussion with her mother, Jacqueline agreed to attend the family GP, who discussed the problems with Jacqueline in some detail. The GP established that Jacqueline's periods had recently stopped due to her precipitous weight loss; that her BMI was 16 kg/m²; and that Jacqueline fulfilled diagnostic criteria for anorexia nervosa (see above).

The GP did a complete physical examination; took blood and urine tests (all of which were normal); assessed the risks to Jacqueline's physical and mental health; and referred Jacqueline to the local mental health service. The GP also directed both Jacqueline and her mother to reliable information about eating disorders on the Internet (see Useful Resources at the end of this chapter) and local support groups for people affected by eating disorders and their families.

What Are the Treatments for Eating Disorders?

Eating disorders are treatable mental disorders. Many people are initially ambivalent about treatment so a good, supportive therapeutic relationship is central. The family and friends of people with eating disorders often experience significant frustration as they seek to help their family member or friend, but commonly struggle to do so. On this basis, it is important that the treating team does not allow such frustration to develop, and maintains a consistent, supportive approach to therapy.

The National Institute for Health and Care Excellence (NICE) in the UK has published detailed guidance on management of 'eating disorders in over 8s',[2] and places strong emphases on comprehensive physical and psychological assessments, as well as assessment of risk to self. The provision of clear information to patients and families is incredibly important, as is getting help as early as possible in the course of the disorder.

At the outset, it is essential that the person's physical health needs are identified and addressed. Undereating, disordered eating, or malnutrition can lead to problems with bones and muscles (for example, weakness, fragile bones or osteoporosis, and developmental problems in younger people); sexual problems (for example, lack of periods and infertility in women; reduced sex drive and erectile dysfunction in men); problems with blood vessels and the heart (for example, low blood pressure, irregular heartbeat and even heart failure); problems with the nervous system (for example, fits, memory problems, poor concentration); blood abnormalities (for example, low blood count or anaemia); and various other problems with virtually every part of the body (kidneys, liver, thyroid, and glucose regulation).

If laxatives are being abused, these should be carefully stopped. Specific physical health problems need to be identified and addressed and, for those who have lost substantial weight or stopped eating, re-feeding needs to be undertaken with care, in a graded, considered fashion, under expert guidance, in order to avoid 're-feeding syndromes' (see below).

People with diabetes require particular monitoring if they develop eating disorders as they are at increased risk of eye complications (for example, retinopathy). Patients who are regularly vomiting require special advice about dental hygiene (for example, avoiding brushing after vomiting; rinsing with non-acid mouthwash after vomiting; reducing acid in the oral environment, that is, the mouth).

In children and adolescents, growth and development need to be carefully monitored; family involvement in care should be encouraged; and the treating team should remain alert for any indicators of abuse (emotional, physical, sexual or other). In pregnancy, anorexia nervosa presents particular risks to mother and child, including heightened risk of miscarriage, premature delivery, having a low birth weight baby and needing a caesarean section. Careful management is essential.

For all people, it is important that physical health problems and risks are identified and managed at an early stage, in parallel with psychiatric treatment of the eating disorder itself. Self-management and self-help are also critical elements at all stages of care. The Royal College of Psychiatrists presents, on its website, a very useful list of 'Do's and 'Don'ts' to assist with self-management of eating disorders.[3] The 'Do's' include:

✓ Sticking to regular mealtimes.

✓ Taking small steps towards a healthier eating (for example, if you can't eat breakfast, just sit at the table for a few minutes at breakfast time and drink a glass of water, and try to progress a little day by day or week by week).

✓ Keeping a diary of what you eat and your thoughts and feelings.

✓ Tring to be open about what you are or are not eating.

✓ Being kind to yourself.

✓ Understanding what a reasonable weight is for you.

✓ Reading stories of other people's recoveries.

✓ Joining supportive self-help groups.

✓ Avoiding websites or social networks that encourage very low body weight.

'Don'ts' include:

✗ Weighing yourself more than once a week.

✗ Spending time checking your body and looking at yourself in the mirror.

✗ Cutting yourself off from family and friends.

Psychiatric treatment, when required, is generally centred on psychological therapy, combined with medication in certain cases, and supported by broad family, community and social support. There is also, since 2010, a National Clinical Programme for eating disorders in Ireland. Each of these elements of treatment is now considered in turn, starting with psychological therapies.

Psychological Therapy for Eating Disorders

Psychological therapies are the cornerstone of treatment of eating disorders, in parallel with monitoring physical health through the patient's weight, height and other indices of physical well-being. The chief psychological therapies for which there are varying degrees of evidence include cognitive behaviour therapy (CBT), cognitive analytic therapy (CAT), interpersonal psychotherapy, focal psychodynamic therapy and family interventions explicitly designed for eating disorders. A multi-disciplinary approach is very useful, often involving judicious advice from a dietician who is familiar with the field.

CBT is the psychological therapy most commonly used in eating disorders. CBT aims to help you to look at your thoughts and feelings in detail, and to develop alternative patterns of thinking or behaving in order to reduce your symptoms (Chapters 2, 3, 5 and 9). CBT is focused on understanding how you think about yourself, the world and other people, and how the things you do affect your thoughts and feelings. As its name suggests, CBT looks at both how you think ('cognition') and how you behave ('behaviour'), seeking to identify and implement changes that can help you to feel better, establish more helpful thinking and behavior patterns, and remain well into the future. The therapy is chiefly focused on the present rather than understanding the past, and it aims to improve your state of mind now and into the future.

In practice, CBT can be done individually or with a group of other people, or, sometimes, with a self-help book or online resources. In anorexia nervosa, CBT generally involves learning more about the disorder itself; understanding how to predict symptoms and when they will intensify; keeping a diary of eating episodes, binges, purging, vomiting and any likely triggers; working towards establishing regular, healthier eating habits; changing the way you think about your behaviour, feelings and symptoms; developing new thinking habits, in a more positive direction; and dealing with day-to-day problems and challenges differently and more positively.

NICE also recommends cognitive analytic therapy (CAT) for anorexia nervosa. In this form of therapy, the therapist works with the patient to identify sequences and chains of events (or thoughts) that underpin problem behaviours such as self-starvation and vomiting. CAT places particular emphasis on the way that problems occur *between* people, as opposed to occurring in an isolated fashion within a single individual. This has significant implications for recognising how problems can be repeated or re-created over time, and establishing how such problems can be re-conceptualised and addressed both now and in the future.

Interpersonal psychotherapy, also recommended by NICE, is another structured, time-limited form of psychological therapy that generally lasts for three to four months. It focuses on the idea that relationships and life events have an effect on mood and that mood, in turn, affects relationships and life events.

NICE also recommends focal psychodynamic therapy which tends to be used in complex cases of anorexia nervosa, and can involve up to 40 sessions, necessitating significant commitment and persistence. The therapy aims to improve understanding of the meaning of food in the person's life, and to help identify alternative ways to express needs and distress, thus facilitating the diminution of eating disorder symptoms.

Family interventions are also recommended by NICE, depending on the features and circumstances of each individual case. Family interventions are commonly first-line treatments for adolescents with anorexia nervosa, along with individual appointments for the patient and any other indicated treatments.

For any psychological therapy to produce benefits, there needs to be a significant degree of engagement and commitment, and this can be challenging in anorexia nervosa, where the person may be ambivalent about treatment, at least initially. Nonetheless, persistence with treatment is likely to produce significant benefits, especially when there is particular focus on the person's own engagement with the process and ensuring that the person themselves feels the cumulative benefits of treatment, however conflictual and subtle these benefits may appear to begin with.

NICE recommends that a majority of persons with anorexia should be treated as outpatients and that psychological treatment should normally be of at least six months duration. If outpatient care does not produce sufficient benefit; or if the person's mental or physical health deteriorates; or if their BMI falls below 13.5 kg/m^2; or if there is significant risk of suicide, inpatient care may be indicated. Inpatient care generally focuses on reducing symptoms and creating an expectation of weight gain during the admission.

It is important to avoid the significant problems associated with excessively rapid re-feeding. Inpatient care should aim for weight gain of 0.5 kg to 1 kg per week (and outpatient care should aim for a gain of 0.5 kg per week). This means an additional 3,500 to 7,000 calories per week, according to NICE. Regular physical monitoring and, in some cases, oral multi-vitamin/multi-mineral supplements are also recommended.

While in hospital, psychological therapy should focus on both symptoms of anorexia nervosa and wider psychosocial matters of relevance to the individual case. Outpatient care following hospitalisation should continue for at least 12 months. For a small number of patients, involuntary mental health care is needed (Chapter 13), and, for a tiny minority, feeding against the will of the patient might be mandated by the High Court. In all such cases, specialised care and supervision are needed.

Treatment of bulimia nervosa involves many of the elements of treatment for anorexia nervosa, with particular emphasis on evidence-based self-help for early symptoms of the disorder. CBT for bulimia nervosa should be offered to those affected. CBT is usually arranged with an individual therapist (for example, clinical psychologist), with a self-help book or manual, in group sessions, or using online resources. In bulimia nervosa, this can involve keeping a diary or a log, and using that to work out healthy ways of thinking about, and dealing with, various circumstances, situations or feelings. According to NICE, treatment should be for 16 to 20 sessions, spread over a period of four to five months.

If response is inadequate, other psychological therapies should be considered such as interpersonal psychotherapy (for eight to 12 months). As with anorexia nervosa, the physical health complications of bulimia nervosa need to be continually borne in mind and addressed if and when they occur during treatment, especially disturbances to fluid and electrolyte balances in patients who are vomiting frequently or taking large amounts of laxatives.

And, as for all patients with eating disorders, risk assessment is important during the treatment of bulimia nervosa, focusing not only on risks to physical health but also on risk of suicide or severe self-harm, which can indicate a need to move to more intensive outpatient care, day-hospital care, or inpatient care for a period of time. Poor impulse control in bulimia nervosa can present particular challenges in any of these therapeutic settings.

Atypical eating disorders should be managed using principles similar to those outlined for anorexia nervosa and bulimia nervosa. Binge eating disorder, for example, is characterised by episodes of excessive eating accompanied by a feeling of lack of control. Such episodes tend to occur, on average, at least once per week for three months. Affected patients should be offered a specially adapted form of CBT for binge eating disorder. Self-help approaches should also be encouraged and psychological therapy may need to be augmented with an antidepressant medication such as the selective serotonin reuptake inhibitors sometimes used in bulimia nervosa, although the long-term effects are unknown. These, and other medications used in eating disorders, are considered next.

Medication for Eating Disorders

The evidence base for the use of medication in anorexia nervosa is very limited and medication on its own is never enough. There are currently (2017) no medications licensed for use in anorexia nervosa in Ireland. Nonetheless, selective serotonin reuptake inhibitors (antidepressants) are sometimes used in people with anorexia nervosa when there are also features of OCD (Chapter 5) or depression (Chapter 2). Use of these medications for anorexia nervosa itself is outside of formal prescribing guidelines. Olanzapine, an antipsychotic medication, is also sometimes used (Chapter 3), although this, too, is outside the formally-recognised indications for the medication and there can be significant side effects such as disproportionate weight gain.

In bulimia nervosa, fluoxetine (a selective serotonin reuptake inhibitor antidepressant) may be indicated in association with psychotherapy for the reduction of binge eating and purging activity in adults (but not children), although the long-term effects are not known. It is also the medication that NICE indicates as first choice in the condition, although the dose in bulimia nervosa may need to be higher than that commonly used in depression (for example, it may need to be 60 mg per day in bulimia nervosa). Sertraline, another antidepressant, is also sometimes used, although it is not licensed for use in eating disorders in Ireland. As with all medications, side effects should be weighed carefully against benefits, especially in younger people, with particular vigilance for any evidence of emerging suicidality. Comprehensive and up-to-date information on all medications is available on the website of the Health Products Regulatory Authority (www.hpra.ie).

As with all mental illnesses, social supports, community organisations and peer support groups provide substantial assistance with eating disorders. In Ireland, Bodywhys is a national voluntary organisation that supports people affected by eating disorders, with the aim that people affected by eating disorders will have their needs met through appropriate, integrated, quality services delivered by a range of statutory, private and voluntary agencies (www.bodywhys.ie). The organisation aims to ensure support, awareness and understanding of eating disorders among the wider community, and advocates for the rights and healthcare needs of people affected by eating disorders.

Bodywhys is committed to the belief that people with eating disorders can and do recover, and the evidence backs them up. Between 40 and 50 per cent of people with anorexia nervosa recover;

up to a further 35 per cent show significant improvement; and approximately 20 per cent develop a chronic disorder, with variable course. Five per cent will, however, die of complications of their disorder. In the long term, some develop osteoporosis. In bulimia nervosa, treatment leads to remission in 30 to 40 per cent, with the benefits of treatment generally well sustained. Outcome is poorer if BMI is low and there is a high frequency of purging.

Case History: Michael

Michael was a 25-year-old engineer who had recently moved job. He presented to his GP saying he felt depressed owing to a recent break-up of a long-term relationship. When his GP asked about Michael's appetite, Michael said that he experienced frequent bouts of overeating, which distressed him terribly as he said he was very keen to control his body weight. As a result of these bouts of overeating, Michael's weight varied a great deal over time, and he felt he was gradually gaining weight. In an effort to counteract this, Michael had started to make himself vomit.

Further discussion revealed that Michael was very preoccupied with eating and spent a great deal of time thinking about food, meals and his weight. He frequently starved himself for days at a time, and used medication he bought on the Internet in order to try to suppress his appetite. He had the medication with him at the GP surgery but when the GP examined it, the label on the medication made no sense whatsoever, much to Michael's disappointment. As best as the GP could guess, it was a multi-vitamin preparation from somewhere in Russia, but she could not be sure. Michael was terrified of becoming 'fat' and had set himself a target weight of 45 kg, well below what would be healthy for a man of his height.

Michael's GP took a detailed history and completed a mental state and physical examination. She took blood and urine tests (all of which were normal); assessed the risks to Michael's physical and mental health; and concluded that Michael had bulimia nervosa. Michael's local mental health services assessed him and offered

treatment with CBT for bulimia nervosa, with an individual thera-
pist. As part of the therapy, Michael kept a diary to help work out
better, reality-based ways of thinking about, and dealing with, vari-
ous circumstances, situations or feelings, especially as they related
to food.

Michael attended 18 sessions of CBT over the following months,
and also accessed the resources and supports provided by Body-
whys (www.bodywhys.ie) (see above). The treating team kept a close
eye on Michael's physical state and blood tests during treatment
but, happily, Michael did not experience any of the disturbances to
fluid and electrolyte balances that can be a feature of bulimia ner-
vosa. While Michael participated reasonably well in the CBT, his
response to the therapy was insufficient, so the treating team also
prescribed an antidepressant medication, fluoxetine, in association
with the psychotherapy.

After some weeks, Michael's dose of fluoxetine reached 60 mg
per day and Michael was educated about, and closely observed for,
any side effects. After a further two months, Michael's symptoms
had improved greatly although not completely: his weight had sta-
bilised, and was gradually approaching the normal range; he was
no longer misusing medication or making himself vomit; and his
binges had become less frequent and less severe.

Michael still felt out of control of his weight at times, but he used
specific cognitive techniques and alternative coping mechanisms to
deal with this. He continued in a CBT after-care programme for
some years following therapy, and gradually gained confidence in
his own ability to recognise and manage his symptoms, should they
ever start to intensify again in the future.

National Clinical Programme for Eating Disorders

Procedures for accessing mental health care for eating disorders
and all other mental disorders are outlined in Chapter 12 of this

book. There is, however, a specific initiative in the area of e[...] disorders in Ireland that merits particular attention.

In 2010, the National Clinical Programme for Mental He[...] was set up as a joint initiative between Health Service Executive (HSE) Clinical Strategy and Programmes Division and the College of Psychiatrists of Ireland. The aim of the national programme is to standardise quality evidence-based practice across the mental health services. The Mental Health Clinical Programme currently (2017) has three programmes centred on:

- Assessment and management of patients presenting to emergency departments following self-harm (Chapter 11)
- Early intervention for people developing first episode psychosis (Chapter 3)
- Eating disorders service spanning child and adolescent and adult mental health services.

The national clinical programme for eating disorders applies to HSE mental health services for children and adults with eating disorders, including anorexia nervosa, bulimia nervosa, binge eating disorder and other eating disorders that benefit from treatment. The programme applies to all clinical stages of the disorder, and seeks to work collaboratively with other relevant clinical programmes in terms of presentations in other settings. The programme focuses on quality of care, access and cost:

- In terms of quality, the programme aims to improve clinical outcomes and recovery through evidence-based treatment by skilled, trained staff; to reduce morbidity (symptoms) and mortality (death rates) through enhanced risk management; to incorporate service-user involvement and feedback about the programme and related services; and to ensure regular evaluation of clinical outcomes.
- In terms of access, the programme aims to improve screening; to ensure timely access to consultation for referrers; to reduce waiting times for assessment and treatment; to provide

a needs-based, stepped care model of service delivery; and to promote seamless transitions across services though guideline development and better coordination.

- In terms of cost, the programme aims to achieve early intervention to improve recovery rates; to use evidence-based treatment to reduce admissions and expedite recovery; to provide day treatment and intensive treatment to reduce inpatient admissions and length of stay; and to reduce relapse rates though all of these measures.

More specifically, the programme's objectives for 2016 were for a working group to design a 'model of care' for HSE eating disorder services, based on international best practice; to establish links with other key clinical programmes (see above); to collaborate with the College of Psychiatrists of Ireland's clinical advisory group for eating disorders; to identify HSE resource requirements for the programme; to define HSE staff competencies, training and professional development requirements; and to support the further roll-out of family-based therapies and enhanced cognitive therapy as first line treatments.

Training is ongoing in these areas, as mental health professionals collaborate and train together in order to expand and deepen existing therapeutic capabilities. The programme also aims to define a core clinical outcome dataset in order to monitor progress with implementation of the programme and assess the effectiveness of the therapies it promotes and provides, accessed through existing mental health teams and structures.

As a result, while treatment for eating disorders can still be quite uneven across Ireland, with significant reliance on the independent sector in places, it is hoped that the national clinical programme for eating disorders will bring renewed focus to this area and lead to continual improvement in the services offered to people with eating disorders and their families. Eating disorders are eminently treatable, and such treatment should be fully available to all who need it.

Useful Resources

It is advisable that anyone who thinks he or she has any of the conditions discussed in this book sees a health care professional. There are many reasons for this, including a need to rule out any other diagnoses, such as physical illnesses. In addition, some people find it easier to talk with a health care professional, especially if they are too uncertain or embarrassed to talk with friends or family members. Often, a brief talk with a GP will 'normalise' the individual's symptoms by reassuring them that they are not alone in what they are experiencing and that help is to hand, if any is needed.

Individuals with any mental disorder or psychological problem, and their families, will find much that is useful on the Internet. As ever, Internet resources need to be evaluated with care and only trusted when the information comes from a reliable source. Reliable information about mental health can be sourced from the websites of the Health Service Executive (www.hse.ie), College of Psychiatrists of Ireland (www.irishpsychiatry.ie), Royal College of Psychiatrists in London (www.rcpsych.ac.uk), National Health Service in the UK (www.nhs.uk) and National Institute of Mental Health in the US (www.nimh.nih.gov).

Evidence-based guidance about specific treatments can be found on the website of the National Institute for Health and Care Excellence (NICE) (www.nice.org.uk). NICE is a UK-based organisation responsible for developing guidance, standards and information on high-quality health and social care, and preventing and treating ill health. Their guidance on eating disorders in adults and children over the age of 8 years can be downloaded from their website free-of-charge: www.nice.org.uk/guidance/cg9/resources/eating-disorders-in-over-8s-management-27103918021

In addition to the above, there is good information about eating disorders available on the Your Mental Health website (www.yourmentalhealth.ie) under 'Eating Disorders'; the HSE website (www.hse.ie) under 'Anorexia Nervosa' and 'Bulimia'; and the NHS

Choices website (www.nhs.uk) under 'Anorexia Nervosa', 'Bulimia' and 'Binge Eating Disorder'. The NHS website includes an especially useful video about anorexia nervosa featuring Professor Janet Treasure, director of the eating disorder unit at the South London and Maudsley National Health Service (NHS) Trust, who talks about anorexia nervosa, including how to spot the symptoms and how the disorder can affect a person's life.

There are also several books which may also be helpful for people with symptoms of eating disorders and their families, including: *Skills-based Caring for a Loved One with an Eating Disorder: The New Maudsley Method* (Second Edition) by Janet Treasure, Gráinne Smith and Anna Crane (Abingdon, Oxon and New York: Routledge, 2017); *Getting Better Bite by Bite: A Survival Kit for Sufferers of Bulimia Nervosa and Binge Eating Disorders* (Second Edition) by Ulrike Schmidt, Janet Treasure and June Alexander (Abingdon, Oxon and New York: Routledge, 2016); *Overcoming Binge Eating: The Proven Program to Learn Why You Binge and How You Can Stop* (Second Edition) by Christopher G. Fairburn (New York: The Guilford Press, 2013); *Fat Is a Feminist Issue* by Susie Orbach (New York: Paddington Press, 1978); *On Eating* by Susie Orbach (London: Penguin Books, 2002).

Endnotes

1 World Health Organisation. *International Classification of Diseases* (10th Edition). Geneva: World Health Organisation, 1992.

2 www.nice.org.uk/guidance/cg9/resources/eating-disorders-in-over-8s-management-27103918021

3 www.rcpsych.ac.uk/healthadvice/problemsdisorders/anorexiaandbulimia.aspx

Chapter 7

ALCOHOL AND DRUG PROBLEMS

Alcohol and drug problems are common, complex and costly. They are also treatable. This chapter looks at four key questions about alcohol and drug problems:

◊ What are the symptoms and signs of alcohol and drug problems?

◊ How common are alcohol and drug problems?

◊ What causes alcohol and drug problems?

◊ What are the treatments for alcohol and drug problems?

Useful resources and sources of further information are provided at the end of the chapter.

What Are the Signs and Symptoms of Alcohol and Drug Problems?

The World Health Organisation (WHO), in its ICD-10 classification system, refers to 'mental and behavioural disorders' due to use of a range of substances, including alcohol, opioids (for example, heroin), cannabinoids (for example, cannabis), sedatives or hypnotics, cocaine, other stimulants (including caffeine), hallucinogens, tobacco, and volatile solvents. To this list, we can add various 'head shop' drugs sold in Ireland and elsewhere, and on the Internet.

For each of these substances, the WHO describes a range of potential problems: intoxication, harmful use, dependence syndrome, withdrawal states, psychotic disorder, amnesic syndrome (memory problems) and various other conditions. Each of these states can be considered in turn.

First off, the WHO describes 'intoxication' as a transient state following use of alcohol (that is, being drunk) or another substance (being 'high'), producing an alteration in consciousness (for example, drowsiness), thinking, perception (sight, hearing, etc.), reactions, or behaviour, as well as various bodily functions. The extent of intoxication is generally related to the amount of the substance taken, and the context is also often relevant (for example, parties, pubs, etc.). Intoxication generally diminishes over time and a single episode of intoxication does not in itself leave permanent damage, unless the person is injured while intoxicated. The WHO notes that many types of substances can produce a variety of intoxicating effects; these effects can change as the dose increases; and the effects of cannabis and hallucinogens are particularly unpredictable.

Before deciding that a person is intoxicated, it is important to rule out other possibilities, such as acute physical illness, low blood glucose or head injury. If the person is indeed intoxicated, the WHO notes that it may be complicated by trauma or other physical injury (for example, falling while drunk); medical consequences of intoxication (for example, vomiting, vomiting blood, inhaling vomit into the lungs); confusion and disturbed perceptions or thinking ('delirium'); fits (convulsions); or, in extreme cases, coma and death owing to one or more of the above. With alcohol, there is also the possibility of 'pathological intoxication' which involves an abrupt onset of aggression and violent behaviour, even following small amounts of alcohol in certain people.

'Harmful use' of a substance is a longer-term problem than a single episode of intoxication, and involves using a substance in such a way as to damage either physical health (for example, liver problems such as hepatitis from drug misuse) or mental health (for example, depression due to alcohol misuse or psychosis due to cannabis misuse; see case histories below). This level of use often prompts criticism from others (for example, family, friends, colleagues) as there are frequently clear negative social consequences such as drunkenness, absenteeism from work, and disruption in the family circle. There can also be physical presentations, such as stomach problems, poor sleep and agitation.

The next level of substance-related problem described by the WHO is 'dependence syndrome' which is a more sustained and harmful pattern of substance misuse than either intoxication or 'harmful use'. Dependence syndrome is defined as a collection of changes to a person's behavior, thinking and body, occurring as the use of a specific substance assumes greater priority than various other activities.

For dependence syndrome, the person needs to demonstrate, over the past year, at least three of the following three criteria outlined by the WHO, at the same time:

- A compulsion or strong desire to take the substance;
- Problems controlling use of the substance (for example, problems resisting taking it, problems stopping taking it, or taking too much);
- Physical symptoms when the person stops using (or reduces use of) the substance (as in a 'withdrawal state'; see below), or the person uses the substance or a similar one to alleviate withdrawal effects;
- Tolerance for the substance; that is, the person needs increased amounts of the substance to achieve the same effects, such as intoxication or avoidance of withdrawal effects;
- Growing neglect of other activities (for example, hobbies) owing to use of the substance, and spending increasing amounts of time acquiring, taking or recovering from use;
- Persisting to use the substance despite clear evidence of harmful and negative effects, such as physical damage to body organs (for example, the liver, in alcohol misuse) or mental state (for example, depression, disordered thinking).

Dependence is often associated with the development of quite rigid patterns of substance use, and there is always a desire to take the substance, a desire that increases during efforts to resist. Episodic use can also occur in the context of dependence and this is known as 'dipsomania'.

Next, the WHO defines a 'withdrawal state' as a set of symptoms that occurs when the person cuts down their intake of a substance, generally after prolonged or substantial use. Withdrawal is one of the features of dependence (see above). The physical features of withdrawal depend on the substance in question, but the psychological features commonly include depression, anxiety and difficulty sleeping. The symptoms are often relieved in the short term by using the substance again. Withdrawal differs from a 'hangover', which is the immediate aftereffects of using a substance, rather than the symptoms associated with ceasing more prolonged or high-dose use (which is withdrawal). Withdrawal can be associated with confusion and disturbed perceptions or thinking ('delirium'), as well as fits (convulsions) in certain cases.

Withdrawal from alcohol may be characterised by a particular syndrome known as 'delirium tremens' ('the DTs') which is an acute, transient, life-threatening state of confusion and physical disturbance associated with stopping or sharply cutting down alcohol, especially stopping abruptly after sustained heavy drinking in someone who is dependent on alcohol. It can start with anxiety, fear, shaking and poor sleep. There may also be fits (convulsions). The three symptoms most characteristic of delirium tremens are (a) confusion and altered consciousness (for example, drowsiness); (b) vivid hallucinations or illusions (for example, seeing, feeling or hearing things that are not there); and (c) significant or substantial shakes (tremor). There can also be agitation, sweating, heart racing, lack of sleep, and delusions (believing things that are not true). Delirium tremens is a terrifying state that can be fatal if the person is not brought to medical attention as a matter of urgency.

The WHO also describes a 'psychotic disorder' associated with substance misuse, that is, a state of mind that involves a significant break with reality in at least one important respect (for example, sustained hallucinations or delusions while not intoxicated and not in acute withdrawal; see above). These psychotic symptoms can occur either during or immediately after substance misuse (usually within 48 hours), and the most common features are auditory hallucinations (hearing things that are not there); misidentifying people or things; delusions (often of a paranoid nature); various physical disturbances (for example, agitation); and altered reactivity (for example, being afraid without cause).

Substance-induced psychotic disorder often resolves significantly within one month and generally resolves within six months. It can, however, persist for longer in some people and under certain circumstances. It is also possible that people misusing alcohol or other substances can develop a 'late onset' of residual or psychotic disorder linked with their substance misuse but occurring after the direct effect of the substance has apparently ended. Symptoms can also include flashbacks (Chapter 5); personality or behaviour disorders (Chapter 9), as seen in organic personality disorder; mood problems (Chapters 2 and 4); dementia (Chapter 8); other sustained cognitive impairments, such as problems with thinking; or late-onset psychotic disorder (see above).

Finally, the WHO describes an 'amnesic syndrome' in association with substance misuse, involving sustained problems with recent memory, among other symptoms. Remote memory (for the distant past) may also be impaired but immediate recall is intact. This condition is characterised by (a) difficulty with learning new material or with knowing what time it is; (b) most other thinking skills being generally intact; and (c) long-term, high dose use of alcohol or other substances. There can also be confabulation, which is when gaps in memory are filled by the person without a desire to deceive, that is, the person's mind generates material to fill memory gaps without the person being fully aware that they are making up memories in order to fill the gaps.

Confabulation may also be a feature of Korsakoff syndrome, a chronic memory disorder caused by severe deficiency of thiamine (vitamin B1), most commonly caused by alcohol misuse. More acutely, deficiency of vitamin B1 can lead to Wernicke's encephalopathy, a similar condition characterised by difficulties with eye movements, unsteadiness and confusion, among other symptoms. Wernicke's encephalopathy is a medical emergency from which only 20 per cent of sufferers recover completely. Treatment involves administering thiamine, among other urgent measures.

Case History: Michael

Michael *was a 21-year-old unemployed man with no history of mental illness. Following two years of unemployment, he became withdrawn and morose, rarely speaking to his parents, with whom he lived. One day, his father noticed a peculiar smell in Michael's room and realised that his son was smoking cannabis daily. He tried to persuade Michael that this was a bad idea and although Michael did not argue with him, he still continued to smoke cannabis every day.*

After some months, Michael began to behave even more strangely than usual. He stopped eating in the house, saying it 'was not safe', and became ever more withdrawn. One day, Michael simply refused to leave his room, and seemed to be arguing loudly with someone who was not there. When his parents asked, through the door, if he was all right, Michael answered: 'You know what's going on. I don't need to tell you. Why are you pretending?' He seemed terrified, and uncertain if his parents really were who they said they were.

Michael's parents consulted their GP who came to the house. At first, Michael would not speak with her, but eventually he opened the door. Concerned for her own safety, the doctor did not enter Michael's room, but spoke with Michel from the doorway. It was soon clear to her that Michael was psychotic, that is, he was experiencing a significant break with reality in at least one important respect: he was paranoid and hallucinating (hearing voices).

Deeply concerned for Michael's well-being, the GP contacted the local community mental health team and eventually persuaded Michael to attend an urgent appointment with them later that day. Following their clinical evaluation and careful risk assessment, it turned out that Michael was indeed psychotic and paranoid, but also, at some level, aware that he needed treatment. While he initially resisted the idea that cannabis had contributed to his psychotic illness, Michael did agree to stop smoking for a trial period, and accepted the antipsychotic treatment and other supports offered by the mental health team, his GP and his parents.

Three weeks later, Michael's psychosis had resolved completely. Michael persisted with the treatment for three months but then, as he was feeling very well, Michael resumed smoking cannabis. His symptoms recurred within three weeks and, on this occasion, were more extensive and severe. Michael was again treated with antipsychotic medication and abstinence from cannabis.

Once again, Michael's acute symptoms resolved quite quickly, within four weeks, and the community mental health team provided additional psycho-education to Michael and his family, strongly emphasising the clear, established links between cannabis use and severe mental disorder (see below). Plainly, Michael's prognosis now depended critically on his ability to abstain from cannabis and continue with treatment, among other factors.

How Common Are Alcohol and Drug Problems?

Alcohol and nicotine are the most commonly used drugs in Ireland. Approximately 77 per cent of adults report having used alcohol in the past year, and 29 per cent report having smoked.[1] Patterns of alcohol use in Ireland remain deeply concerning, despite the fact that the overall number of people using alcohol is falling. According to the Health Research Board (HRB) National Drugs Library compilation of statistics, in 2014/15, 65 per cent of adults had used alcohol in the previous month, compared to 74 per cent in 2002/03.[2] Consumption was highest among men aged 25-34 years (86 per cent) and women aged 35-44 years (82 per cent). Among 15-16-year-old students, 75 per cent of girls and 72 per cent of boys report having tried alcohol, and a very alarming 28 per cent had engaged in 'binge drinking' in the previous month.

In Ireland, a 'standard drink' is 10 grams of pure alcohol; for example, one pub measure of spirits (35.5 ml); a half pint of normal beer; an 'alcopop' (275 ml bottle); or a small glass of wine (12.5 per cent volume). A bottle of wine at 12.5 per cent alcohol contains approximately seven standard drinks. A binge is six or more 'standard drinks' taken in one session (for example, three or more pints of beer, six or more pub measures of spirits, or a bottle of wine).

The low-risk drinking guidelines for adults are up to 11 standard drinks in a week for women and up to 17 standard drinks in a week for men. These drinks should be spread out over the course of the week, with at least two to three alcohol-free days. People under the age of 18 years should avoid alcohol altogether.

Despite falling rates of alcohol use, rates of alcohol-related harm are increasing. In 1995, there were 9,420 people discharged from hospital whose condition was wholly attributable to alcohol; by 2013 this had risen to 17,120 (an increase of 82 per cent). Alcohol also contributes to many other illnesses and problems: over 12 per cent of cases of breast cancer are attributable to alcohol, and at least one-third of presentations to hospitals with deliberate self-harm are alcohol-related (Chapter 11). Alcohol is involved in 35 per cent of deaths by poisoning (more than any other substance) and is a factor in 38 per cent of all deaths on Irish roads, in addition to many other collisions resulting in non-fatal injuries.

Cannabis is the most commonly used illegal drug in Ireland. According to the HRB, in 2014/15 just over one in four people reported having used cannabis in their lifetime, and 8 per cent had used it in the previous year (an increase from 5 per cent in 2002/03).[3] Among 15-16-year-old students, a deeply disturbing 22 per cent of boys and 16 per cent of girls reported having tried cannabis, and 17 per cent had used it in the previous year.

The number of people in Ireland using opiates, most commonly heroin, is not clear. There are approximately 1.3 million opiate users in Europe and in 2001 there were 14,158 heroin-users in Ireland.[4] This increased to 20,790 in 2006. In 2014, there were 90 poisoning deaths where heroin was involved compared to 86 in 2013). Opiates are involved in at least one in every four deaths by poisoning in Ireland, mostly mixed with other drugs.

There is a particular and growing problem, both in Ireland and internationally, with misuse of both prescription painkillers such as morphine and over-the-counter (OTC) painkillers containing codeine. While the sale of OTC painkillers containing codeine has been restricted since 2009, misuse still continues and presents significant problems.

Cocaine is another relatively commonly used drug. In 2014/15, 8 per cent of adults (aged 15-64 years) in Ireland reported having ever tried cocaine, and 1.5 per cent had used it in the previous year.[5] Use is more common in men (11 per cent) than women (5 per cent).

It is difficult to quantify precisely the levels of abuse of sedatives and tranquillisers (for example, benzodiazpeines used to treat anxiety). In 2014/15, it was reported that 14 per cent of the Irish population had used sedatives and tranquillisers at least once, with use more common among women than men.[6] One-third of all poisoning deaths involve diazepam (a benzodiazepine).

Various other substances are used to varying degrees: ecstasy (in 2014/15, 1.8 per cent of adults reported having used ecstasy in the previous year); magic mushrooms (0.5 per cent); amphetamines (for example, 'speed'; 0.2 per cent); 'poppers' (for example, amyl nitrite; 0.5 per cent); LSD (lysergic acid diethylamide; 0.2 per cent); new psychoactive substances (0.7 per cent); solvents (0.2

per cent); and anabolic steroids (0.3 per cent).[7] Further details of many of these substances are provided in the table at the end of this chapter.

'New psychoactive substances' include products bought in 'head shops' or similar outlets online, previously sold as 'bath salts' or 'plant food'. Most of these 'legal highs' (not all of which are legal) are cathinone derivatives (methylone, methylenedioxypyrovalerone, butylone, flephedrone and mephedrone). They have a chemical structure similar to amphetamines (for example, 'speed'), and are commonly sold as either capsules or powder. The growth in head shops in Ireland during the early 2000s and the substantial mental health problems that followed triggered a significant regulatory response by government, and most head shops closed. Nonetheless, people continue to present to Irish hospitals with serious medical and psychiatric sequelae following the use of exceptionally risky substances such as mephedrone, often purchased online or on the streets.

What Causes Alcohol and Drug Problems?

The causes of alcohol and drug problems are not fully understood. In any given individual there are likely to be many contributing factors. The addictiveness of the substances themselves is clearly important: nicotine, for example, is highly addictive both physically and psychologically, which creates real difficulties stopping smoking once one has started (although it certainly can be done, with appropriate support; see below). Recent decades have also seen increased focus on biological contributors to various addictions (for example, genes), although it remains the case that personal psychological and social factors are key shapers of substance misuse and are also critical in determining responses to treatment.

In the case of alcohol, there is now strong evidence of a genetic predisposition to alcohol problems, as certain people's genes mean that alcohol produces more negative effects (for example, hangovers) than is the case in other people, with the result that they are less likely to become dependent. There are, however, also many other factors involved in producing alcohol dependence such as working in certain occupations, including bar work, journalism, medicine and the armed forces. Risk is also associated with certain psychiatric disorders (for example, depression, anxiety) (Chapters 2 and 5), physical illnesses (especially those associated with pain), certain personality traits (for example, impulsivity) and peer-pressure (especially in young adults and teenagers). Patterns of drinking are then strongly reinforced in societies where high intake of alcohol is central to cultural rituals, celebrations or routine socialising, as is commonly the case in Ireland.

Availability and pricing also matter. The Royal College of Physicians of Ireland points out that it is more expensive to buy a cinema ticket or bottled water than alcohol, and that Ireland ranks second place out of 194 countries for binge drinking among people aged 15 years and over.[8] In fact, as a result of heavily-discounted prices, often available in supermarkets, a woman can reach her low risk weekly drinking limit for just €6.30, and a man can reach his for under €10.

In this context, it is worth noting that establishing a minimum price for alcohol ('minimum unit pricing') would have minimal effect on most 'social' drinkers (because drinks in pubs already greatly exceed proposed minimum prices) and would likely have a positive, deterring effect on those who drink large quantities of cheap alcohol: 22 per cent of the Irish population account for 66 per cent of alcohol consumption and these are the people who develop advanced liver disease as a result of drinking vast quantities (more than 140 units per week) of cheap alcohol (less than 50 cent per unit). It is estimated that minimum unit pricing of just €1 per standard drink would save 197 lives per year; save the health service €7.4 million in the first year alone; and reduce absenteeism, crime and – most important of all – the inestimable human suffering that results from the negative effects of alcohol in families: withdrawal, depression (Chapter 2), self-harm (Chapter 11), neglect, abuse and violence, to mention but a few.

The causes of misuse of, and dependency on, substances other than alcohol is similarly multi-factorial and also varies between substances, although certain recurring themes commonly emerge. Throughout history and around the globe, for example, most societies have developed particular, local traditions of substance use, with the result that historical, cultural and social factors are always relevant. In more local terms, peer-pressure and availability are important, as are psychological or psychiatric symptoms which can prompt 'self-medication' with various legal and illegal substances.

Misuse of prescribed medications can also be linked with pre-scribing practices, and misuse of illegal substances can be linked with the general state of policing and criminal justice, as well as community tolerance. Certain personality traits may also predispose towards certain kinds of pleasure-seeking, thus activating the mesolimbic dopaminergic reward pathway, providing short-term reinforcement of the behavior, and ultimately perpetuating the substance use, despite the long-term problems it causes.

These cycles are not, however, inevitable. They can be broken with appropriate determination, treatment and support. Against this background, various treatment approaches to alcohol and drug use are considered next.

What Are the Treatments for Alcohol and Drug Problems?

The best treatments for different forms of substance misuse vary greatly, depending on the substance in question, the stage of the addiction, and the person's own preferences, circumstances and readiness for change. Clearly, prevention is the best strategy, so good public education is vital. There are many misconceptions which need to be remedied. In relation to alcohol, for example, it is now clear that a first drink at early age is associated with later alcohol problems. Therefore, the occasionally fashionable idea that introducing children to alcohol at a relatively early age in the home will encourage responsible drinking in the future is not based in fact. Such a practice is, in fact, harmful: early first drinking is associated with greater likelihood of substance misuse problems in later life.

When it comes to treating established patterns of misuse or dependence, approaches to various specific substances are outlined in the table at the end of this chapter. Tobacco and alcohol, the two most common drugs of addiction, merit more detailed consideration here.

Tobacco

For those who wish to quit smoking tobacco, there are many self-help and group resources available at www.quit.ie. The National Smokers Quitline offers further guidance and support at 1850 201 203. Other supports include counselling, psychotherapy, complementary therapies (such as acupuncture) and support from your GP to withdraw and stay off tobacco.

The most effective approach is probably one-to-one support from a smoking cessation advisor, combined with drug treatments.[9] The smoking cessation advisor is usually free of charge and this service is run by the health system. You can attend smoking cessation clinics for one-to-one sessions that are tailored to your needs, for one to four weeks before your quit date, and then continue for up to one year after you quit. These sessions explore your desire and readiness to quit; take a history of your smoking habit; assess your nicotine addiction; identify your reasons for quitting, any difficulties or risks of relapse; build a personal plan for quitting; measure your carbon monoxide levels; and recommend suitable medical treatment or refer you to a doctor for prescription and follow-up. Group support is also available.

Your GP can also prescribe a smoking cessation treatment, depending on your own personal preference, any previous smoking cessation medication that you have taken, and any side effects they may cause. Nicotine replacement therapy is available over the counter in your pharmacy but you need a prescription from your GP to get it free on the medical card.

Nicotine replacement therapy is the most common smoking cessation treatment and it comes in various different forms, including:

- Transdermal patches (on your skin), which release nicotine for either 16 or 24 hours;
- Chewing gum, with either 2mg or 4mg of nicotine;
- Inhalators, which look like plastic cigarettes through which nicotine is inhaled;
- Tablets and lozenges, to be placed under your tongue;
- Nasal spray, which passes nicotine through the lining of your nose.

Side effects, if any, can include skin irritation (with patches); irritation of nose, throat or eyes (with a nasal spray); disturbed sleep (for example, vivid dreams); upset stomach; dizziness; and headache. If side effects occur, however, they tend to be mild to moderate, and all of these forms of nicotine replacement therapy can be highly effective tools in assisting with quitting tobacco. It is especially advised to stop smoking in pregnancy and while breast-feeding.

Two other medications are also sometimes used: bupropion and varenicline. Bupropion was originally designed to treat depression (Chapter 2), but can also be used as an aid to smoking cessation in combination with motivational support in nicotine-dependent patients. It is advised that the person takes bupropion for 7 to 14 days before trying to quit smoking. A course of treatment usually lasts for seven to nine weeks. Bupropion is not suitable for children and young people under 18 years; for women when pregnant or breastfeeding; for people with anorexia, bulimia, a central nervous system tumour, or severe cirrhosis of the liver; or for people with a higher-than-average risk of seizures (for example, people with epilepsy, serious alcohol misuse problems, or certain other conditions) because bupropion can increase risk of seizures. Side effects can include dry mouth, upset stomach, difficulties sleeping, headaches, difficulties concentrating, dizziness and drowsiness, necessitating caution when operating heavy or complex machinery.

Varenicline is another medication used to assist with smoking cessation in adults, by reducing cravings and the rewarding, reinforcing effects of smoking. If the person has not stopped smoking completely before starting varenicline, they should do so within 7 to 14 days of starting treatment. The recommended duration of varenicline treatment is 12 weeks. If the person successfully stops smoking in this time, it may be prescribed for another 12 weeks to prevent relapse. Varenicline is not suitable for children and young people under 18 years; for women when pregnant or breastfeeding; or for people with epilepsy or advanced kidney disease. Side effects can include nausea and vomiting; headaches; difficulties sleeping (for example, unusual dreams); increased appetite; constipation or diarrhea; swollen stomach, slow digestion and flatulence; dry mouth; tiredness; dizziness; and drowsiness, again necessitating caution when operating heavy or complex machinery

It has also been reported that a number of people experience feelings of depression and suicidal thoughts after beginning treatment with varenicline. While there is no evidence that these symptoms are directly linked with varenicline, anyone feeling depressed or having thoughts of suicide should stop taking varenicline immediately as a precaution and contact their GP.

Finally, if a person does not yet feel ready to stop smoking completely, their GP may suggest a method of quitting known as 'nicotine-assisted reduction'. This involves using nicotine replacement therapy to progressively reduce the number of cigarettes smoked, before eventually stopping smoking altogether.

From a public health perspective, the Royal College of Physicians of Ireland Policy Group on Tobacco takes a strong, evidence-based approach to the problems presented by tobacco in Ireland, and recommends implementation of the Tobacco Free Ireland plan launched by the Minister for Health in 2013; a licensing system for the sale of tobacco products; stricter enforcement of tobacco legislation; publishing details of retail outlets in contravention of tobacco sale legislation; a ban on sale of electronic cigarettes to children; removal of value added tax on nicotine replacement patches; price cap regulation on tobacco industry profits; and a ban on the sale of tobacco products at events/locations primarily intended for persons under 18 years of age.[10] These are sensible, important and potentially powerful measures which would greatly reduce the enormous health and social problems caused by tobacco in Ireland.

Alcohol

The number of people entering treatment with alcohol as their main problem has recently decreased in Ireland, falling from 8,604 in 2009 to 7,541 in 2014 (a decrease of 12 per cent).[11] The number of people admitted to psychiatric hospitals for alcohol treatment is also falling, from 2,767 in 2006 to 1,188 in 2015 (a decrease of 57 per cent). This latter decrease likely reflects the position outlined in the 2006 national mental health policy, *A Vision for Change*, which specifies that treatment for alcohol or drug problems should not form part of core mental health services in Ireland:

> The major responsibility for care of people with addiction lies outside the mental health system. These services have their own funding structure within Primary and Continuing Community Care (PCCC) in the HSE. The responsibility of community mental health services is to respond to the needs of people with both problems of addiction and serious mental health disorders.[12]

Treatment for alcohol misuse or dependence is, therefore, provided through local addiction services which can be accessed following referral by a GP, psychiatrist or other health professional, as well as through self-referral in certain circumstances. Abstinence is the usual and most sensible goal of treatment, and the precise treatments offered depend greatly on the stage of the person's addiction, their readiness for change, their general life circumstances and their previous experiences of efforts to quit.

For acute detoxification from alcohol (that is, stopping drinking immediately after a sustained period of high intake), hospital admission is considered if there is a high risk of delirium tremens (see above) or seizures, or if the person is otherwise vulnerable (for example, a child, cognitively impaired, or severely lacking social support). For many people, however, detoxification is just as effective if it occurs as an outpatient, using reducing doses of a medication such as chlordiazepoxide (for symptoms of acute alcohol withdrawal), appropriate medical supervision, and psycho-social or family support.

Delirium tremens, if it occurs, is an acute withdrawal state (see above) that can be fatal if the person is not brought to medical attention as a matter of urgency. There is a mortality rate of at least 10 per cent if it is not treated correctly. Treatment in hospital is usually with a benzodiazepine (lorazepam), various other medications, and additional supportive measures, along with careful supervision. Unsupervised abrupt withdrawal from alcohol can be fatal; medical support is needed.

Following cessation of drinking, additional treatments to address alcohol problems and support abstinence include motivational interviewing, relapse-prevention strategies, self-help groups, such as Alcoholics Anonymous (AA; www.alcoholicsanonymous.ie) and various medications. It is the psychological and group-based supports that most people find especially useful, particularly AA, which suits the needs of very many (although not all) people with alcohol problems.

The evidence base for some of the medications in this area is quite slim, and they do not benefit everyone, but there are occasions when, in particular circumstances, they can make a significant contribution in conjunction with various other psychological and social supports. Disulfiram (Antabuse), for example, can be used in conjunction with appropriate psychiatric treatment as an adjunct treatment in chronic alcoholism. This medication blocks the processing ('metabolism') of alcohol in the body, resulting in very unpleasant headache, flushing, nausea and anxiety if the person takes alcohol. The effects of the medication can be hazardous if the person drinks while taking it, so disulfiram should be used with caution and with clear explanation to the patient and, where appropriate, family. Acamprosate is a different medication that seeks to reduce cravings and risk of relapse, and can be used as an adjunct to counselling to maintain abstinence in alcohol-dependent patients.

While alcohol treatment most commonly occurs as an outpatient, there are also various residential treatment programmes available. Residential treatment has the merit of taking the person away from their usual sources of alcohol, as they are weaned off their dependence and begin a therapy programme. There can, however, be difficulties with access and challenges with follow-up, among other issues, and it is not unusual for someone to have several episodes of outpatient or residential treatment before sustained abstinence is achieved. It is, nonetheless, well worth persisting with these repeated episodes of treatment, as one never knows which episode of treatment will produce beneficial effect, even if previous ones have not done so: circumstances change constantly and sometimes it can take many years before a person is truly ready for change.

In terms of the long-term outlook, alcohol misuse is associated with increased risk of death from many causes, including heart disease and cancer. Alcohol should be avoided in pregnancy. Regrettably, only 15 per cent of people with alcohol problems seek treatment and those who seek treatment do better overall. Alcohol is a major factor in two-thirds of completed suicides in Ireland, and the risk of suicide when a person is abusing alcohol is eight times greater than if they were not (Chapter 11).

From a public health perspective, alcohol education in schools is an important measure that can significantly reduce alcohol misuse, risky behavior and binge drinking. Other approaches to treatment include motivational interviewing, 12-step programmes and cognitive-behaviour therapy (CBT).

More broadly, the Royal College of Physicians of Ireland Policy Group on Alcohol recommends introduction of minimum unit pricing of alcohol (see above); reduction of alcohol availability; changes to Ireland's culture of alcohol consumption; raised awareness of low risk weekly alcohol levels (see above); embedding of alcohol screening into clinical practice; and development of a model of care for alcohol-related health problems, including (a) clinical guidelines for the treatment of alcohol-related health problems; (b) links between alcohol treatment services in hospitals and the community; (c) aftercare in the community to prevent relapse; and (d) establishing outpatient detoxification services.[13] The College also recommends more funded research into alcohol-related harm, especially alcoholic liver disease, using levies on the alcohol industry to support such research.

Other Drugs

Information about, and treatments for, addictions to drugs other than tobacco and alcohol are outlined in the table at the end of this chapter. Generally speaking, cognitive-behaviour therapy (CBT), motivational interviewing and self-help groups can prove useful strategies for many drug problems. Other, more specific, strategies vary according to the substance in question, the person's history of misuse and abuse, and the social and family circumstances in which the problem developed and is sustained. Problems with the criminal justice system and imprisonment also affect patterns of substance misuse, generally negatively. This is especially the case for people who also have a mental illness: prisons are toxic for the mentally ill.

There is a particular problem with cannabis and, in recent years, the number of people entering drug treatment who report cannabis as their main problem has increased, from 1,058 in 2005 to 2,609 in 2014 (an increase of 146 per cent).[14] Of these, 23 per cent are under the age of 18 years, 80 per cent are male and 51 per cent use cannabis daily.

In August 2016 there were 9,652 patients receiving treatment for opiate use (excluding those in prisons).[15] Some are on methadone for prolonged periods. Of the 16,587 people treated for drug and alcohol misuse in Ireland in 2014, 4,477 reported opiates as their main drug problem, of whom 943 were new cases; 66 per cent were male; 58 per cent were aged between 18 and 34 years; 60 per cent used opiates with other drugs; and 46 per cent used opiates daily. Opiate detoxification generally lasts 4 to 12 weeks and can involve methadone or buprenorphine, among other substances, in conjunction with contingency management and psychosocial support. Naltrexone can help prevent relapse and naloxone can help reverse respiratory depression following opioid overdose. All require close, specialist prescription and supervision in the context of multidisciplinary treatment programmes.

Rates of misuse of other drugs appear lower, but reliable estimates are difficult to formulate. Of the people treated for drug and alcohol misuse in 2014, for example, 743 reported cocaine as their main problem, of whom 369 were new cases; 80 per cent were male; 61 per cent were aged between 18 and 34 years; and 70 per cent used cocaine with other drugs.[16] Cocaine, however, like cannabis, is probably used far more widely than official statistics suggest.

Indeed, rates of use of most drugs are difficult to estimate with certainty and public attitudes towards misuse of all substances can be equally difficult to ascertain, not least because many people deny their own drug misuse or deny Ireland's alcohol and drug problems entirely – at least until someone in their own family is affected.

Against this background, confused discussion about alcohol and drugs in politics and the media is exceptionally unhelpful, especially when such discussion conflates the issue of whether or not a drug is harmful with the issue of whether or not the drug should be illegal, decriminalised or legalised. Public discussion about cannabis provides a good example of the kinds of confusion that can arise and can lead to limited public awareness about real, demonstrated health risks of many drugs, including cannabis.

In 2015, a report from an Oireachtas Justice Committee on the proposed decriminalisation of certain drug use suggested that possession of small amounts of certain illegal drugs (for example, cannabis) for personal use should not be dealt with through the criminal justice system, and small-scale users should be treated with compassion.[17]

This suggestion of a more nuanced approach to low-level drug use is very welcome. There are, however, two key issues relating to cannabis and it is critical that the two are not conflated, as they constantly were during public discussion of these proposals. First, can cannabis affect mental health? Second, should cannabis be decriminalised, legalised or have its legal status changed in any other way? The two questions are linked but they are also separate in certain important ways. Confusing the two questions simply confuses the debate.

From the point of view of mental health, cannabis increases risk of anxiety, depression and severe mental illness, such as schizophrenia and bipolar disorder (manic depression). Some people with early symptoms of mental illness use cannabis in an attempt to self-medicate, but, even taking this into account, cannabis still increases risk. These effects are dose-related: the more cannabis a person uses, the greater the risk.

Like all drugs, cannabis does not affect everyone equally but this does not alter the systematic risks it poses – just as the fact that someone who smokes 40 cigarettes daily may live to age 90 doesn't change the fact that tobacco increases risk of cancer. While certain commentators like to base their comments about cannabis only on certain cherry-picked research studies, the most definitive overall review of studies (both 'positive' and 'negative'), published in 2016, was absolutely clear about the overall public health message from the evidence about cannabis: cannabis can increase risk of serious mental illness.[18]

The fact that decriminalisation or legalisation of cannabis in certain jurisdictions may not result in a detectable upswing in severe mental illness does not affect the link between cannabis and mental ill-health in the slightest: it simply indicates the ubiquity of cannabis use in many countries (including Ireland) even when it is illegal. Nor does the accepted use of cannabis for some very specific medicinal purposes alter the mountain of evidence that cannabis is systematically bad for mental health.

As a psychiatrist, I see the clear negative effects of cannabis on mental health every single week in my clinical work. In my experience, cannabis is also a gateway drug, especially for tobacco. When I can assist people successfully to stop using cannabis, their mental health, energy and mood all improve. They inevitably ask me why information about the ill effects of cannabis are not more widely disseminated. There is, in fact, clear information quite widely available (see Useful Resources at the end of this chapter), but the clear public health message is continually clouded by ideology-based statements by various vested interests.

The answer to the second question, whether or not cannabis should be decriminalised, legalised or have its legal status changed in any other way, is considerably less clear-cut than the question about its effects on mental health (which are clearly negative). Policy about other harmful substances provides limited and generally contradictory guidance about how cannabis should be treated legally: certain extremely harmful substances are legal, for example, tobacco, while others are illegal, for example, heroin. Experiences with banning alcohol have been mixed at best.

The fact that a substance is bad for one's health does not necessarily mean it should be illegal, but it does mean policy steps should be taken to minimise the harm caused. These steps invariably include public education and often also involve some form of regulation, possibly to the point of making the substance illegal. But these steps only make sense if they can be shown to reduce harm. These are complex decisions to be taken by health planners, policy-makers and, ultimately, politicians, with advice from relevant stakeholders.

It is imperative that the clear epidemiological evidence linking cannabis with mental illness forms part of the government's ongoing deliberations on this matter. Robust steps should be taken to educate people about the mental health risks associated with the drug. Mental health is extremely valuable and, based on my clinical experience, I would advise anyone against rolling the dice by using cannabis.

The issues of decriminalisation and legalisation, however, relate not just to medical evidence, but also to other issues, such as the opportunity costs of devoting scarce police and criminal justice resources to relatively low-level offenders, with very little yield in terms of convictions, deterrence, rehabilitation or setting users on a path to mental or social well-being. It may well be the case that these resources could be used in other, more effective ways to address the harm caused by cannabis. The fact that something is bad for you does not automatically mean it should be illegal.

Equally importantly, the question of decriminalisation or legalisation relates to issues of civil liberties, individual responsibility, and the kind of society we want to live in. Crucially, there is an important, complicated balance to be achieved between respecting individual liberty and pursuing legitimate public health concerns, that is, curtailing activities which impact adversely on society, or which place the health and well-being of children, the vulnerable or others at risk.

It is likely that reducing harm associated with different drugs requires different combinations of education and regulation. Whatever is ultimately decided about decriminalising cannabis and various other issues (for example, injecting rooms for opiate users), this is neither the time nor the place for ideology. As every family affected by addiction knows only too well, any proposed measures must be pragmatic, subject to careful evaluation and demonstrated to reduce harm in the real world.

Case History: Joe

Joe was a 52-year-old man who worked as a barman in a hotel. His father had worked in a bar too and Joe had started drinking alcohol at the age of 12. Throughout his teens, Joe drank eight to ten pints two or three nights each week. This continued during his twenties and thirties, even as many of his friends reduced their alcohol intake as they progressed in their jobs, acquired mortgages and had children.

By the time he was in his mid-40s, Joe realised that he commonly experienced a strong compulsion to drink, and he felt increasingly unable to resist the temptation. If he stopped drinking for a day or two, he would get severe withdrawal symptoms, which he felt he could only stop by taking another drink. Nonetheless, he told himself that he would cut down soon and promised himself that he would stop drinking when he turned 50. He didn't.

By the time he was 52, Joe was drinking uncontrollably, feeling guilty about taking ever larger amounts, irritated by people's suggestions that he cut down, and drinking in the mornings in order to get out of bed. Increasingly, he did not show up for work at all, and he no longer contacted his family. It was only when his worried sister called to his house unexpectedly and found him unconscious on the floor that Joe finally acknowledged that he was drinking himself to death and needed urgent help.

Jose went to see his GP who discussed the problem in detail with him and his sister. Following careful risk assessment, they decided that Joe would take some time off work, go to stay with his sister and start a detoxification programme involving chlordiazepoxide and careful monitoring by his GP. Joe also agreed to attend a counsellor and meetings of Alcoholics Anonymous, while his sister went to Al-Anon, which offers understanding and support to families and friends of problem drinkers in an anonymous environment (www. al-anon-ireland.org).

Joe found all of this very difficult. It took him a particularly long time to accept the assistance of his sister, even though she was extremely willing to help and very sensitive to the complexity of the situation in which Joe now found himself. Happily, the treatment programme was successful and Joe remained abstinent from alcohol.

Sustaining his recovery necessitated significant changes to Joe's life. He realised that working in the hotel bar greatly increased the chances of him relapsing into drinking, but he felt that he was not qualified to work in any setting other than a hotel. He eventually brought himself to discuss this challenge with his employer who, it turned out, had been extremely worried about Joe and, in light of Joe's new-found sobriety, was more than happy to assign Joe to other duties in the hotel. This helped greatly to boost Joe's confidence, and he remained abstinent from alcohol and was a daily attender at AA.

Useful Resources

It is advisable that anyone who thinks he or she has any of the conditions discussed in this book sees a health care professional. There are many reasons for this, including a need to out-rule any other diagnoses, such as physical illnesses. In addition, some people find it easier to talk with a health care professional, especially if they are too uncertain or embarrassed to talk with friends or family members. Often, a brief talk with a GP will 'normalise' the individual's symptoms by reassuring them that they are not alone in what they are experiencing and that help is to hand, if any is needed.

Individuals with any mental disorder or psychological problem, and their families, will find much that is useful on the Internet. As ever, Internet resources need to be evaluated with care and only trusted when the information comes from a reliable source. Reliable information about mental health can be sourced from the websites of the Health Service Executive (www.hse.ie/eng/health/az), College of Psychiatrists of Ireland (www.irish-psychiatry.ie), Royal College of Psychiatrists in London (www.rcpsych.ac.uk), National Health Service in the UK (www.nhs.uk) and National Institute of Mental Health in the US (www.nimh.nih.gov).

Evidence-based guidance about specific treatments can be found on the website of the National Institute for Health and Care Excellence (NICE) (www.nice.org.uk). NICE is a UK-based organisation responsible for developing guidance, standards and information on high-quality health and social care, and preventing and treating ill health.

In addition to the above, help and information about stopping smoking is available on www.quit.ie, an excellent website filled with resources and different kinds of support. Information about alcohol is available on the websites of the Royal College of Physicians of Ireland (www.rcpi.ie/policy-and-advocacy/rcpi-policy-group-on-alcohol) and Alcohol Action Ireland (alcoholireland.ie). Information about legislative and other measures to address alcohol problems at national level can be found at: health.gov.ie/healthy-ireland/alcohol

Alcoholics Anonymous is a fellowship of men and women who share their experience, strength and hope with each other that they may solve their common problem and help others to recover from alcoholism (www.alcoholicsanonymous.ie). For families and friends of problem drinkers, Al-Anon offers understanding and support in an anonymous environment (www.al-anon-ireland.org), and Alateen is a fellowship of young Al-Anon members, usually teenagers, whose lives have been affected by someone else's drinking (www.al-anon.alateen.org).

There are several books which may be helpful, including *Overcoming Alcohol Misuse: A 28-Day Guide* by Conor Farren (Kite Books, an imprint of Blackhall Publishing, 2011) and *Living With a Problem Drinker: Your Survival Guide* by Rolande Anderson (Sheldon Press, 2010).

Narcotics Anonymous (NA) is a nonprofit fellowship of men and women for whom drugs had become a major problem. They offer recovery from the effects of addiction through working a twelve-step program, including regular attendance at group meetings (www.na-ireland.org).

There is detailed information about drug use in Ireland and Northern Ireland available in a report titled 'Prevalence of Drug Use and Gambling in Ireland and Drug Use in Northern Ireland' (health.gov.ie/wp-content/uploads/2016/11/Bulletin-1.pdf). Further information about specific drugs and treatment options is available on www.drugs.ie, an independent website managed by the Ana Liffey Drug Project, whose mission is to help individuals, families and communities prevent and/or address problems arising from drug and alcohol use (www.aldp.ie).

The table on the following pages lists the common drugs of abuse in Ireland and treatments that are available.

Important Note: All of the substances discussed in this table and the text of this chapter produce substantial problems with addiction, mental ill health, physical ill health, and overdose, sometimes to the point of death. It is not advisable to use any of them. If you already use them, it is advised that you use the resources available to cut down and quit, in a responsible, supervised and sustainable fashion, in conjunction with your doctor and relevant drug treatment and support services.

The information in this table is adapted with permission from drugs.ie. The drugs.ie website contains a national directory of drug and alcohol treatment services at drugs.ie/services.

Drug Category	Description	What Help Is Available?
Hallucinogens	Hallucinogens can be divided into three broad categories: psychedelics, dissociatives and deliriants. These can cause subjective changes in perception, thought, emotion and consciousness. Examples include PMA (paramethoxyamphetamine), cannabis ('hash', 'hashish', 'blow', 'pot', 'ganja', marijuana, 'grass', 'joint'), 2CB ('bromo'), 'magic mushrooms' (for example, psilocybe, amanita muscaria), methamphetamine ('crystal meth', 'ice'), LSD (lysergic acid diethylamide), 'morning glory' (lysergic acid amide), 'Hawaiian baby woodrose' (lysergic acid amide), ketamine (an anaesthetic) and ecstasy ('E', 3,4-methylenedioxymethamphetamine).	• Self-help support such as Narcotics Anonymous see (see Useful Resources, above) • Counselling or psychotherapy • Complementary therapies, such as acupuncture • Support from your doctor; that is, medical support, as needed. • Residential treatment programmes (clinics) • Aftercare • One to one or group family support • Contact the Drugs Helpline 1800 459 459 to find out about options in your area
Headshop drugs	Also often referred to as 'legal highs', these are usually sold via 'head shops' or the Internet. It is important to note that although these drugs may not be illegal it does not necessarily mean they are safe. Examples include kratom, pills, powders (for example, cathinones), smoke (mixtures of herbs sold as alternatives to cannabis) and various other plant products (for example, salvia divinorum).	• Self-help support such as Narcotics Anonymous (see Useful Resources, above) • Counselling or psychotherapy • Complementary therapies, such as acupuncture • Support from your doctor; i.e. medical support, as needed. • Residential treatment programmes (clinics) • Aftercare • One to one or group family support • Contact the Drugs Helpline 1800 459 459 to find out about options in your area
Opioids	Opioids encompass naturally occurring opium poppy derivatives, such as morphine and codeine, and semi-synthetic opiates like heroin and methadone. They are classed as narcotic analgesics, meaning they decrease pain reaction and sensation. Opioids can produce intense euphoria in a person and a sense of well-being. Side effects include sedation, respiratory depression, severe withdrawal, development of tolerance and dependence issues. Examples include heroin, methadone (used to help reduce cravings in people addicted to heroin, subject to careful regulation and supervision), codeine phosphate (a painkiller) and various other opiates (for example, fentanyl, cyclimorph, oramorph, oxynorm, oxycontin, MST, morphine).	• Self-help support such as Narcotics Anonymous (see Useful Resources, above) • Counselling or psychotherapy • Complementary therapies, such as acupuncture • Support from your doctor to reduce, withdraw, detox and keep off (in the case of methadone, to reduce, stabilise or withdraw) • Residential treatment programmes (clinics) • Aftercare • One to one or group family support • Contact the Drugs Helpline 1800 459 459 to find out about options in your area

Over-the-counter painkillers	These are non-opiate-based, over-the-counter medicines used for mild to moderate pain relief, flu and other symptoms. Prolonged use can lead to dependence. (See also the text of this chapter for information about over-the-counter medications containing codeine.)	• Self-help • Counselling • Complementary therapies, such as acupuncture • Support from your doctor to reduce, withdraw, detox and keep off • Residential treatment programmes • Aftercare • One to one or group family support • Contact the Drugs Helpline 1800 459 459 to find out about options in your area
Sedatives	These are substances that depress the central nervous system (that is, brain and spinal cord), resulting in calmness, relaxation, reduction of anxiety, sleepiness, and slowed breathing. Examples include cannabis, ketamine (an anaesthetic), GHB or GBL (gammahydroxybutyrate, a synthetic drug used as an anaesthetic), kava kava (piper methysticum, yaquona root), benzodiazepines ('roofies', 'downers', 'D5s', 'D10s', 'roche') and alcohol (see main text of this chapter for further discussion of alcohol).	• Self-help support such as Narcotics Anonymous or Alcoholics Anonymous (see Useful Resources, above) • Counselling or psychotherapy • Complementary therapies, such as acupuncture • Support from your doctor; i.e. medical support, as needed (in the case of benzodiazepines, support from your doctor to reduce and withdraw; and in the case of alcohol, support from your doctor to reduce, withdraw or stay off drink) • Residential treatment programmes (clinics) • Aftercare • One to one or group family support (for example, Al-Anon and Alateen for alcohol; see 'Useful Resources', above) • Contact the Drugs Helpline 1800 459 459 to find out about options in your area
Solvents	When inhaled, solvents have a similar effect to alcohol. They make people feel uninhibited, euphoric and dizzy. Examples include gases, gas lighter refills, glue, correction fluids and thinners, petroleum products, aerosols including hairspray, deodorants and air-fresheners.	• Self-help support such as Narcotics Anonymous (see Useful Resources, above) • Counselling or psychotherapy • Complementary therapies, such as acupuncture • Support from your doctor • Residential treatment programmes (clinics) • Aftercare • One to one or group family support • Contact the Drugs Helpline 1800 459 459 to find out about options in your area

Stimulants	Stimulants are drugs that make people feel more awake, alert and energetic. Examples include PMA (paramethoxyamphetamine, similar to ecstasy), BZP (benzylpiperazine), amphetamine ('speed', amphetamine sulphate, 'base', dexedrine, dexamphetamine), 'poppers' (amyl nitrite, butyl nitrite, isobutyl nitrite), methamphetamine ('crystal meth', 'ice'), khat (quat, ghat), ephedrine, ecstasy ('E', 3,4-methylenedioxymethamphetamine), creatine (as a diet supplement), cocaine ('snow', 'coke', 'charlie'), crack cocaine ('freebase', 'base', a smokeable form of cocaine) and anabolic steroids (synthetic versions of the male hormone testosterone).	• Self-help support such as Narcotics Anonymous (see Useful Resources, above) • Counselling or psychotherapy • Complementary therapies, such as acupuncture • Support from your doctor; i.e. medical support, as needed (for example, in the cases of 'poppers' and cocaine, support to withdraw or keep off) • Residential treatment programmes (clinics) • Aftercare • One to one or group family support • Contact the Drugs Helpline 1800 459 459 to find out about options in your area
Tobacco	Nicotine is another stimulant which: • Increases pulse rate and blood pressure; • Increases risk of lung and other cancers, heart diseases, bronchitis, bad circulation and ulcers; • For women, increases risk of heart and circulatory problems when taking contraceptives; • Produces tolerance; i.e. you need to take more to get the same effect • Increases risk of coughs and chest infections; chronic breathing problems (for example, emphysema); heart attack; and death; • Increases risk of miscarriage, premature delivery, stillbirth, low birth weight baby, and cot death. Nicotine is highly addictive both physically and psychologically, and, in the first weeks after stopping, can produce cravings, a bad cough, irritability, and difficulty concentrating. (See main text of this chapter for further discussion of tobacco)	• National Smokers' Quitline 1850 201 203 • Counselling or psychotherapy • Complementary therapies, such as acupuncture • Support from your doctor to withdraw, keep off • Contact the Drugs Helpline 1800 459 459 to find out about options in your area • Visit www.quit.ie

Endnotes

1 health.gov.ie/wp-content/uploads/2016/11/Bulletin-1.pdf

2 http://www.drugsandalcohol.ie/24954/1/FinalAlcohol%20fact-sheet-January%202017.pdf

3 http://www.drugsandalcohol.ie/17307/1/FinalCannabis%20Fact-sheet%20January%202017.pdf

4 http://www.drugsandalcohol.ie/17313/1/Opiates%20Fact-sheet%20%202017.pdf

5 http://www.drugsandalcohol.ie/17308/1/Cocaine%20Fact-sheet%20January%20%202017.pdf

6 http://www.drugsandalcohol.ie/19644/1/sedatives%20and%20tranquillisers%20factsheet%202017.pdf

7 health.gov.ie/wp-content/uploads/2016/11/Bulletin-1.pdf

8 rcpi-live-cdn.s3.amazonaws.com/wp-content/uploads/2015/12/MUP-info-guide.pdf

9 www.hse.ie/eng/health/az/Q/Quitting-smoking

10 www.rcpi.ie/policy-and-advocacy/rcpi-policy-group-on-tobacco

11 http://www.drugsandalcohol.ie/24954/1/FinalAlcohol%20fact-sheet-January%202017.pdf

12 Expert Group on Mental Health Policy. *A Vision for Change.* Dublin: The Stationery Office, 2006 (p.146).

13 www.rcpi.ie/policy-and-advocacy/rcpi-policy-group-on-alcohol

14 http://www.drugsandalcohol.ie/17307/1/FinalCannabis%20Fact-sheet%20January%202017.pdf

15 http://www.drugsandalcohol.ie/17313/1/Opiates%20Fact-sheet%20%202017.pdf

16 http://www.drugsandalcohol.ie/17308/1/Cocaine%20Fact-sheet%20January%20%202017.pdf

17 This passage is adapted, by kind permission of *The Irish Times*, from B.D. Kelly. 'Should we legalise or decriminalise cannabis?' *The Irish Times*, 27 November 2015.

18 Gage, S.H., Hickman, M. and Zammit, S. 'Association between cannabis and psychosis: Epidemiologic evidence'. *Biological Psychiatry* 2016; 79: 549-56.

Chapter 8

DEMENTIA

Dementia is a term used to describe a set of conditions that are both common and commonly misunderstood, including Alzheimer's disease. At present, approximately 55,000 people in Ireland are living with dementia and 500,000 people live in families affected by dementia. This chapter looks at four key questions about dementia:

◊   What are the signs and symptoms of dementia?

◊   How common is dementia?

◊   What causes dementia?

◊   What are the treatments for dementia?

Useful resources and sources of further information are provided at the end of the chapter.

What Are the Signs and Symptoms of Dementia?

The World Health Organisation (WHO) includes 'dementia' under the heading of 'organic, including symptomatic, mental disorders' in its International Classification of Diseases (ICD-10).[1] In 1992, it sub-divided dementia into 'dementia in Alzheimer's disease', 'vascular dementia' (that is, due to disease of blood vessels from, for example, smoking), frontotemporal dementia (including 'Pick's disease'), and dementia in other diseases, such as Creutzfeldt-Jakob disease, Huntington's disease, Parkinson's disease, and human immunodeficiency virus (HIV) disease, and 'unspecified dementia'. There is also now 'dementia with Lewy bodies' (see below).

All of these different forms of dementia can occur either without any additional symptoms or with additional psychiatric features, such as delusional symptoms (believing things that are not true), hallucinatory symptoms (perceiving things that are not there, such as hearing voices), depressive symptoms, or other mixed symptoms, which can be quite different in each individual case.

In broad terms, dementia is a set of symptoms occurring due to disease of the brain, generally of a chronic or progressive nature. It involves disturbances in many areas of brain function including memory, thinking, comprehension (understanding), calculation, orientation, learning, language and judgement. The person's level of consciousness is not altered, that is, these problems are not the results of drowsiness. There may also be problems with control of emotions, social behaviour and motivation, or various combinations of all of these problems.

It can be difficult to identify dementia reliably, especially in the early stages when signs may be subtle or evolving. When considering whether or not a person has dementia, it is important to consider other possible explanations for their symptoms, including physical frailty, depression (Chapter 2) or various other conditions (see below).

The key requirement for a diagnosis of dementia is a decline in thinking and memory that is sufficient to cause problems with, or impairments of, day-to-day physical activities, such as eating, dressing, washing, toileting or personal hygiene. The characteristic memory problems tend to involve impairments in making, storing and retrieving new memories, although old memories can also be affected, especially in the later stages. Thinking is also affected, further complicating the picture and creating additional difficulties with memory and many other areas of function such as diminished reasoning capacity and reduced flow of ideas. There is often difficulty attending to multiple stimuli at the same time, such as tuning into a conversation with several people speaking at once.

Characteristic symptoms and problems need to be present for at least six months, and usually longer, for a clinical diagnosis of dementia. Before such a diagnosis is made, however, it is important to take into consideration any possible mental illness (for example, depression), short-term states of confusion occurring for various reasons ('delirium' or confusion due to an infection), intellectual disability (possibly undiagnosed), the effects of poor education or sensory deprivation (for example, under-stimulated people in drab, institutional environments), or the side effects of medication. Of course, any of the above problems may also co-exist with dementia, further complicating diagnosis.

Dementia in Alzheimer's Disease

Alzheimer's disease is a degenerative brain condition which starts gradually but progresses steadily, sometimes over two to three years, but often over a longer period. The WHO points out that incidence is higher in later life but it can occur in mid-life or even earlier, especially in people with a family history of the disorder. The course tends to be slower in cases with onset in later life, when memory impairment is generally the central feature.

People with early onset (before the age of 65 years) tend to show disturbances in 'higher functions' relatively earlier in the disease, including aphasia (impairment of language), agraphia (impairment of communication through writing), alexia (impairment of reading), and apraxia (diminished ability to perform learned tasks; for example, combing your hair).

For a diagnosis of Alzheimer's disease, the person needs to have the clinical features of dementia (as described above); gradual onset and slow progression of symptoms; no evidence that the condition has another cause, such as abnormal thyroid gland function, high calcium, low vitamin B12 or niacin, syphilis affecting the brain, bleeding in the brain ('subdural haematoma') or excess fluid in the brain ('normal pressure hydrocephalus', see below); and no

174

sudden onset of particular symptoms such as paralysis, sensory loss, or incoordination, early in the illness, which might suggest a stroke or threatened stroke (that is, a blood clot or bleeding in the brain).

It is also important to ensure that the symptoms are not due to depression which can present as 'pseudo-dementia' in some people, owing to poor concentration and poor memory (Chapter 2); short-term confusion for another reason, for example, 'delirium' due to an infection; any other cause of dementia (see below); apparent dementia due to physical illness or the toxic effect of various substances; or intellectual disability (diagnosed or undiagnosed). It can be difficult to diagnose Alzheimer's disease and it often takes considerable time for the full clinical picture to become apparent.

Vascular Dementia

Vascular dementia is another form that includes dementia caused by multiple strokes. It tends to differ from Alzheimer's disease in its onset, symptoms and course. In many cases, there is a history of threatened strokes beforehand, with brief reductions in consciousness, transient paralysis ('weakness' that just passes), or disturbances to sight. The dementia itself might follow a series of small strokes or a single major one, and is characterised by impairment of thinking and memory. As a result, onset can be abrupt, in contrast with the generally gradual onset of Alzheimer's disease.

For a diagnosis of vascular dementia, the person needs to have the clinical features of dementia (as described above). In addition, the pattern of brain impairments tends to be uneven in vascular dementia, so there may be memory loss, specific problems with thinking and other brain functions, and overall intellectual impairment. The person's judgement and insight may be relatively intact. The condition is especially associated with an abrupt start and stepwise progression, reflecting multiple small strokes or threatened strokes, in contrast with the steady progression of Alzheimer's disease. Brain scans can help distinguish between the two conditions, in conjunction with careful consideration of the clinical picture and clinical course.

Vascular dementia is commonly accompanied by high blood pressure, emotional lability (for example, transient depression, explosive laughter, crying), and occasional episodes of confusion caused by further strokes. Personality can be unaffected but the person can also show increased signs of apathy, disinhibition or exaggeration of other personality traits.

Before diagnosing vascular dementia, it is important to ensure that the symptoms are not due to depression (depressive 'pseudo-dementia'; see above and Chapter 2) or other mental illness; short-term confusion for another reason (for example, 'delirium' due to an infection); any other cause of dementia (see above and below); apparent dementia due to physical illness or the toxic effect of various substances; or intellectual disability (diagnosed or undiagnosed).

The WHO describes various sub-types of vascular dementia, including vascular dementia of acute onset, multi-infarct dementia (with more gradual onset, owing to an accumulation of smaller strokes), subcortical vascular dementia (in which brain scans show different parts of the brain affected by the strokes, and the clinical picture can be more like Alzheimer's disease), mixed cortical and subcortical vascular dementia (a mixture of these sub-types), and various other, less common patterns of vascular brain impairment (that is, the effects of poor blood supply to the brain).

Various Other Forms of Dementia

In addition to Alzheimer's disease and vascular dementia, various other forms of dementia have been described including dementia with Lewy bodies, frontotemporal dementia (including Pick's disease), and dementia occurring in Creutzfeldt-Jakob disease, Huntington's disease, Parkinson's disease and HIV disease, among others. Many of these conditions have features in common with both Alzheimer's disease and vascular dementia, but each also has relatively distinctive features or causes which justify their recognition as separate syndromes.

Dementia with Lewy bodies is the third most common cause of dementia after Alzheimer's disease and mixed Alzheimer's and vascular dementia. Dementia with Lewy bodies typically begins after the age of 50 years, more commonly in males. The condition is named after the identification of 'Lewy bodies' or specific clumps of protein in certain brain cells (described by Frederic Lewy in 1912). Key features include changeable problems with thinking and alertness, with more variability from hour to hour than is seen in other forms of dementia; visual hallucinations (that is, seeing things that are not there) in 75 per cent of patients; and movement problems similar to those in Parkinson's disease (see below), but less extensive. There can also be specific disorders of sleep; increased falling and fainting; and bad reactions to certain medications, including over-the-counter and prescribed medications, most especially antipsychotic and antivomiting medications.

Frontotemporal dementia is another form of dementia, often characterised by early appearance of personality changes and relative sparing of intellectual function, at least initially. Pick's disease, a type of frontotemporal dementia, is a progressive dementia that generally commences between the ages of 50 and 60 years. It involves gradual changes in character and social deterioration, which are then followed by impairments of memory, intellect, and language functions, combined with apathy, euphoria and, in some cases, specific movement disorders (muscular jerks, twitches, restlessness or rigidity). Cases with early onset have a poorer prognosis. For a diagnosis of dementia in Pick's disease, the person needs to have an overall picture of progressive dementia (see above); characteristic features of this particular form of dementia (for example, euphoria, emotional changes, coarsening of social behavior, apathy or restlessness); and characteristic changes in behavior, which are generally apparent before memory impairment becomes prominent.

Dementia in Creutzfeldt-Jakob disease is another form of progressive dementia with extensive nervous system involvement, caused by a 'prion', which is an infectious agent. The disease can manifest any time but generally appears in middle or later life (for example, in the fifth decade). The disorder progresses quite rapidly over months or a few years. There is 15 per cent survival for two or more years, although some cases survive for longer (for example, five years). The condition is characterised by its rapid progression, progressive paralysis of limbs and various movement disorders. There can also be unsteadiness, problems with sight and muscle twitches. Diagnosis can be assisted by electroencephalogram (EEG) to measure patterns of electric activity in the brain, lumbar puncture which samples cerebrospinal fluid, and brain scans.

Dementia in Huntington's disease occurs in the context of the widespread brain degeneration that characterizes Huntington's disease. Symptoms commonly appear in the person's thirties or forties, and may commence with psychiatric features such as depression, anxiety, paranoia or personality change. The condition progresses slowly, but generally leads to death around 20 years after symptoms appear. Huntington's disease typically involves choreiform movement disorder (jerky, random, uncontrolled movements), dementia (see above) and, most commonly, a family history of Huntington's. Early signs typically include involuntary choreiform movements of the face, hands and shoulders, or as the person walks. The dementia element tends to involve the frontal lobes of the brain early on, with memory affected later.

Dementia can also occur in Parkinson's disease, especially when severe. Parkinson's disease is a long-term degenerative disorder of the central nervous system (CNS, that is, brain and spinal cord) that mainly affects the motor system. Early symptoms include shaking, rigidity and slowness of movement. Difficulty with walking and dementia may also develop.

Dementia also occurs in certain cases of HIV disease, often with features of poor memory, poor concentration and difficul-

ties with reading and problem-solving, as well as apathy and social withdrawal. There can be psychiatric symptoms (for example,
mood changes, psychosis), seizures (fits), tremor (shakes), unsteadiness and various other signs.

How Common is Dementia?

Fewer than 1 per cent of people develop dementia before the age of
65 years. Incidence increases with age and by the age of 90 years,
up to 25 per cent of people have some degree of dementia. Risk
of dementia in later life is associated with obesity, untreated high
blood pressure, lack of physical and social activity and low educational attainment. In Ireland, approximately 55,000 people are
currently living with dementia and 500,000 people live in families
affected by dementia.

Alzheimer's disease, which is more common in women than
men, accounts for 55 per cent of all cases of dementia; mixed vascular and Alzheimer's disease accounts for 25 per cent (with vascular dementia more common in men than women); dementia with
Lewy bodies accounts for 10 per cent; frontotemporal dementia
accounts for 5 per cent; and other forms of dementia account for
the remaining 5 per cent of cases.

Frontotemporal dementia has an earlier age of onset than other dementias. It accounts for less than 10 per cent of late onset dementias but up to 20 per cent of early onset cases. Approximately
25 per cent of people with Parkinson's disease develop dementia,
rising to 80 per cent of those who are still alive after 20 years of
follow-up with Parkinson's.

In 2006, the new national mental health policy, *A Vision for
Change,* noted that in 2001 there were 21,500 people over the age
of 65 with dementia in Ireland, and this was projected to increase
to 55,750 in 2036.[2] Similarly, the number of people aged 65 or
over with depression was projected to rise from 47,300 in 2001 to
122,540 in 2036.

The accuracy or otherwise of these projections remains to be
seen, however, as it is now increasingly clear that gains in life ex-

pectancy at age 65 years are accompanied by equivalent gains in years free of any cognitive impairment (that is, free of dementia or early dementia), decreased years with mild or moderate to severe cognitive impairment, and gains in years in excellent or good self-perceived health.[3] Even so, there is still a compelling need to devote attention to the mental health needs of ageing persons and people with dementia (especially those with intellectual disability) and their carers.

What Causes Dementia?

The causes of dementia are not fully understood. In any given individual, there may be many contributing factors including genes, lifestyle factors (for example, smoking) and other physical conditions increasing risk of one or more forms of dementia.

The WHO points out that Alzheimer's disease is associated with specific changes in the brain: a reduced number of brain cells in certain brain areas, tangles of proteins within cells, and brain plaques made of 'amyloid' (a form of protein), among other anomalies. There are also changes in brain chemistry associated with the condition, although symptoms can occur even if these changes are minimal, and vice versa. People with Down syndrome (a genetic disorder) are at increased risk of Alzheimer's disease. There are also specific gene anomalies associated with most cases of early onset Alzheimer's and other genes associated with some cases of late onset Alzheimer's, although there is still much research to be done on the ultimate underpinnings of the disorder.

In addition, dementia in Alzheimer's disease may coexist with vascular dementia when, for example, cerebrovascular episodes (small strokes) are superimposed on Alzheimer's disease. These episodes may result in sudden exacerbations of the symptoms of dementia and, according to postmortem findings, both types of dementia coexist in up to 25 per cent of people with dementia. There may also be overlap with other forms of dementia. For example, in cases of dementia with Lewy bodies, not only are Lewy bodies found in the brain after death, but many of the brain changes associated with Alzheimer's disease are also commonly found too.

Frontotemporal dementia affects chiefly the frontal and anterior temporal parts of the brain, and is associated with many different brain abnormalities, including specific lesions known as ubiquitin or tau positive inclusions. Pick's disease, for example, a type of frontotemporal dementia, is caused by gradual deterioration of specific brain areas (the frontal and temporal lobes) in the absence of the brain features of Alzheimer's disease, such as tangles and plaques (see above).

Dementia in Creutzfeldt-Jakob disease is associated with specific neuropathological changes ('subacute spongiform encephalopathy'), caused by a transmissible agent. In addition, 5 per cent to 10 per cent of cases are inherited. Huntington's disease is transmitted by a single autosomal dominant gene, although 10 per cent of cases are caused by mutations (spontaneous change or damage to a gene). The causes of Parkinson's disease are not known, but it is known that cells in certain brain areas (the 'basal ganglia') are affected, with extensive cell death. Dementia in HIV disease is caused by HIV infection and, overall, up to 10 per cent of cases of dementia are attributable to alcohol misuse.

Normal pressure hydrocephalus is a condition caused by excess fluid in the brain resulting from bleeding, head injury or meningitis (inflammation of the brain linings). It can also be of unknown cause, but some cases are treatable. The condition is often associated with mental slowing down, altered walk, loss of interest, incontinence of urine, and relatively mild dementia. Finally, dementia can also result from repetitive head injury (for example, boxing), motor neurone disease, or various physical illnesses (for example, infections, or disorders of the thyroid or parathyroid glands, which can be assessed by your general practitioner with a blood test).

Case History: Niamh

Niamh was a 72-year-old woman, living with her 78-year-old husband, Jim. Neither had any history of problems with physical or mental health. Both were retired but actively involved in the lives of their two daughters, both of whom had children whom Niamh and Jim often minded.

Over the course of two or three months, Jim noticed that Niamh was increasingly forgetful: she frequently lost her glasses or forgot to tell Jim when one of their daughters had phoned. Niamh was also losing weight and losing focus on tasks that she previously enjoyed such as doing crosswords, gardening or meeting her sister for coffee.

One night, Jim awoke to find Niamh had gone downstairs and was looking for her something in the kitchen. When Jim arrived, Niamh became even more confused and suddenly burst into tears, seeming to realise that she did not really know what she was doing. After some discussion, Niamh agreed to go with Jim to see their GP the following day, and they both went back to bed.

The next day, their GP listened to their story with care, and took a complete history from both Niamh and Jim. Following a physical examination of Niamh, the GP took some blood tests and asked them both to return the following week. One week later, the GP reported that the blood tests were all normal and she had a long discussion with Niamh. It transpired that Niamh had been feeling low for several months, was having particular difficulty falling asleep (which was new for her) and had lost significant weight over the previous three months as her appetite had virtually vanished.

The GP felt that Niamh was most likely depressed rather than showing signs of dementia. Following careful risk assessment, the GP referred Niamh for psychological therapy for moderate depression, and also prescribed an antidepressant medication. In addition, the GP provided both Niamh and Jim with advice about social activation and community involvement as a means of improving mood and remaining active in later life.

One month later, Niamh went back to see the GP. She was feeling significantly better, as her symptoms of depression had improved with treatment and there were no longer any features suggestive of dementia. Given that they were both in their 70s, however, the GP, took the opportunity to emphasise to Niamh and Jim the importance of managing risk factors for dementia, that is, stopping smoking, and treating high cholesterol, high blood pressure and diabetes. The GP placed particular emphasis on the importance of personal and social activities, including remaining physically active, reading and doing crosswords (which Niamh had always enjoyed), and making particular efforts to engage in community and cultural events of interest to them.

What Are the Treatments for Dementia?

The first step in management of dementia is to identify if the person has any treatable causes contributing to the dementia. Examples include disorders of the thyroid or parathyroid glands, or various other medical or psychiatric illnesses (see above). Treating depression or other psychiatric symptoms is especially important. If the dementia is part of another, broader disorder, such as Creutzfeldt-Jakob, Huntington's, Parkinson's or HIV disease, appropriate treatment should be provided for that illness (through your GP and medical team).

In addition, even with an established diagnosis of, for example, Alzheimer's disease or vascular dementia, it is still important to address risk factors such as smoking, and treating high cholesterol, high blood pressure and diabetes. Appropriate mental activity, physical exercise and social activation are all very important, as are diet and hygiene.

Treatments for dementia itself focus chiefly on managing or arresting the development of symptoms, as the core dementia process is often substantially irreversible. And, as is the case in much of mental health care, there are three strands to treatment: biological treatments (for example, medication), psychological treatments (for example, cognitive stimulation and behavior management), and social interventions (for example, social supports for patients and families).

Turning to medication first, the UK-based National Institute for Health and Care Excellence (NICE) has produced recommendations on the use of 'donepezil, galantamine, rivastigmine and memantine for the treatment of Alzheimer's disease'.[4] The first three of these medications are 'acetylcholinesterase inhibitors' which act to increase the levels of a specific chemical (acetylcholine) in the brain. This can help arrest or even temporarily reverse some of the cognitive and functional problems in people with mild to moderate Alzheimer's disease. They can also improve behavior and stabilise certain symptoms in some cases.

In Ireland, donepezil, galantamine and rivastigmine are all duly licensed for the symptomatic treatment of mild to moderately severe Alzheimer's dementia. Common undesirable effects of donepezil include diarrhoea, muscle cramps, fatigue, nausea, vomiting and sleep problems. Nausea and vomiting, among other possible adverse effects, are also associated with galantamine and rivastigmine. These medications can also affect heart rhythm. As a result, they need to be used under specialist supervision, with careful weighing up of contra-indications, potential adverse effects, interactions with other medications, and potential benefits. As with all medications, relevant information should be considered with care prior to use (for example, on the website of the Health Products Regulatory Authority, www.hpra.ie).

Treatment should be initiated and supervised by a physician experienced in the diagnosis and treatment of Alzheimer's dementia, and only started if a caregiver is available who will regularly monitor medication intake for the patient. Maintenance treatment can be continued for as long as therapeutic benefit persists, so it is necessary to reassess clinical benefit on a regular basis. Individual responses cannot be predicted and discontinuation should be considered when evidence of a therapeutic effect is no longer present.

NICE also recommends use of memantine, which primarily affects a different brain chemical (glutamate), in people with moderate Alzheimer's disease when the person cannot tolerate or take acetylcholinesterase inhibitors, and in people with severe Alzheimer's disease. NICE specifies that any of these agents should be continued only when they are considered to have a worthwhile effect on the person's cognitive, global, functional or behavioural symptoms, that is, if the person improves significantly or if deterioration is significantly slowed down.

In Ireland, memantine is licensed for treatment of patients with moderate to severe Alzheimer's disease. Common undesirable effects include dizziness, headache, constipation, sleepiness and high blood pressure. The therapy should be initiated and supervised by a physician experienced in the diagnosis and treatment of Alzheimer's dementia. Treatment should only be started if a caregiver is available who will regularly monitor the intake of the medication by the patient. In addition, the patient's tolerance for the medication, and its dose, should be reassessed on a regular basis, preferably within three months of starting treatment.

Rivastigmine is also sometimes used in dementia associated with Parkinson's disease of no known cause, and acetylcholinesterase inhibitors can prove useful in people with dementia with Lewy bodies. The use of these medications, however, requires specialist supervision, as it can move outside of recommended guidelines in some cases.

In addition to the above, other medications, such as antipsychotics (Chapter 3), are sometimes used in people with dementia who demonstrate challenging behavior. NICE, however, in a guidance document titled 'Dementia: Supporting People with Dementia and Their Carers in Health and Social Care', recommends that people with Alzheimer's disease, vascular dementia or mixed dementias with mild-to-moderate non-cognitive symptoms should *not* be prescribed antipsychotic medication, owing to possible increased risks of strokes or death.[5] In addition, people with dementia with Lewy bodies with mild to moderate non-cognitive symptoms should not be prescribed antipsychotic drugs either, owing to their particular risk of severe adverse reactions (see above).

NICE, however, does recommend that people with Alzheimer's disease, vascular dementia, mixed dementias or dementia with Lewy bodies with *severe* non-cognitive symptoms (for example, psychosis, or agitated behavior that is causing significant distress) may be offered treatment with an antipsychotic medication, once the following conditions are met:

- There should be a full discussion with the patient and/or carers about benefits and risks of the medication (for example, risk of strokes or threatened strokes, or possible effects on thinking)
- Changes in thinking ability ('cognition') should be assessed frequently, and the prescribed medication re-considered, if indicated, and possibly changed
- Specific target symptoms should be identified and documented, and changes in these assessed regularly
- Consideration should be given to the possible effects of co-existing conditions on the evolving clinical picture (for example, depression).

In addition, there should also be a careful individual risk/benefit analysis for each patient; the initial dose of medication should be low, and increased upward as needed; and the entire treatment programme should be reviewed frequently and regularly, to ensure continued benefit and minimisation of risk.

Looking at treatment more broadly, NICE places particular emphasis on person-centred care, non-discrimination, the rights of carers, coordination of services and careful management of behavior that challenges. Other key factors in shaping care include funding arrangements, staff training, environmental design, management of risk factors, early identification and genetic counselling (where appropriate).

In acute situations, confused or disturbed behaviour by people with dementia can present real problems at home, in the hospital or in nursing homes, with confusion, wandering, hostility or aggression. These issues are by no means inevitable, but they do occur, often in response to external factors such as changes in environment, physical illness or other developments with which the person has difficulty coping. Management strategies depend on the specific situation. For the general management of agitation, NICE recommends aromatherapy, multisensory stimulation, therapeutic use of music and/or dancing, animal-assisted therapy or massage, depending on the situation and the person's interests or preferences.

Looking at treatment more broadly in terms of psychological therapies, there can be a role for behavioural management techniques, for example, addressing wandering by increasing exercise during the day, or decreasing stimulants such as caffeine. Cognitive stimulation is also important, and can include group activities to stimulate people with dementia and engage them in various activities. Individual cognitive activity is also important, even after diagnosis. Memory aids and reminiscence therapy can play useful roles in orienting and re-orienting patients with impaired awareness of time, person or location. Day hospitals, day centres and community groups can also prove very helpful.

Most care for dementia is provided as an outpatient, through primary care services (for example, GPs and primary care teams) or outpatient clinics (medicine of the elderly services, dedicated dementia services or community mental health teams for older adults). Occasionally, there is a need for hospital admission or admission to inpatient mental health services. Reasons for admission include severe dementia, complications relating to physical health or co-existing mental illness, specific levels of risk to self or others and various other factors. In 2015, there were 567 admissions of adults with 'organic mental disorders', which include dementia, to psychiatric inpatient units and hospitals in Ireland.[6] Over half (55 per cent) were male, 18 per cent were involuntary admissions under the Mental Health Act 2001 (Chapter 13) and the most common length of stay was 31 days.

From the perspective of social treatment and support, there may be a need to address issues such as housing, social isolation, legal issues and financial matters. There is an excellent overview of a broad range of such issues in *Ageing and Caring: A Guide for Later Life* by Professor Des O'Neill, (Orpen Press, 2013). This excellent book covers a wide variety of relevant topics ranging from loneliness to driving, from behavior problems in dementia to life in nursing homes, and from advance care planning to financial affairs. Ireland's new Assisted Decision-Making (Capacity) Act 2015 is also relevant in this context, and is discussed later in Chapter 14.

Overall, and notwithstanding the various services available at present, there is still a strong need for better support for people with dementia and their families and carers. There is a particular need to focus on the requirements of younger people who develop dementia at an early age, whose needs may differ in certain respects from those of older adults. Support for carers is critical in all forms of dementia. Primary care, secondary (hospital-based) care, outreach interventions, home support, respite care, and realistic, acceptable long-term care options are all needed, depending on the needs of the individual, their evolving condition, and their family situation. *The importance of sustained, meaningful support for the families and carers of people with dementia cannot be over-stated.*

Case History: Harold

Harold was a 67-year-old man who lived with his long-term partner, Bob. Harold had just one brother and both his parents had died relatively young. Harold had recently retired from his job as an accountant, at which he had always excelled.

Over the course of around four months, Bob began to notice that Harold's memory was not as sharp as it once was. Uncharacteristically, Harold began to forget various social engagements. This was most unlike Harold, but Bob said nothing until one day he noticed Harold apparently struggling to remember Bob's name – although Harold thought of it moments later.

Bob discussed this with Harold, who had also been worried about himself. They went to see their GP who took a careful history from both Harold and Bob, carried out a physical examination, and performed a series of blood tests (all of which were normal). The GP referred Harold to the local 'medicine for the elderly' team, and the team's clinical psychologist performed an extensive set of memory tests, which showed significant memory problems.

Over the following months, Harold's memory problems gradually worsened and he began to experience difficulties with day-to-day physical activities, such as eating and washing. He had continual problems remembering new information, although his memory for events in the more distant past appeared intact. Harold's speech became less rich than it had been, and he was no longer buzzing with ideas (as he previously had been). He could, nonetheless, still communicate adequately and was able to attend to his day-to-day tasks with some gentle prompting from Bob, although he found social situations particularly difficult.

At his follow-up appointment with the medicine for the elderly team, the physician and clinical psychologist told Harold that he had signs of dementia, likely Alzheimer's disease. They put into place a programme of management of risk factors (stopping smoking, and treating high cholesterol, high blood pressure and diabe-

tes); cognitive activation (mental exercises); physical activity (weekly swimming, which Harold had always enjoyed); psycho-education about dementia (for both Harold and Bob); and treatment with donepezil to try to help arrest or even temporarily reverse some of the cognitive (thinking) and functional problems associated with Harold's condition. Harold also discussed the kind of care he would like to receive in the future, in the event that he was to lose mental capacity to make treatment decisions. He made a will and an enduring power of attorney, making Bob and his brother attorneys (Chapter 14).

Most of all, though, Harold and Bob agreed that Harold would continue to engage in all of his day-to-day activities in the normal fashion as best he could for as long as feasible, with the support of Bob and the supervision of his medical team and GP. Harold was determined to remain physically and mentally active as best as possible under the circumstances, because both he and Bob understood that this would optimise Harold's functioning in the long term, and keep him as well as he could be for as long as possible into the future.

Mental Health Services in Later Life

Health and social services for older people in Ireland are an area in need of careful attention in the years to come, especially in relation to dementia. To this end, Ireland's first *Irish National Dementia Strategy* was launched in December 2014. The strategy aims to meet the needs of the 55,000 people currently living with dementia in Ireland and the expected increase of people who will live with dementia in the future.[7]

The new policy has a background in various earlier policy initiatives in this area. In 1988, a Working Party on Services for the Elderly published a 'policy for the elderly' titled *The Years Ahead... A Policy for the Elderly,* building on a 1968 report *Care of the Aged,* which had stated that 'it is better, and probably much cheaper, to help the aged to live in the community than to provide for them in hospitals or other institutions.'⁸ Two decades later, the 1988 Working Party noted that the 1968 policy had:

> recommended improvements in existing services, payments and the provision of new services and allowances where they identified a need. Many of these recommendations have been implemented and as a result, services for the elderly have been transformed.⁹

The 1988 policy proposed a series of additional measures promoting 'comprehensive and coordinated' services for the elderly; maintaining health; housing; 'care at home', in the community and in general hospitals; community hospitals; and the need for partnership. The 1988 policy placed particular emphasis on 'care of the elderly mentally ill and infirm', and articulated the importance of specialist services for dementia.

Implementation was, however, challenging, and a 1998 review raised issues about both the pace of change and the adequacy of the vision outlined in *The Years Ahead*.¹⁰ Nonetheless, in 2003, Professors Des O'Neill and Shaun O'Keeffe reported that, despite a relatively low level of popular advocacy for older people, specialist medical and psychiatric services had indeed developed in Ireland, and geriatric medicine had become the largest medical specialty in hospital practice.¹¹ Ongoing challenges in the field related to policy implementation, funding, staffing and development of community and long-term care.

In 2006, the new national mental health policy, *A Vision for Change*, outlined a clear vison of 'mental health services for older people' but while definite progress was made in subsequent years, full implementation proved challenging. In April 2013, the government's *National Positive Ageing Strategy* again placed considerable emphasis on mental health in later life and included the maintenance of 'physical and mental health and wellbeing' as a 'national goal'.¹²

The 2013 strategy also noted the broad range of factors relevant to achieving this 'national goal', especially in the context of mental health:

> While dementia and Alzheimer's disease are a significant cause of disability among the older population, depression is the most common mental health problem in those aged 65 years and over. It is of note that recent Irish research found a high prevalence of undiagnosed depression and anxiety in the older population. Consistent with physical health, a range of factors contribute to good or poor mental health, such as environmental, economic and social determinants, including the physical environment, geography, education, occupation, income, social status, social support, culture and gender.

Also in 2013, the College of Psychiatrists of Ireland published its *Workforce Planning Report 2013-2023*, noting that 'old age psychiatry' is an expanding area and requires consideration to be given to the number of specialists in old age psychiatry that will be required to meet the needs of this population.[13] More specifically, the College stated that only approximately 50 per cent of the required consultant psychiatrist posts needed for old age psychiatry work were currently provided.

In December 2014, the *Irish National Dementia Strategy* identified four 'key principles to underpin and inform the full range of health and social care services provided to people with dementia, their families and carers. These include the following:

- An integrated, population-based approach should be taken to dementia service provision;
- Services, including palliative care services, should be tailored to deliver the best possible outcomes for people with dementia and their families and carers;
- All communications with those with dementia should be as accessible as possible;

- All those dealing with people with dementia across health and social care settings should be appropriately trained.[14]

The 2014 Strategy also identified five 'priority actions which are considered to be capable of delivery within existing resources, or by reconfiguring the resources which are currently available', broadly based on the following:

- Clear responsibility for dementia will be assigned within the Health Service Executive, both at management level and at the front-line, to manage the progress of individual patients through their care journey;

- Clear descriptions of care pathways will be prepared, and clear information and effective assistance will be made available to GPs and to people with dementia and their families and carers to identify and access available services and supports;

- Measures will be taken to promote a better understanding of dementia, including modifiable risk factors, and to remove the stigma sometimes associated with the condition;

- The way in which resources are deployed and services configured will be reviewed to ensure that available resources are used to optimal effect;

- Research to inform the design and delivery of dementia services in Ireland will be supported and given appropriate priority.

It is to be hoped that these measures will be advanced with enthusiasm in the coming years, because there is still much work to be done to provide a full range of health and social services to older adults in Ireland, especially those with dementia, and their families and carers, all of whom face considerable challenges at present.

Useful Resources

It is advisable that anyone who thinks he or she has any of the conditions discussed in this book sees a health care professional.

There are many reasons for this, including a need to out-rule any other diagnoses, such as physical illnesses. In addition, some people find it easier to talk with a health care professional, especially if they are too uncertain or embarrassed to talk with friends or family members. Often, a brief talk with a GP will 'normalise' the individual's symptoms by reassuring them that they are not alone in what they are experiencing and that help is to hand, if any is needed.

Individuals with any mental disorder or psychological problem, and their families, will find much that is useful on the Internet. As ever, Internet resources need to be evaluated with care and only trusted when the information comes from a reliable source. Reliable information about mental health can be sourced from the websites of the Health Service Executive (www.hse.ie/eng/health/az), College of Psychiatrists of Ireland (www.irishpsychiatry.ie), Royal College of Psychiatrists in London (www.rcpsych.ac.uk), National Health Service in the UK (www.nhs.uk) and National Institute of Mental Health in the US (www.nimh.nih.gov).

Evidence-based guidance about specific treatments can be found on the website of the National Institute for Health and Care Excellence (NICE) (www.nice.org.uk). NICE is a UK-based organisation responsible for developing guidance, standards and information on high-quality health and social care, and preventing and treating ill health.

The Alzheimer Society of Ireland works across Ireland in local communities providing dementia-specific services and supports and advocating for the rights and needs of all people living with dementia and their carers (www.alzheimer.ie). It is a national non-profit organisation which also operates the Alzheimer National Helpline, offering information and support to anyone affected by dementia, at 1800 341 341. In addition to the above, the Health Service Executive offers a range of resources relating to dementia on its website: www.hse.ie/dementia.

For an excellent guide to well-being in later life in Ireland, see: *Ageing and Caring: A Guide for Later Life* by Professor Des O'Neill (Orpen Press, 2013). For further information on the themes discussed in the section of this chapter dealing with 'Mental Health Services in Later Life', see: *Hearing Voices: The History of Psychiatry in Ireland* by Brendan Kelly (Irish Academic Press, 2016), Chapter 8 ('The Future of Psychiatry in Ireland'). For an overview of research into dementia, see: *The Fragile Brain: The Strange, Hopeful Science of Dementia* by Kathleen Taylor (Oxford University Press, 2016).

Endnotes

1 World Health Organisation. *International Classification of Diseases* (10th Edition). Geneva: World Health Organisation, 1992.

2 Expert Group on Mental Health Policy, *A Vision for Change* (Dublin: The Stationery Office, 2006), p. 116.

3 Jagger, C., Matthews, F.E., Wohland, P., Fouweather, T., Stephan, B.C.N., Robinson, L., Arthur, A. and Brayne, C. on behalf of the Medical Research Council Cognitive Function and Ageing Collaboration. 'A comparison of health expectancies over two decades in England: Results of the Cognitive Function and Ageing Study I and II'. *Lancet* 2016; 387: 779-86. See also: O'Neill, D. 'Playing constituency politics to the detriment of our hospitals'. *The Irish Times*, 8 March 2016.

4 www.nice.org.uk/guidance/ta217

5 www.nice.org.uk/guidance/cg42

6 Daly, A. and Craig, S. HRB Statistics Series 29: Activities of Irish Psychiatric Units and Hospitals 2015. Dublin: Health Research Board, 2016 (Tables 2.6a, 2.8 and 2.14a).

7 Irish National Dementia Strategy Working Group. *Irish National Dementia Strategy*. Dublin: Department of Health, 2014.

8 Inter-Departmental Subcommittee on the Care of the Aged. The Care of the Aged. Dublin: The Stationery Office, 1968 (p. 13).

9 Working Party on Services for the Elderly. *The Years Ahead... A Policy for the Elderly*. Dublin: The Stationery Office, 1988 (p. 16).

10 Ruddle, H., Donoghue, F. and Mulvihill, R. *The Years Ahead Report: A Review of the Implementation of its Recommendations*. Dublin: National Council on Ageing and Older People, 1998.

11 O'Neill, D. and O'Keeffe, S. 'Health care for older people in Ireland.' *Journal of the American Geriatric Society* 2003; 51: 1280-6.

12 Department of Health and Healthy Ireland. *The National Positive Ageing Strategy*. Dublin: Department of Health, 2013 (p. 20).

13 College of Psychiatrists of Ireland. *Workforce Planning Report 2013-2023*. Dublin: College of Psychiatrists of Ireland, 2013 (pp. 9-11).

14 health.gov.ie/wp-content/uploads/2014/12/30115-National-Dementia-Strategy-Eng.pdf.

Chapter 9

OTHER MENTAL ILLNESSES
AND CONDITIONS

Definitions of mental illnesses change continually (Chapter 1). This chapter looks at key issues concerning various mental illnesses and conditions that are not covered in other chapters, including personality disorders, perinatal mental illness (mental illnesses during and following pregnancy), delusional disorders, and various other conditions such as seasonal affective disorder, work stress, gender identity disorders and disorders of sexual preference. Useful resources and sources of further information are provided at the end of the chapter.

Personality Disorders

Personality disorders are controversial conditions that can be difficult to define as they overlap to a significant extent with 'normal' personality. While some people take the view that the very concept of 'personality disorder' is not a useful or reasonable one to begin with, the WHO does include 'disorders of adult personality and behaviour' in its *International Classification of Diseases* (ICD-10).[1] They are described as clinically significant conditions and behaviour patterns which are generally persistent and are expressions of a person's characteristic lifestyle and mode of relating to self and others. In other words, they are aspects of a person's personality.

The WHO goes on to specify that personality disorders are deeply ingrained and enduring behavior patterns, which manifest as inflexible responses to a wide variety of social and personal situations. They are significant or extreme deviations from the way that average people in a given culture perceive, think, feel and relate to others. These behaviour patterns are generally stable and involve multiple aspects of behaviour and psychological functioning. For the most part, they date from childhood, they are not the result of other mental disorders and they generally cause subjective distress and problems with social function and performance into adulthood.

Before making a diagnosis of personality disorder, it is important to (a) consider *all* aspects of a person's functioning; (b) consider as many sources of information as possible; and (c) take account of a person's behavior over time: personality disorder refers to *long-standing, stable* patterns of maladaptive behaviour, and not just occasional periods of unusual behavior to which everyone is prone.

Several specific personality disorders have been described, based on their most common features. In practice, it is common for a person to demonstrate some but not all of the features of one personality disorder, or selected features of more than one. The diagnostic categories presented by the WHO and outlined here are just guidelines; they are not set in stone (Chapter 1).

In general, though, once it is clear that the problems identified are not attributable to brain damage, brain disease or another mental disorder, specific personality disorders are characterised by (a) notably disharmonious attitudes and behaviour, generally involving a number areas of functioning (for example, impulse control, thinking habits, patterns of relating to others); (b) a long-standing history of these patterns and problems; (c) evidence that these patterns span several areas of the person's life and are maladaptive in those areas (that is, cause actual problems); (d) evidence that these problems commenced in childhood or late adolescence, and have persisted into adulthood; (e) evidence of personal distress resulting from these issues; and, often, (f) problems in social and occupational performance resulting from these behaviors and personality features. Clearly, diagnosing personality disorders is a culturally-dependent activity, as behavioural norms vary considerably across cultures.

For specific disorders, the WHO goes on to outline specific criteria, suggesting that at least three are needed for a diagnosis. Criteria for **paranoid personality disorder** include (a) excessive sensitiveness to rebuffs and setbacks; (b) a tendency to bear grudges for long periods; (c) suspiciousness and a tendency to misconstrue the actions of other people as hostile even when they're not; (d) an excessively tenacious sense of personal rights that is out of keeping with the context; (e) recurring, unfounded suspicions about a partner's sexual fidelity; (f) excessive self-importance and self-reference; and (g) preoccupation with unfounded conspiratorial explanations of events. Of course, many people have some but not all of these features at various points in time, so, for a diagnosis of 'paranoid personality disorder', a person needs to have the general features of personality disorder (above) as well as three of these more specific features of 'paranoid personality disorder'.

The diagnostic approach to other personality disorders is similar; the person needs to have the general features of personality disorder (above) as well as three of the specific features listed by the WHO for each personality disorder. Criteria for **schizoid personality disorder**, for example, include (a) few activities, if any, provide pleasure to the person; (b) emotional detachment, coldness or flattening; (c) diminished capacity to express either warm or angry feelings towards other people; (d) ostensible indifference to criticism or praise; (e) diminished interest in having sexual experiences; (f) a persistent preference for solitary activities; (g) disproportionate preoccupation with introspection and fantasy; (h) diminished number of, or desire for, close, confiding relationships; and (i) notable insensitivity to social conventions and norms.

Dissocial personality disorder is an especially well known condition which tends to involve significant conflict between a person's behaviour and social norms. It is also known as antisocial personality disorder and psychopathy. This condition is characterised by (a) notable lack of concern for other people's feelings; (b) persistent and gross irresponsibility with disregard for social norms; (c) lack of capacity to maintain lasting relationships, despite being able to establish them; (d) low tolerance for frustration and a tendency towards aggression; (e) lack of capacity to experience guilt or to learn from experience (for example, punishment); and (f) a tendency to blame others or construct plausible rationalisations for problems resulting from these factors.

Emotionally unstable personality disorder, by contrast, involves a tendency to act impulsively; emotional instability; diminished ability to plan ahead; and outbursts of anger, especially when impulsive acts are criticized. There are two subtypes of emotionally unstable personality disorder described: *impulsive* type and *borderline* type, both of which are associated with impulsiveness and diminished self-control. The 'impulsive' subtype, however, is especially characterised by emotional instability and diminished impulse control; there are also commonly outbursts of threatening or hostile behavior. The 'borderline' subtype involves emotional instability, often with disturbances to the person's self-image, goals and desires (including sexual preferences); there are also commonly feelings of emptiness, a tendency towards involvement in intense, unstable relationships, recurrent emotional crises, fear of abandonment and repeated threats or acts of self-harm.

Histrionic personality disorder involves (a) theatrical dramatisation of emotions; (b) easy suggestibility; (c) increased, shallow emotional reactivity; (d) persistent appetite for excitement and being the centre of attention; (e) excessive seductiveness; and (f) excessive concern with physical attractiveness.

Anankastic personality disorder is characterised by (a) excessive feelings of caution and doubt; (b) disproportionate preoccupation with lists, organisation, details, etc.; (c) a counter-productive degree of perfectionism; (d) disproportionate conscientiousness at the expense of personal pleasure and relationships; (e) disproportionate pedantry; (f) stubbornness and rigidity; (g) unreasonable expectations that others will comply with the person's approach; and (h) insistent intrusion of unwelcome impulses or thoughts.

Anxious (avoidant) personality disorder involves (a) pervasive and persistent feelings of apprehension and tension; (b) a conviction that the person is socially inept or inferior; (c) disproportionate preoccupation with social criticism or rejection; (d) a need to be certain of being liked before becoming involved with others; (e) limitations on lifestyle owing to a need for physical security; and (f) avoiding occupational or social activities involving significant interpersonal contact.

Dependent personality disorder is characterised by (a) allowing or encouraging other people to make most of the key decisions about the person's life; (b) subordination of the person's own needs to those of others, with undue compliance with the wishes of others; (c) being unwilling to make even reasonable demands of others; (d) feeling helpless or uncomfortable when alone; (e) preoccupation with fears of abandonment; and (f) diminished capacity for day-to-day decisions without excessive reassurance and advice.

The WHO also describes various other specific personality disorders (for example, organic personality disorder due to brain disease, damage or dysfunction); mixed personality disorders; enduring personality changes (for example, after catastrophic experiences or psychiatric illness); and habit and impulse disorders, including pathological gambling, pathological fire-setting (pyromania), pathological stealing (kleptomania), and an excessive tendency to pull out hairs, owing to mounting tension (trichotillomania).

It has been estimated that approximately 5 per cent of the adult population have a personality disorder to at least a mild degree. The rate may be higher in certain groups; for example, almost 50 per cent of people in prisons might be considered to have a personality disorder. These figures are estimates: it can be extremely difficult to diagnose personality disorders, and real questions need to be asked about making such a diagnosis in certain cases. How does making the diagnosis really help the person? Does it lead to better understanding, treatment, and reduced distress, as is sometimes the case? Or does it simply lead to pointless labelling, further stigma and increased distress?

These questions are especially relevant given that the causes of personality disorder are not fully understood. In any given individual, there is likely to be a mix of genetic factors (that is, running in the family) and environmental factors, such as childhood adversity, abuse, trauma, life events, persistent relationship problems and unhelpful coping strategies. Studies of twins suggest a certain genetic component to the risk of personality disorder, but the development of poor coping strategies in childhood is also likely significant.

Against this background, treatment or management of personality disorder can be just as challenging as diagnosis, if not more so. Consistency and structure are important elements of treatment, not least because these are the very areas that are often impaired in many people with specific personality disorders. A tolerance for frustration is also helpful in many cases and this, again, is something that is commonly impaired in personality disorders.

Treatment should follow the bio-psycho-social approach to management, that is, there are 'biological' treatments (such as medication), psychological treatments (such as cognitive therapies) and social interventions, all of which can be combined to suit the needs and circumstances of any given individual. The chief use of medication in personality disorders is to treat any co-occurring mental illness, such as depression (Chapter 2). While mood-stabilising medication used in bipolar disorder (Chapter 4) is sometimes used for impulsivity in personality disorders, the evidence base for this is very limited and it is not systematically recommended.

In emotionally unstable personality disorder, psychological therapies can prove very helpful, including adaptions of cognitive behavioural therapy (CBT) (Chapters 2, 5 and 6) and dialectical behaviour therapy (DBT). DBT is somewhat similar to CBT and also involves group sessions, building skills such as mindfulness, and developing coping strategies other than deliberate self-harm for dealing with emotional instability. DBT is a challenging therapy but it can be highly effective.

In dissocial personality disorder, engagement with treatment is often challenging, but good engagement predicts good treatment outcomes. People with dissocial personality disorder who also have a history of offending behavior can engage in group-based CBT therapies with a focus on reducing antisocial behavior and offending, with some success.

Most treatment of personality disorders is delivered on an outpatient basis, but admission to psychiatric facilities can occur if symptoms are severe, the condition is treatment-resistant or it appears that there is a risk of harm to self or others than can be diminished by admission (for example, during a particular crisis). In 2015, there were 1,379 admissions to adult psychiatry inpatient facilities in Ireland with 'personality and behavioral disorders' (70 per cent female), of which 80 per cent were readmissions.[2] The most common length of stay with personality disorder was just 7 days, compared to 15 days for all mental disorders. There were 20 admissions of children or adolescents with this diagnosis in 2015 (again, 70 per cent female), of which 25 per cent were readmissions.

Social support can be very important for some people with personality disorder, especially those which marked emotional instability, so assistance with matters such as housing can prove very helpful in conjunction with the other treatment and management approaches outlined above.

Perinatal Mental Illness

Recent decades have seen increased research into mental health and ill health during and following pregnancy. In Ireland, one in six pregnant women (16 per cent) attending maternity services is at probable risk of depression during pregnancy, according to research conducted by a Trinity College Dublin research team and Irish obstetric services in 2016. Ireland has the second highest birth rate in Europe, with an average of just under 68,000 births per year. This means that in one year, over 11,000 women could be experiencing or at risk of depression during pregnancy.

This is important owing not only to the negative effects of depression itself but also to increasing evidence that depression during pregnancy can influence obstetric health and may compromise the physical and mental health of the infant. However, screening for antenatal depression is not routine in Ireland's maternity hospitals and perinatal mental health services are under-resourced in comparison to other comparable EU countries, according to the research clinicians.

The 'Well Before Birth' study – the first such study to be carried out in the country – shows that prevalence rates of depression among women giving birth in Ireland are high, and may be higher than those recorded in other Organisation for Economic Co-operation and Development (OECD) countries which show prevalence rates of ante-natal (pre-delivery) depression ranging between 10 and 15 per cent.

For the Irish study, over 5,000 pregnant women at all stages of pregnancy attending six maternity hospitals or centres were questioned. The researchers used the Edinburgh Postnatal Depression Scale (EPDS) as a recognised screening tool for depression. A score of 13 or over was used as an indication of probable depression, which is at the higher-end of an indication of probability.

Data were collected between January and September 2016, and 5,007 women aged between 18 and 49 were surveyed. Almost two-thirds (63 per cent) had an undergraduate degree or higher, indicating that this was a population skewed towards higher socio-economic status. Participants were recruited from the National Maternity and Rotunda Hospitals, Dublin; Cork University Hospital; Mayo General Hospital, Castlebar; University Hospital Limerick; and Community Antenatal Clinics in Tallaght, County Dublin.[3]

Professor Veronica O'Keane, Professor in Psychiatry at Trinity, the lead research investigator, said that women in Ireland should be screened for depression early in their antenatal care plan and should be encouraged to seek help:

> Properly caring for the mental health of women during pregnancy protects the longer-term mental health of both mother and child. Antenatal depression, as we are seeing with this study, is common. Rates of depression during pregnancy among women in Ireland are at least as high, and probably higher, than in other EU countries.

> We now know that hormonal changes that happen during pregnancy can actually contribute to the development of depression', she points out. 'This is why it is so important that depression is screened for during pregnancy and that women are encouraged to look for support. If we don't do this as a systematic part of our antenatal care-plan, we are putting women at risk, not only of suffering distress, but of being compromised before birth and so less able to cope with the additional stresses of caring for a baby.

Emerging and increasing scientific evidence has shown that women who suffer from depression during pregnancy have an increased risk of various complications including pre-eclampsia (high blood pressure in pregnancy, leading to other problems), caesarean section and epidural during labour, preterm delivery and low birth weight. For the baby, it can lead to neuro-developmental and behavioural disadvantage during infancy, and increased risk of mental health problems in childhood and later life.

The Irish study also showed that risk of depression increases with advancing pregnancy, with 12.9 per cent at risk in the first trimester, 13.8 per cent in the second trimester, and 17.2 per cent in the third. This compares with rates of 12 and 14 per cent in a landmark UK study (the Avon Longitudinal Study of Parents and Children). In addition, the Irish study shows that rates of depression are higher among women from lower socio-economic groups and with lower educational attainment. Rates of depression are also higher for younger pregnant women, particularly those under 18 years of age (22 per cent), and women who have had higher numbers of pregnancies and births.

These data emphasise the need for improved detection of new cases of depression during pregnancy and better treatment services. Women who are already taking antidepressants prior to pregnancy should consult their doctor or psychiatrist as soon as they decide to start trying for a baby, or learn they are pregnant, to discuss any risks associated with taking or stopping the medication during pregnancy or while breastfeeding. Some medications that are used to stabilise mood may increase the risk of physical defects and developmental problems in the baby (Chapter 4). After discussion with the doctor, it may be decided to change or stop the medication, but medical advice is needed, especially during pregnancy.

The first line of treatment for many cases of depression during pregnancy is often psychological therapy, along with practical support and information about pregnancy and childbirth, and careful assessment of risk of suicide. Antidepressants can also be used, under medical supervision. Use of antidepressants is now relatively common in pregnancy, with some 10 per cent of women in the US prescribed antidepressants at some point during pregnancy, mainly selective serotonin reuptake inhibitors (SSRIs) (Chapter 2).

Indeed, depending on the person's mental state, stage of pregnancy and personal preferences, antidepressants or other medications can prove life-saving in certain circumstances, following sensible balancing of risks: untreated depression is a severe, debilitating condition that can be fatal, and while there can never be definitive proof that any medications are 100 per cent safe in pregnancy, it is clear that untreated mental disorder not only involves great suffering for both mother and baby, but can prove fatal, through suicide.

There is now growing experience with the use of various treatments for mental disorders during pregnancy, with good therapeutic effects. Careful consultation and specialist supervision are needed in order to both minimise risks and ensure that women have timely access to the support and treatments that they and their babies need.

With regard to termination of pregnancy owing to suicidality, the Citizens Information Board advises that abortion is illegal in Ireland except where there is a real and substantial risk to the life (as distinct from the health) of the mother.[4] This includes a risk arising from a threat of suicide. The Protection of Life During Pregnancy Act 2013 regulates the limited circumstances in which a pregnancy can be legally terminated in Ireland. The Department of Health has published guidance for health professionals about the operation of the 2013 Act. Women may not be prevented from travelling abroad to get an abortion. It is not lawful to encourage or advocate an abortion in individual cases, but it is lawful to provide information in Ireland about abortions abroad, subject to strict conditions.

Following the end of the pregnancy ('postpartum'), women can experience a range of psychological and psychiatric problems, including postpartum 'blues', postpartum depression and postpartum 'psychosis'. Women with a previous history of serious mental illness (for example, severe depression or psychosis) are at especially high risk of relapse after giving birth.

In the first instance, ***postpartum 'blues'*** are very common, occurring in between 50 and 70 per cent of women, generally between three and five days after delivery. This transient but highly distressing condition generally involves emotional lability, irritability, crying and worries about coping with the baby. These symptoms tend to be very acutely distressing, but usually resolve within a few days or a week or two. Reassurance, support and understanding are generally all that are needed. It is helpful if, prior to the birth of the baby, the parents-to-be are warned that postpartum blues might occur for a few days after the delivery, that additional support is needed during this period and that it generally passes.

Postpartum depression occurs in 10 to 15 per cent of new mothers, generally in the first six weeks after giving birth, but can present many months later. Postpartum depression has many of the symptoms of depression that occur in other circumstances (Chapter 2). In the postpartum setting, there may also be particular anxiety or guilt about the baby, a feeling of being an inadequate mother, disproportionate worry about the health of the baby, reluctance to feed or hold the baby or, less commonly, thoughts of harming the baby. Postpartum depression is more common in mothers who have a history of depression and are poor or unemployed, and with low educational attainment. It is also more common if the woman is in a dissatisfying or violent relationship, has few friends, or if the baby is premature or ill.

Postnatal depression is often not detected, especially if it mislabeled as postpartum 'blues'. Up to one-quarter of cases persist for more than a year, if not treated. The first line in management in many cases is psychological therapy along with careful assessment of risk to the mother and baby. Suicide can also occur either during pregnancy or postpartum, and needs to be considered as a significant risk (as is the case with all persons who are depressed). In all postpartum conditions, potential risks to the baby also need to be considered, assessed and managed.

Use of antidepressants and other medications is also possible during the postpartum period, when clinically indicated. Careful assessment and specialist supervision are needed, especially if breastfeeding. Again, while there can never be definitive proof that any medications are 100 per cent safe for the baby while breastfeeding, there is growing experience with various treatments for mental disorders in the postpartum period, with good therapeutic effects. Women who are breastfeeding can be advised about timing feeds to avoid peak medication levels in milk, and how to recognise adverse reactions in babies, if they occur.

The same applies to use of medication in ***postpartum psychosis***. Psychosis is a state of mind in which a person loses contact with reality in at least one important respect for a period of time, while not intoxicated with alcohol or drugs, and while not affected by an acute physical illness that better accounts for the symptoms (for example, having a high fever). Psychosis can be associated with schizophrenia (Chapter 3), depression (Chapter 2), mania (Chapter 4) and certain other conditions. It can also occur postpartum (that is, following delivery).

Postpartum psychosis is most common in women with previous psychosis, first-time mothers and those who have had instrumental deliveries. The overall incidence of postpartum psychosis is approximately one per 1,000 births, and onset can be abrupt, often between two and four weeks following delivery. There are often mood symptoms (depression or mania) in addition to symptoms of psychosis, and it is very important to assess risk to mother and baby in what can be a very serious episode of mental illness. As with postpartum depression, hospitalisation may be needed, ideally in a 'mother and baby' unit unless there are specific reasons why this cannot occur (for example, if there is risk to the baby or if such units simply do not exist).

Treatment often involves practical support, psychological interventions and antipsychotic medication (Chapter 3), all under specialist supervision. Again, no antipsychotics are definitively safe in breastfeeding, but untreated psychosis can be fatal, so pragmatic risk balancing and specialist advice are both needed. Electroconvulsive therapy (ECT) may also be needed in certain, severe cases, and can be very effective (Chapter 2). The outcome in postpartum psychosis is very good in the short term, once treatment is provided promptly and effectively.

As regards fathers, up to 10 per cent of fathers experience prenatal or postnatal depression, especially when the mother is depressed or there are relationship problems. In all of these situations, specialist mental health services have much to offer to both mothers and fathers, ranging from advice about practical support and baby care, to psychological and other treatments for depression or psychosis, if needed.

More specific guidance on many of these conditions is available from your GP, mental health services attached to maternity hospitals or units, or local community mental health teams. In addition, the Health Service Executive (HSE) website has an especially good section on postnatal depression.[5] The UK's National Health Service (NHS) 'Choices' website also has excellent, extensive information about 'mental health problems and pregnancy', outlining symptoms of, and treatments for, all of these disorders occurring during pregnancy and the postpartum period.[6]

In addition, the NHS website has a very helpful video about postnatal depression, in which women talk about their experiences and perinatal psychiatrist Dr Margaret Oates explains how the condition can be treated quickly with the right help. Both websites also have useful guides to premenstrual syndrome (PMS), the menopause ('change of life'), and other related matters.

Delusional Disorders

Delusions are fixed, false beliefs which are held with conviction and which persist despite evidence to the contrary. They can occur as part of other mental disorders such as severe depression (Chapter 2), schizophrenia (Chapter 3) or bipolar affective disorder (Chapter 4), or they can occur on their own. Some delusions might not cause any difficulties but the WHO does include 'persistent delusional disorders' in its *International Classification of Diseases* (ICD-10) as a specific category of mental disorder.[7] These are conditions in which long-standing delusions are the only, or the most conspicuous, clinical characteristic, and where the person does not have another mental disorder such as schizophrenia, a mood disorder or an organic (physical) brain disorder (for example, a tumour) that better accounts for the delusions.

In ***delusional disorder***, the delusions can be varied in content; they can be paranoid, hypochondriacal (that is, health-focused), grandiose or jealous in character, among many other possibilities. There may be other symptoms from time to time, including, for example, low mood or hallucinations (that is, perceptions without appropriate external stimuli, often consistent with the delusion). For this diagnosis, the delusions need to be present for three months and must not be attributable to the person's culture or sub-culture. Onset can be later in life ('late paraphrenia') and delusions can focus on bodily concerns ('dysmorphophobia'). Some forms, such as delusional jealousy, are associated with significant risk and require careful treatment and monitoring.

Many of the key issues relating to delusional disorder can be demonstrated by considering one of the better known variations of delusional disorder, known as **erotomania**. This is a relatively rare condition which occasionally commands public attention owing to its relationship with stalking. From earliest times, however, references to erotomania are found in the work Hippocrates, Plutarch and Galen and, in 1921, Bernard Hart, an English psychiatrist, described 'old maid's insanity', a condition very similar to what is now known as erotomania or de Clerambault's syndrome.

In erotomania, the patient ('subject') develops the delusional belief that he or she is loved from afar by another person ('object'). The subject is generally female, though males predominate in forensic samples (for example, in courts, prisons or secure hospitals). The object is generally perceived to belong to a higher social class, often seems unattainable (for example, a teacher or priest), and is usually believed to be the first to declare love. The patient will often cite farfetched 'proof' of the object's affections, and may paradoxically interpret rejections as covert declarations of love.

The delusional love in erotomania is generally intense and may or may not be reciprocated by the patient. Many people with erotomania only come to attention when they engage in socially disruptive acts, such as repeated letter writing, persistent telephoning or public harassment. The relationship between erotomania and stalking is a source of constant speculation and legitimate concern, and a relationship between erotomania and homicide has also been reported.

The incidence of erotomania is unclear. In the early 1970s, it was thought that modern freedom of sexual expression might reduce the incidence of erotomania. Although this does not appear to be the case, it still appears that the overall incidence of erotomania is low.

Erotomania may coexist with other psychiatric disorders, including schizophrenia (Chapter 3), bipolar affective disorder (Chapter 4), Fregoli syndrome (the delusion that different people are a single person in disguise), Capgras syndrome (the delusion that someone has been replaced by an identical impostor), *folie à deux* (shared delusions or hallucinations) and various other conditions. Erotomania can also occur as part of the clinical picture in dementia in Alzheimer's disease (Chapter 8), epilepsy, meningioma (a type of brain tumour), head trauma and alcoholism (Chapter 7), as well as certain drugs.

There are many psychological theories about erotomania. Some commentators note that the condition often arises in the context of loneliness and social isolation, and it has even been suggested that it can serve as a compensation for disappointments in life.

Management of erotomania is based on treatment of any other associated mental illness in the first instance (for example, treatment of depression; Chapter 2). It has been suggested that delusional disorders (including erotomania) respond preferentially to pimozide, a specific antipsychotic medication that is not very commonly used any more.

More recently, however, there is increased interest in the use of newer, atypical antipsychotic medications in the treatment of erotomania and other delusional disorders (see Chapter 3). In addition, psychological and social treatments may be very useful in conjunction with antipsychotic agents, particularly in patients whose delusions are maintained, at least in part, by social isolation or loneliness.

Many authors describe limited success in the treatment of erotomania, suggesting that delusions tend to persist or can recur. Nonetheless, treatment tends to reduce socially unacceptable behaviours, even though the delusions themselves may persist. It has also been suggested that erotomania, if controlled, might serve to provide solace to some lonely individuals who would otherwise feel entirely unloved.

It is possible that, in time, advances in neuroscience may well demonstrate that primary erotomania is biologically indistinguishable from schizophrenia or other psychotic disorders. Another possible development is the increased use of newer antipsychotic medications and other treatments in the management of erotomania and other delusional disorders, along with psychological therapies such as cognitive behavioural therapy (CBT) for specific delusions.

If the disorder pursues a chronic or relapsing course, it is hoped that the relatively attractive side effect profile of these approaches will help improve compliance with treatment programmes, reduce risk and improve outcomes for all who are affected.

There are many other mental disorders described in the literature, and it is not possible to cover all of them in this book. Some affect both adults and children and are discussed elsewhere. For example, attention deficit hyperactivity disorder (ADHD) in adults in discussed in the chapter on children (Chapter 10) for purposes of convenience only; the condition is now fully recognised as a real and substantial problem for adults as well as children.

The remainder of this chapter is devoted to a number of described conditions about which some readers might have questions. These include seasonal affective disorder, stress and conditions that the WHO, in ICD-10, terms 'gender identity disorders' and 'disorders of sexual preference'.

Seasonal Affective Disorder

Seasonal affective disorder (SAD) is a condition which has many of the features of depression but occurs chiefly or exclusively in winter. It commonly involves low mood, loss of enjoyment and interest in life, and diminished energy, sociability and interest in sex. Unlike most people with depression, those with SAD are more likely to experience increased sleep and appetite, along with craving for chocolate and high carbohydrate foods (for example, sugary food, white bread). There is usually an improvement in spring and one person in every three with SAD feels more energetic than usual in spring and summer.

Like depression, SAD is more common in women than men, and appears related to reduced light in winter. Treatment can involve self-help techniques (for example, walking during daylight hours in winter) or light therapy: a 'light box' can provide light (2,500 to 10,000 lux) that is like sunlight, but without the ultra-violet rays. It is usually used for 20 to 30 minutes or more per day, depending on the light intensity, ideally at breakfast time. Medical advice is needed. Improvement can occur within a week, although antidepressant medications are also sometimes used, especially selective serotonin reuptake inhibitors (in adults) (Chapter 2).

Stress

Stress is a state of tension or strain resulting from adverse or demanding circumstances, and it occurs primarily when demands appear to exceed resources. A certain amount of stress can help achieve better performance at work or leisure activities, but stress becomes problematic when it is too great, too sustained or produces psychological or physical symptoms. Common symptoms include headaches, irritation, agitation, feeling breathless, fast heartbeat, tense muscles, excessive sweating, difficulty sleeping, stomach upset, racing thoughts, diminished concentration and general nervousness.

The Health and Safety Authority (HSA) advises that work-related stress can result from:

- *Stress from doing your job*, possibly related to monotonous work, too much work, or not enough time;
- *Stress from work relationships*, possibly related to poor teamwork, complex hierarchies, working alone, or harassment and bullying;
- *Stress from working conditions*, possibly related to shift work, dealing with serious injuries, illnesses and deaths, or the threat of violence and aggression.[8]

Other relevant factors include organisational cultures, career structure, home-work interface, task design and work schedules, as well as employee factors.

It is exceptionally difficult to find reliable estimates of the prevalence of stress. Levels of stress fluctuate in most people's lives, and a certain amount of stress is both necessary and healthy. Some surveys suggest that up to 80 per cent of people report significant stress, but these figures are limited by vague definitions of what stress really is and when it is to be considered problematic. It appears likely that most employees experience excessive stress at times, and there is no doubt that certain jobs predispose to stress more than others, especially positions in which the employee has low control over their work-flow (for example, working in the army or in a call centre).

In terms of prevention, the Safety, Health and Welfare at Work Act 2005 requires employers to put in place systems of work which protect their employees from hazards which could lead to mental or physical ill-health. There is also an obligation on employers to 'risk assess' all known hazards including psychosocial hazards which might lead to stress. There is, however, sill much work to be done in this area. In 2014, research from Aware, the national organisation which provides support, education and information on depression and related conditions, showed that half of Irish businesses considered stress and mental health a priority in the workplace, but some 84 per cent did not have a wellness policy or programme in place.[9]

At a personal level, it is important to ensure that work life is carefully balanced with personal and family life, and to recognise that stress can come from any or all of these. Good diet, exercise, lifestyle and socialising are all very important in preventing, managing and reducing stress. In the workplace, there needs to be clear respect for the dignity of each person, appropriate employee involvement with work structures, and fair management procedures for all.

If stress does become a problem, it is important to identify it early on and take steps to address it. This can involve changes in both work and personal life, regardless of which area is the primary source of stress, as both are likely to be affected. The Health Service Executive (HSE) advises:

- Early identification of stress so as to spot the causes and address them when possible (for example, keeping a calendar, or seeking support from family, friends or GP);
- Talking to someone, or writing your concerns out in words;
- Keeping your well-being in mind, and developing good mental health habits (for example, exercising, relaxing, having a good diet, sleeping, doing breathing exercises, and avoiding excessive alcohol or drugs);
- Finding professional support if the problems persist despite these measures (for example, from your GP).[10]

It can also be useful to discuss matters with your employer, as many are now aware that addressing stress at an early stage is not only required by law, but is also good practice and makes economic sense: an increasingly stressed worker is neither constructive nor productive, and will likely require leave from work, possibly for extended periods.

Work stress is a pernicious problem which certainly can be managed but is best prevented. A healthy, balanced lifestyle is the best protector from stress.

Gender Identity Disorders and Disorders of Sexual Preference

The WHO includes 'gender identity disorders' as a category of mental disorder in its *International Classification of Diseases* (ICD-10).[11] This category includes a range of conditions, such as transsexualism, which is a desire to be accepted and live as a member of the opposite sex, generally underpinned by a sense of discomfort with, or inappropriateness of, one's anatomic sex. There is often a desire to have hormonal treatment and/or surgery. For this diagnosis to be made, the WHO specifies that transsexual identity should have been present persistently for at least two years and must not be attributable to another identifiable cause.

It is worth noting that many of these categories are – rightly – highly contested and are subject to change over time. After all, homosexuality was classified as a mental illness by the American Psychiatric Association until 1973 and by the WHO until 1990. In addition, American classification systems now approach this whole area quite differently to the WHO, and it is likely that both approaches will be revised again in the future.

The key issue in relation to many of the categories in this and other areas is distress caused to self or others; if there is distress, this can justify offering support or psychological treatment, although, even then, labelling something as a 'mental illness' still might not be justified, appropriate or helpful for anyone.

The WHO also includes a category of 'disorders of sexual preference' which include *fetishism*, which it defines as a reliance on non-living objects as stimuli for sexual arousal and gratification (for example, shoes). Fetishism should be 'diagnosed' only if the fetish is the most important source of sexual stimulation or is essential for a satisfactory sexual response. *Exhibitionism* is a persistent or recurrent tendency to expose the genitalia to strangers and/or people in public places, without intending or inviting closer contact; this behaviour is generally limited to heterosexual males. *Voyeurism* is a persistent or recurring tendency to look at people engaging in sexual or intimate behaviour (for example, undressing). *Sadomasochism* is a preference for sexual activity that involves bondage or the infliction of pain or humiliation. *Frotteurism* involves rubbing up against people for sexual stimulation in crowded public places (for example, on buses). *Paedophilia* is a sexual preference for children, but more detailed, specialised consideration of this – and the various other matters outlined in this section – are beyond the scope of the present book.

Some of the Useful Resources at the end of this chapter might prove helpful, but more specialist advice, via a GP, is likely to be needed as management of these conditions requires quite specialised input (for example, behaviour therapy, or antiandrogen medication in certain cases of paedophilia). The same is true of sexual dysfunction, which can have physical and psychological components and can often be addressed effectively through a careful combination of physical investigations and treatments and psychological approaches, as indicated in each particular case.

Useful Resources

It is advisable that anyone who thinks he or she has any of the conditions discussed in this book sees a health care professional. There are many reasons for this, including a need to out-rule any other diagnoses, such as physical illnesses. In addition, some people find it easier to talk with a health care professional, especially if they are too uncertain or embarrassed to talk with friends or family members. Often, a brief talk with a GP will 'normalise' the individual's symptoms by reassuring them that they are not alone in what they are experiencing and that help is to hand, if any is needed.

Individuals with any mental disorder or psychological problem, and their families, will find much that is useful on the Internet. As ever, Internet resources need to be evaluated with care and only trusted when the information comes from a reliable source. Reliable information about mental health can be sourced from the websites of the Health Service Executive (www.hse.ie/eng/health/az), College of Psychiatrists of Ireland (www.irishpsychiatry.ie), Royal College of Psychiatrists in London (www.rcpsych.ac.uk), National Health Service in the UK (www.nhs.uk) and National Institute of Mental Health in the US (www.nimh.nih.gov).

Evidence-based guidance about specific treatments can be found on the website of the National Institute for Health and Care Excellence (NICE) (www.nice.org.uk). NICE is a UK-based organisation responsible for developing guidance, standards and information on high-quality health and social care, and preventing and treating ill health.

In addition to the above, there is further information about the Protection of Life During Pregnancy Act 2013 available on the website of the Citizens Information Bureau, along with links to further information and guidance: www.citizensinformation.ie/en/health/health_services/women_s_health/abortion_information_the_law.html

There are interesting, fictional accounts of erotomania in the novel *Enduring Love* by Ian McEwan (London: Jonathan Cape, 1997) and the French film, *He Loves Me ... He Loves Me Not* (Sony Pictures Entertainment, 2002).

The Seasonal Affective Disorder Association offers information and support about seasonal affective disorder (SAD) for professionals and the public (www.sada.org.uk), and the Royal College of Psychiatrists (www.rcpsych.ac.uk) has an especially good leaflet about the condition on their website: www.rcpsych.ac.uk/healthadvice/problemsdisorders/seasonalaffectivedisorder.aspx

With regard to work stress, the Health and Safety Authority (HAS; www.hsa.ie) has produced a very useful document titled *Work-Related Stress: A Guide for Employers* (www.hsa.ie/eng/Publications_and_Forms/Publications/Occupational_Health/Work_Related_Stress_A_Guide_for_Employers.pdf).

The organisation One in Four professionally supports men and women who have experienced sexual abuse during childhood (www.oneinfour.ie).

In addition to the above, there are several other books relating to the themes of this chapter which may also be helpful, including: *Beyond Borderline: True Stories of Recovery from Borderline Personality Disorder* edited by John G. Gunderson and Perry D. Hoffman (New Harbinger, 2016); *Down Came the Rain: My Journey Through Postpartum Depression* by Brooke Shields (Michael Joseph, 2005); *Winter Blues: Everything You Need to Know to Beat Seasonal Affective Disorder* (Fourth Edition) by Norman E. Rosenthal (The Guilford Press, 2013); *Flagging Stress: Toxic Stress and How to Avoid It* by Dr Harry Barry (Liberties Press, 2010); *Sexual Dysfunction: A Guide for Assessment and Treatment* (Third Edition) by John P. Wincze and Rita B. Weisberg (The Guilford Press, 2015).

Endnotes

1 World Health Organisation. *International Classification of Diseases* (10th Edition). Geneva: World Health Organisation, 1992.

2 Daly, A. and Craig, S. HRB Statistics Series 29: Activities of Irish Psychiatric Units and Hospitals 2015. Dublin: Health Research Board, 2016 (Tables 2.6a, 2.6b, 2.14a and 5.3).

3 The study was compiled by the REDEEM research group, based in the Trinity College Institute of Neurosciences (TCIN), Trinity College Dublin and the Irish Obstetric Services from Dublin, Cork, Limerick and Castlebar. The Trinity Team was led by Professor Veronica O'Keane and the Obstetric Services Team was led by Professor Fionnuala McAuliffe, Obstetrician and Gynaecologist at the National Maternity Hospital. This prevalence survey is part of a longer-term research study being undertaken by the REDEEM Group, Trinity, investigating the effects of depression on pregnant women, the foetus and the infant.

4   www.citizensinformation.ie/en/health/health_services/
    women_s_health/abortion_information_the_law.html

5   www.hse.ie/eng/health/az/P/Postnatal-depression

6   www.nhs.uk/Conditions/pregnancy-and-baby/pages/mental-
    health-problems-pregnant.aspx#

7   World Health Organisation. *International Classification of Diseases* (10th Edition). Geneva: World Health Organisation, 1992.

8   www.hsa.ie/eng/Your_Industry/Healthcare_Sector/Work_Related_Stress

9   www.aware.ie/half-of-irish-companies-consider-stress-and-mental-health-in-the-work-place-to-be-a-high-priority

10 www.yourmentalhealth.ie/about-mental-health/common-problems/mental-health-problems/stress

11 World Health Organisation. *International Classification of Diseases* (10th Edition). Geneva: World Health Organisation, 1992.

Chapter 10

Children and Adolescents

Most children and adolescents are mentally well, psychologically balanced and resilient. All that most children and adolescents require for good mental health is a stable, loving family, good relationships at school and with friends, and a sense of belonging. Stability and the absence of conflict in the home are key.

For the minority of children and adolescents who develop psychological problems or mental illness, even despite these advantages, it is critical that services are appropriate, accessible, sensible and effective. This chapter considers the psychological problems and mental illnesses most commonly described in children and adolescents, and outlines management and treatment strategies used to address these. Useful resources are provided at the end of the chapter.

Attention Deficit Hyperactivity Disorder

Approximately 10 per cent of boys and 6 per cent of girls aged between 5 and 10 years have a behavioural or emotional disorder of some description, and the excess in boys is attributable almost entirely to 'attention deficit hyperactivity disorder' (ADHD) and conduct disorders (below). Also known as 'hyperkinetic disorder', ADHD is one of the most controversial concepts in contemporary mental health. This disorder appears to be more common in boys than girls, but estimates of its prevalence vary widely: in certain parts of the US, up to 30 per cent of boys have been diagnosed with the disorder. That is a genuinely disturbing statistic because over-diagnosis is harmful for *all* children, not only for those wrongly diagnosed, but also for those whose genuine problems risk being dismissed as part of a wave of over-diagnosis that is clearly driven, at least in part, by non-medical considerations.

As a result of this and various other trends, ADHD generates endless discussion and debate. Some of this debate is important and admirably focussed on the well-being of children and adults with the cluster of specific problems currently labelled 'ADHD'. But much of the discussion seeks to use the concept of 'ADHD' to make broader arguments about the nature of our societies, arguments that have little to do with psychological well-being or mental health. While these latter discussions are certainly important from sociological and anthropological perspectives, they often cloud consideration of the important mental health and learning issues at hand, especially for children during valuable school years.

From a clinical perspective, some commentators argue that the diagnosis of ADHD is grossly over-used and simply medicalises certain long-recognised behavioural issues which should be dealt with in other, non-'medical' ways. Some say ADHD does not even 'exist'. Clearly, these commentators have a point to a certain extent: ADHD, like all mental illnesses, is defined based on a set of commonly co-occurring symptoms rather than any fixed, specific biological abnormality; that is, there are no scans or blood tests for ADHD. As a result ADHD 'exists' only as a clinical concept or a description of a set of symptoms that are commonly reported to occur together.

But on the other hand, the clinical description of ADHD is a very compelling one, and many commentators point to the undeniable existence of hyper-kinetic (hyperactive) behaviour problems in a small but significant number of children and adults. They argue that, regardless of the label used (currently ADHD but likely to change), any treatment strategies that assist the child or adult to manage problem behaviours, experience less distress and get on with life are greatly to be welcomed.

I tend to agree with the latter group on a pragmatic rather than ideological basis: yes, the diagnostic terminology will change again with time; yes, the clinical description of ADHD will evolve further and is, at best, imprecise; yes, ADHD is probably over-diagnosed, especially in the US; and, yes, critics have a certain point when they say that ADHD does not, in a certain sense, 'exist' as a defined biological entity.

But all of that is to miss the central point, which concerns human suffering: it is an undeniable reality that certain children and adults present with many of the features currently called ADHD and their impairment and distress are very real. Moreover, there are management strategies which can reduce this distress and these should be provided, regardless of whether or not any specific diagnostic label is used. In this context, it is important any disempowering effects of a diagnosis such as ADHD are outweighed by therapeutic benefits following diagnosis. And, equally, it must be clear that receiving a diagnosis of ADHD (or anything else) does *not* mean that all personal responsibility for behaviour is removed. All of the arguments 'against' ADHD should be considered with care but should not prevent or delay delivery of treatments which reduce the distress experienced by people with these symptoms.

At all times, it must be remembered that ADHD, as with all psychiatric diagnoses, is simply a cluster of symptoms that commonly co-occur. Many children have some but not all of the required symptoms, while others have additional symptoms that might just as reasonably have been included in the original definition of ADHD but weren't (and might well be included in the future when criteria are revised again). For any given child (as with any given adult), the key issue is *not* whether this person precisely ticks all the boxes for all the current criteria for ADHD or any other disorder. Rather, the key question is: If this person's symptoms accord roughly with most of the criteria listed for a given disorder such as ADHD, does making such a diagnosis lead us to a management plan or treatment strategy that will be helpful *for this person*?

In other words, what is the point of 'diagnosing' this disorder in this person at this time? How does it *benefit* this person? This is critical: defined diagnoses are not set in stone; diagnostic criteria are changeable guidelines, *not* to be used in a tick-box fashion; and specific diagnoses are only useful insofar as they direct us towards an understanding or treatment or management plan that will help this particular person with whatever symptoms are causing distress. One must be pragmatic and focus on reducing distress and suffering. Ideological arguments about ADHD certainly have their place but they are secondary to the therapeutic considerations and reduction of suffering.

All that being said, and all the critics being duly noted, the key clinical features of ADHD have been described many times in recent decades and now include a fairly reliable cluster of features centred on inattention, distractibility, impulsivity and over-activity. The WHO, in its diagnostic manual, the *International Classification of Diseases* (ICD-10), emphasises the disorder's early onset, and its combination of poorly modulated, overactive behaviour, combined with marked inattention and lack of persistent task involvement.[1] The problem here is that most children demonstrate some if not all of these characteristics at one point or other. The diagnostic threshold for ADHD lies in the presence of more of these features than is common; their early onset (usually in the first 5 or 7 years of life); their pervasiveness in multiple settings (at least two settings, for example, school and home); their persistence over time; and their severity and effects, resulting in significant disruption to the child's home life, school life, etc.

The inattention associated with ADHD is evident in the fact that children with the disorder generally break off from activities, leaving them unfinished; lose interest quickly; and move from activity to activity at a rate out of keeping with their age and IQ. The over-activity is especially apparent in situations requiring calm and concentration, or ones requiring particular self-control. In ADHD this over-activity is out of keeping with the child's age and IQ, and is excessive in the particular situation. It is also relatively common for children with ADHD to also have other disorders, such as conduct disorders or language delay, which can complicate the picture.

The causes of ADHD are not fully known. For at least some children, there appears to be a genetic component, although – as with all other mental disorders – social and personal circumstances also play a part. While parental alcohol abuse is to be avoided, there is no evidence that parenting styles have any influence on the genesis of ADHD, so parents have no reason to feel guilty or responsible if their child is diagnosed with ADHD. In addition, the precise role (if any) of environmental factors such as diet has yet to be determined. As a result, our current understanding of the roots of ADHD is generally unsatisfactory and does not yet provide a clear guide for prevention or the development of new treatments, although understanding will hopefully grow in the coming decades.

Despite this lack of knowledge, there is mounting evidence to support certain treatment approaches to ADHD. Education and training programmes for children and families are central, in combination with classroom interventions by teachers and special needs assistants. These interventions focus on behavioural strategies to reduce and manage problem behaviours, as well as promoting pro-social behaviour and enhanced learning. Co-existing difficulties, such as language delay, can be especially difficult to identify and address owing to the presence of ADHD, but these must still be included in the treatment and management plan from the earliest stage possible: we are treating a child, not an illness.

Treatment can be challenging for all concerned, including, most especially, the child. In February 2016, the National Institute for Health and Care Excellence (NICE) in the UK published very useful, updated, evidence-based guidance on 'attention deficit hy-

peractivity disorder: diagnosis and management'.[2] NICE emphasises the importance of identifying possible ADHD and referring
appropriately; careful diagnosis (which should not be based solely
on rating scales, which are helpful rather than definitive); advice
about diet, behaviour and general care; specific treatments, including psychological treatments, parent-training/education programmes and medication; and careful transition to adult services
for young people with the disorder.

In terms of diagnosis, NICE advises *against* universal screening
for ADHD: most children are fine and there is a real risk of over-diagnosis. If the child's problems with behaviour or attention appear
to indicate ADHD, a school special needs coordinator and the parents should be notified early on. They should then consider a period
of watchful waiting for up to 10 weeks, as well as offering parents
or carers referral to a parent training/education programme. This
referral should not wait for a formal diagnosis of ADHD as such a
programme may be of use for the parents or carers of children who
do not have ADHD but still present significant challenges.

If problems persist, a diagnosis of ADHD should only be made
in secondary care, for example, by a paediatrician, child psychiatrist or other appropriately qualified member of a child and adolescent mental health team. Diagnosis should be based on full clinical and psychosocial assessment, developmental and psychiatric
history and assessment of mental state. Social, family, educational
and occupational circumstances, as well as physical health, should
all be considered. Rating scales may also be helpful but are not, on
their own, definitive.

NICE recommends that, following diagnosis, a balanced diet,
good nutrition and regular exercise are important. There are no
foods that all children with ADHD should be advised to avoid, but
if a particular child appears to be affected by a particular food, the
matter should be discussed with a dietitian and the child and adolescent mental health team. For pre-school children, drug treatment is not recommended but parents or carers should be referred

to a parent training/education programme. It is important that the child's nursery or pre-school teacher is also involved in the plan and any special educational needs are identified and addressed both at school and at home.

For school-age children with ADHD and moderate impairment, NICE recommends group-based parent-training/education programmes as the usual first-line intervention. This can include group psychological treatment (cognitive behavioural therapy or social skills training) for younger children and individual psychological treatment for older age groups. Treatment with medication may be tried next for those with moderate levels of impairment or severe symptoms. For those with severe impairment, medication is recommended as a first-line intervention, along with parent-training/education programmes. If this is not acceptable to the patient or parents/guardian, psychological interventions can be tried but NICE warns that these are not as effective as medication for those with severe impairment. In all cases, it is important that, with consent, the child's teacher is aware of the plan; classroom behavioural interventions, when possible, are very helpful.

Before commencing medication, it is important that there is a full history and medical examination, including assessment of heart rate, blood pressure, height, weight and family history (for example, of cardiac disease). An electrocardiogram (ECG or heart tracing) is advised if there is a relevant family history, along with a risk assessment for substance misuse or medication diversion (that is, the child giving the tablets to someone else).

NICE notes that the choice of medication depends on a series of factors and, broadly, recommends methylphenidate, atomoxetine and dexamfetamine within their licenced indications. At time of writing, all three of these medications are licensed for use in certain children aged 6 years and over in Ireland, subject to specific conditions and as part of comprehensive treatment programmes. Up-to-date licensing information should always be sought from the website of the Health Products Regulatory Authority (www.hpra.ie).

NICE recommends methylphenidate for ADHD without significant co-existing problems or when it is accompanied by conduct disorder (see below). Either methylphenidate or atomoxetine is recommended if the ADHD is accompanied by tics, Tourette's syndrome (a neurological disorder with involuntary tics and vocalisations; see below), anxiety disorder, misuse of stimulants, or risk of stimulant diversion. Methylphenidate and dexamfetamine appear to increase levels of dopamine, a specific chemical in the brain, while atomoxetine increases noradrenaline, another brain chemical, among other effects.

It is important to monitor for side effects. With atomoxetine, there should be particular vigilance for irritability, agitation, suicidal thinking, self-harming behaviour or unusual changes in behaviour, particularly in the months after commencement or following a change in dose. This should be explained to parents or carers who should bring any such side effects to the attention of healthcare professionals as soon as they occur. Parents and carers should also be aware of the possibility (albeit rare) of liver damage with atomoxetine; signs can include abdominal pain, nausea, malaise, jaundice or darkening of the urine.

For adults with ADHD, NICE recommends that medication (under specialist supervision) should be the first line of treatment, unless the person prefers a psychological approach. As with children, there should be a detailed pre-medication assessment, and the overall treatment plan should include not just medication but also elements addressing behavioural, psychological, educational and occupational needs. Methyphenidate is recommended by NICE as the medication of choice, but is not licensed for new treatment in adults in Ireland at time of writing. NICE suggests that if first-line treatment does not prove sufficient or the patient cannot tolerate it, atomoxetine (licensed for adults in Ireland, under certain conditions) or dexamfetamine (not licensed for adults in Ireland) can be considered. For atomoxetine, there should be careful warnings similar to those outlined for children (see above), especially in younger people and early in treatment. As with children, careful, specialist supervision is needed.

NICE also provides additional guidance for situations when there is a poor response to treatment, when a child with ADHD is transitioning to adult mental health services, titration of medication doses, monitoring side effects, discontinuation issues, future research directions and various other matters.

In terms of outcome, hyperactivity in children usually decreases by adolescence but for some children ADHD persists into adulthood. Treatment, as outlined above, can help significantly, but the diagnosis is often missed in adulthood, as it may present in the form of apparent antisocial behaviour. Notwithstanding these challenges, it is important that the diagnosis is made: ADHD, although currently over-diagnosed in some places (for example, parts of the US), causes substantial difficulties for those who suffer from it, and for their families. Early, effective and sensible treatment is important, as is greater understanding of the nature and effects of this puzzling, evolving disorder.

Conduct Disorders

Conduct disorders are childhood conditions characterised by repetitive and persistent patterns of dissocial, disruptive, aggressive or defiant conduct. As with all childhood disorders, the child's stage of development needs to be taken into consideration before reaching a diagnosis. According to ICD-10, the behaviour, at its most difficult, should represent a major violation of age-appropriate social expectations, and significantly exceed the threshold for ordinary childish mischief or adolescent rebellion.

Isolated criminal or antisocial acts are not sufficient for a diagnosis of conduct disorder; there needs to be an enduring *pattern* of behaviour. This can include excessive fighting or bullying; cruelty to other people or animals; severe destruction of property; setting fires; stealing; multiple episodes of lying; running away from home and truanting from school; unusually severe and frequent temper tantrums; provocative and defiant behaviour; and severe, persistent disobedience. These behaviours need to persist for six months or longer to create a case for the diagnosis.

In some cases, conduct disorder can be confined to the family context and the child may or may not be integrated into a peer group ('socialised' and 'unsocialised' conduct disorder, respectively). 'Oppositional defiant disorder' is the type of conduct disorder most characteristically seen in children under the age of 9 or 10 years. This involves notably disobedient, defiant, provocative behaviour without the more severe aggressive or dissocial acts that violate the rights of others, or the law, and are seen in other forms of conduct disorder. But, as with all conduct disorder, the behaviour of the child must clearly lie outside the range of what is normal for the child's personal context, age and IQ.

While the underlying causes of conduct disorder are unclear, it is often associated with lower socio-economic groups, family disharmony and parental alcohol dependence. Treatment is focussed on a psycho-social understanding of the child's problems, and can include group or individual parent training and education. A cognitive-behavioural approach and teaching in social skills can help reduce aggressive behaviours and improve socialisation in unsocialised conduct disorder. In adolescence, antipsychotic and antidepressant medications are sometimes used, but the evidence for these is slim.

In terms of outcome, conduct disorder may well resolve in time, but it is also the case that problem behaviours may persist into adult life, and may be associated with later substance misuse and crime. Children with oppositional defiant disorder tend to get on better than those with other forms of conduct disorder, although outcomes are enormously variable in practice and a great deal depends on the stability and supportiveness of the family situation.

Emotional and Anxiety Disorders

Children can develop any of the mental illnesses seen in adults, including anxiety and depression, in addition to patterns of emotional disorder which appear somewhat specific to childhood. The latter include separation anxiety, phobic anxiety disorder of childhood and social anxiety disorder of childhood.

Separation anxiety occurs when fear about separation clearly exceeds normal levels and is associated with difficulties in social functioning. The anxiety is generally focussed on family members and reflects a preoccupying worry that a specific person (for example, parent) will come to harm or fail to return, or that the child will become separated from the person in some other way (for example, kidnapped or lost). There may also be refusal to go to sleep, fear of being alone, nightmares and various physical symptoms. Behavioural and family interventions are indicated when symptoms become significantly disabling or troubling for the child. Similar approaches are recommended for sibling rivalry, if it exceeds the normal level of rivalry seen between children, especially following the arrival of a younger sibling.

Other anxiety disorders can also present in childhood, including specific phobias (for example, phobias of the dark or strangers), generalised anxiety (often accompanied by reports of stomach pain), and obsessive-compulsive disorder (OCD; Chapter 5). Great care must be taken with diagnosis of OCD, however, as isolated obsessions and compulsions are very common in childhood, for example, not walking on cracks between paving stones, touching things with one hand and then the other ('an even mind'), or counting. If, however, the obsessions and compulsions reach a pathological level, cognitive behavioural therapy (CBT) (with family involvement) can help. There is also an evidence base for certain antidepressant medications in OCD (for example, sertraline for children aged 6 years or over, or fluvoxamine for children over 8 years old) which can be used under specialist supervision (see below) when the situation is especially challenging.

Bereavement reactions can also occur in children and are characterised by poor sleep, bed-wetting, temper tantrums, diminished school performance and/or behaviour problems. Grieving can be a complex, lengthy process and it is important to give the child genuine opportunity to discuss their anxieties, which may relate to the possible loss of other key figures, quite sophisticated reflections on the inevitability of death, or concerns centred on the remaining parent following a parental loss.

School refusal is sometimes regarded as a mental illness specific to childhood but is probably better seen as a behaviour pattern which can incorporate many elements, ranging from separation anxiety to conduct problems. In younger children, school refusal can have many of the features of separation anxiety, but school transitions can also be relevant (for example, at ages 11 or 12 years), as can low self-esteem, bullying and depression (especially in older children). A majority of children have good outcomes following abrupt or gradual resumption of school attendance. A minority go on to have persistent difficulties with school or agoraphobia as adults. In all cases, it is important to recognise the child's particular stage of development, the importance of school and social environments as settings for their symptoms, and the need for a management plan that recognises both the child's distress and the imperative to continue with education and social participation.

Depression

Depression can occur in childhood and adolescence, and can display many of the features of the various other disorders discussed above, especially emotional and anxiety disorders. See Chapter 2 for a broader discussion of common symptoms and features of depression more generally.

In March 2015, NICE updated its guidance on 'Depression in children and young people: identification and management' and emphasised the importance of training healthcare professionals in a range of settings (schools, primary care, community settings) to recognise both the symptoms of depression and its risk factors, such as bullying, abuse, substance misuse or parental depression.[3]

In terms of treatment, there is a strong focus on psychological therapies rather than medication in children and adolescents, combined with support in family and educational contexts. More specifically, NICE describes a stepped care model that balances risk of under-treatment with the complexities of treatment in this age group. For mild depression, NICE recommends watchful waiting, general supportive therapy, or cognitive behavioural therapy (CBT) delivered in a group setting. Guided self-help is another option, combined with general family assistance and school support. If the child's depression is moderate or severe, however, NICE recommends brief psychological therapy and, possibly, fluoxetine, an antidepressant medication (under specialist supervision). For treatment-resistant depression, intensive psychological therapy may be needed, or other medication (for example, other antidepressants or even augmentation with antipsychotic medication, under specialist supervision).

Licences for these medications in specific age groups should be checked on the website of the Health Products Regulatory Authority (www.hpra.ie). At time of writing, fluoxetine is licensed in Ireland for children and adolescents aged 8 years and above, for moderate to severe major depressive episode, if depression is unresponsive to psychological therapy after four to six sessions. The medication should be offered to a child or young person with moderate to severe depression only in combination with concurrent psychological therapy.

The use of psychiatric medication in children is perennially controversial but many of the same basic principles apply as with adults: medication should only be used when it is as clear as possible that the benefits exceed the risks. In children with severe depression, the stakes are very high, as valuable months of education can be missed and the normal trajectory of childhood development can be disturbed. On the other hand, all medications are associated with various side effects and risks, and the risk profiles for these medications in children can differ significantly from the risk profiles in adults. All of this necessitates careful, constructive thought focussed clearly on the well-being and education of the child. Careful, attentive, specialist supervision is needed.

If moderate to severe depression in a child does not respond to psychological therapy, NICE recommends careful multi-disciplinary review, and states that issues such as family discord or parental mental ill health should be identified and addressed. Alternative psychological therapy should also be considered, but if none of these steps produce sufficient benefit, fluoxetine is an option if the child is over the age of 12 years. This medication is sometimes used very cautiously in younger children (5 to 11 years) but it has not been proven effective in this age group. NICE advises that fluoxetine is the only antidepressant for which there is evidence that benefits outweigh risks in children with depression.

Antidepressants should only be offered in combination with psychological therapy following consultation with a child and adolescent psychiatrist, and with careful arrangements for follow-up monitoring (for example, weekly contact). There is particular need to monitor for the emergence of any suicidal behaviour, self-harm or hostility, especially at the start of treatment. A warning about suicidality associated with particular antidepressants (selective serotonin reuptake inhibitors) in children was issued by the US Food and Drug Administration (FDA) in 2003 and this was endorsed by the Irish Medicines Board later that year. The Medicines and Health Regulatory Agency in the UK also recommended withdrawing use of all selective serotonin reuptake inhibitors in children with depression, except for fluoxetine.

In 2005, the Irish Medicines Board (now Health Products Regulatory Authority) issued one of a number of warnings about antidepressants in young people and recommended changes to product information to include (a) a warning to remind prescribers that common antidepressants (selective serotonin reuptake inhibitors and selective noradrenaline reuptake inhibitors) should not be used in children and adolescents under 18 years of age; (b) a statement that if a clinical decision to treat is taken, patients should be carefully monitored for suicidal symptoms; (c) a statement that studies have shown increased risk of suicide attempts, suicidal thoughts and hostility (aggression, oppositional behaviour, anger); and (d) a statement indicating that long-term safety in children and adolescents has not been proven. Further warnings and up-to-date information are available from their website, www.hpra.ie, including information regarding increased suicidal thoughts with antidepressants and advice to seek care urgently if someone is affected in this way.

In 2015, an important research study looked at the effects of such warnings on prescription of antidepressants to children in Ireland.[4] The study showed that use of antidepressants in children declined by 45 per cent between 2002 (before the warnings) and 2008 (after the warnings). In 2008, Ireland's rate of antidepressant prescribing in children was lower than that in the US, similar to that in the UK, and higher than those in Denmark and Germany. Also in 2008, the warning from the Irish Medicines Board was reiterated and revised, extending the warning up to age 25 years. It was re-emphasised by the Board in 2009 that close supervision of patients is recommended, and caregivers are advised to monitor for clinical disimprovements, suicidal behaviour or thoughts, and unusual changes in behaviour (and to seek medical advice immediately).

If the antidepressant produces substantial improvement which is sustained for eight weeks, it should then be continued for a minimum of a further six months in order to consolidate recovery. If fluoxetine does not produce sufficient improvement, and if symptoms persist, careful consideration can be given to other treatments, although the evidence base for these is much weaker, and careful, specialist advice and supervision are needed.

More detailed guidance on the use of medication in children is beyond the scope of this book, especially as medications are sometimes used 'off licence' (that is, outside of formal guidelines) in cases of severe distress which are not covered by current treatment advice, prescribing protocols, or official medication licences. This level of treatment of childhood depression should only be undertaken by specialist, multi-disciplinary teams, and child and adolescent psychiatrists. Guidance in this matter is continually evolving so the advice in this book might well be incomplete or out-of-date at time of reading. It is advised to check the website of the Health Products Regulatory Authority (www.hpra.ie) in order to see the most up-to-date position about specific medications, and to consult with specialist services for detailed or more specific advice on this important, complex topic.

Much of the treatment of childhood depression occurs as an outpatient. Inpatient care can be indicated if the child or young person presents an especially high risk of suicide, serious self-harm or self-neglect, or when intensive, highly-supervised treatment is needed. Suicide is rare in children and self-harm is more common, especially among girls. There are few studies of suicide among children in Ireland, but one 2008 study found that suicide rates in children rose between 1993 and 2008, especially among older boys (aged 15 to 17 years), whose rate reached 13.5 suicides per 100,000 population per year during the period 2003-2008.[5] The equivalent rate for girls was 5.1, which is lower but is also an increase since 1993-1998.

These figures indicate that while suicide remains a rare event among children, it is certainly not unknown and may well be increasing. This stands in marked contrast with Ireland's overall suicide rate, which is decreasing in recent years (Chapter 11). Recognising and treating depression in children is an important element in addressing suicide in this age group. It is also important to recognise and treat bipolar affective disorder (manic depression), which is rare in children but can occur, and needs to be managed with care and understanding (see Chapter 4 of this book for information about bipolar affective disorder more generally).

Other Mental Disorders in Children and Adolescents

Elective or selective mutism (not speaking) can occur at any age, and is sometimes prominent in certain situations (for example, school) but not others (for example, home). The condition is generally diagnosed only if the elective mutism lasts for more than one month (a month that is not the first month of school); interferes with educational or social activity; and is not attributable to lack of knowledge. Developmental delay is often a feature, as is shyness, and social phobia may develop in the future. Treatment, which should involve both family and school (if indicated), focuses not on speaking itself but on reducing the anxiety associated with speaking. Removing pressure to speak and addressing anxiety are central. There is good advice about this for families and others on the National Health Service 'NHS Choices' website.[6] Prognosis is generally good.

Other conditions seen in children include reactive attachment disorder, which is characterised by difficulties in a child's pattern of relationships, generally commencing before the age of 5 years. Treatment for this centres on consistent parenting.

Enuresis is the medical term used for bed-wetting or daytime involuntary bladder emptying, which occurs in 10 per cent of 5-year-olds, 5 per cent of 10-year-olds, and 1 per cent of 18-year-olds. Twice as common in boys as girls, treatment centres on ensuring there is no physical cause (for example, infection); regularising fluid intake and toileting; 'star charts' to encourage adhering to the treatment plan; alarm devices activated by moisture, to discourage bed-wetting; and, if the condition is severe, short-term medication such as desmopressin (from age 5, under specialist guidance).

The HSE website offers clear and useful information about bed-wetting (www.hse.ie/eng/health/az/B/Bedwetting), as does the NHS Choices website (www.nhs.uk/Conditions/Bedwetting), which also covers encopresis (www.nhs.uk/Conditions/encopresis), the medical term for depositing faeces (poo) in inappropriate places despite being able to control bowel movements normally. Most children are continent of faeces by age 4 years, although 2 per cent of boys and 1 per cent of girls display encopresis at the age of 8 years. Treatment centres on ensuring there is no physical cause (for example, Hirschprung's disease, a nerve problem in the bowels); ignoring soiling as much as possible, so that the child realises this is not an effective way to express anger or other emotions; improving child-parent relationships in other ways; and use of 'star charts' to modify behaviour.

Tic disorders are conditions characterised by repetitive, stereotyped and purposeless movements or vocalisations (for example, blinking, shrugging shoulders or involuntarily saying words). Complex tics include jumping or gesturing obscenities. Suppressing tics leads to increased anxiety. Tics may be temporary (lasting up to one year) or chronic (more than one year), and they affect up to one child in every five before the age of 10 years. Tics are more common in boys than girls.

Tourette's Syndrome is a specific tic disorder involving multiple motor tics and one or more vocal tics for more than one year. The syndrome affects 1 per cent of children between the ages of 5 and 18 years and there is often a family history of tics or OCD. The causes are unclear, but the syndrome usually commences around age 7 years with facial tics and 11 with vocal tics, which may include coprolalia (involuntary swearing). There may also be co-existing ADHD, OCD or other disorders. Management centres on education for patient and family; comprehensive behavioural intervention (along the lines of cognitive behaviour therapy); treatment of co-existing ADHD or OCD, if these are present; and medications, such as clonidine (unlicensed for children in Ireland) or certain antipsychotic medications (limited licenses in Ireland), under specialist supervision.

Developmental Disorders

The area of developmental disorders has received considerably increased attention in recent decades, with particular attention paid to 'autism spectrum disorders' such as Asperger's Syndrome. It is, in the first instance, important to remember that many children will have some but not all of the features of these 'developmental disorders' at various stages of childhood, so great care needs to be taken when reading descriptions of them or when discussing these disorders with other people. Many children also go through phases which can appear decidedly peculiar at the time, but which resolve over the following months, and these children subsequently get along fine. Others, with persisting difficulties causing substantial disruption, can have specific, demarcated reading difficulties or dyslexia, or substantial problems with arithmetic calculations (dyscalculia) but no other features of developmental disorders; for these children, educational and psychological inputs should focus on the specific needs identified.

Some children, however, may demonstrate some or all of the features of 'autism spectrum disorders', a broad term which is generally taken to include autism and Asperger's Syndrome. While diagnosis can be challenging, ICD-10 outlines quite helpful diagnostic guidelines for 'childhood autism', noting that developmental problems in autism become apparent before the age of 3 years, with particular impairment of social interactions, for example, failing to respond to the emotions of others or to the social context; diminished social use of language skills; reduced make-believe and imitative play; impaired emotional responses; and diminished richness of communication (reduced gesturing, etc.). There are also repetitive, restricted patterns of behaviour and interests; excessive rigidity in routines and rituals; and, sometimes, problems with eating, sleeping, tantrums and, occasionally, self-injury (for example, wrist biting).

The clinical picture and severity of autism can vary enormously, but diminished emotional and communicative responsiveness to others is generally a central feature. There is impaired intelligence (low IQ) in some but certainly not all cases. ICD-10 also outlines 'atypical autism' which lacks some of the characteristic features of autism because it generally occurs in people with co-existing severe intellectual disability which might prevent them from displaying all the features of autism. Rett's Syndrome is a rare, related condition in girls, associated with loss of hand skills and speech, among other symptoms, at the age of 7 to 24 months, along with growth anomalies and interrupted social development; this condition follows a different course to autism and requires specialist care.

Asperger's Syndrome is, perhaps, the most controversial and discussed feature of the 'autism spectrum'. ICD-10 associates the diagnosis with qualitative abnormalities of reciprocal social interaction similar to those seen in autism, accompanied by a repetitive, restricted repertoire of activities and interests. There is, however, generally no disturbance of language development or cognitive development, apart from a narrowing of focus. Intelligence levels are generally normal but the condition can be associated with clumsiness.

The big problem with this diagnosis is that many people with Asperger's Syndrome take the position – very reasonably – that they do not have a 'disorder' at all. They hold the view that they are simply neuro-developmentally different from some other people, with a different mix of strengths and weaknesses. Some people with autism share this view. They do not regard themselves as 'disordered' or 'mentally ill' and they urge others to accept their neuro-diversity. Others, however, express great relief at a diagnosis of Asperger's Syndrome, seeing it as an explanation of why they have had long-standing difficulties with emotions and communications, despite being normally intelligent or – as is often the case – exceptionally intelligent or capable in specific ways. Such exceptional abilities can also occur in autism but are far more common, and possibly even the norm, in Asperger's Syndrome.

All of this brings us back to the central issue of what diagnoses in psychiatry actually mean (if anything), given that they are based on commonly co-occurring clusters of symptoms rather than specific, demonstrated biological anomalies: there are no scans or blood tests for most mental disorders, including autism and Asperger's Syndrome. As a result, and as already discussed at the start of this chapter, the key question is this: if this person accords roughly with most of the criteria listed for a given disorder, does that lead us to a management plan or treatment strategy that will be helpful for this person? Does it help with self-understanding? How does making this diagnosis at this time *benefit* this person?

In the case of children diagnosed with autism, there are clear reasons for reaching a clear and early diagnosis. First, recognising autism in a child reassures the parents that challenges they are facing with their child *are not in any way their fault*. While the causes of autism are not fully known, it now appears that genetics and pre-birth problems can be involved. And it is also clear that the disorder is *not* attributable to parental behaviour: most parents of children with autism are genuinely excellent parents who respond to the (often considerable) challenges of autism with astonishing ability, forbearance and love. They – and their children and broader families – deserve all the support and consideration that can be provided to them.

Second, early recognition of autism is important because intensive behavioural treatment (over 25 hours per week) can assist significantly with communication and cognitive skills in autism, as well as rewarding appropriate and discouraging inappropriate behaviour (known as 'applied behaviour analysis'). The HSE website helpfully explains this and a range of other potential treatments including TEACCH (an educational intervention emphasising structured learning with visual prompts), speech and language therapy, and medication: while there are no medications for core features of autism, certain antidepressants are sometimes used (outside of licensing guidelines, under specialist supervision) for repetitive thoughts and behaviour, and for problems related to aggression (for example, tantrums, self-harming).[7] Family support is also critical in optimising outcomes and quality of life for all concerned.

For all these interventions, it is important that the full range of areas affected by autism are addressed, including communication, social interaction, cognitive and academic skills. Unfortunately, a 2012 HSE 'National Review of Autism Services' concluded that:

> geographically, current services can vary from robust, comprehensive and integrative to isolated, patchy and ineffective. Moreover, differing models and approaches to the provision of health services are evident across Local Health Office (LHO) areas and HSE areas. This current model is no longer appropriate or sustainable in providing equity of access and intervention.[8]

On the positive side, the report recommended:

> a consistent clear pathway on how services can be accessed for children ... through the reconfiguration of autism services for children and young people.

It is to be hoped that future years see further progress in building on this report and providing equitable, effective services for those with autism. The importance of this cannot be overstated. People with autism (and other enduring neurodevelopmental differences) and their families are among the most neglected citizens in our democracy: they deserve better services and supports if they are to achieve their full potential, participate more fully in society, and enjoy the optimal, fully realised lives to which they are entitled.

Accessing Child and Adolescent Mental Health Services

Access to child and adolescent mental health services is primarily through referral by a GP, as outlined for adults in Chapter 12. The vast majority of children and adolescents with psychological or mental health problems are treated in primary care without referral to specialist mental health services. Many GPs and primary care teams provide various forms of care themselves, including counselling, support, medication and other treatments. They can also refer the child or adolescent to other local sources of treatment and support.

In terms of the most appropriate pathway for referral onward, the HSE provides a useful 'Summary of Appropriate Referrals to Child Psychology/Counselling in Primary Care and Specialist Child and Adolescent Mental Health Teams' in a 2012 guidance document on 'Advancing the Shared Care Approach between Primary Care and Specialist Mental Health Services'.[9] The HSE advises that problems appropriate for child counselling in primary care (through GP referral, as opposed to Child and Adolescent Mental Health Services) include mild to moderate problems with depression and low self-esteem; general anxiety and mild/specific phobias; behaviour problems; bereavement and loss; coping with injury or illness; stress; and trauma. Problems appropriate for Child and Adolescent Mental Health Services include moderate to severe problems with significant mood disorder; anxiety disorders (for example, OCD); ADHD; eating disorders; psychotic disorders; suicidal ideation/intent and/or deliberate self-harm.

Throughout these referral processes it is imperative that the best interests of the child or adolescent are central to the process. In the rare cases when psychiatric admission is indicated, such admission should ideally occur in a dedicated child and adolescent mental health unit. In 2015 there were 503 inpatient admissions of persons aged under 18 years to Irish psychiatric hospitals and units, of which 407 (81 per cent) were to specialised child and adolescent inpatient units.[10] The remainder were admitted to adult facilities, which is deeply regrettable. Admission diagnoses included depression (32 per cent); neuroses, for example, anxiety disorders (13 per cent); eating disorders (12 per cent); and schizophrenia (9 per cent). Of the 503 admissions of persons under the age of 18 years, 17 (3 per cent) were involuntary, of whom 41 per cent had depression and 29 per cent had schizophrenia. While schizophrenia is rare in children, it can occur, especially in teenagers, and specialist treatment is needed (Chapter 3).

Overall, there is an urgent and long-standing need to provide adequate specialised inpatient facilities for children and adolescents with mental illness so that it is no longer necessary to admit them to adult facilities. Enhanced outpatient care is also needed, centred on multi-disciplinary services that are appropriate, accessible and effective in meeting the needs of children, adolescents and their families. The establishment in 2016 of a National Taskforce on Youth Mental Health by Minister Helen McEntee, Minister of State for Mental Health and Older People, represents an important commitment to progress in this area.

Useful Resources

It is advisable that anyone who thinks he, she or their child has any of the conditions discussed in this book sees a health care professional. There are many reasons for this, including a need to rule out any other diagnoses, such as physical illnesses. In addition, some people find it easier to talk with a health care professional, especially if they are too uncertain or embarrassed to talk with friends or family members. Often, a brief talk with a GP will 'normalise' the individual's symptoms by reassuring them that they are not alone in what they are experiencing and that help is to hand, if any is needed.

Individuals with any mental disorder or psychological problem, and their families, will find much that is useful on the Internet. As ever, Internet resources need to be evaluated with care and only trusted when the information comes from a reliable source. Reliable information about mental health can be sourced from the websites of the Health Service Executive (www.hse.ie), College of Psychiatrists of Ireland (www.irishpsychiatry.ie), Royal College of Psychiatrists in London (www.rcpsych.ac.uk), National Health Service in the UK (www.nhs.uk) and National Institute of Mental Health in the US (www.nimh.nih.gov).

There is extensive information about accessing mental health services in Ireland at www.yourmentalhealth.ie. Services which can be accessed directly include the following:

- Childline provides a free and confidential listening service to children and young people up to the age of 18. Their free helpline is 1800 666 666. For their Teentxt service, text the word 'Talk' to 50101. Childline Online Chat (www.childline.ie) is open daily between 10.00 am and 10.00 pm.

- Jigsaw is a network of programmes across Ireland designed to ensure that every young person has somewhere to turn to and someone to talk to. There are Jigsaw projects in many communities across Ireland and further information can be accessed at www.jigsaw.ie.

- ReachOut.com provides quality mental health information aimed at helping young people get through tough times.

- SpunOut.ie offers a range of health information for young people, covering mental health, sexual health, exam stress and general lifestyle information.

The National Institute for Health and Care Excellence (NICE) guidance on 'attention deficit hyperactivity disorder: diagnosis and management' (February 2016) is, like all NICE guidance, available to download free of charge from their website: www.nice.org.uk/Guidance/cg72. NICE guidance on 'depression in children and young people: identification and management' is also available on the website: www.nice.org.uk/guidance/cg28. The NICE website is an excellent, free resource.

The HSE (www.hse.ie) and NHS Choices websites (www.nhs.uk) make enormous amounts of reliable, sensible information available to the public, covering many of the disorders mentioned in this chapter, as well as more common issues such as sleep problems in children (www.nhs.uk/Conditions/pregnancy-and-baby/Pages/sleep-problems-in-children.aspx), among other topics.

The late, renowned neurologist Oliver Sacks wrote a fascinating account of Tourette's Syndrome ('Witty Ticcy Ray') in his masterful book, *The Man Who Mistook His Wife for a Hat* (Gerald Duckworth, 1985). Sacks also wrote about this case in the *London Review of Books* (19 March 1981); all of Sacks' essays and books are richly worth reading.

There is now a vast literature on autism, Asperger's Syndrome and various developmental disorders; for example: *Autism and Creativity: Is There a Link between Autism in Men and Exceptional Ability?* by M. Fitzgerald (Brunner-Routledge, 2004); *Far from the Tree: Parents, Children and the Search for Identity* by A. Solomon (Chatto and Windus, 2013); *Neurotribes: The Legacy of Autism and How to Think Smarter About People Who Think Differently*, by S. Silberman (Avery/Penguin Random House LLC, 2015); *The Reason I Jump* by Naoki Higashida (Sceptre, 2013). The material in this book was written by a child with autism. It is a superb. touching book. It was translated by K.A. Yoshida and David Mitchell, and has an introduction by David Mitchell.

For all of these sources of information, it is wise to read the information provided in a careful, measured way, and to consult your GP if you feel your child has specific problems or requires information, help or support in relation to any emotional, psychological or psychiatric issues.

Endnotes

1   World Health Organisation. *International Classification of Diseases* (10th Edition). Geneva: World Health Organization, 1992, pp. 262-3.

2   https://www.nice.org.uk/guidance/cg72

3   https://www.nice.org.uk/guidance/cg28

4   O'Sullivan, K., Boland, F., Reulbach, U., Motterlini, N., Kelly, D., Bennett, K. and Fahey T. 'Antidepressant prescribing in Irish children: Secular trends and international comparison in the context of a safety warning'. *BMC Pediatrics* 2015; 15:119.

5   Malone, K.M., Quinlivan, L., McGuinness, S., McNicholas, F. and Kelleher, C. 'Suicide in children over two decades: 1993-2008'. *Irish Medical Journal* 2012; 105: 231-3.

6   www.nhs.uk/conditions/selective-mutism

7   www.hse.ie/eng/health/az/A/Asperger-syndrome

8   www.hse.ie/eng/services/Publications/Disability/autismservices.html, p. 57.

9   HSE Working Sub Group on Mental Health in Primary Care. Advancing the Shared Care Approach between Primary Care and Specialist Mental Health Services: A Guidance Document. Dublin: HSE, 2012 (p. 19).

10 Daly, A. and Craig, S. HRB Statistics Series 29: Activities of Irish Psychiatric Units and Hospitals 2015. Dublin: Health Research Board, 2016 (p. 18).

Chapter 11

SUICIDE AND DELIBERATE SELF-HARM

The rate of suicide in Ireland has been in decline for several years, but deliberate self-harm and suicide are still urgent problems. This chapter examines several key areas relating to suicide and deliberate self-harm, including:

◊   What are suicide and deliberate self-harm?

◊   What should I do if someone says they are suicidal?

◊   How common are suicide and deliberate self-harm?

◊   Can suicide and deliberate self-harm be predicted and prevented?

◊   Homicide and murder-suicide.

Useful resources and sources of further information are provided at the end of the chapter.

What Are Suicide and Deliberate Self-harm?

Suicide is intentional self-killing and features in every society for which there is recorded history. Deliberate self-harm is the intentional infliction of non-fatal harm on oneself and includes a wide variety of methods such as overdosing and self-cutting. Suicide and deliberate self-harm in Ireland merit a separate book for themselves, both because the topics are important and because their histories in Ireland are significantly under-researched.

In the early 1900s, it was generally thought that Ireland had a low suicide rate, which is said to have increased significantly as the twentieth century progressed, with some fluctuation. In 1954, the Central Statistics Office reported the annual average number of deaths from suicide in Ireland was 89 between 1921 and 1930 (giving a rate of 3.0 per 100,000 population per year), 98 between 1931 and 1940 (3.3 per 100,000 population per year), and 77 between 1941 and 1950 (2.6 per 100,000 population per year).[1] Suicide was likely under-reported during this period and, in 1967, the Central Statistics Office introduced a new form (Form 104) to improve recording accuracy and facilitate study. During much of this period, suicide was a felony under Irish law and attempted suicide was a misdemeanour; both offences were abolished in 1993 with the Criminal Law (Suicide) Act.

In 1962, the Samaritans were established in Ireland and their volunteers provide a listening service to anyone who contacts them; many, but not all, of those who contact them are suicidal (www.samaritans.org; telephone 116 123; email jo@samaritans.org). By 2016, there were 20 Samaritans branches across Ireland with 2,400 active volunteers doing extraordinarily skilled, selfless work; their contribution to Irish society is literally beyond measure.

In 1996, the Irish Association of Suicidology was founded by Dr John Connolly, Dr Michael Kelleher and Mr Dan Neville TD, to work with community, voluntary and statutory bodies to inform, educate and promote positive suicide prevention policies. It is a forum where various organisations can come together and exchange knowledge regarding any aspect of suicidology gained from differing perspectives and experiences (www.ias.ie).

Today, there are a number of sources of information and statistics about suicide and deliberate self-harm, including the National Suicide Research Foundation, an independent, multidisciplinary research unit that investigates the causes of suicide and deliberate self-harm in Ireland (www.nsrf.ie). The National Office for Suicide Prevention (NOSP) was set up in 2005 within the Health Service

Executive (HSE) to oversee the implementation, monitoring and coordination of 'Reach Out: National Strategy for Action on Suicide Prevention, 2005-2014', Ireland's first national suicide prevention strategy. NOSP is now a core part of the HSE National Mental Health Division, strongly aligned with mental health promotion and specialist mental health services (www.nosp.ie).

The limits of the definitions of suicide and deliberate self-harm are the subject of continual debate. For example, most people would agree that intentionally cutting one's wrists constitutes deliberate self-harm, but what about smoking cigarettes? Most people are aware that smoking reduces life expectancy due to smoking-related diseases like heart disease and cancer. Does this mean that smoking is also a form of deliberate self-harm?

There are similar questions about the definition of suicide. For example, if a person who routinely uses illegal drugs is aware that their level of drug use is such that they could easily die of an 'accidental' overdose, does that mean that if they are found dead following drug use the death is a form of suicide?

In this context, it is useful to consider the concept of a 'sub-intended' death. This can occur when a person might not identify a single moment when they decide to end their own life, but rather makes a series of choices which indicate, at the very least, significant ambivalence about living and dying, for example, routine excessive use of alcohol or drugs, despite knowing the risks.

Thus, a death that results from a person knowingly taking risks can be considered a 'sub-intended' death, that is, a death which is linked to a partial death-wish. Many deaths fit this category, especially among persons with substance misuse who lose sight of reasons to live, without ever having a fully articulated, fully conscious desire to die.

What Should You Do If Someone Says They Are Suicidal?

If someone tells you that they are suicidal, it is incredibly important that you take them seriously and listen to them. Doing this is more important than whatever you were doing before the person told you how they were feeling, no matter what that was. You need to settle down and take some time with this.

At all times, listening and devoting time to people who are depressed or suicidal is absolutely vital. Remain calm and collected. If you think someone might be suicidal but you are not certain, asking them directly does *not* increase risk and does *not* 'put the idea into their head'. For example, if a person says they are feeling very depressed and hopeless about the future, you can ask: 'Are there times when you feel so low that you feel you can't carry on? That you want to end your life, or kill yourself?'

Again, contrary to what many people think, asking in this direct fashion does *not* increase risk, nor does asking the person to tell you more about how they're feeling if they are hesitant or unclear. Most people are hugely relieved to talk about their distressing thoughts with someone who has the capacity to listen and not be overwhelmed by what is said. Someone who will actively listen, really hear what they say, and demonstrate that they care.

Language matters greatly. Mostly listen. When you speak, avoid platitudes. For example, do not say: 'Don't worry; everything is okay'. Clearly, everything is *not* okay. Saying that everything is okay just confirms the person's worst fear: that you're not really hearing them. As they see it, everything is most certainly *not* okay. It is also generally not helpful to tell people that things could be worse. You don't know if that is true and, even if it is, the person probably thinks things cannot possibly get any worse which is why they feel the way they do. It might not be true, but it is how they feel right now.

And you are not there to argue with them. For now, you are there *just to be there*, and that might well be enough for the moment. Listening is the most important thing you can do. You can challenge some of their interpretations or beliefs some other day, when matters are less acute.

After a while, make one or two very pragmatic, short-term suggestions, for example: 'Let's go for a walk while you tell me more about this.' At the outset, avoid making more long-term suggestions, such as: 'Maybe you should quit your job' or 'Why not leave your husband?' These are issues for another day. Be generally hopeful but remember that simplistic solutions to long-term problems can seem trite and unrealistic. Just focus on today. Do not panic or let yourself get overwhelmed. Do not blame the person. Remain calm, pragmatic and hopeful as you speak and make a plan of action.

When making a plan of action, there is good advice on the website of SpunOut.ie about what to do when someone is feeling suicidal.[2] In the first instance, if the person has already taken steps to end their own life (for example, taken an overdose) it's important to call 999 immediately to get them medical attention, or take them straight to an emergency department in a hospital.

If they have not already taken steps to end their life but remain suicidal, it is useful to stay with the person and remove means of self-harm from their immediate vicinity (for example, tablets). It is also useful to assist the person in accessing one of the support services available, depending on the situation.

The Samaritans (www.samaritans.org) provide a listening service to anyone who contacts them, many of whom are contemplating suicide. Pieta House (www.pieta.ie) also offers support for anyone who is suicidal. Other sources of support include GPs and community mental health teams.

In the more acute situation, most large and regional hospitals have psychiatry services operating 24 hours a day, seven days a week, 365 days a year (Chapter 12). Where the local inpatient unit is located within a general hospital, emergency and out-of-hours psychiatry assessments generally occur in the emergency department. This is often a difficult setting for such assessments to occur, but staff try to make the circumstances as therapeutic as possible. For inpatient units that are not located in general hospitals (for example, stand-alone psychiatric hospitals), emergency assessments sometimes occur in the hospital itself or in a neighbouring general hospital.

It is important at all times to remain calm and supportive, and really listen to what is being said. By confiding in you, the person has placed you in a very privileged and responsible position. And remember, while this might be the first time you have had a conversation like this, thoughts of suicide and self-harm are, regrettably, far more common than most people imagine. The statistics for Ireland are considered next, followed by a discussion about predicting or preventing suicide.

How Common Are Suicide and Deliberate Self-harm?

Globally, over 800,000 people die due to suicide every year, and for every suicide there are many more people who engage in deliberate self-harm. Suicide is the second leading cause of death among 15- to 29-year-olds around the world.

Rates of suicide and deliberate self-harm change significantly over time. In broad terms, recent years have seen a reduction in the rate of suicide in Ireland, despite the economic recession of 2008-13. But rates of suicide and deliberate self-harm are not evenly distributed across age groups and there are particular reasons to be concerned about younger adults.

Turning to deliberate self-harm first, NOSP's 2015 'Annual Report' analysed trends in suicide and self-harm in Ireland from 2002 to 2015, for which it presented provisional figures drawn from National Self-Harm Registry Ireland (www.nsrf.ie).[3,4] In 2015, there were 11,189 presentations to hospitals in Ireland due to self-harm, involving 8,791 individuals. This gives an overall rate of 204 episodes of self-harm per 100,000 population per year, which is essentially the same as the rate in 2002, six years prior to the recession.

Just over half (55 per cent) of presentations with deliberate self-harm are by women. The highest rate among females is in the 15 to 19 age group, which has a rate of 718 episodes of deliberate self-harm per 100,000 population per year, meaning that one in every 139 girls in this age group presents to a hospital with deliberate self-harm in a given year. The highest rate among men is among 20- to 24-year-olds, at 553 per 100,000 per year, or one in every 181 men in that age group.

The 'National Self-Harm Registry Ireland Annual Report 2015' states that two acts of deliberate self-harm in every three involve taking an overdose, one in every three involves alcohol and one-quarter involve self-cutting.[4] There is a higher incidence of deliberate self-arm in urban compared to rural areas, and the highest numbers of presentations to hospitals are on Mondays and Sundays.

Turning to suicide, NOSP's 2015 'Annual Report' states that there were 554 suicides in 2011, 541 in 2012, 487 in 2013, 459 in 2014 and 451 in 2015.[5] This is a 19 per cent decrease over five years despite likely population growth. The 2015 report also notes that the rate of suicide in 2005 was 11.6 per 100,000 population per year, and by 2015 this had fallen to 9.7 per 100,000 population per year, following some fluctuation over the course of the decade.

Consistent with previous years, the 2015 suicide rate in men (16.4 per 100,000 population per year) was substantially higher than that in women (3.2 per 100,000 population per year). While under-reporting likely remains an issue, it is noteworthy that the rate of undetermined deaths (which might well include some suicides) also fell over the past decade, from 3.2 per 100,000 population per year in 2005 to 1.5 in 2015.

How does Ireland compare internationally? In its 2013 'Annual Report', NOSP presented figures comparing the Irish suicide rate with those of other European countries.[6] This comparison showed that Ireland's overall suicide rate was relatively low by European standards, eleventh lowest in the EU. In the 15 to 19 age group, however, Ireland's rate was the fourth highest in the EU, in dramatic contrast with Ireland's overall rate and with rates in that age group in other countries.

In 2015, Ireland's suicide rate among males aged 15 to 24 years increased to 21.5 per 100,000 population per year, compared to

16.4 for all males in Ireland and 3.6 for females aged 15 to 24 years. Rates among men also increased in the 25 to 34 age group, to 24.2 per 100,000 population per year in 2015.

The precise effects of the economic recession of the early 2000s on suicide and deliberate self-harm remain unclear, but particular and legitimate concern has emerged about suicide and deliberate self-harm in young people, especially young men and children.

Despite the overall decrease in suicide in Ireland in the early years of the twenty-first century, then, rates of youth suicide and deliberate self-harm remain a real source of concern, especially as rates of youth suicide are persistently very high in Ireland compared to other EU countries. This merits greater investigation and coordinated psychological, social and educational supports for young people in communities, schools and colleges, and through social media.

Can Suicide and Deliberate Self-harm Be Predicted or Prevented?

Given the research findings outlined above, there have been extensive efforts to build models to try to predict suicide and deliberate self-harm, and so to provide better care. Key risk factors for non-fatal deliberate self-harm include female gender, younger age, poor social support, major life events, poverty, being unemployed, being divorced, mental illness and previous deliberate self-harm.

Key risk factors for suicide include male gender, poor social support, major life events, chronic painful illness, family history of suicide, mental illness and previous deliberate self-harm. For both suicide and deliberate self-harm, availability of means is also significant (for example, easy availability of tablets to take overdoses).

In terms of mental illness, suicide is associated with major depression (long-term risk of suicide, 10-15 per cent), bipolar affective disorder (10-20 per cent), schizophrenia (10 per cent) and alcohol dependence syndrome (15 per cent).[7] In addition, individuals who engage in deliberate self-harm have a 30-fold increased risk of completed suicide over the following four years.[8]

Despite these associations from the research, the majority of people with these risk factors will *not* die by suicide, because the increases in risk associated with these factors are small and, despite its tragedy and implications, suicide is (from a mathematical viewpoint) a statistically rare event, with fewer than 500 suicides per year in a population of 4.7 million. As a result, it is statistically impossible to predict suicide at the level of the individual.

There have been very many studies of this, and all yield similar results. One classic study followed-up almost 5,000 psychiatry inpatients after discharge, using a combination of known risk factors to try to predict suicide in this especially high risk group.[9] While this study succeeded in predicting 35 out of 67 subsequent suicides, their model also generated over 1,200 'false positives', that is, it predicted suicide in over 1,200 individuals who did *not* die by suicide.

The reason for this is that suicide is, statistically, a rare event and rare events are either very difficult or impossible to predict. The risk factors for suicide (male gender, poor social support, etc.) are both non-specific and common in the population, so the vast majority of people with these risk factors will *not* die by suicide. This is true even for people who have thoughts of suicide, as the proportion of people with suicidal thoughts who go on to actually complete suicide is less than one in 200. This suggests that simple population screening for suicidal thoughts is unlikely to be either effective or efficient in identifying individuals at risk of suicide.

Overall, then, it is impossible to predict suicide in any individual case. It is often the case that bereaved families believe that there were signs that they missed or that health professionals should have predicted the outcome in cases of suicide. Statistically, however, there is no way that anyone can predict suicide in an individual case.

So, if risk is impossible to predict accurately at individual level, what can be done? Plenty. See, for example, the advice earlier in this chapter about what to do if some tells you that they are suicidal. In addition, while risk assessment might not be accurate in a statistical sense, there is still much that can be done to reduce the general risk of suicide.

First, despite the impossibility of statistical or actuarial prediction in individual cases, careful, realistic clinical assessments and explorations of risk factors are still very useful for guiding treatment and providing support to people who present with suicidal crisis or mental illness. However, even following careful psychiatric clinical evaluation, exploration of risk factors, full treatment, risk management, communication with family and/or others (possibly necessitating breach of confidentiality; see Chapter 12), and meticulous follow-up, it is still entirely possible that any given individual will engage in deliberate self-harm or suicide. All of the assessments, risk management and treatment services should, of course, be provided as appropriate to each individual case and they might well reduce risk in a general sense. But, even so, the outcome cannot be predicted in any given case. Even with the very highest standard of assessment and care on any given day, suicide and deliberate self-harm can still occur on that same day and cannot be predicted.

In an overall sense, however, good mental health care, good communication with families and good follow-up might help to reduce the general risk of suicide. In 2010, the College of Psychiatry of Ireland (as it was then called) noted that 'effective treatment of depression is an important means of reducing suicide rates' and addressed the much-discussed role of antidepressant medication in adults in some detail:

> Untreated depression can have a fatal outcome. Those experiencing moderate to severe depression frequently describe having thoughts of self-harm. Antidepressants are effective in the treatment of depression. The effective treatment of depression is an important means of reducing suicide rates. A huge volume of research in recent years has failed to establish a causal link between antidepressant use and suicide. At an individual level, the period early in treatment may be a

time of relatively high risk, as treatment tends to start when the person's depression is severe and treatment takes some weeks to work. As treatment takes effect and energy and motivation return, people who have recently commenced antidepressant treatment may be more able to act on suicidal thoughts that are inherent to their condition. That the early recovery period is potentially a period of increased risk for suicidality is something of which all doctors should be aware. The College of Psychiatry of Ireland, in unison with the advice of the Irish Medicines Board, recommends close monitoring of all individuals commenced on antidepressant therapy. There is no evidence of a link between antidepressant use and homicide.[10]

Good treatment of depression in primary care (by GPs and their teams) is also essential in trying to reduce suicide rates (Chapter 2), as is treatment of substance abuse, including alcohol misuse (Chapter 7). Other specific mental disorders should also be treated in their own ways, as outlined in other chapters in this book, for example, use of lithium in bipolar disorder (manic depression) might help reduce suicidal thoughts or behaviour in this group (Chapter 4).

In emotionally unstable personality disorder, psychological therapies can prove very helpful, including adaptions of cognitive-behaviour therapy (CBT) (Chapters 2, 5 and 6) and dialectical-behaviour therapy (DBT) (Chapter 9). DBT is somewhat similar to CBT and also involves group sessions, building skills such as mindfulness, and developing coping strategies other than deliberate self-harm for dealing with emotional instability. DBT is a challenging therapy but it can be highly effective for reducing self-harm in certain conditions, including (but not limited to) emotionally unstable personality disorder.

From a public health perspective, public education and measures to limit access to means of self-harm are very important and effective. Regulations governing paracetamol sales are an excellent example as they greatly reduce harm resulting from

paracetamol overdose. Placing barriers at known suicide locations (for example, certain bridges) is another very effective
method for deterring self-harm and suicide. Research shows that a
great number of people who are deterred or delayed in this fashion
will reconsider their suicidal thoughts and many will *not* proceed
to find other means of self-harm.

Good primary care, good mental health care and appropriate
public health measures are, then, essential for addressing the problems of suicide and deliberate self-harm at national level in Ireland. These measures should be aimed at everyone, not just those
with thoughts of suicide or deliberate self-harm. Often, there are
no warning signs.

In 2015, a new suicide prevention strategy was launched by
Healthy Ireland, the Department of Health, HSE and NOSP, titled
'Connecting for Life: Ireland's National Strategy to Reduce Suicide,
2015-2020'.[11] The strategy involves preventive and awareness-rais-
ing work with the population as a whole, supportive work with local communities, and targeted approaches for priority groups. The
strategy proposes high-quality standards of practice across service
delivery areas and, most importantly, an underpinning evaluation
and research framework. In parallel, the budget for NOSP was increased from €3.7 million in 2010 to €11.5 million.

Also in 2015, Derek Beattie, a social researcher, and Dr Patrick
Devitt, a psychiatrist, made a substantial contribution to the public conversation about suicide with their book *Suicide: A Modern
Obsession* (Liberties Press, 2015). In 2016, Dr Declan Murray, another psychiatrist, noted the profound difficulties with estimating
suicide risk and recommended that assessment and management
of patients presenting with suicidal thoughts, feelings and behaviour should focus on reducing or tolerating emotional pain.[12]

This is key. Addressing the psychiatric, psychological and emotional underpinnings of suicidal feelings is an essential element of
care, complementing public health measures (such as limiting access to means). This is especially important among those present-

ing to Irish hospitals with deliberate self-harm, as we know that they are at especially high risk of further deliberate self-harm and suicide.

At present, according to the 'National Self-Harm Registry Ireland Annual Report 2015', 73 per cent of people who present to Irish hospitals with deliberate self-harm receive an assessment in the emergency department.[13] Of these, approximately 23 per cent are admitted to a general hospital, 9 per cent are admitted to a psychiatric inpatient unit, 1 per cent do not permit admission, 13 per cent leave before a recommendation is made, and 55 per cent are not admitted. The more lethal the method of self-harm used, the greater the likelihood of psychiatric admission.

Follow-up assessments, support for families, communication with GPs, good outpatient mental health care, and involvement of dedicated self-harm nurses are all essential elements in care plans following deliberate self-harm. Media guidelines on reporting suicide have been produced by the Irish Association of Suicidology and the Samaritans in order to minimise further harm and reduce the possibility of copycat acts.[14] The HSE has also produced clear guidelines on responding to suicide 'clusters', focused on proactive response plans in local health areas.[15]

Despite such increased public and professional discussion, however, much remains to be done to provide effective, coordinated support to those at risk of suicide and those bereaved. In 2016, it was estimated that there were up to 300 different groups providing support for those at risk. Clearly, a coordinated, effective and compassionate approach is needed, linking community and state resources with each other in order to optimise efforts to address this problem which has been a long-standing issue in the history of psychiatry in Ireland, as has been the case elsewhere.

Approaches rooted outside of core mental health services will be vital in this process: addressing alcohol problems and other addictions, reducing homelessness, reforming the criminal justice system and improving access to social care.

This matters to us all. Everyone knows a family affected by suicide. Grief following suicide is especially complex and difficult. Families often experience shock, loss, guilt, shame, anger and many other emotions. They may not feel able to identify with families who are bereaved in other ways. They may feel isolated and that there is a lack of understanding.

Those who are bereaved by suicide are by no means alone, but it can be difficult to reach out to others. Support groups can prove very helpful, as can discussions with your GP or other members of the primary care or mental health teams. Pieta House (www.pieta.ie) also offers support, both for those bereaved and those who are feeling suicidal.

One in four people will develop a mental illness at some point in life. There is no 'them'; there is only 'us'.

Homicide and Murder–Suicide

There has long been an association between mental illness and dangerousness in the public mind, even in advance of any systematic studies of the matter. Research over recent decades, however, has shown that individuals with mental illnesses such as schizophrenia are just slightly more likely to engage in acts of violence compared to individuals without such illnesses.

People with mental illness are, however, far more likely to be the *victims* of crime compared to those without mental illness. At population level, the proportion of violent crime attributable to mental illnesses such as schizophrenia is *extremely low* and much is attributable to co-occurring drug misuse, which increases the risk of violence in individuals with and without mental illness.

Because violence is such a rare event in mental illness, it is extremely difficult to predict it: the most detailed predictive models, which include almost all known risk factors for violence in schizophrenia, can only explain approximately one-quarter of the variation in violence between individuals with schizophrenia. It is mostly unexplained and unpredictable.

Even if there was a predictive model that was 90 per cent sensitive and 90 per cent specific (both of which are unrealistically high levels of prediction in any field of medicine), the rarity of homicide by individuals with severe mental illness means that such a model would generate at least 2,000 false positives for every true positive; that is, the model would predict that 2,001 mentally ill individuals were at high risk of committing homicide but in fact only one would have gone on to commit homicide.[16]

Against this background, it is apparent that individuals with mental illnesses such as schizophrenia present a small increased risk of violence, but such violence is impossible to predict at the level of the individual. The situation is similar in relation to murder–suicide, which is when an individual kills another person and then takes their own life. We know that this is a very tragic, very rare event, but precisely how common is it internationally and in Ireland? And can it be predicted or prevented?

In the US, the rate of murder–suicide is approximately 0.2 to 0.3 per 100,000 population per year.[17] This rate is considerably higher than that in England and Wales, where there were 60 murder–suicides between 1 January 2006 and 31 December 2008, giving a rate of 0.04 per 100,000 population per year.[18] The rate in Ireland is more difficult to establish with certainty.

If the US rate applied to Ireland, with our population of 4,757,976 people (based on the 2016 census), we would expect, at a minimum, 9.5 murder–suicides per year. If the England and Wales rate applied, we would expect 1.9 per year in Ireland.

In February 2017, the National Suicide Research Foundation reported that there have been at least 23 murder–suicides in Ireland since 2004.[19] This gives a rate of at least 1.8 per year (approximately 0.04 per 100,000 population per year), which is similar to the rate in England and Wales, but considerably lower than that in the US. It is worth noting that the National Suicide Research Foundation's figure is an 'at least' figure, so the true number may be higher. It seems likely, however, that any underestimate is small, and that Ireland's rate is essentially the same at that of England and Wales, that is, just under two murder–suicides per year.

Can murder–suicide be predicted? Looking across the international literature, it is clear that most perpetrators of are men (88 per cent), most commonly in their mid-40s. The most common life event in the run-up to the murder–suicide is the loss of, or a significant change in, a close personal relationship.

Up to two-thirds of perpetrators have a history of mental illness (most commonly depression) but fewer than 12 per cent have had contact with specialist mental health services in the year prior to the murder–suicide. A majority (between 77 per cent and 90 per cent) have never had any contact with mental health services.

It is therefore unclear how many perpetrators of murder–suicide are truly mentally ill. Unthinkable acts are commonly committed by people who are not mentally ill, and some cases of murder–suicide may relate more to domestic violence than to mental illness. In these circumstances, it is possible that targeted interventions and supports in cases of domestic violence might help prevent escalation to the point of murder–suicide in certain families.

Given these statistics and research findings, can murder–suicide be predicted or prevented? Unfortunately, as is the case with any event that is so rare (with two cases per year in a population of 4.7 million people), accurate prediction is impossible at the individual level. Even with the best use of current evidence, the various factors linked with murder–suicide (male gender, mid-40s, past depression) are so common that it is simply not possible to predict with any degree of accuracy if a given individual will engage in murder–suicide.

So, if prediction is impossible, is prevention impossible too? Possibly not. Given that many people who engage in murder–suicide have a history of depression, it is possible that better treatment of depression might help prevent it. While it is certainly not proven that better treatment of depression can prevent murder–suicide, it is difficult to see how there could ever be such proof since it is impossible to count events that have been prevented, especially rare ones like murder–suicide.

In any case, there are already many good reasons for better treatment of depression, including reducing suffering, improving quality of life and, possibly, preventing suicide (see above). As a result, better treatment of depression can and should remain a key element in primary care and mental health services. In other words, there are already many compelling reasons for better treatment of depression and better routine provision of good mental health care, and these may also help reduce the risk of murder–suicide and homicide, even though this possible benefit remains unproven (and possibly unprovable).

In terms of targeted interventions, the National Suicide Research Foundation notes that 90 per cent of murder–suicide involving mothers and 60 per cent involving fathers are associated with a desire to alleviate real or imagined suffering in their children. This suggests that this clinical feature should present particular cause for concern. Again, however, it remains the case that the vast majority of people who express such concern about their children will *not* engage in murder–suicide, so the predictive value of this feature as a risk factor is (again) unproven.

We do know, however, that there is a need for better support services for those bereaved by murder–suicide, focused on timely and direct provision of information, practical assistance in the aftermath of the tragedy, and sustained psychological support for family members and affected friends (for example, school friends and staff).

Previous murder–suicide have led to calls for greater emphasis on child risk assessment in psychiatric evaluations. While there is no evidence that child risk assessment can statistically predict the risk presented by murder–suicide or reduce its incidence, assessing child welfare when a parent is severely mentally ill certainly deserves more attention than it currently receives. This is not based on the idea that such assessment can reduce risk of murder–suicide, but is based, rather, on meeting the needs of all family members, therefore delivering better general mental health care, and possibly thus reducing the general risk of murder-suicide, homicide and, indeed, suicide. Calls for greater involvement of families in mental health care are also entirely justified and apt for similar reasons, and this topic is discussed in some detail in Chapter 12.

The HSE has produced clear and helpful guidelines on responding to murder–suicide, focused on proactive response plans in local health areas.[20] The National Suicide Research Foundation has provided advice on sensitive and factual reporting in order to minimise further harm.[21] They note that graphic or detailed reporting can trigger copycat acts; sensational reporting can distort facts; and media professionals should consider potential effects on vulnerable readers. Media guidelines on reporting suicide have been produced by the Irish Association of Suicidology and the Samaritans.[22]

Overall, it is important to remember that while various measures discussed above may well reduce the likelihood of homicide, murder–suicide or copycat acts in the general population, it remains impossible to predict the risk for any given individual. As is the case with suicide, it is often the case that bereaved families believe that there were signs that they missed or that health professionals should have predicted the outcome in cases of homicide or murder–suicide. Statistically, however, there is no way that anyone can predict suicide, homicide or murder–suicide in an individual case.

As a result, even following careful psychiatric clinical evaluation, exploration of risk factors, full treatment, risk management, communication with family and/or others (possibly necessitating breach of confidentiality; see Chapter 12), and meticulous follow-up, it is still entirely possible that any given individual will engage in deliberate self-harm, suicide, murder–suicide or homicide. This is true in both inpatient and outpatient settings. Arguably, admission to an inpatient psychiatry unit can sometimes add to a person's distress rather than decrease it. It is impossible to maintain a 100 per cent safe environment even in a high-observation psychiatry inpatient unit.

All of the assessments, risk management and treatment services should, of course, be provided as appropriate to each individual case and might reduce risk. But, even so, the outcome cannot be predicted in an individual case: even with the very highest standard of assessment and care on any given day, deliberate self-harm, suicide, murder-suicide or homicide can still occur on that same day.

More specific issues relating to people with mental illness who offend, forensic psychiatry, and the Criminal Law (Insanity) Acts 2006 and 2010 are beyond the scope of the present book. Information about fitness to be tried, the verdict of 'not guilty by reason of insanity', 'diminished responsibility' in murder cases, and the role of the Mental Health Review Board is available on the website of the Citizens Information Board.[23]

Useful Resources

For anyone who is feeling suicidal, the Samaritans (www.samaritans.org) provide a listening service to anyone who contacts them (telephone 116 123; email jo@samaritans.org). Pieta House (www.pieta.ie) also offers support, both for those who are feeling suicidal and those who are bereaved (telephone 1800 247 247).

It is advisable that anyone who thinks they have any of the conditions discussed in this book sees a health care professional. There are many reasons for this, including a need to rule out any other diagnoses, such as physical illnesses. In addition, some people find it easier to talk with a health care professional, especially if they are too uncertain or embarrassed to talk with friends or family members. Often, a brief talk with a GP will 'normalise' the individual's symptoms by reassuring them that they are not alone in what they are experiencing and that help is to hand, if any is needed.

Individuals with any mental disorder or psychological problem, and their families, will find much that is useful on the Internet. As ever, Internet resources need to be evaluated with care and only trusted when the information comes from a reliable source. Reliable information about mental health can be sourced from the websites of the Health Service Executive (www.hse.ie/eng/health/az), College of Psychiatrists of Ireland (www.irishpsychiatry.ie), Royal College of Psychiatrists in London (www.rcpsych.ac.uk), National Health Service in the UK (www.nhs.uk) and National Institute of Mental Health in the US (www.nimh.nih.gov).

Evidence-based guidance about specific treatments can be found on the website of the National Institute for Health and Care Excellence (NICE) (www.nice.org.uk). NICE is a UK-based organisation responsible for developing guidance, standards and information on high-quality health and social care, and preventing and treating ill health.

Information about suicide around the world is available from the World Health Organisation (www.who.int/topics/suicide/en) and there is further information available from Ireland's National Suicide Research Foundation (www.nsrf.ie) and National Office for Suicide Prevention (www.nosp.ie).

In addition to the above, there are several books which may also be helpful, including: *The Savage God: A Study of Suicide* by Al Alvarez (Weidenfeld and Nicolson, 1971); *A Concise Guide to Understanding Suicide: Epidemiology, Pathophysiology, and Prevention* edited by Stephen H. Koslow, Pedro Ruiz and Charles B. Nemeroff (Cambridge University Press, 2014); *The International Handbook of Suicide Prevention* (Second Edition) edited by Rory C. O'Connor and Jane Pirkis (John Wiley and Sons, 2016).

Endnotes

1   Kelly, B. *Hearing Voices: The History of Psychiatry in Ireland.* Dublin: Irish Academic Press, 2016 (Chapter 8).

2 http://spunout.ie/health/article/help-my-friend-is-feeling-suicida
   l?gclid=CMuHqr3IrtICFc297Qod66sAVQ

3 http://www.hse.ie/eng/services/list/4/Mental_Health_Services/
   NOSP/about/annualreports/nosp-report-2015.pdf

4 http://nsrf.ie/wp-content/uploads/reports/NSRF%20Registry%20
   Report%202015.pdf

5 Some figures are provisional.

6 http://www.hse.ie/eng/services/list/4/Mental_Health_Services/
   NOSP/about/annualreports/nospannual2013.pdf

7 Williams, P. *Suicide and Attempted Suicide*. London: Penguin,
   1997.

8 Cooper, J., Kapur, N., Webb, R., Lawlor, M., Guthrie, E., Mack-
   way-Jones, K. and Appleby, L. 'Suicide after deliberate self-harm:
   A 4-year cohort study'. *American Journal of Psychiatry* 2005; 162:
   297-303.

9 Pokorny, A.D. 'Prevention of suicide in psychiatric patients: Report of a prospective study', in Maris, R.W., Berman, A.L., Matls-
   berger J,T. and Yufit, R.I., eds., *Assessment and Prediction of Suicide*. New York: Guilford Press, 1992 (pp. 105-29).

10 College of Psychiatry of Ireland, *Antidepressant Medication –
   Clarification*. Dublin: College of Psychiatry of Ireland, 2010.

11 http://health.gov.ie/wp-content/uploads/2015/06/Connecting-
   for-Life_LR.pdf

12 Murray, D. 'Is it time to abandon suicide risk assessment?' *British
   Journal of Psychiatry Open* 2016; 2: e1-2.

13 http://nsrf.ie/wp-content/uploads/reports/NSRF%20Registry%20
   Report%202015.pdf

14 http://www.samaritans.org/your-community/samaritans-ireland-
   scotland-and-wales/samaritans-ireland/media-guidelines-ireland

15 http://www.hse.ie/eng/services/list/4/Mental_Health_Services/
   NOSP/Resources/Respondingmurdersuicidesuicideclusters.pdf

16 Szmukler, G. 'Homicide enquiries'. *Psychiatric Bulletin* 2000; 24: 6-10.

17 Eliason, S. 'Murder–suicide: A review of the literature'. *Journal of the American Academy of Psychiatry and the Law* 2009; 37: 371-6.

18 Flynn, S., Gask, L., Appleby, L. and Shaw, J. 'Homicide–suicide and the role of mental disorder: A national consecutive case series'. *Social Psychiatry and Psychiatric Epidemiology* 2016; 51: 877-84.

19 http://www.nsrf.ie/wp-content/uploads/Briefings/Briefing%20Murder-Suicide%20and%20Media%20Reporting%20NSRF%2001-02-2017.pdf

20 http://www.hse.ie/eng/services/list/4/Mental_Health_Services/NOSP/Resources/Respondingmurdersuicidesuicideclusters.pdf

21 http://www.nsrf.ie/wp-content/uploads/Briefings/Briefing%20Murder-Suicide%20and%20Media%20Reporting%20NSRF%2001-02-2017.pdf

22 http://www.samaritans.org/your-community/samaritans-ireland-scotland-and-wales/samaritans-ireland/media-guidelines-ireland

23 http://www.citizensinformation.ie/en/justice/criminal_law/criminal_trial/criminal_insanity_and_mental_health.html

Chapter 12

MENTAL HEALTH SERVICES IN IRELAND

The history of mental health services in Ireland is dominated by the shadow of the large mental hospitals that overshadowed so many Irish towns during the 1800s and 1900s. Prior to the emergence of these institutions, the mentally ill were commonly committed to gaols or private establishments, or incarcerated in private homes. In 1817, Robert Peel (1788-1850), Chief Secretary, prevailed upon the House of Commons of the United Kingdom of Great Britain and Ireland to set up a Select Committee to look into the position of 'the lunatic poor in Ireland'. The Right Honourable Denis Browne (a Mayo Member of Parliament) presented the Committee with evidence about the plight of the mentally ill in rural areas of early nineteenth-century Ireland:

> There is nothing so shocking as madness in the cabin of the peasant, where the man is out labouring in the fields for his bread, and the care of the woman of the house is scarcely sufficient for the attendance on the children. When a strong young man or woman gets the complaint, the only way they have to manage is by making a hole in the floor of the cabin not high enough for the person to stand up in, with a crib over it to prevent his getting up, the hole is about five feet deep, and they give the wretched being his food there, and there he generally dies. Of all human

271

calamity, I know of none equal to this, in the country parts of Ireland which I am acquainted with.[1]

This was the position prior to the public asylums for the mentally ill that emerged in the 1800s. While the thinking behind the asylums was generally well-meaning, the new institutions soon grew well beyond their original capacity and by the late 1800s were extremely overcrowded, deeply antitherapeutic and in desperate need of reform.[2] Admission numbers continued to rise until the late 1950s, when Ireland had the highest known level of psychiatric bed availability internationally.[3] At this point, for various reasons, the era of the large mental hospital in Ireland finally began to draw to a close. Between 1963 and 2003 the number of psychiatric inpatients decreased from 19,801 to 3,658, representing a five-fold decrease, or 82 per cent.[4] There were many reasons for this, including changing public attitudes, new treatments, increased emphasis on human rights, economic factors and general social change in Ireland and across Europe. By 31 December 2015, there were just 2,337 patients in approved adult psychiatry inpatient units in Ireland, as well as 73 under-18s in specialised child and adolescent inpatient units.[5]

Even more importantly, most mental health care is now delivered outside of inpatient settings, in GP surgeries, primary care centres, community-based facilities and various other locations. Against this background, this chapter provides a guide to mental health services as they currently operate in Ireland, looking firstly at national mental health policy, and then moving on to how to access public mental health care, family involvement in care, provision of services to particular groups (for example, persons with intellectual disability, ethnic minorities, members of the Traveller community and those in need of forensic mental health care) and, finally, the roles of mental health service-user groups. But firstly, Ireland's mental health policy: *A Vision for Change.*

Mental Health Policy: *A Vision for Change* (2006)

In 2006, the Irish government published a new national mental health policy, titled *A Vision for Change: Report of the Expert Group on Mental Health Policy*.[6] Over two decades earlier, the preceding policy, *Planning for the Future*, had suggested that mental health services should be comprehensive and community-oriented, aimed at delivering continuous, coordinated, multidisciplinary care.[7] The policy recommended that the population be divided into sectors, each comprising 25,000 to 30,000 people; psychiatric care should be delivered by consultant-led multidisciplinary teams; dedicated crisis teams should be developed; and additional specialised services should be developed to cover more than one sector. Day hospitals were to provide intensive outpatient treatment essentially equivalent to inpatient care for certain patients.

While the two decades following the publication of *Planning for the Future* saw considerable changes in the delivery of mental health care, not all of the report's recommendations were implemented. In 2006, a fresh policy document, *A Vision for Change*, again sought to create a new, community-oriented framework for promoting positive mental health in all sectors of society and providing accessible specialist services for those who need them.

The vision underpinning the 2006 policy underlined the need for a population-based approach to mental health, involving not only mental health services but also primary care (GP surgeries) and community supports. It emphasised the importance of partnership with service-users, carers and broader groups of stakeholders. Links between mental health and education, poverty, unemployment, housing and social exclusion were explored; mental health promotion discussed; and various protective factors and risk factors for mental illness identified.

The policy recommended that a comprehensive range of services should be available at primary care (GP) level for those who do not require specialist services; a consultation/liaison model should ensure formal links between specialist services and primary care, especially in relation to discharge planning; suitably trained staff should be available in primary care settings to meet mental health needs; and relevant education, training and research should be developed.

In terms of adult mental health services, the report recommended that one multidisciplinary community mental health team be provided per 50,000 population, with two consultant psychiatrists per team. It recommended the provision of 50 beds per 300,000-person catchment area, comprising 35 beds for general adult mental health services (including six close observation beds), eight beds for mental health services for older people, five beds for persons with intellectual disability and two beds for individuals with eating disorders. These modest numbers were a far cry from the enormous asylums of Ireland's past.

The 2006 report also made a series of other recommendations, including provision of one 'crisis house' per 300,000 population (each with 10 places) and, nationally, four intensive care rehabilitation units (30 beds each); eight high support intensive care residences (10 places each); two early intervention services; and various other facilities. In terms of rehabilitation psychiatry, the report recommended one multidisciplinary team, three community residential units (10 places each), and one service-user provided support centre per 100,000 population, as well as one to two day centres (with a total of 30 places) per 300,000 population.

In addition to the above, the report addressed services for specific groups, including older people, people with intellectual disability, the homeless, people with substance misuse disorders and people with eating disorders, as well as forensic mental health services and liaison mental health services. Attention was paid to special categories of service provision including people with both severe mental illness and substance abuse problems, people with neuropsychiatric disorders requiring specialist services and borderline personality disorder. In terms of suicide prevention, the report supported implementation of the recommendations of the *National Strategy for Action on Suicide Prevention* (2005).

As well as making specific recommendations about levels of service provision in these and other areas, the report explored more general principles that should inform mental health care. Particular attention was paid to multidisciplinary teamwork, care-planning, the process of recovery and development of needs-based models of service delivery. In terms of implementation, the policy recommended that mental health catchment areas should be established (with populations of 250,000-400,000) and these should be managed by multidisciplinary Mental Health Catchment Area Management Teams, and a National Mental Health Services Directorate should be established.

From the outset, it was apparent that implementation of *A Vision for Change* would require substantial extra funding and the report suggested that resources be remodelled to increase equity, with special attention paid to areas of socio-economic disadvantage with a high level of mental health need. It was also apparent that implementation would have implications for manpower, education and training, and these areas were all explored in the document; in particular, it was suggested that a multi-profession manpower plan be put in place. Finally, *A Vision for Change* emphasised the importance of mental health information systems and research, and recommended that a national mental health minimum data set be prepared in consultation with stakeholders.

Did any of this actually happen in the decade since this rather expansive *Vision* was outlined? Did the ambitious 2006 policy produce meaningful change on the ground?

In the first instance, the policy was generally welcomed as representing an important shift away from institution-based psychiatry and towards community-based care (although this was not, in fact, new, having been part of national policy since 1966). More encouragingly, however, shortly after the policy was launched, a monitoring group was established to assess implementation and the degree to which specific policy measures truly improved services. From the outset, it was plain that the sequencing of various measures in the *Vision* was likely to be critical. It was imperative, for example, that community mental health services would be substantially strengthened prior to any changes in levels of inpatient care, and pre-existing disparities in levels of service provision across different geographical areas resolved.

At national level, however, the overall rate of implementation of *A Vision for Change* was soon criticised as being too slow. In 2008, one extensive study of 32 mental health services reported that just 16 per cent of services had received the resources promised in order to implement the new policy; 32 per cent had not even been promised such resources and nor was there tangible evidence of the requisite enhancement of clinical teams; and there was significant concern about low levels of staff recruitment.[8]

In September 2009, a report by Indecon International Consultants, submitted to Amnesty International, made some similar points, highlighting that while some progress had certainly been made, significant deficits remained in relation to the number of community mental health teams and their composition.[9] The report contended that there was still an over-reliance on traditional acute and long-stay inpatient facilities, and it presented a series of recommendations for future developments, including setting new, realistic implementation targets.

The rate of implementation was also a key concern of the Independent Monitoring Group (IMG) established as part of *A Vision for Change* in March 2006. In June 2012, the IMC, in its sixth annual report, concluded that implementation of the policy was still 'slow and inconsistent'.[10] The IMG pointed in particular to the 'continued absence of a National Mental Health Service Directorate with authority and control of resources. Such a body has the potential to give strong corporate leadership and act as a catalyst for change':

The absence of a comprehensive, time-lined and costed implementation plan has made it difficult to put in place a consistent framework for the development of all mental health specialities and has led to a lack of coherency in the planning and development of community based services. Existing community mental health teams are poorly populated with an estimated 1,500 vacant posts. These are mostly allied health professional posts. Consequently, the service that is delivered through medical and nursing posts is not based on multiple interventions as envisaged in [*A Vision for Change*]...There is an absence of the ethos of recovery and poor development of recovery competencies in service delivery resulting in a reactive rather than proactive approach to the needs of individuals and their families (p. 3).

On a more positive note, there was:

evidence of many local and regional initiatives being developed in line with [*A Vision for Change*]. These are principally 'bottom-up' developments led by local leadership.

The IMG noted that:

the HSE in combination with the Mental Health Commission has driven the continued closure of unfit for purpose facilities in favour of modern community-based approaches. In respect of capital developments, progress has and is being made in the area of general adult mental health services, child and adolescent mental health services and forensic mental health services.

There was, however, still much to be done to advance other areas of the policy:

What is still required to achieve full implementation of [*A Vision for Change*] is an operational framework for the development of recovery competencies for all staff both at entry training level and ongoing in-service development. As a matter of urgency, the specialist mental health services for older people, rehabilitation and recovery, eating disorders, intellectual disability, co-morbid severe mental illness and substance abuse problems and others described in [*A Vision for Change*] need to be fully developed and delivered. Government Departments, other than the Department of Health and the Department of the Environment, Community and Local Government need to focus on their responsibilities for the implementation of [*A Vision for Change*] (pp. 3-4).

Many of these themes also appeared in a further, independent study of implementation by Dr Helen Johnston published in 2014, which identified a significant body of opinion that saw implementation as slow, haphazard and uneven.[11] That study also identified a need for authoritative, accountable leadership as a key factor for implementation and, in 2013, the HSE appointed a National Director for Mental Health.

By 2015 the Mental Health Division of the HSE had responsibility for all HSE mental health services, including area-based mental health services (approved inpatient residential centres, all community-based teams), child and adolescent mental health, general adult psychiatry, psychiatry of old age, the National Forensic Mental Health Service, National Counselling Service and National Office for Suicide Prevention. The HSE Mental Health Management Team, led by the National Director, comprised a Head of Planning, Performance and Programme Management, Head of Operations, Quality and Service Improvement, Interim Head of Service User, Family Member and Carer Engagement, and National Clinical Adviser and Clinical Programme Group Lead for Mental Health.

In 2010, there was further progress with the launch of See Change, Ireland's national programme working to change minds about mental health problems (www.seechange.ie). Also in 2010, the National Clinical Programme for Mental Health was set up as a joint initiative between HSE Clinical Strategy and Programmes Division and the College of Psychiatry of Ireland (as it was then called; now College of Psychiatrists of Ireland). The overarching aim of the national programmes was to standardise high quality evidence-based practice across mental health services in relation to (a) assessment and management of patients presenting to emergency departments following self-harm; (b) early intervention for people developing first episode psychosis; and (c) management of persons with eating disorders (spanning child and adolescent and adult mental health services). These programmes aim to address identified areas of high need and provide a programmatic response in which integration with other services is key to successful delivery and reform.

Notwithstanding these developments, substantial challenges remained. In 2014, the Chairman of the Mental Health Commission (Mr John Saunders) pointed to some of the outstanding challenges in relation to *A Vision for Change*:

> The implementation of policy to date is still reliant on innovative and imaginative clinical and administrative leadership at regional and local levels. There is considerable commitment to the policy. Despite these actions the policy is being implemented unevenly and inconsistently across the country and there is a requirement for innovative actions to be supported and reinforced by strong corporate governance at national level.[12]

While acknowledging recent progress in relation to governance and certain other areas, the Chairman stated that 'the [Mental Health] Commission is also concerned regarding a number of specific areas of service provision which impinge on human rights and where, in 2013, standards fell below what is acceptable' (p.7). These areas included individualised care plans (implemented appropriately in an estimated 60 per cent of approved centres), unacceptable use of seclusion and restraint, continued admission of children to adult facilities (22 per cent of all child admissions in 2013), the absence of reformed, enacted mental capacity legislation, and various issues relating to staffing.

Overall, then, while progress was made with *A Vision for Change* in the decade following publication, and while there is now increased emphasis on recovery in mental health services, further work is still needed. The process of reform must always be a continuous one.

But even after all this policy analysis, the next question is, for many, the most crucial one: how, precisely, does one access mental health services in Ireland? What do you actually *do*?

How to Access Mental Health Care in Ireland

The primary way to access public (free at point-of-delivery) mental health services in Ireland is to present to a GP or primary care team with symptoms that you think might be attributable to a mental health problem. These matters are rarely clear or simple, and it is common for people to be uncertain about whether their symptoms amount to a mental health problem and whether they will benefit from treatment. This should not be an obstacle to discussing your concerns with a GP; all GPs are trained in mental health care and can provide reassurance, advice, treatment and further referral, as required. They will not think you are 'mad'.

The vast majority of people with mental health problems are treated in primary care without referral to specialist mental health services. Many GPs and primary care teams provide various forms of care themselves including counselling, support, medication and other treatments. They can also refer you to other local sources of treatment and support.

For adults with medical cards, the HSE provides the 'Counselling in Primary Care' (CIPC) scheme for assistance with mild to moderate psychological difficulties. This is a short-term counselling service that provides up to eight counselling sessions with a professionally qualified and accredited counsellor or therapist. It is suitable for people who are experiencing difficulties such as depression, anxiety, panic reactions, relationship problems, loss issues and stress. Information leaflets and referral forms for this service are available through GP practices and primary care teams, and on the HSE website.[13]

The HSE also provides the 'National Counselling Service' (NCS) which is a professional, confidential counselling and psychotherapy service available free of charge in all regions of the country. Established in 2000, this service employs over 70 counsellor/therapists who are highly qualified and experienced in working with developmental trauma. Healthcare professionals can refer clients but people can also refer themselves directly by calling a free-phone number.[14]

Since the establishment of the NCS, its primary clients have been adults who experienced abuse whilst in the care of the state as children. The core mission of the NCS is:

> to listen to, value and understand those who have been abused in childhood, in particular those abused in institutional care. The National Counselling Service aims to assist clients to live more satisfying lives and, in learning from their experiences, strives to prevent further abuse in Ireland.

In addition to the CIPC and NCS, there are various other community-based resources for adults, adolescents and children with mental health problems in different parts of Ireland. These differ from area to area. Some require referral from a GP; others do not. GPs, other primary care team members and public health nurses can advise about the availability of such services locally and how to access them. (For children and adolescents, see also Chapter 10.)

A minority of people with mental health problems who attend their GP may be referred to a community mental health team for more specialist care. The HSE has a network of community mental health teams spanning the entire country and which team you are referred to depends on your postal address. You do not need to know which 'catchment area' you live in; your GP will direct the referral appropriately and, if there is any doubt, the local mental health service will have a list of addresses covered by various clinics and can redirect the referral to the correct clinic. Once a

GP referral letter is received, the community mental health team for that area will most commonly schedule an outpatient appointment to assess what treatment, if any, is needed, and what advice they can give.

For the most part, the initial assessment by the community mental health team is performed by a doctor, although, increasingly, at least in certain areas, other members of the team might see the patient first. Mental health services in Ireland seek to use a multidisciplinary approach, whereby a number of trained, accredited professionals offer their particular skills in a co-ordinated and complementary way. Teams commonly include some or all of the following mental health professionals:

- *Clinical psychologist:* This is a person with a university degree in psychology and a further, specialist qualification in mental health. The clinical psychologist is involved in psychological assessment and provision of therapies such as cognitive-behaviour therapy (that is, focussed on thinking and behaviour patterns) (Chapter 2), family therapy, and other forms of psychological therapy. The clinical psychologist can also often advise about other psychological services available locally, outside of strictly-defined 'mental health services'.

- *Mental health social worker:* Mental health social workers can carry out a range of functions including assessment, family work, education, counselling, 'case management' (to ensure continuity of care and co-ordination of services) and assisting with housing, social welfare, job training and employment, among other matters. They often have an intensely pragmatic focus on relevant aspects of patients' day-to-day lives, as well as on mental and social well-being more broadly.

- *Occupational therapist:* Occupational therapists focus on building people's ability to cope with everyday activities, especially when they experience practical difficulties due to mental illness. The aim is to enable the person to have as independent, productive and satisfying a lifestyle as possible, to deepen or strengthen sustainable recovery from mental illness, and optimise social, educational and occupational function.

- *Mental health nurse:* Mental health nurses provide nursing and psychological care to patients, support and encouragement to families, and work in the full range of mental health care settings, including day hospitals, day centres, outpatient clinics and inpatient units. Community mental health nurses follow-up patients after discharge from hospital, providing care at home and continued support for patients, families and communities.

- *Psychiatrist:* Psychiatrists are medical doctors who have completed additional training in the treatment of mental illness. They differ from clinical psychologists who are specialists in mental processes and behaviour but are not medical doctors. Both psychiatrists and clinical psychologists work in mental health services and their roles are similar in certain respects but different in others (for example, psychologists cannot prescribe medication in Ireland whereas psychiatrists can). A fully trained psychiatrist is most commonly a 'consultant' and their name will be on the register of medical specialists maintained by the Medical Council (which is publicly available).[15]

Which of these team members (or various others) participate in your care will depend on your initial assessment and ongoing needs. Most mental health care is provided on an outpatient basis (that is, without admission to hospital at any point), through outpatient clinics, day hospitals, day centres or other outpatient facilities. Outpatient clinics in mental health operate in a fashion similar to outpatient clinics in other areas of medicine, with patients attending appointments to see doctors or other members of the multi-disciplinary team. Family members and others can also seek appointments to discuss care with the doctor and patient, and these meetings are often held with the patient at the time of the patient's own appointment but are sometimes scheduled for other times too.

Some mental health services offer 'assertive outreach' care, which involves more intensive care provided in the patient's home, possibly involving daily visits from members of the community mental health team, along with increased availability for telephone consultation and enhanced support for patients and families. These services are not yet fully developed in all areas but are highly effective and empowering once they are appropriately structured and resourced. The term 'home care' is sometimes used for a related model of care focussed on community-provision of mental health care which would previously have necessitated hospital admission but can sometimes be provided at home instead, resulting in less disruption to the person's day-to-day life.

Day hospitals and day centres are other common features of community mental health services in Ireland. *Day hospitals* are outpatient facilities that offer more intensive services than those provided in outpatient clinics. The patient will generally attend the day hospital several days per week and the precise services provided will depend on the patient's needs. Typical features include group therapies, various other group activities, consultations with specific staff members (for example, nurses, psychiatrists, clinical psychologists) and a range of different forms of counselling and support. Day hospitals aim to provide a level of focussed, short-term care that is almost equivalent to that provided in an inpatient unit but with the patient continuing to stay at home. Day hospital attendance may therefore prevent the need for inpatient admission or facilitate early discharge from inpatient care for certain patients.

Day centres involve many activities similar to those in day hospitals, but these are provided at a less intense level. Rather than approaching the level of inpatient care, day centres aim at being sustainable in the medium to long term, and often focus on continuing care for people with enduring mental health problems or enduring social needs as a result of mental illness or various psychological problems. Day centres are focussed on recovery and reintegration into social and family life over a more sustained period of time.

For a minority of people, these community supports are not enough and admission to a psychiatric hospital or inpatient unit is needed. In 2015, there were 17,860 admissions to Irish psychiatric units and hospitals, a rate of 389 per 100,000 total population, which was a small increase on the previous year.[16] The majority of such admissions (88 per cent) were on a voluntary basis, just like any other admission to hospital, that is, the person agrees to be admitted to hospital and accepts treatment willingly. Involuntary admission is discussed separately in Chapter 13.

Voluntary psychiatric admission can occur following an assessment within the mental health service (for example, following an outpatient clinic visit at which the team member recommends admission) or following a visit to a GP, who might arrange direct admission to the psychiatry inpatient unit or provide a letter of referral for emergency assessment at the emergency department of a general hospital or at a local psychiatric facility (for example, a stand-alone psychiatric hospital). If the admission is arranged during regular 'working hours' (9.00 am to 5.00 pm, Monday to Friday), it is usually planned by the referring doctor in communication with the community mental health team and/or staff the inpatient facility.

For out-of-hours assessments and admissions, psychiatry hospitals or units have doctors on duty 24 hours a day, seven days a week, 365 days a year. Precise arrangements for emergency assessments and admissions vary from place to place, but all services have some form of emergency assessment available. Where the inpatient unit is located within a general hospital, emergency and out-of-hours psychiatry assessments generally occur in the emergency department. This is often a difficult setting for such assessments to occur, but staff try to make the circumstances as therapeutic as possible. For inpatient units that are not located in general hospitals (for example, stand-alone psychiatric hospitals), emergency assessments sometimes occur in the hospital itself or sometimes in a neighbouring general hospital. It is common for a

GP who is making an emergency referral to telephone to find out where the emergency assessment will occur, if the GP and patient are not already familiar with the service.

Sometimes it is necessary for the patient to be assessed by other teams in the hospital before seeing the mental health team (for example, following self-harm, overdose, accident, or acute medical illness). This medical or surgical assessment can occur in the emergency department before psychiatric assessment takes place. Most emergency psychiatric assessments are initially performed by doctors, usually trainees in psychiatry who work under the supervision of consultant psychiatrists. Increasingly, however, emergency assessments are performed by nurses and nurse specialists, especially ones trained in the assessment and management of deliberate self-harm (Chapter 11).

Following emergency psychiatric assessment, the patient can be discharged home (often with a plan for follow-up care by either a GP or mental health team), admitted to the inpatient unit in the hospital where the assessment took place, or admitted to a different inpatient unit if the patient's address indicates that they live within the 'catchment area' of a different mental health service. For involuntary admissions, the pathway to care is often different and somewhat more complex, although the same key elements are generally involved: assessment by a GP, emergency psychiatric assessment, and a final decision about admission or discharge at the inpatient unit (Chapter 13).

Once admitted as a voluntary patient, the inpatient experience in a psychiatry unit is similar in many respects to that in any other part of a general hospital. Doctors, nurses and various other healthcare professionals see the patient, assessments are made and treatments are offered. Consent is required for treatment (see Chapter 13 for exceptions to this), family and friends can visit during visiting hours and some patients leave the ward from time to time to go to the hospital shop (if there is one) or make brief trips outside the hospital with family or friends (for example, for fresh air), as appropriate.

Most hospitals are no-smoking zones but many psychiatry in-patient units still manage to create some form of sheltered (usually outdoor) facility for smoking. Smoking is, however, strongly dis-couraged, and most units actively offer supports for quitting. Most inpatient units also arrange weekly multi-disciplinary team meet-ings at which the treating team discusses care with the patient and members of the patient's family, as appropriate, if the patient so wishes (see below).

Length of stay in psychiatric inpatient units varies significantly but is quite short for the vast majority of patients: 30 per cent are discharged within a week of admission and 67 per cent are dis-charged within a month.[17] The Mental Health Commission has a *Code of Practice on Admission, Transfer and Discharge to and from an Approved Centre* which recommends that 'a comprehensive and structured discharge plan should be developed as a component of the individual care and treatment plan [which is a legal require-ment for all inpatients]. Discharge planning should commence as soon as possible after admission.'[18] A 'pre-discharge assessment' is also recommended:

- A resident [patient] and his/her family/carer and/or cho-sen advocate, *where appropriate* (that is, with the resident's consent), should be actively involved in the discharge pro-cess and a written record should be made of any involve-ment in the resident's clinical file.

- Involvement should include the option to attend and be in-volved in discharge meetings, ongoing discussion regard-ing the discharge plan with the multi-disciplinary team and key worker, and the opportunity for the resident and his/her family/carer and/or chosen advocate to voice any con-cerns they may have regarding discharge.

- Every effort should be made to identify the support needs of the family/carer, *where appropriate*, prior to discharge.

- Comprehensive information should be provided by the key-worker to the resident and his/her family/carer and/ or chosen advocate, *where appropriate* (that is, with the resident's consent), in plain understandable language upon discharge, which should include generic and individualised information.

- The key-worker should discuss the information provided with the resident and his or her family/carer and/or chosen advocate, *where appropriate* (that is, with the consent of the resident), prior to discharge to ensure that the resident understands the information given and to address any questions or concerns he/she may have prior to discharge.

- Approved centres should provide the resident, his/her family/carer and/or chosen advocate *where appropriate* (that is, with the consent of the resident), with a minimum of 2 days notice of discharge. If this does not occur, the reason(s) for it should be clearly documented in the resident's clinical file.' [emphasis in the Mental Health Commission's original].

Despite every effort being made to ensure that inpatient facilities and experiences reach an acceptable standard, there are occasions when services fall short of what might be expected. In these situations, it is your right as a patient or service user of the HSE to make a complaint and the HSE has developed a network of Complaints Officers and various other ways to receive and act upon complaints.[19] Facilities that are not directly run by the HSE have an obligation to provide similar facilities for complaints. In addition, the Inspector of Mental Health Services inspects inpatient facilities every year.

All of the above applies to *public* mental health care, funded by the HSE and provided by either the HSE directly or by other agencies acting on the HSE's behalf. It is also possible to access *private* mental health care in Ireland, through a number of private psychiatric hospitals, clinics and other facilities across the country. It is not possible to outline in detail the services available in all of these private facilities, so suffice it to say that many provide inpatient and outpatient services similar to those provided in public mental health services, and that much of the information above applies to many private psychiatric facilities also. The larger services, especially those involved in involuntary inpatient care, are subject to inspection by the Inspector of Mental Health Services.

There are also many private psychological therapists operating in Ireland, including clinical psychologists, psychotherapists, counsellors, analysts and any number of different alternative therapists. Many of these therapists are highly responsible, reliable and effective practitioners. Some, however, are not, chiefly because many areas within this sector are either regulated poorly or not regulated at all.[20] If you want to attend a private therapist, it is generally a good idea to ask your GP or local mental health team if they can recommend a therapist that they know to be appropriately qualified, reliable and effective. If, on the other hand, you are seeking to navigate this rather complex area yourself – which is not advised – here are some general guidelines that might help.

First, always look at a therapist's accreditation before considering attending. If someone claims to be a medical doctor, you can check this on the website of the Medical Council (www.medical-council.ie) under 'Search Registered Doctors'; this website will also let you check if the doctor is a trained 'specialist' in psychiatry. If someone claims to be a psychologist, you can check this on the website of the Psychological Society of Ireland (www.psihq.ie), and while not all psychologists wish their details to be disclosed publicly on the website, you can still confirm someone's registration status by emailing info@psihq.ie. For other kinds of therapists, there are various regulatory bodies which can be consulted, but easily the best way to pick a therapist to attend privately is to (a) select one recommended by your GP or mental health team; (b) select one that also works in the public sector (and has therefore been properly accredited, Garda-vetted, etc.); or (c) select one that a family member or friend has previously attended and found to be helpful and reliable.

Second, beware of excessive or clearly outlandish claims of cures. Many people who seek psychological therapy or support are at highly vulnerable moments in their lives, and there is no shortage of practitioners who – consciously or subconsciously – take advantage of this by making exaggerated claims for their therapies. Many of these are well-intentioned people who have come under the influence of 'rescue fantasies', which is when a therapist's genuine desire to help slowly transforms into a belief that the therapist is the only person who can 'rescue' you or cure you of your problems. Most psychological therapy works incrementally rather than dramatically, and claims of miracle cures should always be regarded with suspicion. People who sweepingly dismiss all other forms of therapy in favour of their own are especially suspicious: one size does not fit all. Also, beware of anyone charging dramatically more or dramatically less than the market rate for similar therapies; both extremes are equally suspicious.

Finally, if you are attending a therapist and you feel something is not right, leave at once. Just get up and walk away. If the therapist seeks contact outside therapy sessions, seeks to become involved in your life in other ways, or in any way steps outside expected boundaries, you should simply leave and discuss the matter immediately with your family and/or GP. This is by no means an uncommon situation and if the therapist is linked with a regulatory or accreditation body you should report them at once. Regrettably, I have found that, for the most part, experiences of this sort generally occur with 'therapists' who are not linked with any regulatory or accreditation body, in which case a report to the Gardaí may be in order.

It is important to emphasise again that the vast majority of private psychological therapists are highly responsible, reliable and effective practitioners, who perform important work extremely well. It is, however, in everyone's interests that the people attending such services are not harmed or betrayed by them, and to know how to assist in eliminating the unacceptable behaviours that would otherwise tarnish the reputation of the entire sector.

Family Involvement in Mental Health Care

Delivery of mental health care is greatly enhanced when there is family involvement in care delivery, whenever this is possible and appropriate. Family members are often key care-givers and supporters, and their lives can be profoundly affected by treatment decisions. They have, therefore, a legitimate and generally positive role in mental health care. Even so, this is often an area of great uncertainty and occasional conflict, especially if patients request that the treating team does not communicate with the family at all, despite the family having reasonable and entirely legitimate concerns about treatment. This tension has increased recently due to Irish legislation's general move away from consideration of the 'best interests' of the patient as the overarching principle of care, in favour of greater emphasis on autonomy, although the two concepts are not, of course, antithetical.

The Mental Health Commission, in its *Code of Practice on Admission, Transfer and Discharge to and from an Approved Centre* recommends that the patient 'should be encouraged to involve his/her family/carer in his/her care and to inform them of the admission, *where appropriate*'; that the patient's 'family/carer and/or chosen advocate should be involved in the admission process and in the development of the care and treatment plan' with the patient's consent; and that 'advocacy services should be made available'.[21] Similar recommendations regarding discharge-planning were already outlined above, with the Mental Health Commission strongly emphasising family involvement '*where appropriate*' (emphasis in the Mental Health Commission's original).

As there can sometimes be tensions between patients and families, especially if family members have instigated the involuntary admission process under the Mental Health Act 2001 (Chapter 13), the 2015 *Report of the Expert Group on the Review of the Mental Health Act 2001* also considered the matter of 'contact with families and doctor/patient confidentiality' in some detail, and made several recommendations:

- Where it is deemed appropriate, there should be proactive encouragement for the patient at all stages to involve his/her family/carer and/or chosen advocate in the admission process and in the development of the care and treatment plan with the patient's consent.

- All relevant professional bodies involved in mental health care should write into their codes of practice guidelines for practitioners the need to involve families/carers in the development of care and treatment plans with the patient's consent especially in cases of serious and enduring mental health problems.

- The Mental Health Commission should bring this matter before the Health, Social Care and Regulatory Forum to highlight the importance of the points made and to explore how best the relevant provisions could be expressed in codes of ethics/practice and guidance in this area by each of the professional regulatory bodies.

- The Mental Health Commission should develop more detailed guidance in this area for application right across the mental health sector.[22]

For doctors, the Medical Council has quite detailed guidelines concerning confidentiality, communication and other matters, and states that:

> confidentiality is central to the trust between you and your patients and a core element of the doctor/patient relationship. However, sharing information, in appropriate circumstances, is also important, both for patient care and for the safety of the patient and others.[23]

The Council goes on to say that:

> while the concern of the patient's relatives and close friends is understandable, you must not disclose information to them without the patient's consent. If the patient does not

consent, you should respect their decision, except where failure to disclose information would put the patient or others at risk of serious harm.

Disclosure without consent may be required either by law (for example, when ordered by a judge) or 'in the public interest':

> Disclosure in the public interest may be made to protect the patient, other identifiable people, or the community more widely. Before making a disclosure in the public interest, you must satisfy yourself that the possible harm the disclosure may cause the patient is outweighed by the benefits that are likely to arise for the patient or for others. You should disclose the information to an appropriate person or authority, and include only information needed to meet the purpose.

When information is disclosed in this fashion, the doctor 'should inform patients of the disclosure, unless this would cause them serious harm, or would undermine the purpose of the disclosure'. There are various other, more specific areas of guidance for doctors, including in relation to 'end of life care', where the Council emphases that 'communicating with patients and their families is an essential part of good care'. There is also further guidance in relation to 'open disclosure and duty of candour':

> Patients and their families, where appropriate, are entitled to honest, open and prompt communication about adverse events that may have caused them harm. When discussing events with patients and their families, you should:
>
> • Acknowledge that the event happened;
> • Explain how it happened;
> • Apologise, if appropriate; and
> • Assure patients and their families that the cause of the event will be investigated and efforts made to reduce the chance of it happening again.

More generally, Professor Patricia Casey of University College Dublin, writing in the *Irish Journal of Psychological Medicine* (journal of the College of Psychiatrists of Ireland), suggests a balanced approach to these issues, focussed clearly and pragmatically on the principles of 'beneficence' (keeping the welfare of the patient central) and 'non-maleficence' (not doing harm):

> Between no disclosure and total disclosure there is leeway to engage with both the patient and their carers while respecting the over-arching principle of confidentiality balanced against the vital involvement of carers.
>
> The confidentiality rule does not extend to refusing to take telephone calls or neglecting to respond to communication from carers expressing concern. Practices such as these would create an inappropriate barrier that would compromise patient care. Listening is not precluded by confidentiality, even when a capacitious patient refuses consent to share information. In these circumstances not only must the doctor listen to carers' concerns but if they are grave enough the doctor should act on these concerns.
>
> The possibility of advance directives in respect of confidentiality is one that could be considered. When patients are well between episodes of illness, the limits and extensions of confidentiality could be discussed and recorded in their medical records. The extent to which these would be binding law is unclear but, provided they are reviewed regularly to identify changes in the relationship between the patient and their carer, the good will of the treating doctor would be in no doubt. Arguably, this would afford significant protection for the doctor faced with a complaint or litigation in respect of confidentiality.
>
> Confidentiality is clinically and ethically challenging and as we deal with increasingly complex psychiatric illnesses and an informed public, the time may have come for specific training in responding to confidentiality issues.[24] Managing confidentiality should not be cast as a competition between patients and carers.[25] When faced with a dispute or dilemma involving a patient and the information that we believe

a carer should be given we should consult with colleagues and with textbooks of ethics and document carefully in the patient's records the issues and concerns. Just saying 'no' to a carer isn't good enough.[26]

Mental Health Services for Specific Groups

Mental health services for specific groups present particular issues which merit separate consideration. People with intellectual disabilities, for example, can develop the full range of mental illnesses and psychological problems, but the nature of presenting symptoms can vary significantly. In 2006, *A Vision for Change* noted that up to 50 per cent of people with severe and profound intellectual disabilities will have a mental health problem at some point during their lives, as will 20 to 25 per cent of those with mild and moderate intellectual disability:[27]

> Most of the mental health services for people with intellectual disability are provided by the voluntary and non-statutory sector (for example, by religious orders, parents associations, etc.).
>
> The voluntary sector has largely determined the shape of intellectual disability services. Service-level agreements are negotiated between the HSE and voluntary agencies to provide care to those with intellectual disability. Multidisciplinary teams in intellectual disability services provide person-centred care that is focused very much on the social, vocational, educational and residential needs of the individual but in general they do not deal with specialist mental health needs.
>
> For people in residential care, mental health care is supported by a relatively small number of psychiatrists with a special interest in the psychiatry of intellectual disability. Most of these psychiatrists work in voluntary agencies that do not have multidisciplinary MHID [mental health of intellectual disability] teams, nor do they have access to

the range of facilities required for comprehensive mental health assessment, treatment and care.

While the contribution of the voluntary sector has been extensive in this area, there is ample scope for greater coverage and coordination from a national perspective, especially for those with mild intellectual disability who still tend to come under the remit of generic rather than specialist mental health services. The 2006 policy made several recommendations to improve matters, focussed on gathering comprehensive and meaningful data, promotion of mental well-being, and registration with GPs, as well as development of specialist teams for adults and children with intellectual disability, and specialist forensic services:

> A spectrum of facilities should be in place to provide a flexible continuum of care based on need. This should include day hospital places, respite places, and acute, assessment and rehabilitation beds/places. A range of interventions and therapies should be available within these settings. [...] In order to ensure close integration, referral policies should reflect the needs of individuals with intellectual disability living at home with their family, GPs, the generic intellectual disability service providers, the MHID team and other mental health teams such as adult and child and adolescent mental health teams.

While significant progress has been made over the past decade, including in the area of forensic care, there remains much to be done in this historically neglected area. The mental health of ethnic minorities is another area that has become the subject of increased focus in recent decades owing to the advent of increased migration into Ireland in the late 1900s and early 2000s. The mental health needs of migrants were duly highlighted in 2006 in *A Vision for Change* and again in 2008 the HSE's *National Intercultural Health Strategy, 2007-2012*.[28]

This persisting issue was further underlined in a 2013 study of 178 Irish and migrant mental health service users, which found that a high percentage of both Irish (47 per cent) and migrant groups (70 per cent) had experienced two or more psychologically traumatic life events in their lives, a notably high level of trauma.[29] Forced migrants displayed more traumatic life events, post-traumatic symptoms, and higher levels of post-traumatic stress disorder than their voluntary migrant and Irish counterparts, with over 50 per cent experiencing torture prior to arrival in Ireland.

For the most part, mental health services for this group are provided by generic mental health services. In marked contrast with the situation in other countries, however, there is no evidence that people who were born outside Ireland experience higher rates of involuntary psychiatric care in Ireland, although there is evidence that they do not access voluntary mental health care as commonly as might be expected, possibly owing to inadvertent barriers to care (for example, differing cultural interpretations of suffering, language problems, etc.).[30]

Spirasi, on Dublin's North Circular Road, is Ireland's national centre for the treatment of survivors of torture (www.spirasi.ie). Established in 1999 to address the needs of the growing number of asylum-seekers and refugees in the country, Spirasi provides assistance to survivors of torture through a number of core services relating to physical, psychological, social and occupational well-being. There is, however, still need for more systematic national provision of specialist mental health care to this population, especially those in 'direct provision' who can have particular mental health needs.

The Irish Traveller community is another group with specific mental health needs that are both under-recognised and urgent: the suicide rate in male Travellers is more than six times that in the general population.[31] Generic mental health services are available to Travellers residing in the relevant catchment areas, but there are also Traveller-specific resources and initiatives which are especially important in terms of facilitating meaningful access to much-needed support services. Exchange House Ireland, for example, has provided Traveller-specific, professional, front-line family support, crisis intervention, education, training and services for over 35 years (www.exchangehouse.ie). This service is funded by the HSE (among other sources) and delivers a broad range of Traveller-specific services and supports.

The National Traveller Suicide Awareness Project uses a community development approach to address the issue of Traveller suicide and promotes initiatives which support suicide prevention, intervention and postvention in a coordinated way (www.travellersuicide.ie). It works within the Family Support Service and is supported by the Youth Service and Education Service. In addition, a dedicated Traveller Counselling Service, launched in February 2008, has now developed into a community-based counselling service for the Traveller community (www.travellercounselling.ie).

More broadly, Pavee Point is a national, non-governmental organisation committed to the realisation of human rights for Irish Travellers and Roma living in Ireland, with a strong emphasis on supporting mental health (www.paveepoint.ie). Traveller community health workers employed through the Primary Health Care for Travellers Project have worked in partnership with Temple Street Hospital to develop an information leaflet for Travellers on the hospital's self-harm team, and a bullying resource for Traveller parents was developed through the Eastern Regional Traveller Health Network and the Traveller Health Unit. The Traveller Men's Health Project also places strong emphasis on mental health, but still more need to be done to address mental health need and suicide rates in this population. The broad emphasis that Pavee Point places on achieving social rights for Travellers will play a key role in creating a societal context conducive to better mental and physical health among Travellers. The challenge is a social one as much as it is a medical one, if not more so.

Another group whose mental health needs are, perhaps, some of the least understood in the country is prisoners and various others in contact with the Gardaí and criminal justice system. Forensic psychiatry is that branch of mental health care concerned with the recognition and treatment of mental illness in the context of offending behaviour, often in the setting of prisons. People with mental illness are grossly over-represented in prison populations and there is a strong socioeconomic gradient, with people from deprived areas more likely to have mental illness *and* to be committed to prison. Moreover, the lower the level of mental health services in an area, the greater the likelihood of admission to the Central Mental Hospital, Dundrum, a secure inpatient forensic psychiatric facility[32] (Chapter 15).

Legislation in this area was substantially reformed through the Criminal Law (Insanity) Act 2006 which introduced significant change, replacing the 'guilty but insane' verdict with 'not guilty by reason of insanity', and providing for the concept of 'diminished responsibility' in murder cases, among other reforms. More specific issues relating to people with mental illness who offend, forensic psychiatry, and the Criminal Law (Insanity) Act 2006 are beyond the scope of the present book. Information about fitness to be tried, the verdict of 'not guilty by reason of insanity', 'diminished responsibility' in murder cases, and the role of the Mental Health Review Board is available on the website of the Citizens Information Board.[33]

The 2006 legislation was undoubtedly an important step forward and, as a result of this and various other developments, the late 1900s and early 2000s saw the National Forensic Mental Health Service develop into a highly progressive service by national and international standards, with specialised, multidisciplinary inpatient treatment, award-winning prison in-reach services and a comprehensive research programme.

Nonetheless, substantial challenges remain, especially with regard to drug misuse and mental health problems in Irish prisons, which still house alarming numbers of mentally ill offenders. This is deeply regrettable: prisons are toxic for the mentally ill. In June 2015, planning permission was granted for a 120-bed national forensic hospital in Portrane, County Dublin, as well as two 10-

bed specialist units for persons with intellectual disabilities and children and adolescents. The project included progressing design work for three 30-bedded Intensive Care Rehabilitation Units in Cork, Galway and Portrane, and represented the most substantial step forward for Ireland's forensic mental health services in several decades. Much has been achieved in this complex area in recent decades, but there remains much to be done.

There are various other groups whose mental health needs merit closer attention in the years to come. These include lesbian, gay, bisexual and transgender (LGBT) people. In 2011, the College of Psychiatry of Ireland, HSE and the Gay and Lesbian Equality Network (GLEN) published guidelines 'to inform psychiatrists of what they need to know when providing a mental health service to a lesbian, gay or bisexual (LGB) person'.[34] They advised 'psychiatrists to challenge any antigay bias they may have' so as to avoid behaviour such as 'presuming patients are heterosexual' or 'failing to appreciate any non-heterosexual form of behaviour, identity, relationship, family or community'. Psychiatrists were also advised to:

- Be aware of LGB mental health issues and gay-specific stressors.
- Respond supportively when patients disclose they are LGB.
- Take a gay-affirmative approach.
- Demonstrate that their practice is inclusive of LGB people.

In 2016, a *National Study of the Mental Health and Well-being of Lesbian, Gay, Bisexual, Transgender and Intersex People in Ireland* reported that between 12 and 35 per cent of participants showed evidence of severe or extremely severe depression, anxiety and stress, with the youngest age group (14-18 years) showing the most psychopathology and notably low scores on satisfaction, happiness and self-esteem.[35] A lifetime history of self-harm was reported by one-third (34 per cent) of participants, which represents an increase on the 27 per cent previously reported in the LGBT population in Ireland. While there is little doubt that services have improved considerably in recent decades, there is still, clearly, much work to be done.

Service-user Groups

Recent decades have seen a welcome increase in the number of mental health service-user groups in Ireland. Groups focussing on specific mental illnesses are mentioned in various specific chapters throughout this book. More generally, Mental Health Ireland is a national voluntary organisation comprising a 92 mental health associations throughout Ireland, led by volunteers (www.mentalhealthireland.ie). Its associations fundraise to organise outings and events for those with mental health problems in their communities.

Shine is another national organisation dedicated to upholding the rights and addressing the needs of those affected by mental ill health (www.shine.ie) (Chapter 3). Formerly Schizophrenia Ireland, Shine aims to empower people with mental ill health and their families through support, information and education. It advocates for social change, promoting and defending the right of all those affected by mental ill health to equal rights and quality services. The organisation promotes the development of self-help groups for people with mental ill health and their family members and carers; empowers through support, information and education; promotes rights to person-centred services which support recovery; engages in public awareness activities aimed at challenging stigma and discrimination; and seeks to influence positive policy changes in the provision of mental health services.

Aware, another support and advocacy organisation, developed in response to a clear need for information, understanding and support among persons affected by depression or bipolar disorder and their families (www.aware.ie) (Chapters 2 and 4). The organisation expanded across Ireland and seeks to create a society where people affected by stress, depression, bipolar and mood disorders are better understood, supported, free from stigma (Chapter 15) and encouraged to access appropriate therapies. The organisation's work involves information, education and support, and it organises group meetings, a telephone and email support service and a number of programmes based on principles of cognitive behavioural therapy. Aware also works in schools and offers education and training programmes in workplaces nationwide.

Mad Pride Ireland was founded by Mr John McCarthy, a powerful advocate for the mentally ill who argued for the normality of madness, a theme duly taken up by thousands of supporters at events in Cork, Tullamore and Portlaoise (www.madprideireland. ie). The Mad Pride approach is based on the idea that the best way to advance understanding of issues surrounding mental health is by engaging the community through active participation in a fun environment. This is achieved by holding family events that are inclusive, fun and suitable for everyone, including children, teenagers, adults and families.

The National Service Users Executive was founded with the aim of informing the National Health Service Directorate and the Mental Health Commission on issues relating to service-user involvement and participation in planning, delivering, evaluating and monitoring services, as well as implementing best practice guidelines at the service-user and provider interface (www.nsue.ie).

GROW is another mental health organisation that helps people with mental health problems (www.grow.ie). Founded in Australia in 1957, GROW now has a national network of over 130 groups in Ireland and its principal strength lies the support members give each other from their own experience.

The Mental Health Trialogue Network Ireland is a community development initiative in mental health which aims to empower communities to become proactive in communicating about mental health through an open dialogue and participatory process called 'trialogue' (www.trialogue.co). These groups aim to change the perception that only those who work in the field of mental health are experts in mental health: mental health concerns everyone, regardless of background and experience.

Hearing Voices Ireland was founded in 2006 by Mr Brian Hartnett with the goal of fostering acceptance of voice hearing as a valid human experience (www.voicesireland.com). By 2015, there were 'hearing voices' groups across Ireland, in Cork, Donegal, Dublin, Kerry, Kildare, Kilkenny, Longford, Tipperary and Belfast. These form part of a larger international 'hearing voices' movement, with 29 national networks and over 270 national, regional, and local hearing voices networks, groups, research and training centres, and trainers throughout the world. This movement reflects an exceptionally powerful reinterpretation of the experience of hearing voices which used to be invariably linked with major mental illness but is now subject to more nuanced interpretations, formulated chiefly by those having such experiences themselves.

Mental Health Reform (then named the Irish Mental Health Coalition) was also founded in 2006 and emerged during a period when there was little public advocacy on behalf of better mental health services, little political will for reform, and little presence of mental health as an issue covered in the media (www.mentalhealthreform.ie). The coalition was founded in part in response to the recognition in *A Vision for Change* that 'there is no equivalent advocacy for improving mental health services as exists for various other health services'. With a shared objective to campaign for the improvement of mental health services in Ireland, the formation of the coalition reflected its members' collective desire to ensure the new mental health policy translated into real change for people using mental health services.

Established with just five members initially, Mental Health Reform soon grew to more than 50 member organisations including most of the national mental health not-for-profit organisations and professional associations along with many other not-for-profit organisations who have a strong interest in better mental health supports for their clients. The aim of the coalition is to provide a coordinated public voice advocating for reform of the entire mental health system.

Useful Resources

There is extensive information about accessing mental health services in Ireland at www.yourmentalhealth.ie. Useful books relating to mental health policy in Ireland and elsewhere include: *Mental Health in Ireland: Policy, Practice and Law* edited by Agnes Higgins and Shari McDaid (Gill & Macmillan, 2014); *American Psychosis: How the Federal Government Destroyed the Mental Illness Treatment System* by E. Fuller Torrey (Oxford University Press, 2014); *Principles of Mental Health Law and Policy* edited by Lawrence Gostin, Peter Bartlett, Phil Fennell, Jean McHale and Ronnie Mackay (Oxford University Press, 2010); *Mental Health Policy and Practice* by Helen Lester and Jon Glasby (Palgrave Macmillan, 2006); *Mental Health and Social Policy in Ireland* edited by Suzanne Quin and Bairbre Redmond (University College Dublin Press, 2005).

Can't You Hear Them? The Science and Significance of Hearing Voices by Simon McCarthy-Jones (Jessica Kingsley Publishers, 2017) provides excellent, extensive information on hearing voices.

The national mental health policy, *A Vision for Change* (2006), can be downloaded from the website of the Department of Health: http://health.gov.ie/future-health/reforming-social-and-continuing-care-2/mental-health-a-vision-for-change/a-vision-for-change/

The Mental Health Commission's website (www.mhcirl.ie) provides access to their *Code of Practice on Admission, Transfer and Discharge to and from an Approved Centre* (under 'For Health Professionals', 'Codes of Practice'), as well as a wealth of other resources relating to voluntary and involuntary admission, the Mental Health Act 2001, and various other specific aspects of mental health services in Ireland.

The HSE website provides details of the *Advancing Recovery in Ireland* movement, which brings together people who provide mental health services, those who use them, and their families and community supports, to work on how to make the services better: www.hse.ie/eng/services/list/4/Mental_Health_Services/advancingrecoveryireland

Finally, the highly progressive EOLAS project (http://www. eolasproject.ie/) aims to design an information programme in collaboration with users of services and family members; deliver the programme using a co-facilitation model involving both clinicians and peer facilitators; recruit and educate both clinician and peer facilitators from within mental health services; conduct an independent evaluation of the programme from the perspectives of all stakeholders; and integrate EOLAS into HSE mental health service provision (see also Chapter 15).

Endnotes

1   Select Committee on the Lunatic Poor in Ireland, Report from the Select Committee on the Lunatic Poor in Ireland with Minutes of Evidence Taken Before the Committee and an Appendix. London: House of Commons, 1817 (p. 23).

2   Kelly, B. *Hearing Voices: The History of Psychiatry in Ireland*. Dublin: Irish Academic Press, 2016.

3   Brennan, D. *Irish Insanity: 1800-2000* (Routledge Advances in Sociology). Routledge, 2014 (p. 2).

4   Kelly, B.D. 'Penrose's Law in Ireland: An ecological analysis of psychiatric inpatients and prisoners'. *Irish Medical Journal* 2007; 100: 373-4.

5   Daly, A and Craig, S. HRB Statistics Series 29: Activities of Irish Psychiatric Units and Hospitals 2015. Dublin: Health Research Board, 2016 (p. 19)

6   Expert Group on Mental Health Policy. *A Vision for Change*. Dublin: The Stationery Office, 2006.

7   Study Group on the Development of the Psychiatric Services. *The Psychiatric Services – Planning for the Future*. Dublin: Stationery Office, 1984.

8   Barry, S. and Murphy P. (on behalf of the Faculty of Clinical Directors of the College of Psychiatry of Ireland). 'A Gloomy View:

Rhetoric or reality in relation to the advancement of *A Vision for Change'*. Dublin: College of Psychiatry of Ireland, 2009.

9   Indecon International Consultants. 'Review of Government Spending on Mental Health and Assessment of Progress on Implementation of *A Vision for Change'*. Dublin: Indecon/Amnesty International, 2009.

10 Independent Monitoring Group. '*A Vision for Change*: Sixth Annual Report on Implementation' (2011). Dublin: Department of Health, 2012 (p. 3).

11 Johnston, H. *All Vision but No Change? Determinants of Implementation: The Case of Ireland and Mental Health Policy.* Dublin: Institute of Public Administration, 2014.

12 Mental Health Commission. 'Mental Health Commission Annual Report 2013 Including Report of the Inspector of Mental Health Services'. Dublin: Mental Health Commission, 2014 (p. 6).

13 www.hse.ie/eng/services/list/4/Mental_Health_Services/counsellingpc

14 www.hse.ie/eng/services/list/4/Mental_Health_Services/National_Counselling_Service

15 www.medicalcouncil.ie/Public-Information/Check-the-Register

16 Daly, A. and Craig, S. HRB Statistics Series 29: Activities of Irish Psychiatric Units and Hospitals 2015. Dublin: Health Research Board, 2016 (p. 10).

17 Daly, A. and Craig, S. HRB Statistics Series 29: Activities of Irish Psychiatric Units and Hospitals 2015. Dublin: Health Research Board, 2016 (Table 2.9).

18 Mental Health Commission. 'Code of Practice on Admission, Transfer and Discharge to and from an Approved Centre'. Dublin: Mental Health Commission, 2009 (p. 39).

19 www.hse.ie/eng/services/yourhealthservice/feedback/Complaint

20 This problem will, hopefully, be addressed soon: P. Cullen. 'Counselling profession to be regulated'. *The Irish Times*, 2 September 2016.

21 Mental Health Commission. 'Code of Practice on Admission, Transfer and Discharge to and from an Approved Centre'. Dublin: Mental Health Commission, 2009 (p. 30).

22 Expert Group on the Review of the Mental Health Act 2001. 'Report of the Expert Group on the Review of the Mental Health Act 2001'. Dublin: Department of Health, 2015 (p. 81). I was nominated to the Expert Group on the Review of the Mental Health Act 2001 by the College of Psychiatrists of Ireland and appointed to the group by Minister Kathleen Lynch, Minister for Primary Care, Social Care (Disabilities and Older People) and Mental Health, in 2012. This book is written in a personal capacity, as a psychiatrist, and views expressed here or elsewhere do not necessarily represent the views of the Expert Group on the Review of the Mental Health Act 2001 or the College of Psychiatrists of Ireland. See also: Kelly, B.D. 'Revising, reforming, reframing: Report of the Expert Group on the Review of the Mental Health Act 2001' (2015). *Irish Journal of Psychological Medicine* 2015; 32: 161-6.

23 Medical Council. *Guide to Professional Conduct and Ethics for Registered Medical Practitioners* (8th Edition). Dublin: Medical Council, 2016 (p. 25).

24 Stiberg, E., Holand, U., Olstad, R. and Lorem, G. 'Teaching care and cooperation with relatives: Video as a learning tool in mental health work'. *Issues in Mental Health Nursing* 2012; 33: 528-35.

25 Chatzidamianos, G., Lobban, F. and Jones, S. 'A qualitative analysis of relatives', health professionals' and service users' views on the involvement in care of relatives in bipolar disorder'. *BMC Psychiatry* 2015; 15: 228.

26 Casey, P. 'Beneficence and non-maleficence: confidentiality and carers in psychiatry'. *Irish Journal of Psychological Medicine* 2016; 33: 203-6. Reproduced with the permission of Cambridge Univer-

sity Press and the agreement of Professor Patricia Casey and the College of Psychiatrists of Ireland.

27 Expert Group on Mental Health Policy. *A Vision for Change*. Dublin: The Stationery Office, 2006 (pp. 124-34).

28 Health Service Executive, 'National Intercultural Health Strategy, 2007-2012'. Dublin: Health Service Executive, 2008.

29 Wilson, F.E., Hennessy, E., Dooley, B., Kelly, B.D. and Ryan, D.A. 'Trauma and PTSD rates in an Irish psychiatric population: a comparison of native and immigrant samples'. *Disaster Health*, 2013; 1:74-83.

30 Kelly, B.D., Emechebe, A., Anamdi, C., Duffy, R., Murphy, N. and Rock, C. 'Custody, care and country of origin: Demographic and diagnostic admission statistics at an inner-city adult psychiatry unit'. *International Journal of Law and Psychiatry* 2015; 38: 1-7

31 All Ireland Traveller Health Study Team. Our Geels: All Ireland Traveller Health Study. Dublin: Our Geels: All Ireland Traveller Health Study; Department of Health and Children; Department of Health, Social Services and Public Safety; HSE; UCD; DCU, 2010 (p. 94).

32 O'Neill, C., Sinclair, H., Kelly, A. and Kennedy, H. 'Interaction of forensic and general psychiatric services in Ireland: Learning the lessons or repeating the mistakes?' *Irish Journal of Psychological Medicine* 2002; 19: 48-54.

33 http://www.citizensinformation.ie/en/justice/criminal_law/criminal_trial/criminal_insanity_and_mental_health.html

34 http://www.irishpsychiatry.ie/wp-content/uploads/2016/12/Lesbian-Gay-Bisexual-Patients-The-Issues-for-Mental-Health-Practice-Full-doc.pdf

35 Higgins, A., Doyle, L., Downes, C., Murphy, R., Sharek, D., DeVries, J., Begley, T., McCann, E., Sheerin, F. and Smyth, S. *The LGBT Ireland Report: National Study of the Mental Health and Wellbeing of Lesbian, Gay, Bisexual, Transgender and Intersex People in Ireland*. Dublin: GLEN and BeLonG To, 2016 (p. 23).

Chapter 13

INVOLUNTARY MENTAL HEALTH CARE AND PROTECTION OF HUMAN RIGHTS

Involuntary admission has been a feature of mental health care for as long as the history of the mentally ill has been recorded. Nonetheless, only a small minority of people with mental illness will ever experience involuntary care: in 2015, there were 17,860 psychiatric admissions in Ireland, of which 2,144 were on an involuntary basis.[1] As a result, 12 per cent of all admissions and 13 per cent of first admissions were involuntary. These proportions were exactly the same as those in 2014. This yields an involuntary admission rate of 46.7 per 100,000 population per year. Schizophrenia has the highest rate of involuntary admission, at 20.2 per 100,000 population per year, followed by mania at 7.7 per 100,000 population per year and depressive disorders at 4.8 per 100,000 population per year.

Ireland's rate of involuntary admission, at 46.7 per 100,000 population per year, is low by international standards. In England, there were 110 detentions per 100,000 population in the year leading up to 31 March 2015, which is over double the rate in Ireland.[2] Bradford, in West Yorkshire, reported 264.5 involuntary admissions per 100,000 population – over five times the Irish rate.

Notwithstanding Ireland's low rate of involuntary admission, the involuntary admission process is still an exceptionally important one, and one which many people find difficult to navigate and understand. This chapter outlines the process of involuntary psychiatric admission in Ireland, examines protections of human rights for those involuntarily admitted and treated, highlights gaps in the existing law and outlines recent proposals to revise and update the Mental Health Act 2001.

The Involuntary Admission Process in Ireland

The Mental Health Act 2001 governs civil (non-criminal) involuntary psychiatric admission and treatment in Ireland. There is a separate process under criminal law, the Criminal Law (Insanity) Acts 2006 and 2010 (Chapters 11 and 12). More specific issues relating to people with mental illness who offend, forensic psychiatry, and the Criminal Law (Insanity) Acts 2006 and 2010are beyond the scope of the present book. Information about fitness to be tried, the verdict of 'not guilty by reason of insanity', 'diminished responsibility' in murder cases, and the role of the Mental Health Review Board is available on the website of the Citizens Information Board.[3]

In relation to civil (non-criminal) involuntary care, the Mental Health Act 2001 comprises six parts dealing with (1) 'preliminary and general' issues, such as definitions and principles; (2) 'involuntary admission of persons to approved centres' (that is, admission to psychiatric inpatient units and hospitals); (3) 'independent review of detention', especially 'mental health tribunals' which review involuntary admissions; (4) 'consent to treatment', especially for involuntary patients; (5) regulations governing 'approved centres'; and (6) 'miscellaneous' matters, such as 'bodily restraint and seclusion', 'clinical trials', 'clinical directors', 'leave of High Court for certain proceedings', 'offences' and a scheduled 'review of operation of Act' (which was published in 2015 and is discussed towards the end of this chapter).

Preliminary and General

The preliminary section of the 2001 Act is primarily concerned with principles and definitions. The key principles of the legislation are set out in Section 4, and centre on 'the best interests of the person':

1. In making a decision under this Act concerning the care or treatment of a person (including a decision to make an admission order in relation to a person), the best interests of the person shall be the principal consideration with due regard being given to the interests of other persons who may be at risk of serious harm if the decision is not made.

2. Where it is proposed to make a recommendation or an admission order in respect of a person, or to administer treatment to a person, under this Act, the person shall, so far as is reasonably practicable, be notified of the proposal and be entitled to make representations in relation to it and before deciding the matter due consideration shall be given to any representations duly made under this subsection.

3. In making a decision under this Act concerning the care or treatment of a person (including a decision to make an admission order in relation to a person) due regard shall be given to the need to respect the right of the person to dignity, bodily integrity, privacy and autonomy.

The term 'mental disorder' is used throughout the legislation and includes 'mental illness, severe dementia or significant intellectual disability':

Mental illness is defined as:

a state of mind of a person which affects the person's thinking, perceiving, emotion or judgment and which seriously impairs the mental function of the person to the extent that he or she requires care or medical treatment in his or her own interest or in the interest of other persons.

Severe dementia is:

a deterioration of the brain of a person which significantly impairs the intellectual function of the person thereby affecting thought, comprehension and memory and which

311

includes severe psychiatric or behavioural symptoms such as physical aggression.

Significant intellectual disability is:

a state of arrested or incomplete development of mind of a person which includes significant impairment of intelligence and social functioning and abnormally aggressive or seriously irresponsible conduct on the part of the person.

Mental health services are defined as:

services which provide care and treatment to persons suffering from a mental illness or a mental disorder under the clinical direction of a consultant psychiatrist.

Treatment is:

the administration of physical, psychological and other remedies relating to the care and rehabilitation of a patient under medical supervision, intended for the purposes of ameliorating a mental disorder.

For the purposes of the Act, a child is defined as:

a person under the age of 18 years other than a person who is or has been married.

A relative is:

a parent, grandparent, brother, sister, uncle, aunt, niece, nephew or child of the person or of the spouse of the person whether of the whole blood, of the half blood or by affinity.

For the purposes of making an application for involuntary admission (see below), the term spouse:

does not include a spouse of a person who is living separately and apart from the person or in respect of whom an application or order has been made under the Domestic Violence Act 1996.

Involuntary Admission of Persons to Approved Centres

A person can be involuntarily admitted to an 'approved centre' on the grounds that the person is suffering from a 'mental disorder' fulfilling certain criteria (below), but a person *cannot* be so admitted *solely* on the grounds that he or she '(a) is suffering from a personality disorder' (Chapter 9); (b) 'is socially deviant', or (c) 'is addicted to drugs or intoxicants' (Chapter 7). The Act does not provide a definition of the term 'socially deviant'.

The involuntary admission procedure for adults is essentially a three-step process, involving a series of assessments which need to be recorded on a series of forms, all of which can be downloaded from the website of the Mental Health Commission (www.mhcirl. ie, under 'For Health Professionals', 'Forms', 'Statutory Forms (1-18)').

The first step is an 'application' for involuntary admission and this can be made by a spouse, civil partner, relative (Form 1); 'authorised officer' (member of the health service who can be reached through a community mental health team) (Form 2); member of the Garda Síochána (Irish police force) (Form 3); or anyone else ('member of the public') who fulfils certain conditions outlined in the Act (Form 4; for example, in circumstances where no one in the other categories can be found to make an application). Most importantly, the 'applicant' (for example, the family member seeking to have someone involuntarily admitted) must have observed the person within 48 hours of making the application.

The applicant should fill out the application form in clear, direct language and use legible handwriting. There are spaces to enter various personal details and to explain why the applicant thinks that the person named in the form requires involuntary admission and treatment. It is also necessary to know the name of the 'approved centre' to which the person is to be admitted. This information is available from a mental health team, GP or the website of the Mental Health Commission (www.mhcirl.ie, under 'Registration of Approved Centres', 'Register of Approved Centres').

The application forms do not require any detailed knowledge of psychiatry or mental health issues and the language should be clear and direct. If the applicant has previously filled out another application form and presented it to a GP who then declined to take the matter further (that is, the GP declined to fill out a 'recommendation', which is the second step in the involuntary admission process), the applicant must detail this on the new application form. It is worth reading over the application form after it is completed to check there are no errors, bearing in mind that the form will later be seen by the person's legal representative and possibly the person themselves.

The second step in the involuntary admission process involves presenting the completed application form to a registered medical practitioner who does not work at the 'approved centre' (for example, GP) and arranging for the person to be examined by that doctor. Sometimes, the applicant will have received the application form from the GP in the first place, in which case the applicant needs to complete the application form and then return it to the GP.

It is the responsibility of the applicant (for example, family member) to arrange assessment of the person by the doctor, most commonly the GP. The required 'examination' can occur at the GP surgery if the applicant can persuade the person to go there or it can occur elsewhere if, for example, the GP visits the person's home. The Act defines an 'examination' as 'a personal examination [...] of the process and content of thought, the mood and the behaviour of the person concerned'. If the person will not attend the GP and if the GP cannot gain access to the person to perform an 'examination', the entire involuntary process might simply come to an end at this point. In this case, it might be worth trying again later that day or on the next day, or seeing if the patient would see another GP.

If none of this works, then the only other option is to involve the Gardaí, but this is only possible under certain circumstances involving 'a serious likelihood' of 'immediate and serious harm'. More specifically:

> where a member of the Garda Síochána has reasonable grounds for believing that a person is suffering from a mental disorder and that because of the mental disorder there is a serious likelihood of the person causing immediate and serious harm to himself or herself or to other persons, the member may either alone or with any other members of the Garda Síochána (a) take the person into custody, and (b) enter if need be by force any dwelling or other premises or any place if he or she has reasonable grounds for believing that the person is to be found there. Where a member of the Garda Síochána takes a person into custody under [this section of the 2001 Act], he or she or any other member of the Garda Síochána shall make an application [...] to a registered medical practitioner for a recommendation.

Therefore, the Gardaí can only become formally involved in the application when there is 'a serious likelihood' of 'immediate and serious harm'. This higher threshold for involvement of Gardaí compared to other potential applicants reflects the fact that Gardaí have greater powers than any other applicant: Gardaí can enter someone's home by force if needed and take the person to the Garda station in order to have them examined by a doctor there. This leaves, however, a gap in the legislation in a situation where a family either cannot do an application or cannot get the person to see a GP (for example, because the person will not admit anyone to the house) but the person does not appear to present 'a serious likelihood' of 'immediate and serious harm' sufficient to merit Garda involvement (for example, certain cases of chronic self-neglect without overt threats or violence). In this circumstance, it is possible that involuntary admission simply cannot proceed at that time because the person does not fulfil criteria for the involuntary admission process under the 2001 Act, despite being possibly very mentally ill.

Presuming that the doctor (for example, GP) does gain access to the patient following an application, the doctor's examination:

> shall be carried out within 24 hours of the receipt of the application and the registered medical practitioner concerned shall inform the person of the purpose of the examination unless in his or her view the provision of such information might be prejudicial to the person's mental health, well-being or emotional condition.

The key question faced by the doctor on the recommendation form (Form 5) and (later) by the consultant psychiatrist on the 'admission order' (Form 6), is whether the person has 'mental illness, severe dementia or significant intellectual disability' (that is, 'mental disorder') *and* fulfils criterion (a) or (b) or both:

> (a) because of the illness, disability or dementia, there is a serious likelihood of the person concerned causing immediate and serious harm to himself or herself or to other persons;

> or

> (b) (i) because of the severity of the illness, disability or dementia, the judgment of the person concerned is so impaired that failure to admit the person to an approved centre would be likely to lead to a serious deterioration in his or her condition or would prevent the administration of appropriate treatment that could be given only by such admission, and (ii) the reception, detention and treatment of the person concerned in an approved centre would be likely to benefit or alleviate the condition of that person to a material extent.

If the doctor concludes that the person fulfils criterion (a) or (b) or both, the doctor can make a 'recommendation' for involuntary admission (Form 5) and a copy of the recommendation:

> shall be sent by the registered medical practitioner concerned [for example, GP] to the clinical director of the

approved centre concerned [that is, psychiatric inpatient unit or hospital] and a copy of the recommendation shall be given to the applicant concerned [for example, family member].

Such a recommendation 'shall remain in force for a period of 7 days' (that is, there are seven days to bring the person to the psychiatric inpatient unit or hospital named on the forms before the 'recommendation' expires).

If the doctor concludes that the person does not fulfil criterion (a) or (b), then the doctor does not complete the recommendation for involuntary admission. If the applicant is unhappy with this decision, the applicant can seek to have the person seen by another GP, but must inform the second GP (on a new application form) about the decision of the first GP to decline to complete the first 'recommendation'.

Following the 'recommendation' for involuntary admission, 'the applicant concerned [for example, family member] shall arrange for the removal of the person to the approved centre' within seven days. It is up to the applicant, in the first instance, to arrange transport to the 'approved centre'. Given that this is an *involuntary* admission, however, there is every likelihood that the applicant will be unable to arrange such transport owing to non-cooperation by the person concerned. In this circumstance, the GP and the consultant psychiatrist at the 'approved centre' can take steps to admit the person.

More specifically:

> where the applicant concerned [for example, family member] is unable to arrange for the removal of the person concerned, the clinical director of the approved centre specified in the recommendation or a consultant psychiatrist acting on his or her behalf shall, at the request of the registered medical practitioner who made the recommendation [for example, GP], arrange for the removal of the person to

the approved centre by members of staff of the approved centre.

For this to occur, the consultant psychiatrist must have a copy of the application form, the recommendation form signed by the doctor (for example, GP), and sufficient clinical information about the case to perform a preliminary risk assessment of the situation. If the psychiatrist and GP believe:

> there is a serious likelihood of the person concerned caus-ing immediate and serious harm to himself or herself or to other persons, the clinical director or a consultant psychia-trist acting on his or her behalf may, if necessary, request the Garda Síochána to assist the members of the staff of the approved centre in the removal by the staff of the person to that centre and the Garda Síochána shall comply with any such request.

Under such circumstance, the Garda Síochána can, if neces-sary, enter the person's dwelling by force and ensure the removal of the person to the approved centre, in collaboration with staff.

After the completed application and recommendation forms are received by the consultant psychiatrist, and after the patient has arrived at the 'approved centre', the third and final step in the involuntary admission process can occur: 'a consultant psychia-trist on the staff of the approved centre shall, as soon as may be, carry out an examination of the person' and shall either (a) com-plete an 'admission order' if 'he or she is satisfied that the person is suffering from a mental disorder' (Form 6) or (b) 'refuse to make such order'. The patient cannot be detained for more than 24 hours without such an examination taking place and such an order being made or refused.

If an admission order is made, it authorises 'the reception, de-tention and treatment of the patient concerned and shall remain in force for a period of 21 days'. This period may be extended by a 'renewal order' for a period of up to three months, then up to six months, and then up to 12 months, under certain conditions.

The involuntary admission process is a complex, important one, which is commonly misunderstood. It is extremely important for both patients and families to understand that no individual person – family member, Garda, GP – has the power to 'sign someone in' to hospital under civil mental health legislation. Various people, including family, can *commence* the involuntary admission process by making an application for involuntary admission (as described above), and a doctor's signature is required for the recommendation, but the ultimate decision about involuntary admission lies with the consultant psychiatrist. Even the consultant psychiatrist, however, cannot involuntarily admit someone from the community without the first two steps being completed, with the result that *no single individual can 'sign in' anyone anywhere.* There are now, moreover, proposals to reform the 2001 Act to create a mandatory duty for the consultant psychiatrist to consult with another member of the multi-disciplinary mental health team before completing any involuntary admission order, further broadening involvement in the process (see below).

Once an involuntary admission order is completed (Form 6) and the patient notified in writing, the consultant psychiatrist must inform the Mental Health Commission of the order and the Mental Health Commission will then (a) refer the matter to a mental health tribunal; (b) assign a legal representative to the patient, 'unless he or she proposes to engage one'; and (c) direct that an independent psychiatrist examine the patient, interview the patient's consultant psychiatrist and review the patient's records.

Within 21 days of an involuntary admission, a mental health 'tribunal shall review the detention of the patient' and, 'if satisfied that the patient is suffering from a mental disorder' and that appropriate procedure has been followed, shall 'affirm the order' (that is, state that involuntary admission can continue); if the tribunal is not so satisfied, the tribunal shall 'revoke the order and direct that the patient be discharged from the approved centre concerned.' There must be a tribunal within 21 days of each admission order and each renewal order.

The treating psychiatrist can 'revoke' the involuntary admission or renewal order at any time and *must* do so when the patient no longer fulfils relevant criteria, at which point the patient can leave the approved centre or choose to remain as a voluntary inpatient. If the order is revoked prior to review by a mental health tribunal, the scheduled tribunal is cancelled but the patient can (within 14 days) request a tribunal to review the matter at a future date. Tribunals are considered in more detail below.

Part 2 of the Mental Health Act 2001 goes on to address a range of other areas of relevance to this process, including provisions for appeal to the Circuit Court where, regrettably, the onus of proof lies on the patient to prove that he or she does *not* have mental disorder (an exceptionally difficult and arguably impossible task); transfer of involuntary patients between approved centres (for example, from one hospital to another); and powers to prevent voluntary patients from leaving approved centres for up to 24 hours, to allow either their treating consultant psychiatrist to discharge them or the opinion of another consultant psychiatrist to be sought.

This means that a voluntary inpatient can be detained if they request to leave, fulfil criteria for involuntary admission and an opinion from a second consultant psychiatrist supports this decision. There are currently proposals to change this procedure to make it more like the three-step involuntary admission procedure from the community (which has also been used in this situation), thus increasing procedural equality (see below).

Independent Review of Detention

When introduced, the Mental Health Act 2001 made provision for the appointment of a 'Mental Health Commission', the principal functions of which are:

to promote, encourage and foster the establishment and maintenance of high standards and good practices in the delivery of mental health services and to take all reasonable steps to protect the interests of persons detained in approved centres under this Act.

More specifically, the Mental Health Commission appoints persons to serve on mental health tribunals; maintains a panel of psychiatrists to perform independent medical examinations of involuntary patients; assists in organising free legal aid for involuntary patients; provides appropriate advice to relevant ministers; and prepares and reviews periodically codes of practice for the guidance of persons working in the mental health services.

One of the central functions of the Commission is to appoint mental health tribunals 'to determine such matter or matters as may be referred to it by the Commission'. One of the chief functions of tribunals is to review the detentions of patients involuntarily admitted to approved centres under the 2001 Act. Each tribunal comprises three members, including (a) one consultant psychiatrist; (b) one barrister or solicitor (of not less than seven years' experience); and (c) one other person who does not fall into categories (a) or (b) and is neither a registered doctor nor a registered nurse. Decisions are made by majority voting. A tribunal can direct a patient's treating psychiatrist that the patient must appear at a tribunal at a given place and time, direct any persons to appear at a tribunal to give evidence, direct any person to produce any documents relevant to the work of the tribunal, and 'give any other directions for the purpose of the proceedings concerned that appear to the tribunal to be reasonable and just'.

The Mental Health Commission duly directs that an independent psychiatrist examines each patient detained under the Act, interviews the patient's consultant psychiatrist and reviews the patient's records at the approved centre. Then, within 21 days of the involuntary admission or renewal order being made, a mental health tribunal reviews the involuntary admission of the patient and, 'if satisfied that the patient is suffering from a mental disorder' and that appropriate procedure has been followed, shall affirm the order (that is, state that the involuntary admission can continue); if the tribunal is not so satisfied, the tribunal shall 'revoke the order and direct that the patient be discharged from the approved centre concerned'. The person can also remain as a voluntary inpatient if he or she wishes.

Under the legislation, tribunal hearings are held 'in private' in the approved centre (that is, psychiatric inpatient unit or hospital). The patient is provided with free legal representation through a free legal aid scheme. In practice, there is often unclearness among patients and families about who attends tribunals and who does not. First, the three members of the tribunal must be present, as must the patient's treating psychiatrist. The patient's legal representative is also present, unless the patient has dispensed with their services. The patient may attend if he or she wishes but does not have to. No one else has an automatic right to attend.

If someone else wishes to attend the tribunal (for example, the applicant, a family member, other healthcare staff), they must come to the approved centre at the time the tribunal is due to occur and make a request of the clerk to attend. The most usual course of events then is that the clerk conveys the request to the tribunal chairperson, who will often consult with the patient and/ or the patient's legal representative before deciding whether or not the person can attend the tribunal. The treating consultant psychiatrist has no decision-making power in this matter and cannot predict in advance whether the tribunal chairperson will permit someone to attend the tribunal. Additional staff members (for example, community mental health nurses), advocates or various others may also request to attend the tribunal, but whether or not they can do so is a matter for the tribunal to decide on the day.

Following the hearing, the tribunal will either affirm the involuntary admission or renewal order (that is, state that the involuntary admission can continue) or else revoke it (that is, permit the patient to leave the approved centre or choose to remain as a voluntary inpatient). Around one in every ten orders reviewed by tribunals is revoked. The tribunal can revoke an admission or renewal order owing to either (a) an apparent failure to follow the procedures in the legislation to the extent that an injustice might have resulted (minor aberrations such as misspellings can be overlooked provided they do 'not affect the substance of the order' and do 'not cause an injustice'); or (b) the tribunal reaching the conclusion that the patient does not fulfil the *clinical* criteria for involuntary admission (as set out above) *on the day of the tribunal*; that is, they do not base this decision on the reported clinical picture on the day the admission or renewal order was made, but rather on the day of the tribunal, which can be up to 21 days after the order was made (as it is hoped that clinical improvement will have occurred by then).

Therefore, a revocation does not mean that the patient did not fulfil clinical criteria for involuntary admission on the day that the admission or renewal order was made, but rather that the patient no longer fulfils such criteria *on the day of the tribunal* or there were substantive procedural aberrations when the order was made. In reaching its decision, the tribunal must have regard to the independent psychiatric report prepared earlier during the involuntary admission, as well as the input from the patient's legal representative and treating psychiatrist, as well as anyone else it heard from including, most importantly, the patient (unless the patient chooses not to attend or does not speak).

After the tribunal, the patient's legal representative will generally explain the outcome to the patient. It is, however, very common that further explanation is required later in the day and this is often provided by the treating psychiatrist, nursing staff or other members of the multi-disciplinary team at the approved centre. If the order is affirmed by the tribunal the patient remains detained and therefore must remain in hospital.

The patient's legal representative can advise the patient about the possibility of proceeding to the Circuit Court for an appeal if the patient so desires. More specifically, 'a patient may appeal to the Circuit Court against a decision of a tribunal to affirm an order made in respect of him or her on the grounds that he or she is not suffering from a mental disorder'; that is, the patient cannot appeal to the Circuit Court on the grounds of the service's alleged failure to follow the procedures in the legislation (this could, however, be heard in the High Court), but can appeal to the Circuit Court on the grounds that he or she no longer fulfils clinical criteria for involuntary admission. The patient's legal representative can arrange an independent psychiatric assessment for the patient to assist with the Circuit Court case (funded by the legal aid scheme).

The Circuit Court, having listened to the evidence, can either revoke or affirm the order, based on its conclusions as to whether the patient fulfils involuntary admission criteria *on the day of the Circuit Court case*; that is, as with the tribunals, the Circuit Court does not base its decision on the reported clinical picture on the day that the admission or renewal order was made, but rather on the day of the appeal hearing. A High Court appeal against a Circuit Court order can only be made on a 'point of law' and not on clinical grounds (and there is also the possibility of free legal support for High Court cases).

Overall, mental health tribunals and the associated appeals systems are a key element in the human right protections offered by the Mental Health Act 2001. I have attended many tribunals both as treating psychiatrist and as tribunal psychiatrist, and have prepared independent reports for tribunals, but the fact that tribunals are conducted 'in private' prevents me from providing any more details about the hearings themselves. What I can say, however, is that making them work effectively for patients requires considerable teamwork, explanation and support, but that it is richly worth the effort as they provide an important forum at which key issues relating to treatment, liberty and service provision are worked out. Various reforms to the tribunal system, to make them work better, were proposed in 2015 and these are summarised below.

In terms of other forms of oversight apart from tribunals, the 2001 Act made provision for the establishment of an Inspector of Mental Health Services to replace the pre-existing Inspector of Mental Hospitals. The functions of the Inspector of Mental Health Services are 'to visit and inspect every approved centre at least once in each year ... and to visit and inspect any other premises where mental health services are being provided as he or she thinks appropriate'. Each year, the inspector shall 'carry out a review of mental health services in the State' and 'furnish a report in writing to the Commission'. These inspections occur annually, the reports are made public and the Inspectorate represents another important layer of oversight and governance of the mental health system.

Consent to Treatment

The Mental Health Act 2001 provides detailed guidelines in relation to 'consent obtained freely without threats or inducements' and specifies that:

> the consent of [an involuntary] patient shall be required for treatment except where, in the opinion of the consultant psychiatrist responsible for the care and treatment of the patient, the treatment is necessary to safeguard the life of the patient, to restore his or her health, to alleviate his or her condition, or to relieve his or her suffering, and by reason of his or her mental disorder the patient concerned is incapable of giving such consent.

As a result, even if someone is admitted on an involuntary basis as outlined above, they can receive treatment without consent *only* if they lack mental capacity to provide such consent; that is, just being unwilling to accept treatment is insufficient to justify treatment without consent: the person must be actually mentally *incapable* of making such decisions. This is in marked contrast to many other jurisdictions, such as England and Wales, where an involuntary patient with full mental capacity can be treated against their wishes; this is *not* the case in Ireland. The result is that, in practice, a great deal of negotiation about treatment occurs, even in the context of an involuntary admission.

There are additional provisions relating to particular treatments. Psychosurgery (which is now very, very rare) can only be carried out if an involuntary patient consents in writing and the surgery is authorised by a mental health tribunal. ECT (Chapters 2, 3 and 4) can be administered to an involuntary patient only if (a) the patient consents in writing, or (b), if the patient is 'unable' (that is, lacks mental capacity) to provide consent and the treatment is approved by the treating consultant psychiatrist and one other consultant psychiatrist.

Similarly, if 'medicine has been administered to [an involuntary] patient for the purposes of ameliorating his or her mental disorder for a continuous period of 3 months, the administration of that medication shall not be continued' unless either (a) the patient consents in writing, or (b) if the patient is 'unable' (that is, lacks mental capacity) to provide consent, the treatment is approved by the treating consultant psychiatrist and one other consultant psychiatrist.

Approved Centres and Other Matters

The Mental Health Act 2001 provides detailed guidelines in relation to 'approved centres' which are hospitals or other inpatient facilities 'for the care and treatment of persons suffering from mental illness or mental disorder'. The Mental Health Commission maintains a register of approved centres and may attach conditions to the registration of specific centres, including the performance of maintenance or refurbishment, or the specification of minimum staffing numbers and/or maximum resident numbers.

The final part of the 2001 Act addresses a range of other miscellaneous but important issues, including the use of bodily restraint and seclusion, participation in clinical trials, the appointment of clinical directors and instigation of civil proceedings.

In relation to seclusion and bodily restraint, the Act specifies that:

a person shall not place a patient in seclusion or apply mechanical means of bodily restraint to the patient unless such seclusion or restraint is determined, in accordance with the rules made under [this legislation], to be necessary for the purposes of treatment or to prevent the patient from injuring himself or herself or others, and unless the seclusion or restraint complies with such rules.

According to the Mental Health Commission, 'seclusion' is:

the placing or leaving of a person in any room alone, at any time, day or night, with the exit door locked or fastened or held in such a way as to prevent the person from leaving.[4]

This practice is now carefully governed by detailed rules which are available on the website of the Mental Health Commission (www.mhcirl.ie, under 'For Health Professionals', 'Rules'), which also provides rules governing use of 'mechanical means of bodily restraint' and a 'code of practice' governing 'physical restraint' (www.mhcirl.ie, under 'For Health Professionals', 'Codes of Practice'). All of these practices are monitored by the Commission, which reports on their use and makes these reports publicly available on its website.

Regarding clinical trials, the 2001 Act states that:

notwithstanding section 9 (7) of the Control of Clinical Trials Act 1987, a person suffering from a mental disorder who has been admitted to an approved centre under this Act shall not be a participant in a clinical trial.

It is understood that, in this section of the Act, the term 'patient' refers to patients admitted on an involuntary basis under the 2001 Act.

Regarding the instigation of civil proceedings, the Act states that:

no civil proceedings shall be instituted in respect of an act purporting to have been done in pursuance of this Act save by leave of the High Court and such leave shall not be refused unless the High Court is satisfied: (a) that the proceedings are frivolous or vexatious, or (b) that there are no reasonable grounds for contending that the person against whom the proceedings are brought acted in bad faith or without reasonable care.

There is now a considerable body of High and Supreme Court cases clarifying various aspects of the 2001 Act.

Children

The Mental Health Act 2001 contains several sections relating specifically to children, where a 'child' is defined as 'a person under the age of 18 years other than a person who is or has been married'. In essence, a child can be admitted as a 'voluntary' patient at the behest of the child's parents or guardian. There are two methods for the involuntary admission of children: one pertaining to children in the community, the other to children who are already voluntary patients in an approved centre.

For a child in the community (for example, at home) whose parents or guardian are concerned that he or she is mentally ill, it should be suggested that the child sees a GP, who may refer to a child and adolescent psychiatrist who may (in a minority of cases) suggest voluntary psychiatric admission. If the parents and guardian are in agreement with this but the child does not cooperate, the legislation indicates that the child can still be admitted 'voluntarily', based solely on parental consent. If this proves inoperable (for example, if a 17-year-old 'child' physically objects), contact can be made with the local health service (that is, HSE), via the GP or child and adolescent mental health team, to express concern.

Following such an expression of concern (or a similar expression of concern from another source), the 2001 Act states that:

> where it appears to a health board [HSE] with respect to a child who resides or is found in its functional area that (a) the child is suffering from a mental disorder, and (b) the

child requires treatment which he or she is unlikely to receive unless an order is made under this section, then, the health board may make an application to the District Court ("the court") for an order authorising the detention of the child in an approved centre [that is, involuntary admission of the child to an inpatient psychiatric unit or hospital].

The definition of 'mental disorder' for children (that is, the clinical criteria for involuntary admission) are the same as those for adults (outlined in Section 3 of the 2001 Act; above).

For involuntary admission of a child to occur, it is necessary that 'the child has been examined by a consultant psychiatrist who is not a relative of the child and a report of the results of the examination is furnished to the court by the health board'. The Act also states that:

where (a) the parents of the child, or either of them, or a person acting *in loco parentis* refuses to consent to the examination of the child, or (b) following the making of reasonable enquiries by the health board, the parents of the child or either of them or a person acting *in loco parentis* cannot be found by the health board, then, a health board may make an application [to the District Court] without any prior examination of the child by a consultant psychiatrist.

In this circumstance:

the court may, if it is satisfied that there is reasonable cause to believe that the child the subject of the application is suffering from a mental disorder, direct that the health board arrange for the examination of the child.

When the court has considered the resultant psychiatric report and any other evidence presented to it, and if the court concludes:

that the child is suffering from a mental disorder, the court shall make an order that the child be admitted and detained for treatment in a specified approved centre for a period not exceeding 21 days.

This process might take some time to complete, so in the interim:

> the court, of its own motion or on the application of any
> person, may give such directions as it sees fit as to the care
> and custody of the child who is the subject of the applica-
> tion pending such determination, and any such direction
> shall cease to have effect on the determination of the ap-
> plication.

In practice, this process can be very difficult for families to operate, especially in the case of an older child (aged 16 or 17) who
is physically uncooperative with assessment. In these instances,
the Gardaí can, on occasion, become involved in order to facilitate safe assessment by a psychiatrist and provision of a report to
the District Court. Garda involvement is, however, an exceptional
measure and other methods of resolving matters are greatly to be
preferred if they are at all possible.

Once an order is issued by the court, the child can be trans-
ferred to an approved centre, ideally (but by no means invariably) an approved centre specifically for children and adolescents.
While the initial 21-day order is in force, 'the health board' (that is,
HSE) can apply 'for an extension of the period of detention of the
child the subject of the application' and 'the court may order that
the child be detained for a further period not exceeding 3 months'
(and, subsequently, 6 months) following a further psychiatric report. Psychosurgery and ECT require court approval. There are no
mental health tribunals for children; review by the District Court
is seen as sufficient protection of rights.

The second route to involuntary care for a child pertains to
children who are already voluntary inpatients in approved centres.
More specifically:

> where the parents of a child who is being treated in an ap-
> proved centre as a voluntary patient, or either of them, or
> a person acting *in loco parentis* indicates that he or she

wishes to remove the child from the approved centre and a consultant psychiatrist, registered medical practitioner or registered nurse on the staff of the approved centre is of opinion that the child is suffering from a mental disorder, the child may be detained and placed in the custody of the health board for the area in which he or she is for the time being.

In practice, the child is usually detained in the approved centre for up to 72 hours and, unless the health board then returns the child to their guardian, the health board must apply to the District Court, with a psychiatric report, and the involuntary admission process is, from that point, essentially the same as that described above for the involuntary admission of a child in the community (for example, at home).

Discussion

The incremental introduction of the Mental Health Act 2001 between 2001 and 2006 stimulated a range of responses from various stakeholders in Ireland's mental health services. In general, there was broad acceptance of the need to update existing legislation in order to better protect patients' rights and increase adherence to the UN 'Principles for the Protection of Persons with Mental Illness and the Improvement of Mental Health Care' (1991). There were, however, clear gaps in the legislation which did not address in detail the process of voluntary admission, did not establish a minimum standard of care to which patients were entitled and did not allow for shorter periods of detention explicitly for assessment purposes.

In fact, the 2001 Act is quite crisply focussed on two key issues: revised procedures for involuntary admission and strengthened governance mechanisms, especially mental health tribunals and changes to inspection processes. Its overarching aim was to enhance protections of the human rights of the mentally ill, especially those who receive involuntary care. Over a decade since full implementation in 2006, did the 2001 Act achieve its goal?

In 2005, the WHO published a systematic set of human rights standards for national mental health legislation in its 'Resource Book on Mental Health, Human Rights and Legislation', which outlined a detailed statement of human rights issues which, according to the WHO, need to be addressed at national level.[5] Since then, it has become apparent that full implementation of the Mental Health Act 2001 has brought Ireland into much greater, but still incomplete, compliance with these standards.

In its 'Resource Book', the WHO sets out its 'Checklist for Mental Health Legislation' comprising specific human rights standards which, according to the WHO, need to be met in each jurisdiction. These standards are clearly based on previous UN and WHO statements and centre on the provision of mental health care that is reasonable, equitable and in accordance with international standards. Inevitably, mental health legislation plays a key role in meeting these standards.

In Ireland, civil mental health legislation (chiefly the Mental Health Act 2001) now meets 80 (48.2 per cent) of the 166 relevant standards for adults.[6] Areas of relatively high compliance include definitions of mental disorder, procedures for involuntary admission and treatment, and clarity regarding offences and penalties. Areas of medium compliance relate to mental capacity and consent (Chapter 14), and certain aspects of oversight and review (which exclude long-term voluntary patients, who can experience *de facto* restrictions of liberty). Areas of low compliance relate to promoting rights, voluntary patients (especially non-protesting, incapacitated patients) and protection of vulnerable groups. These deficits reflect the 2001 Act's focus on involuntary admission procedures and governance processes, rather than voluntary patients and broader social rights (Chapter 15).

Overall, then, the 2001 Act performs quite well in areas of traditional concern in mental health services (chiefly involuntary care) but there is still much progress to be made in relation to the human rights of the mentally ill more broadly, especially social and economic rights (Chapter 15). These issues have come strongly to the fore following the adoption of the UN Convention on the Rights of Persons with Disabilities (CRPD) by the UN General Assembly in 2006. The CRPD commits ratifying countries 'to promote, protect and ensure the full and equal enjoyment of all human rights and fundamental freedoms by all persons with disabilities, and to promote respect for their inherent dignity'. It specifies that 'persons with disabilities include those who have long-term physical, mental, intellectual or sensory impairments which in interaction with various barriers may hinder their full and effective participation in society on an equal basis with others'.

In the context of psychiatry, it seems clear that this definition does not include all people with mental illness, because many mental illnesses (for example, adjustment disorder) are not 'long-term'. The CRPD does not, however, present its definition of 'persons with disabilities' as a comprehensive one but specifies that the term 'persons with disabilities' *includes* people with 'long-term' impairments; others, presumably, will also fit this definition.[7] As a result, it is likely that some people with mental illness meet the definition at least some of the time (for example, some people with chronic schizophrenia or an intellectual disability) but others do not (for example, a person with adjustment disorder).

The CRPD also states 'that disability is an evolving concept and that disability results from the interaction between persons with impairments and attitudinal and environmental barriers that hinders their full and effective participation in society on an equal basis with others'. This definition decouples 'persons with disabilities' from any specific diagnoses and moves the definition of disability into a social context, implicitly recognising that it is societal attitudes and barriers that generate most of the 'disability' experienced by people with physical or mental impairment (and not the impairment itself). Ireland signed the CRPD in 2007 but has not yet ratified it (at time of writing, in early 2017).

The CRPD raises an important issue relating to involuntary mental health care as it states that 'the existence of a disability shall in no case justify a deprivation of liberty'. If certain people with 'mental disorder' under the Mental Health Act 2001 (for example, some people with chronic schizophrenia) fit the UN definition of 'persons with disabilities', then the 2001 Act is inconsistent with the CRPD in this respect, given the clear links that the 2001 Act draws between mental disorder, risk and involuntary admission (see above). This is also the case for mental health legislation in England, Wales, Scotland, Northern Ireland and most other jurisdictions, all of which violate this article of the CRPD.

In 2009, the UN High Commissioner for Human Rights underlined this issue by objecting explicitly to any link between 'preventive detention' and risk to self or others stemming from 'mental illness':

> Legislation authorising the institutionalisation of persons with disabilities on the grounds of their disability without their free and informed consent must be abolished. This must include the repeal of provisions authorising institutionalisation of persons with disabilities for their care and treatment without their free and informed consent, as well as provisions authorising the preventive detention of persons with disabilities on grounds such as the likelihood of them posing a danger to themselves or others, in all cases in which such grounds of care, treatment and public security are linked in legislation to an apparent or diagnosed mental illness.[8]

This UN position stands in remarkable contrast to the history of mental health services in Ireland and most other countries, where involuntary care has always been based on the presence of mental illness and associated risk. It is not, however, entirely clear what proportion of persons with mental illness are 'persons with disabilities' under the CRPD, and acute psychiatric admission in Ireland is not considered 'institutionalisation'.

In addition, denial of care (especially to the most distressed) on the basis of the CRPD would be grossly inconsistent with the fundamental aims and purpose of the Convention: people with disabilities are entitled to all the levels and modalities of care that are available to everyone, without distinction of any description. On this basis, abolishing involuntary care in order ostensibly to comply with the CRPD would be historically radical, counterproductive and, it would seem, unlikely step.

The second key issue that the CRPD raises for Ireland from a mental health perspective relates to mental capacity legislation, which became the subject of considerable attention in the early 2000s. On 30 December 2015, new legislation in this area, the Assisted Decision-Making (Capacity) Act 2015, was signed by President Higgins, and this interesting, challenging development is considered in some detail in the next chapter of this book. Before proceeding to that, however, it is worth examining in some detail current gaps in Irish mental health law and recent initiatives to update the Mental Health Act 2001 in order to address some of the unresolved human rights and other issues with the legislation.

Reform of Irish Mental Health Law

Mental health law is both challenging to draft and challenging to implement. In addition to the human rights concerns outlined above, some of the key issues that patients raise in relation to the Mental Health Act 2001 include difficulty understanding how the involuntary admission system works, problems knowing precisely what to expect from mental health tribunals, and a feeling that renewal orders of one-year duration are too long. Families commonly comment about difficulty understanding the system, problems with transport to inpatient facilities, and what to do if their family member is mentally ill and not accepting treatment, but not yet mentally ill enough to fulfil criteria for involuntary admission. Similar concerns are expressed by mental health professionals as well as GPs, other health professionals in primary care settings, Gardaí and various other stakeholders in the mental health system.

Some of these issues relate to provision of information, and the website of the Mental Health Commission (www.mhcirl.ie) addresses many key matters, with useful, practical information in multiple languages. But some of these common concerns also point to more substantive issues with the 2001 Act itself, which can only be addressed through revisions to the legislation. And so, in July 2011, the Irish government announced a root-and-branch review of the 2001 Act, to be rooted in human rights. In March 2015 the 'Report of the Expert Group on the Review of the Mental Health Act 2001' was duly published.[9]

The 2015 report presented 165 recommendations relating to virtually all areas of the 2001 Act. It recommended that 'insofar as practicable, a rights based approach should be adopted through-out any revised mental health legislation', and that the principle of 'best interests' should be replaced by 'the following list of guiding principles of equal importance' to 'be specified in the new law':

- The enjoyment of the highest attainable standard of mental health, with the person's own understanding of his or her mental health being given due respect
- Autonomy and self determination
- Dignity (there should be a presumption that the patient is the person best placed to determine what promotes/compromises his or her own dignity)
- Bodily integrity
- Least restrictive care.

The report recommended that 'mental illness' should be redefined as 'a complex and changeable condition where the state of mind of a person affects the person's thinking, perceiving, emotion or judgment and seriously impairs the mental function of the person to the extent that he or she requires treatment'. The report also proposed new criteria for involuntary admission and treatment, so that for involuntary admission to occur a person would have to fulfil *all three* of the following criteria:

- The individual is suffering from mental illness of a nature or degree of severity which makes it necessary for him or her to receive treatment in an approved centre which cannot be given in the community; and

- It is immediately necessary for the protection of life of the person, for protection from a serious and imminent threat to the health of the person, or for the protection of other persons that he or she should receive such treatment and it cannot be provided unless he or she is detained in an approved centre under the Act; and

- The reception, detention and treatment of the person concerned in an approved centre would be likely to benefit the condition of that person to a material extent.

The report also recommended a number of other changes including redefinitions of 'treatment' and 'voluntary patient' (now to require mental capacity); additional protections for patients who are not involuntary but lack mental capacity ('intermediate patients', who would have tribunals); mandatory multi-disciplinary input into involuntary admission decisions; earlier tribunals (to be renamed 'mental health review boards'); shorter involuntary admission orders; specific measures relating to children; more inspection of community mental facilities; better access to information; and provisions to ensure that any involuntary patient who has mental capacity to refuse ECT or medication has their decision respected.

With regard to the process of involuntary admission, the report recommended that family members should no longer sign forms to apply for the involuntary admission, but should instead contact an 'authorised officer' of the health service who would, 'after consultation with family/carers where possible and appropriate, make the decision on whether or not an application for involuntary admission of the person should be made'. This change would mark a radical shift from practices which generally involve a family member signing a form to instigate the involuntary admission process, leading (understandably) to the (mistaken) impression of people being 'signed in' by their families. As discussed above, this is not, in fact, the case, but the change suggested in the 2015 report would remove even the *perception* of family members 'signing in' their relative, while still offering patients and families a clear path to accessing care.

The report also made several recommendations relating to mental health tribunals including:

- Tribunals should be renamed 'mental health review boards' (to reduce stigma);

- While decisions about the nature and content of treatment remain within the remit of the multi-disciplinary mental health team, review boards should have the authority to establish whether there is an individual care plan in place and if it is compliant with the law' (in accordance with the pre-existing requirements of Statutory Instrument No. 551/2006 – Mental Health Act 2001 (Approved Centres) Regulations 2006, part 3);

- Review boards should also establish that the views of the patient as well as those of the multi-disciplinary team were sought in the development of the care plan;

- The patient's detention must be reviewed by a review board no later than 14 days after the making of the admission order or renewal order (as opposed to the current 21 days);

- A patient should have a legal right to have a review board deferred for specified periods (two periods of 14 days) if that is his/her wish;

- The following individuals must attend a review board: legal representative of the patient [and] responsible treating clinician. The following individuals may attend a review board: patient, who must always have a right to attend the review board; advocate, at the invitation of the patient exercising his/her right to such support; the independent psychiatrist who undertook pre-review board assessment, if the review board so requests; [and] the author of the psychosocial report [see below] or, if they are unable to attend, another member of the multi-disciplinary team may attend on their behalf, if the review board so requests;

- The patient's detention must be subject to an assessment report by an independent psychiatrist with input (to be officially recorded) from another mental health professional of a different discipline to be carried out within 5-7 days of the review board hearing (currently, the independent report can occur at any point prior to the tribunal, and mandatory multi-disciplinary involvement would be new);

- A psychosocial report should also be carried out by a member of the multidisciplinary team from the approved centre who is registered with the appropriate professional regulatory body... This report should concentrate on the non-medical aspects of the patient's circumstances;

- The revised legislation should provide for the oversight of the integrity of the process of review boards by the Mental Health Commission in line with best practice. This would include a mechanism to allow information in relation to decisions of review boards to be published in anonymised form which will ensure patient confidentiality. This will allow such decisions to be available for the Mental Health Commission and/or the public to view.[10]

Various other elements in the report related to the definition of treatment (to include 'ancillary tests'); exclusion criteria (to prevent detention *solely* on the grounds of 'intellectual disability'); requirement for mental capacity assessments for those who appear to have diminished mental capacity on admission; a new definition of 'voluntary patient' (to require mental capacity); creation of a new category of patient known as 'intermediate' patient, who 'will not be detained but will have the review mechanisms and protections of a detained person' ('such patients would not have the capacity to consent to admission and equally do not fulfil the criteria for involuntary detention'); and revised regulations governing medical and psychiatric treatment during the period when the involuntary admission process is occurring (balancing the right to acute care with protection of other rights).

Other recommendations related to broader multi-disciplinary involvement in decision-making; strengthening individual care-planning procedures; clarifying the position regarding consent to treatment; revising the process for transition from voluntary to involuntary inpatient (so that it would be more like involuntary admission from the community, thus increasing procedural equality); abolishing 12-month renewal orders for involuntary patients; reducing absence with leave for involuntary patients to 14 days; shifting the onus of proof from the patient in Circuit Court appeals; improving information and complaints systems; placing greater emphasis on inspections of community mental health facilities; various suggestions relating to contact with families and patient confidentiality (Chapter 12); and revised processes relating to children which are outlined in detail in the report, available on the website of the Mental Health Commission.[11]

The lengthy, detailed report was published in March 2015. The recommendation that any detained patient who has mental capacity to refuse ECT or medication (for more than three months) has their decision respected was implemented in 2016 in the Mental Health (Amendment) Act 2015. The other recommendations await implementation. It is likely that advancing these measures will occur in conjunction with the other significant legislative development in this area that is currently underway: the Assisted Decision-Making (Capacity) Act 2015. This is considered next.

Useful Resources

There is a great deal of useful, reliable information on the website of the Mental Health Commission: www.mhcirl.ie. The Commission has published a guide to the Mental Health Act 2001 which is available in English, Irish, Arabic, Chinese, French, Polish and Russian; all are available on their website.

There are also several books examining mental illness, human rights and the law in Ireland and elsewhere: *Mental Illness, Hu-*

man Rights and the Law by Brendan D. Kelly (RCPsych Publications, 2016); *New Law and Ethics in Mental Health Advance Directives: The Convention on the Rights of Persons with Disabilities and the Right to Choose* (Explorations in Mental Health Series) by Penelope Weller (Routledge, 2015); *Dignity, Mental Health and Human Rights: Coercion and the Law* by Brendan D. Kelly (Routledge, 2015); *Irish Insanity: 1800-2000* (Routledge Advances in Sociology) by Damien Brennan (Routledge, 2014); *Mental Health and Human Rights: Vision, Praxis and Courage* edited by Michael Dudley, Derrick Silove and Fran Gale (Oxford University Press, 2012); *Psychiatry and the Law* (Second Edition) by Patricia Casey, Paul Brady, Ciaran Craven and Aisling Dillon (Blackhall Publishing, 2010); *The Mental Health Acts 2001-2009: Case Law and Commentary* by Damien A. Ryan (Blackhall Publishing, 2010); *Mental Disability and the European Convention on Human Rights* (International Studies in Human Rights, Volume 90) by Peter Bartlett, Oliver Lewis and Oliver Thorold (Martinus Nijhoff Publishers, 2007).

Endnotes

1   Daly, A and Craig, S. HRB Statistics Series 29: Activities of Irish Psychiatric Units and Hospitals 2015. Dublin: Health Research Board, 2016.

2   Community and Mental Health Team, Health and Social Care Information Centre. Inpatients Formally Detained in Hospitals under the Mental Health Act 1983, and Patients Subject to Supervised Community Treatment: Uses of the Mental Health Act: Annual Statistics, 2014/15. Leeds: Health and Social Care Information Centre, 2015.

3   http://www.citizensinformation.ie/en/justice/criminal_law/criminal_trial/criminal_insanity_and_mental_health.html

4   http://www.mhcirl.ie/File/Revised_Rules_SecMR.pdf

5   World Health Organisation. *WHO Resource Book on Mental Health, Human Rights and Legislation.* Geneva: World Health Organisation, 2005.

6   Kelly, B.D. 'Mental health legislation and human rights in England, Wales and the Republic of Ireland'. *International Journal of Law and Psychiatry* 2011; 34: 439-54.

7   Kelly, B.D. 'An end to psychiatric detention? Implications of the United Nations Convention on the Rights of Persons with Disabilities'. *British Journal of Psychiatry* 2014; 204: 174-5.

8   UN High Commissioner for Human Rights. Annual Report of the UN High Commissioner for Human Rights and reports of the Office of the High Commissioner and the Secretary-General: Thematic Study by the Office of the United Nations High Commissioner for Human Rights on enhancing awareness and understanding of the Convention on the Rights of Persons with Disabilities. UN, 2009.

9   Expert Group on the Review of the Mental Health Act 2001. Report of the Expert Group on the Review of the Mental Health Act 2001. Dublin: Department of Health, 2015. I was nominated to the Expert Group on the Review of the Mental Health Act 2001 by the College of Psychiatrists of Ireland and appointed to the group by Minister Kathleen Lynch, Minister for Primary Care, Social Care (Disabilities and Older People) and Mental Health, in 2012. This book is written in a personal capacity, as a psychiatrist, and views expressed here or elsewhere do not necessarily represent the views of the Expert Group on the Review of the Mental Health Act 2001 or the College of Psychiatrists of Ireland. Material in this chapter is drawn from: Kelly, B.D. 'Revising, reforming, reframing: Report of the Expert Group on the Review of the Mental Health Act 2001' (2015). *Irish Journal of Psychological Medicine* 2015; 32: 161-6. doi.10.1017/ipm.2015.16. ©, College of Psychiatrists of Ireland 2015, published by Cambridge University Press. Reprinted with permission.

10 See: P. Cullen. 'State to strengthen mental health patients' rights'. *The Irish Times*, 6 August 2016.

11 www.mhcirl.ie/File/rpt_expgroupreview_mha2001.pdf

Chapter 14

ASSISTED DECISION-MAKING (CAPACITY) ACT 2015

The Mental Health Act 2001 (Chapter 13) governs involuntary psychiatric treatment and mechanisms for ensuring standards of care, through the Mental Health Commission and Inspector of Mental Health Services. The Assisted Decision-Making (Capacity) Act 2015, which was signed by President Higgins in 2015 (subject to a commencement date), addresses a somewhat different issue: people who have diminished mental capacity for any reason (not just mental disorder) and who therefore experience difficulty making specific decisions (relating to any area, not just healthcare), and who thus require support in making those decisions.

This chapter sets out the general principles of the 2015 Act; explains the three levels of decision-making support articulated in the legislation; discusses enduring powers of attorney and advance healthcare directives; looks at interactions between the 2015 Act and the Mental Health Act 2001; and, finally, explores the broader implications of the 2015 Act. At time of writing this book (early 2017) the 2105 Act was not yet commenced (for the most part), but preparatory work was well under way.

In essence, the Assisted Decision-Making (Capacity) Act 2015 seeks to create a responsive, multi-level framework to provide support and assistance for people with impaired mental capacity, for whatever reason (for example, dementia, intellectual disability, head injury). It also introduces new measures relating to enduring power of attorneys (that is, giving other people decision-making authority which will endure when the person has developed impaired mental capacity) and advance healthcare directives (that is, making treatment decisions now that will apply in the future when the person has developed impaired mental capacity).[1]

The 2015 Act was designed to replace Ireland's outdated Ward of Court system by which, under the Lunacy Regulation (Ireland) Act 1871, the wardship court gained jurisdiction over *all* matters in relation to the 'person and estate' of a person who was deemed to lack mental capacity. The ward of court framework was in gross violation of the UN Convention on the Rights of Persons with Disabilities (2006); did not adequately define 'capacity'; was poorly responsive to changes in capacity; made unwieldy provision for appointing decision-makers; and had insufficient provision for review. It was generally unfit for purpose and had to go. The Assisted Decision-Making (Capacity) Act 2015 was developed to replace it and to bring Ireland into greater accordance with international human rights standards.

General Principles

In sharp contrast with the pre-existing Ward of Court system, the Assisted Decision-Making (Capacity) Act 2015 places the 'will and preferences' of persons with impaired mental capacity firmly at the heart of all decision-making in relation to 'personal welfare' (including healthcare) and 'property and affairs'. Capacity is to be 'construed functionally'; that is, it is decision-specific. This means that a person's mental capacity might be impaired in relation to financial matters, but might be perfectly intact in relation to healthcare, or vice versa. In other words, mental capacity is no longer an 'all or nothing' concept. More precisely, the Act states that:

> a person lacks the capacity to make a decision if he or she is unable (a) to understand the information relevant to the decision, (b) to retain that information long enough to make a voluntary choice, (c) to use or weigh that information as

344

part of the process of making the decision, or (d) to communicate his or her decision (whether by talking, writing, using
sign language, assistive technology, or any other means).

A person is not to be considered as lacking in mental capacity
just by making, or considering, an unwise decision. If the person
has mental capacity, they can make all the unwise decisions they
want, regardless of how much these decisions might annoy or dis-
may other people (including family).

The 2015 Act specifies that all interventions by other people
under the Act must be 'in good faith and for the benefit of the
relevant person'. These are important, empowering principles, ensuring that the 'will and preferences' and 'benefit of the relevant
person' lie at the heart of all decisions concerning them.

Three Levels of Decision-making Support

In order to help realise these principles, the Assisted Decision-
Making (Capacity) Act 2015 outlines three levels of supported
decision-making: 'decision-making assistant', 'co-decision-maker' (joint decision-making) and 'decision-making representative'
(substitute decision-making).

The first of these is the lowest level of decision-making support: a decision-making assistant. For the decision-making assistant, any adult 'who considers that his or her capacity is in question or may shortly be in question may appoint another person' to
be a decision-making assistant to assist with making one or more
than one decision about 'personal welfare' (including healthcare) or
'property and affairs, or both'. So this might occur when someone
realises that they are becoming forgetful and sometimes need help
with certain decisions. Many people already rely informally on the
help of spouses, family or friends in this situation; appointing one
of them as a decision-making assistant formalises this arrangement
and, possibly, indicates to other people that the decision-making
assistant is now the key advisor (and not anyone else who might
seek to exert unwelcome influence or advance another agenda).

The precise roles of the decision-making assistant are to (1) assist with obtaining relevant information; (2) advise and explain relevant information and considerations; (3) ascertain the 'will and preferences' of the person who appointed them, and assist with communicating such 'will and preferences'; (4) assist with making and expressing the decision; and (5) try to ensure that 'relevant decisions are implemented'. The decision-making assistant is, then, *an advisor only*: their role is to advance the 'will and preferences' of the person who appointed them, rather than to advance or impose their own view on the matter. Any decision made 'with the assistance of the decision-making assistant is deemed to be taken by the [person who appointed them] for all purposes'.

As a result, the decision-making assistant does not have any actual decision-making responsibility: they are an advisor and this arrangement simply formalises something that already occurs very commonly, as most of us rarely make large decisions without advice from, and discussion with, others. It is envisaged that most 'decision-making assistants' will be spouses, family members or trusted friends.

The second level of supported decision-making support is a 'co-decision-maker', or joint decision-maker, who can be appointed in one of two ways. In the first instance, similar to the decision-making assistant process, any adult 'who considers that his or her capacity is in question or may shortly be in question may appoint a suitable person' to be a 'co-decision- maker' to 'jointly make' one or more decisions regarding 'personal welfare' (including 'healthcare') or 'property and affairs, or both'.

Unlike the decision-making assistant, however, the co-decision-maker makes the decision 'jointly' with the appointer, as well as advising the appointer, 'explaining relevant information and considerations', ascertaining the appointer's 'will and preferences', assisting and discussing, and making 'reasonable efforts to ensure that a relevant decision is implemented as far as practicable'. When such a co-decision-making agreement in relation to a particular area (for example, healthcare) is registered, any decision made in that area without the participation of both the appointer and the co-decision-maker is invalid.

In essence, the co-decision-maker plays all the roles that the decision-making assistant plays but – crucially – also makes the final decision 'jointly' with the person who appointed them. And while the co-decision-maker must always 'acquiesce with the wishes of the appointer' (unless 'it is reasonably foreseeable that [the decision] will result in serious harm to the appointer or to another person'), the resultant decision is still a 'joint' one, involving both the co-decision-maker and the person who appointed them.

A number of documents and statements need to be supplied to register a co-decision-making agreement, including 'a statement by a registered medical practitioner and a statement by [another] healthcare professional' that:

> (1) the appointer has capacity to make a decision to enter into the co-decision-making agreement, (2) the appointer requires assistance in exercising his or her decision-making in respect of the relevant decisions contained in the co-decision-making agreement, and (3) the appointer has capacity to make the relevant decisions specified in the co-decision-making agreement with the assistance of the co-decision-maker.

So, in order to set this up, the person must attend a doctor and another healthcare professional, both of whom must believe that the person lacks the mental capacity to make the relevant decisions on their own but has the mental capacity to set up the co-decision-making agreement, and that the provision of a co-decision-maker would enable joint decision-making.

The other pathway to appointing a co-decision-maker involves the Circuit Court. For this pathway, any one of a number of persons with 'a *bona fide* interest in the welfare of a relevant person' (for example, family member, healthcare professional) can seek to apply to the Circuit Court in relation to the person's mental capacity, and, if a hearing proceeds, the Circuit Court 'may make one or both of the following declarations: (1) a declaration that the relevant person the subject of the application lacks capacity, unless the assistance of a suitable person as a co-decision-maker is made available' or (2) that the person 'lacks capacity, even if the assistance of a suitable person as a co-decision-maker were made available to him or her'.

The Court can use expert reports in reaching its decision. In the event of declaration (a), the Court allows the person some time to appoint a co-decision-maker and register a co-decision-making agreement. If the person does not do so, or if there is no suitable person to act as a co-decision-maker, or if the Court makes declaration (b) in the first place, the Court can proceed to the third level of decision-making support: the 'decision-making representative', or substitute decision-making.

But before moving on to consider the role of decision-making representative, it is worth pausing to note one or two further points about the process to this stage. First, in addition to the above, the Circuit Court has the power simply to make any given decision itself, if that course of action is deemed necessary in the circumstances, for example, if the decision is an urgent one and there is no time to put in place the necessary level of decision-making support. No one should have a decision delayed or be denied treatment owing to this process.

Second, the activities of co-decision-makers are to be overseen by the director of the Decision Support Service, a new office within the Mental Health Commission, which will review co-decision-making agreements after the first year and at least every three years thereafter. The co-decision-maker must also submit an annual report on their activities. Finally, either the co-decision-maker or the person who appointed them can revoke a co-decision-making agreement at any time (subject to certain provisions in the 2015 Act).

For the third and highest level of decision-making assistance, a decision-making representative can be appointed if the Circuit Court so decides, following a hearing. The role of the decision-making representative is to 'ascertain the will and preferences of the relevant person' and 'assist the relevant person with communicating such will and preferences'. In addition, 'a decision-making representative shall make a relevant decision on behalf of the relevant person and shall act as the agent of the relevant person in relation to a relevant decision'. So the decision-making representative not only ascertains the 'will and preferences' of the person and assists the person with communicating them, but actually makes the decision on the person's behalf, in accordance with the person's 'will and preferences', insofar as these are ascertainable (if at all).

As with the other levels of decision-making assistance, there are various 'restrictions' on decision-making representatives. For example, unless an 'advance healthcare directive' directs otherwise, the decision-making representative 'shall not refuse consent to the carrying out or continuation of life-sustaining treatment or consent to the withdrawal of life-sustaining treatment for the relevant person'. This appears to exclude the possibility of a decision-making representative agreeing with a 'do-not-resuscitate order', unless the person has made specific and explicit advance provisions in relation to the matter.

In addition, a decision-making representative:

> shall not do an act that is intended to restrain the relevant person unless there are exceptional emergency circumstances and (a) the relevant person lacks capacity in relation to the matter in question or the decision-making representative reasonably believes that the relevant person lacks such capacity, (b) the decision-making representative reasonably believes that it is necessary to do the act in order to prevent an imminent risk of serious harm to the relevant person or to another person, and (c) the act is a proportionate response to the likelihood [and] seriousness of such harm.

With regard to oversight, a decision-making representative must make an annual report and the Circuit Court must review declarations of impaired capacity at least every year or, 'if the court is satisfied that the relevant person is unlikely to recover his or her capacity', every three years. There are, in addition, various other requirements and regulations for each of the three levels of decision-making assistance (and for 'enduring power of attorney' and 'advance healthcare directives'; see below), including qualifying and disqualifying criteria, and mechanisms for support, oversight, review, complaints, objections, appeals and decisions by the Circuit Court. There is also a legal aid scheme and there are transitional arrangements for current wards of court. These are all integral and vital elements of the proposed framework. Much depends on the development of rules, guidance, codes of practice and ongoing training programmes for those involved, as well as public education and feedback.

Enduring Powers of Attorney

In addition to the three levels of decision-making support, the other two key areas addressed in the Assisted Decision-Making (Capacity) Act 2015 are 'enduring powers of attorney' and 'advance healthcare directives'.

An enduring power of attorney is a mechanism for appointing someone else to make certain decisions on one's behalf in the future, after one's mental capacity has diminished. For an enduring power of attorney, an adult ('donor') with mental capacity can give another person:

> (1) general authority to act on the donor's behalf in relation to all or a specified part of the donor's property and affairs; or (2) authority to do specified things on the donor's behalf in relation to the donor's personal welfare or property and affairs, or both.

> [This] enduring power of attorney shall not enter into force until (1) the donor lacks capacity in relation to one or more

of the relevant decisions which are the subject of the power, and (2) the instrument creating the enduring power of attorney has been registered.

A number of documents and statements are required to create an enduring power of attorney under the 2015 Act, including a statement 'by a registered medical practitioner that in his or her opinion at the time the power was executed, the donor had the capacity to understand the implications of creating the power', and a similar statement by another 'healthcare professional'. The instrument is to be registered with the director of the Decision Support Service by the attorney once the attorney believes the donor lacks capacity. There are specific restrictions on attorneys in relation to 'personal welfare decisions' (including 'restraint') and 'property and affairs'. 'An enduring power of attorney may be varied or revoked by the donor, where the instrument creating the enduring power of attorney has not been registered and where the donor has capacity to make the variation or revocation' (subject to various regulations and procedures outlined in the legislation).

In terms of oversight, an attorney must submit various reports to the director of the Decision Support Service, including annual reports, once the arrangement is activated. Overall, then, the 2015 Act revises arrangements for enduring powers of attorney and introduces new mechanisms for accountability and oversight, hopefully making the system more useful, workable and accountable, and assisting people with mental capacity who wish to appoint decision-makers who will take specific decisions in the future, after mental capacity has been impaired.

Advance Healthcare Directives

The final key area addressed in the 2015 Act is 'advance healthcare directives'. These are ways to indicate in advance the kind of treatments one wishes to request or to decline after one has lost mental capacity to make such decisions.

Under the 2015 Act, an advance healthcare directive is 'an advance expression made by the person [of] his or her will and preferences concerning treatment decisions that may arise in respect of him or her if he or she subsequently lacks capacity'. There are detailed regulations and procedures in the Act, which specifies that a:

> refusal of treatment set out in an advance healthcare directive shall be complied with if the following three conditions are met: (1) at the time in question the directive-maker lacks capacity to give consent to the treatment; (2) the treatment to be refused is clearly identified in the directive; (3) the circumstances in which the refusal of treatment is intended to apply are clearly identified in the directive.

'A request for a specific treatment', on the other hand, 'is not legally binding but shall be taken into consideration'.

In addition, 'an advance healthcare directive is not applicable to life-sustaining treatment unless this is substantiated by a statement in the directive by the directive-maker to the effect that the directive is to apply to that treatment even if his or her life is at risk'. That is, if the directive states that life-sustaining treatment is not to be given in particular circumstances, this must be very clearly spelled out by the person in precisely these terms in the directive.

The person who makes the directive can appoint 'a designated healthcare representative [with] the power to ensure that the terms of the advance healthcare directive are complied with'. This 'designated healthcare representative' can 'advise and interpret what the directive-maker's will and preferences are regarding treatment' and 'consent to or refuse treatment, up to and including life-sustaining treatment, based on the known will and preferences of the directive-maker as determined by the representative by reference to the relevant advance healthcare directive'. 'An advance healthcare directive is not', however, 'applicable to the administration of basic care to the directive-maker', where 'basic care' includes '(but is not limited to) warmth, shelter, oral nutrition, oral hydration and hygiene measures but does not include artificial nutrition or artificial hydration.'

Overall, advance healthcare directives allow a person to outline in advance their will and preferences regarding specific treatments in specific circumstances. They are, however, limited to predictable circumstances, and events in life often confound easy prediction. Ideally, advance healthcare directives would form part of a broader programme of advance healthcare planning, which would involve an overall understanding between a person and their healthcare providers about general preferences regarding care. Such broader planning would incorporate sufficient flexibility to apply in unpredictable future circumstances and cover unexpected advances in health or social care practices in the future.

Interaction between the 2015 Act and the Mental Health Act 2001

In general, the Assisted Decision-Making (Capacity) Act 2015 applies to people with mental illness precisely as it does to everyone else, with one exception: advance healthcare directives relating to mental healthcare for involuntary patients. This is quite a complex exception to the general scheme of the 2015 Act but it is an important one.

If a person's treatment is regulated under Part 4 the Mental Health Act 2001 (that is, if the person is subject to an involuntary admission order under the 2001 Act) or if the person 'is the subject of a conditional discharge order' (under Section 13A of the Criminal Law (Insanity) Act 2006), an advance healthcare directive is not legally binding, except 'where a refusal of treatment set out in an advance healthcare directive by a directive-maker relates to the treatment of a physical illness not related to the amelioration of a mental disorder of the directive-maker,' in which case 'the refusal shall be complied with.'

What this means is the following. First, for voluntary psychiatry patients (who constitute the vast majority of psychiatry patients), advance healthcare directives refusing specified treatments relating to physical or mental healthcare are entirely valid, just as they are for everyone else. Requests for specific treatments should, similarly, 'be taken into consideration' in the normal fashion. Second, for involuntary patients, advance healthcare directives are entirely valid when they pertain to refusals of specific treatments relating to physical healthcare (for example, cardiac care, cancer care, etc.) and, again, requests for specific physical healthcare treatments should 'be taken into consideration'. Advance healthcare directives are not binding, however, for involuntary patients when they pertain to refusal of treatments relating solely to mental healthcare, although they can still be taken into consideration as expressions of preference.

Case Study: David

This is, perhaps, best illustrated with a hypothetical example. David, a 20-year-old man with no history of mental illness or drug misuse. became increasingly withdrawn, uncommunicative and isolative over a period of two months. One day, he told his father that the family was being watched but that there was nothing to fear. The forces watching them were benign and posed no threat. David's father persuaded David to see the family's GP, who commenced treatment and made a referral to mental health services. David attended willingly and accepted outpatient care, including home-support from a community mental health nurse and antipsychotic medication.

David recovered from this first episode of psychosis and returned to college. Eight months later, however, he reported that the family was again being watched but this time those watching them were less benign, and he felt he could not continue to live like this. He spent increasing amounts of time on the Internet looking up suicide methods. Following discussion with the community mental health nurse, David agreed to voluntary admission to the local psychiatry inpatient unit.

David spent four weeks there as a voluntary inpatient. At first, he reported relief at being away from the alleged surveillance but anxiety about the imagined risk to his family soon re-emerged.

David's antipsychotic medication was changed and he was linked with a clinical psychologist, who discussed ways of managing persistent symptoms and dealing with his illness. After four weeks in hospital as a voluntary patient, David recovered again, was discharged and resumed his studies. Two years later, David was relapse-free and graduated from his course.

Under the Assisted Decision-Making (Capacity) Act 2015, David could, at this point, with full mental capacity, make out an advance healthcare directive indicating specific treatments (for example, a certain antipsychotic medication) that he would wish to refuse under specific, clearly identified circumstances (for example, another relapse resulting in voluntary admission). Such a refusal of treatment, once clearly made with full mental capacity, would be legally binding, as long as David remained a voluntary patient. If, however, David became an involuntary patient under the Mental Health Act 2001, such a refusal of treatment for mental illness would no longer be legally binding.

If David's advance healthcare directive, made when he had full mental capacity, related to physical health care (for example, refusing a specific treatment for asthma) and if he required asthma treatment while detained under the Mental Health Act 2001 (for a mental illness unrelated to asthma), his decision refusing the asthma treatment would have to be respected, provided the conditions for a valid advance healthcare directive were met; that is,

> *(1) at the time in question the directive-maker lacks capacity to give consent to the treatment; (2) the treatment to be refused is clearly identified in the directive; (3) the circumstances in which the refusal of treatment is intended to apply are clearly identified in the directive.*

If the asthma treatment was a 'life-sustaining treatment' in the circumstances, the refusal would, in order to be valid, have to be 'substantiated by a statement in the directive by the directive-maker to the effect that the directive is to apply to that treatment even if his or her life is at risk'.

In order to assist with the interpretation and implementation of an advance healthcare directive, David could have appointed 'a designated healthcare representative [with] the power to ensure that the terms of the advance healthcare directive are complied with'. This 'designated healthcare representative' could 'advise and interpret what the directive-maker's will and preferences are regarding treatment' (on the basis of the advance healthcare directive) and 'consent to or refuse treatment, up to and including life-sustaining treatment, based on the known will and preferences of the directive-maker as determined by the representative by reference to the relevant advance healthcare directive.'

Implications of the 2015 Act

Overall, the Assisted Decision-Making (Capacity) Act 2015 reflects a significant advance in placing the 'will and preferences' of the person with impaired mental capacity at the heart of decision-making. This development is long overdue and increases Ireland's compliance with the UN Convention on the Rights of Persons with Disabilities, although compliance will still be incomplete, even following the 2015 Act.[2] Key challenges will centre on the complex decision-making required by patients, families, carers, healthcare staff, Circuit Court judges and the director of the Decision Support Service. The implementation of advance healthcare directives will also present a challenge as, ideally, these would form part of a broader model of advance care planning that would incorporate the flexibility required for unknowable future circumstances and advances in care.

The issue of logistics is also critical. In 2014, there were 512,681 discharges from medical inpatient care in Ireland and studies from other jurisdictions indicate that between 30 per cent and 51 per cent of medical inpatients lack mental capacity to make healthcare decisions.[3] In 2015, there were 17,860 psychiatric admissions in Ireland and studies from other jurisdictions indicate that 29 per cent of psychiatry patients lack mental capacity to make healthcare decisions.[4] In addition, there were approximately 27,000 people in nursing homes in Ireland in 2014, and studies from other jurisdictions indicate that over 60 per cent of these people lack mental capacity to make healthcare decisions.[5] These are large numbers.

In theory, all of these people, as well as people who lack mental capacity in primary care and other settings (including non-medical settings), will require supports under the 2015 Act. While it is likely that a decision-making assistant will be sufficient for most, it is not at all clear how many will require greater levels of support, how many Circuit Court hearings will be needed, what level of legal representation is required, or how the entire, rather elaborate system will really operate in practice.

It is also worth noting that certain areas are not covered by the 2015 Act, which specifies that:

> unless otherwise expressly provided, nothing in this Act shall be construed as altering or amending the law in force on the coming into operation of this section relating to the capacity or consent required as respects a person in relation to any of the following: (a) marriage; (b) civil partnership; (c) judicial separation, divorce or a non-judicial separation agreement; (d) the dissolution of a civil partnership; (e) the placing of a child for adoption; (f) the making of an adoption order; (g) guardianship; (h) sexual relations; (i) serving as a member of a jury'. And 'nothing in this Act shall be construed as altering or amending the law relating to the capacity of a person to make a will.

In the end, perhaps the greatest challenge presented by the 2015 Act lies in balancing the principle of autonomy with the principles of beneficence and mutuality, to result in support and care that are consistent with the person's values and are effective, humane and dignified. Such challenges are inevitable with any development of this magnitude which seeks to systematise many of the principles that already define good health and social care practice in Ireland, but are placed on a more explicit footing with the 2015 Act. These are historically important changes, which need to be implemented in an effective, empowering fashion in order to realise their full potential, especially for particular groups, such as people with intellectual disability and co-existing mental disorder.

This latter group merits particular attention in the context of the new legislation. In 2006, *A Vision for Change* recommended that 'delivery of mental health services to people with intellectual disability should be similar to that for every other citizen.' Services:

> should be provided by a specialist mental health of intellec-
> tual disability (MHID) team that is catchment-area based.
> These services should be distinct and separate from, but
> closely linked to, the multidisciplinary teams in intellectual
> disability services who provide a health and social care ser-
> vice for people with intellectual disability.

Over a decade later, it is hoped that the 2015 Act, once it is commenced, will strengthen the agency of the intellectually disabled and their families, and assist in providing them with mental health, medical and social care, as well as further promoting their rights in a society that has ignored their rights and needs all too often in the past.

Useful Resources

There are several books and others resources of relevance to the themes explored in this chapter, including: *New Law and Ethics in Mental Health Advance Directives: The Convention on the Rights of Persons with Disabilities and the Right to Choose* (Explorations in Mental Health Series) by Penelope Weller (Routledge, 2015); *Challenges to the Human Rights of People with Intellectual Disabilities* edited by Frances Owen and Dorothy Griffiths (Jessica Kingsley Publishers, 2009).

There is information about Ireland's Assisted Decision-Making (Capacity) Act 2015 on the websites of the Citizen's Information Board (www.citizensinformation.ie/en/health/legal_matters_and_

health) and Inclusion Ireland (www.inclusionireland.ie/capacity). The legislation is also discussed in this paper: Kelly, B.D., 'The Assisted Decision-Making (Capacity) Act: What it is and why it matters', *Irish Journal of Medical Science* 2017; 186: 351-6.

Endnotes

1   Material in this chapter is drawn from: *Irish Journal of Medical Science*, 'The Assisted Decision-Making (Capacity) Act: What it is and why it matters', Volume 186, 2017, pages 351-356, by B.D. Kelly, © Royal Academy of Medicine in Ireland 2016. With permission of Springer.

2   Kelly, B.D. 'An end to psychiatric detention? Implications of the United Nations Convention on the Rights of Persons with Disabilities'. *British Journal of Psychiatry* 2014; 204: 174-5.

3   Healthcare Pricing Office (HSE). Activity in Acute Public Hospitals in Ireland: Annual Report, 2014. HSE, 2015; Owen, G.S., Szmukler, G., Richardson, G., David, A.S., Raymont, V., Freyenhagen, F., Martin, W. and Hotopf, M. 'Decision-making capacity for treatment in psychiatric and medical in-patients: Cross-sectional, comparative study'. *British Journal of Psychiatry* 2013; 203: 461-7; Bilanakis, N., Vratsista, A., Athanasiou, E., Niakas, D. and Peritogiannis, V. 'Medical patients' treatment decision-making capacity: A report from a general hospital in Greece'. *Clinical Practice & Epidemiology in Mental Health* 2014; 10: 133-9.

4   Daly, A. and Craig, S. HRB Statistics Series 29: Activities of Irish Psychiatric Units and Hospitals 2015. Dublin: Health Research Board, 2016; Okai, D., Owen, G., McGuire, H., Singh, S., Churchill, R. and Hotopf, M. 'Mental capacity in psychiatric patients: Systematic review'. *British Journal of Psychiatry* 2007; 191: 291-7.

5   BDO. Health's Ageing Crisis. BDO, 2014; Christensen, K., Haroun, A., Schneiderman, L.J. and Jeste, D.V. 'Decision-making capacity for informed consent in the older population'. *Bulletin of the American Academy of Psychiatry and the Law* 1995: 23: 353-65.

Chapter 15

STIGMA AND STRUCTURAL VIOLENCE: MENTAL ILLNESS AND SOCIETY

M ental illness is associated with symptoms that can be troubling and difficult to treat, but treatments *are* effective. Recovery is always possible. In fact, most of the problems associated with mental illness are not core features of such illnesses at all, but problems with the ways in which symptoms are interpreted by other people who simply do not understand the nature of mental illness. As a result, most of the disability associated with mental illness is not attributable to mental illness itself, but to how it is interpreted by others and how society responds to the mentally ill.

This situation reflects the strong stigma associated with mental illness, as people with mental illness commonly face misunderstanding, prejudice and isolation. Those with enduring illness find themselves at increased risk of homelessness, imprisonment and social exclusion. This deeply regrettable situation is considered in some detail in this chapter, along with ways in which this kind of social injustice or 'structural violence' against the mentally ill can be addressed.

Stigma

A 'stigma' is an identifying characteristic that is wrongly seen as a mark of shame or discredit. Stigma has an enormous impact on the experience and treatment of mental illness. Stigma can lead

360

to prejudicial or discriminatory behaviour on the part of others, a subsequent failure to seek medical or social assistance in times of crisis, and feelings of loneliness and isolation which many are reluctant to share. The nature and extent of perceived stigma are dependent on a variety of personal, social and cultural factors.

Stigma is closely associated with misunderstandings about the nature of mental illness and its treatment. For example, it has been repeatedly shown that many people wrongly believe that 'multiple personalities' are a common feature of schizophrenia. Such misunderstandings contribute greatly to the growth of ill-informed attitudes about mental illness in general and schizophrenia in particular.

Stigma adversely affects the lives of people with mental illness. People with schizophrenia who perceive stigma report significantly lower quality of life compared to those who do not perceive stigma. This is entirely understandable as daily experiences of prejudice and discrimination inevitably have a powerful effect on self-esteem and personal satisfaction.

Stigma is conferred by many different signs, including a diagnosis of illness, the taking of medication, or even attendance at psychiatric clinics or services. In October 1998 the Royal College of Psychiatrists launched its 'Changing Minds' antistigma campaign, designed to address the issues around stigma through consultation and collaboration with key stakeholders: patients, patients' groups, carers, healthcare providers, parents, teachers, employers and the general public. The breadth of involvement emphasised the cross-discipline nature of stigma, and the need to involve multiple groups in addressing the complex problems it poses.

Initially, the campaign aimed to focus on six major conditions: depression, schizophrenia, anxiety, dementia, eating disorders and alcohol/drug misuse. Various projects were undertaken to address a range of issues related to stigma, and to reduce the gap between public opinion and health workers' knowledge of mental illness. Campaigns such as this, undertaken with careful planning and appropriate consultation, can contribute substantially to the reduction of stigma and significantly improve quality of life for people with mental illness.

Public education is another key element in the reduction of stigma, as public attitudes are shaped by a combination of personal experience of mental illness and environmental inputs, such as media images. Indeed, newspaper articles, blogs, television programmes and movies are among the most powerful shapers of public opinion. Treatment programmes that incorporate social skills development also have a particular role in reducing the effects of stigma: both increased social skills and reduced negative symptoms can help diminish the amount of 'social distance' reported by persons with enduring mental illness.

In the end, stigma is a complex social, political and personal construct, which reflects cultural, social and personal political factors that are often independent of the realities of mental illness. Addressing stigma requires broad, cross-discipline involvement and ongoing efforts at accurate public education about the signs and symptoms of mental illness and the nature and purpose of psychiatric treatment.

Combatting stigma is a constant process and recent years have seen considerably more public discussion about mental health and illness in Ireland, with key opinion leaders such as Niall Breslin, sports star, musician and author of *Me and My Mate Jeffrey: A Story of Big Dreams, Tough Realities and Facing My Demons Head On* (Hachette Books Ireland, 2015), speaking openly about mental health problems and solutions. Similarly, Lily Bailey, model, journalist and former Trinity student, has written compellingly about her recovery from severe obsessive compulsive disorder, in *Because We Are Bad: OCD and a Girl Lost in Thought* (Canbury Press, 2016).

There is a compelling need for similar public discussion about a broad range of conditions such as personality disorder, bipolar disorder, schizophrenia and various other psychological problems and mental illnesses. Ultimately, it is 'experts by experience' who have unique knowledge and experience of mental illness who, along with their families, can have particular impact on reducing stigma.

Structural Violence

Stigma is closely related to the other concept at the heart of this chapter: 'structural violence'. Structural violence is the term given to forces such as poverty, racism, socioeconomic inequality and discrimination which necessarily have an influence on people's health.[1] More specifically, the impact of illnesses such as HIV/AIDS in Haiti and tuberculosis in prisons in the former Soviet Union has been clearly related to the social, economic and political forces that shape the landscape of risk for developing these illnesses, and the context in which health care is provided (or fails to be provided).[2]

Issues such as poverty, gender inequality, lack of access to treatment, political violence and social exclusion not only affect patterns of susceptibility and exposure to illness, but also limit the effectiveness of health care systems and reduce access to services, especially among the poor.

In the context of mental illness, both homelessness and imprisonment are substantially more common among the mentally ill than the general population. This situation is, for the most part, not attributable to mental illness itself but rather to the ways in which mental illness is patterned, interpreted and treated by societies, resulting in denial of rights, denial of opportunity, and broad-based social exclusion of the mentally ill and their families. Let's consider homelessness first.

Homelessness

People with mental illness, especially enduring mental illness, are at increased risk of homelessness in every country around the world in which this has been studied. Overall, approximately 11 per cent of homeless people have schizophrenia, compared to under 1 per cent of the general population. Treatment can be very challenging as homeless patients with schizophrenia are often the most difficult to engage with treatment and are especially vulnerable owing to their homelessness. Moreover, homelessness is more common among people with younger onset of schizophrenia, more severe symptoms and co-existing substance misuse problems – all of which make engagement and treatment even more challenging among the homeless, although it is by no means impossible.

The link between homelessness and substance misuse also has implications for both the assessment of healthcare need and delivery of services, as substance misuse is significantly associated with aggression and violence in first episode psychosis (for example, early schizophrenia). In addition, individuals with schizophrenia who misuse drugs are more likely to engage in aggressive or violent acts compared to individuals with schizophrenia who do not misuse drugs, although the overall proportion of societal violence attributable to mental illness remains low (Chapter 11). In addition, having a substance misuse problem as well as schizophrenia increases the likelihood that the person will be the victim of crime themselves, and this risk is increased even further by homelessness – creating a deeply challenging vicious circle of illness, substance misuse, victimisation and social exclusion.

The reasons for homelessness among the mentally ill are many and varied. Some people might, owing to the illness itself, experience difficulty sustaining a tenancy or remaining in the family home, especially if there is also a problem with substance misuse. In addition, there is clear evidence that people with severe mental illness encounter particular problems accessing community care services following discharge from hospital and additional difficulties adapting to housing following prolonged periods of homelessness. All of these issues substantially complicate the process of reintegration into society, especially following a period of hospitalisation or, indeed, imprisonment. Much of this difficulty is attributable to relatively poor links between mental health and social services in many countries, including Ireland. Many people with enduring mental illness are also dependent on 'rent allowance' to afford private rented accommodation and this can add to the challenges of finding somewhere to stay.

The degree of disconnectedness between the homeless mentally ill and mainstream society is profound and disturbing. In 2008, Dr Austin O'Carroll and Dr Fiona O'Reilly studied the health of the homeless in Dublin in the context of Ireland's economic boom and reported that the proportion of homeless people in Dublin with mental illness actually increased rather than decreased during the so-called 'boom'.[3]

In 1997, 35 per cent of homeless people had depression, and by 2005 this had increased to 51 per cent. In 1997, 32 per cent of homeless people had anxiety and by 2005 this had increased to 42 per cent. In 1997, 32 per cent of homeless people had current or past problems with drug misuse, and by 2005 this had doubled, to 64 per cent. These findings demonstrate clearly the extent to which the homeless mentally ill were left behind during Ireland's so-called economic boom of the late 1990s and early 2000s.

In 2006, A Vision for Change, the national mental health policy, recognised the problems presented by high rates of mental illness among the homeless:

> Homeless people with mental health problems are exposed to all the same difficulties that other homeless people encounter but have more trouble meeting their needs because of their mental health condition. [...] Alcohol abuse has been cited as the single most prevalent health problem for homeless persons. [...] Alcohol and substance abuse may be the primary cause of their homelessness and contribute to or cause their health problems; it may also be the case that alcohol and substance abuse may be a result of a person's homelessness. [...] Homeless people are more likely to be hospitalised, but less likely to use community-based mental health services, than the general population. Lack of resources for survival and inability to access existing services

to meet their needs have been cited by homeless people as a factor in their high readmission rate to psychiatric hospitals (p. 144).

The policy recommended a series of measures to address the problem, including that:

- A database should be established to assist with making evidence-based recommendations;

- The pre-existing plan, 'Making it Home: An Action Plan on Homelessness in Dublin 2004-2006' (published by the Homeless Agency in 2004) 'should be fully implemented and the statutory responsibility of housing authorities in this area should be reinforced';

- A range of suitable, affordable housing options should be available to prevent the mentally ill becoming homeless;

- The community mental health team (CMHT) 'with responsibility and accountability for the homeless population in each catchment area should be clearly identified. Ideally this CMHT should be equipped to offer assertive outreach. Two multidisciplinary, community-based teams should be provided, one in North Dublin and one in South Dublin, to provide a mental health service to the homeless population' (these now exist, at Usher's Island and Parkgate Hall; the ACCESS team);

- All community mental health teams should adopt practices to help prevent service users becoming homeless, such as guidelines for the discharge of people from psychiatric in-patient care and an assessment of housing need/living circumstances for all people referred to mental health services;

- Integration and coordination between statutory and voluntary housing bodies and mental health services at catchment area level should be encouraged (pp. 145-6).

Despite progress with many of these measures, substantial challenges remain. In 2016, a study at the acute mental health unit in Tallaght Hospital, Dublin showed that 38 per cent of acute psychiatry inpatients had unmet accommodation needs.[4] These accounted for 98 per cent of delayed discharges with the result that delayed-discharge inpatients with unmet accommodation needs accounted for some 28 per cent of all inpatients at any given time. This is deeply regrettable: when a person's mental illness had been treated and they are ready for discharge, it is actively unhelpful and disempowering for them to remain in an inpatient unit. There are also significant opportunity costs when acute inpatient psychiatry beds are occupied by people who no longer need that level of care and simply need appropriate accommodation in the community.

The solution to these problems is to develop better links between mental health and social services, especially housing services. There are specific initiatives in this regard in certain mental health services (for example, Tallaght), but there is still much more work to be done. There is also need for greater support for the mentally ill who seek private rented accommodation, or wish to live at home with their families but can only do so with enhanced support. Housing is a right, and it is a right that is commonly violated among people with enduring mental illness in Ireland. All too often, one of the knock-on consequences of this is imprisonment.

Imprisonment

People with mental illness are grossly over-represented in prison populations, who have much higher rates of depression, psychosis and substance misuse than the general population. In 2006, Professor Harry Kennedy, clinical director of the National Forensic Mental Health Service, pointed out that, at that time, Ireland committed over 300 people to prison each year with a six-month prevalence of severe and enduring mental illness, such as schizophrenia.[5] Among remand prisoners (prisoners awaiting court appearances), the rate was twice that seen in other countries.

There is a number of possible explanations for the high rates of mental illness among prisoners. In the first instance, people with major mental illness, such as schizophrenia, may be slightly more likely to engage in certain offences than individuals without mental illness, even though, at societal level, the proportion of violence attributable to the mentally ill is still very small (Chapter 11). Most people with mental illness are far more likely to be the victims of crime than the perpetrators of it. The vast majority are not at all violent and, among those who are, the risk factors for violence are the same as those in the general population: young age, male gender, being single, poverty and substance misuse.

Other factors, apart from the effects of illness, are of much greater significance in accounting for the disproportionate numbers of the mentally ill in prisons. For example, people with mental illness are more likely than those without mental illness to be arrested in similar circumstances, and remand is more likely even when lesser offending is associated with mental illness. Homelessness is a key contributor to this problem. This results in disproportionate imprisonment of the mentally ill, often because there appears to be no other more appropriate option available to hard-pressed Gardaí or judges following arrest. It is also relevant that rates of arrest are higher among people with schizophrenia who misuse substances compared to those who do not, further highlighting the complex care needs of this group.

There is, in addition, a phenomenon known as 'Penrose's Law', named after Professor Lionel Penrose (1898-1972) who studied data from 14 European countries and concluded that the number of persons in mental 'institutions' was inversely correlated with the number in prisons; that is, when the number of people in asylums falls, the number in prisons rises.[6] In Ireland, most large psychiatric institutions started to close in the 1960s so that between 1963 and 2003 the number of psychiatric inpatients decreased from 19,801 to 3,658 (a five-fold decrease, or 82 per cent) and – consistent with Penrose's law – the number of prisoners duly rose, from

534 to 3,176 (a five-fold increase, or 495 per cent).[7] Plainly, there is a relationship between the provision of psychiatric services and the numbers of mentally ill persons in prisons. This does not mean that large psychiatric hospitals are the answer, but rather that community mental health services need to be improved to provide better, earlier treatments and prevent the mentally ill ending up in prison unnecessarily.[8]

Taken together, these factors demonstrate that the extraordinarily high rates of mental illness among prisoners are attributable, for the most part, to prevailing service structures and processes rather than the clinical features of mental illnesses themselves. From a historical perspective, there is substantial evidence that society has *always* tended to place individuals with mental illness into some form of detention, ranging from the small, private asylums of the eighteenth century to the large-scale, public 'mental institutions' of the nineteenth and twentieth centuries. And this trend has, if anything, worsened in recent decades, as fewer of the mentally ill are admitted to psychiatric facilities, but more are committed to prisons.

In Ireland, when someone arrives in prison their health needs are assessed and services offered within the prison, as appropriate, including mental health inreach services. Inpatient mental health care for prisoners and certain others is provided at the Central Mental Hospital (CMH) in Dundrum, Dublin, but it remains the case that there are still large numbers of mentally ill persons in prisons. This is deeply regrettable: prisons are toxic for the mentally ill. There is still much progress to be made in this area.

In 2006, *A Vision for Change*, the national mental health policy, recognised the importance of dedicated mental health service for prisoners and others with related needs:

> Forensic mental health services (FMHS) are primarily concerned with the mental health of persons who come into contact with law enforcement agencies, the Garda Síochána, the Courts and the Prison Service. FMHS teams

also provide consultation services to generic mental health services on the assessment and management of mentally ill persons whose disorder is characterised by challenging and aggressive behaviour. FMHS, in addition to providing secure in-patient care, should have a strong community focus, and should be provided by multidisciplinary teams offering specialist assessments and consultation services to generic mental health teams, specialist assessments for court diversion schemes, and a service to prisons within the region (p. 136).

The 2006 policy made a series of recommendations, including:

1. Every person with serious mental health problems coming into contact with the forensic system should be accorded the right of mental health care in the non-forensic mental health services unless there are cogent and legal reasons why this should not be done. Where mental health services are delivered in the context of prison, they should be person-centred, recovery-oriented and based on evolved and integrated care plans.

2. FMHS should be expanded and reconfigured so as to provide court diversion services and legislation should be devised to allow this to take place. [There has been progress in this area in recent years.]

3. Four additional multidisciplinary, community-based forensic mental health teams should be provided nationally on the basis of one per HSE region.

4. The CMH should be replaced or remodelled to allow it to provide care and treatment in a modern, up-to-date humane setting, and the capacity of the CMH should be maximised. [Some of this is in process.]

5. Prison health services should be integrated and coordinated with social work, psychology and addiction services to ensure provision of integrated and effective care. Efforts should be made to improve relationships and liaison

between FMHS and other specialist community mental health services.

6. A dedicated residential 10-bed facility with a fully re-sourced child and adolescent mental health team should be provided with a national remit. An additional commu-nity-based, child and adolescent forensic mental health team should also be provided.

7. A 10-bed residential unit, with a fully resourced multi-disciplinary mental health team should be provided for care of intellectually disabled persons who become se-verely disturbed in the context of the criminal justice sys-tem.

8. Education and training in the principles and practices of FMH should be established and extended to appropriate staff, including An Garda Síochána.

9. A senior garda should be identified and trained in each Garda division to act as resource and liaison mental health officer (pp. 142-3).

These recommendations are important. Significant progress has been made since 2006, especially in relation to forensic ser-vices for the intellectually disabled and court diversion schemes. In addition, in June 2015, planning permission was granted for a 120-bed national forensic hospital in Portrane, County Dublin, and two 10-bed specialist units for persons with intellectual dis-abilities and children and adolescents. This project also included progressing design work for three 30-bedded Intensive Care Reha-bilitation Units in Cork, Galway and Portrane.

Notwithstanding these developments, substantial challenges remain.[9] In 2012, study of 171 young male offenders in St Patrick's Institution in Dublin, aged 16 to 20, showed that 23 per cent were at 'ultra-high risk' of psychosis (Chapter 3) as evidenced by ratings of unusual thought content, hallucinations, disorganised speech and various other features, as well as functional impairment.[10] Pre-dictably, there was a strong association with multiple substance misuse. The authors recommended that much greater attention needed to be paid to the health needs of young offenders.

The key requirements here are for further enhancement of community mental health teams, further development of court diversion schemes, and expanded, improved forensic psychiatry inpatient facilities. In the absence of these resources, the mentally ill will continue to experience disproportionate loss of liberty in Irish prisons, preventable exposure to criminal behaviours while spending indefensible periods in custody, deteriorating mental health in toxic prison settings, and increased risk of worsening substance misuse by association with other prisoners both during and after time in prison.

The National Forensic Mental Health Service is a progressive, focussed and effective element within Ireland's mental health services: it deserves greater resources to deliver much-needed care to this troubled, troubling population.

Fighting for Social Justice

Remedying the stigma, social injustices and 'structural violence' experienced by the mentally ill and their families is a challenging, important and increasingly urgent task. This is a task for everyone: patients, families, carers, mental health professionals, politicians, policy-makers and the public in general. Various groups engaged with these and other issues in mental health are discussed in Chapter 12.

One of the key organisations in this field, Mental Health Reform (originally named the Irish Mental Health Coalition), was founded in 2006, at a time there was little public advocacy on behalf of better mental health services, little political will for reform, and little presence of mental health as an issue covered in the media.[11] The establishment of the coalition reflected its members' collective desire to ensure the new mental health policy, *A Vision for Change*, translated into real change for people using mental health services. Mental Health Reform soon grew to more than 50 member organisations including most of the national mental

372

health not-for-profit organisations and professional associations along with many other not-for-profit organisations who have a strong interest in better mental health supports for their clients. It aims to provide a coordinated public voice advocating for reform of the entire mental health system. More than 10,000 people are also connected to the coalition through social media, reflecting a growing movement for better mental health services (www.mentalhealthreform.ie).

Participation in movements such as this are key ways of exerting pressure on politicians, policymakers and the media to ensure that mental health services and social services for the mentally ill remain to the forefront of public policy developments in Ireland. Other important, empowering initiatives within mental health services include the Advancing Recovery in Ireland movement, which supports recovery-oriented mental health services, and the EOLAS project which was initiated in 2011 by the Kildare West Wicklow mental health team, with Dr Pat Gibbons, consultant psychiatrist, as chairperson of the project group (www.eolasproject.ie).

EOLAS ('knowledge' in Irish) was developed in collaboration with users of mental health services, family members, mental health support organisations, clinicians and academia. Its objective is to design, deliver and evaluate mental health information and support programmes to assist in the recovery journey of those diagnosed with schizophrenia spectrum and bipolar disorders, and also their family members and friends. The EOLAS programmes are co-facilitated by a peer facilitator and a clinical facilitator: clinicians bring their professional expertise and family members and service-users are experts by experience. Following a positive evaluation by the School of Nursing and Midwifery at Trinity College Dublin (2015), this programme is now being rolled out across Ireland. Initially funded by Genio (www.genio.ie), EOLAS today forms part of the HSE programme for mental health.

These are important, empowering initiatives within Ireland, linked with similar developments abroad. At international level, there are also very useful resources relating to mental health services and social justice on the WHO website, especially through their mental health portal which provides access to a wealth of material relating to mental health policy, mental health in emergencies and, in particular, the WHO Mental Health Gap Action Programme (mhGAP), which aims at scaling up services for mental, neurological and substance use disorders (www.who.int/mental_health/en). There is a strong emphasis on social justice and human rights for the mentally ill.

Ultimately, the key mechanisms for achieving continued development of mental health services, enhanced supports for families and greater social justice for the mentally ill lie in the realm of politics and political action. And, in addition to exerting pressure through organisations such as Mental Health Reform, and using WHO materials to advocate for improvements, there is a central role for voting as a means to generate change. Politicians are uniquely sensitive to letters and petitions from constituents, and are highly responsive to any suggestion that they could represent their constituents better by pursuing a particular course of action. For this mechanism to be effective, however, it is important to register to vote in the first place.

There are, in general, very few data about political activity and voting patterns among the mentally ill and those secondarily affected by mental illness (for example, family, friends, carers). This paucity of data is explained, at least in part, by the fact that the lives of people with mental illness are not solely defined by illness, so there may not be a direct or readily detectable link between mental illness and voting choices. Nonetheless, existing evidence suggests that the voting patterns of individuals with mental illness tend to differ somewhat, though not hugely, from voting patterns of the overall population, with a general tendency towards the liberal side of the political spectrum.[12]

One study, for example, found that outpatients with enduring mental illness in Germany were more likely to vote for left-wing parties compared with the general population, suggesting that the political choices of the mentally ill reflect a set of priorities that is somewhat, although not dramatically, different to that of the overall population.[13] Another study identified smaller differences in voting preferences among inpatients with mental illness in Israel,[14] whereas in Canada the proportions of votes cast in psychiatric hospitals for various political parties were virtually the same as in the surrounding areas.[15]

Interestingly, there is evidence that psychiatric inpatients are particularly well-informed voters and a majority report positive subjective feelings following voting, including a sense of responsibility, belonging to a community and pride.[16] Nonetheless, voting rates among psychiatry inpatients can be as low as 3 per cent.[17] In 2014, one Irish study found that only 10 per cent of psychiatry inpatients who were surveyed voted in the 2011 general election, in which national turnout was 70 per cent.[18] Many patients were unaware of their right to vote. These are interesting, disturbing and provocative findings, of considerable relevance to ongoing efforts to address and remedy the social and political exclusion of the mentally ill.

Progress is, however, entirely possible. In a notably progressive initiative, patients at the Central Mental Hospital (inpatient forensic psychiatry facility) were facilitated to vote for the first time in general elections in 2007, following a European Court of Human Rights ruling in 2005. Voting took place in the same way as voting at any other polling station and was overseen by the county sheriff. Voter turnout was high, at 75 per cent.[19] Two years later, voter turnout at the Central Mental Hospital remained high in European and local elections, and on the eve of the poll, three election candidates attended a question and answer session in the hospital. A similar debate among candidates took place at the Central Mental Hospital prior to the general election in 2016.

Clearly, persons directly or indirectly affected by mental illness represent an extremely large political constituency – a constituency that political organisations rarely address during political campaigns. One reason for this may be a perception among politicians that individuals with enduring mental illness do not vote. Failure to vote among the mentally ill, however, is likely attributable, in large part, to remediable secondary correlates of mental illness (for example, homelessness), lack of knowledge or administrative problems, rather than primary symptoms of mental illness itself. In Israel, for example, the most common reason for inpatients with mental disorder not voting is a lack of identity cards.[20]

This relevance of contributory factors such as these demonstrates that the systematic disenfranchisement of the mentally ill represents a problem that is, in large part, remediable. This situation needs to be addressed not only by mental health service-users and service-providers, but also by advocacy services and other stakeholders through (a) improved staff awareness of patients' voting rights; (b) provision of relevant information to patients, especially inpatients, and families and carers; (c) where indicated, assessments of voting capacity, using standardised, well-proven tools such as the Competency Assessment Tool for Voting;[21] and (d) voter-registration programmes, all of which have important roles to play in the re-enfranchisement process.[22]

Another reason for the relatively low profile of mental health issues in political debate may relate to an apparent political consensus about mental health policy, for example, a consensus that traditional services need to be expanded, or that custodial approaches are needed for safety reasons. The manufacture of such a *faux* consensus may simply represent a way to avoid debating the real, challenging social and political issues raised by mental illness. It is, in any case, highly unlikely that any apparent political consensus on an issue as complex as mental health is an accurate reflection of true social consensus, and it is only by repeatedly raising issues related to mental health that real political debate will evolve.

Overall, active political participation is a crucial and potentially transformative path to better protecting and promoting the rights of the mentally ill. Voting is one important, empowering element of such political participation. In the words of Rudolf Virchow (1821-1902), the German pathologist, anthropologist and politician: 'Medicine is a social science, and politics nothing but medicine on a large scale.'

Ways to Combat Stigma

- *Actions speak louder than words, but both words and actions are needed: do not discriminate against people with mental illness; accommodate mental illness-related needs just as you would accommodate needs stemming from physical conditions (for example, a broken leg); and avoid discriminatory language.*

- *If you are a journalist or otherwise involved in media, media guidelines on reporting suicide have been produced by the Irish Association of Suicidology and the Samaritans, in order to minimise further harm and reduce the possibility of copycat acts.[23] Issues relating to mental ill health require ongoing media attention, provided media discussion is conducted in a fashion that is respectful, dignified and mindful of the mentally ill.*

- *The National Alliance on Mental Illness in the US (www.nami. org) points to nine key ways to fight stigma:*

  ◊ *Talk openly about mental health issues;*

  ◊ *Educate yourself and others about mental health and mental illness;*

  ◊ *Be conscious of your use of language;*

  ◊ *Encourage equality in how people perceive mental illness and physical illness;*

  ◊ *Show empathy and compassion for people living with a mental health condition;*

◊ Stop the criminalisation of people who live with mental ill-ness;

◊ Push back against the way that people with mental illness are portrayed in the media;

◊ See the person, not just the illness;

◊ Advocate assertively for mental health reform.

Useful Resources

There are several useful books on the themes of social justice and mental illness, including: *From Psychiatric Patient to Citizen: Overcoming Discrimination and Social Exclusion* by Liz Sayce (Palgrave, 2000); *Mental Health and Inequality* by Anne Rogers and David Pilgrim (Palgrave Macmillan, 2003); *Mental Illness, Discrimination and the Law: Fighting for Social Justice* by Felicity Callard, Norman Sartorius, Julio Arboleda-Flórez, Peter Bartlett, Hanfried Helmchen, Heather Stuart, José Taborda and Graham Thornicroft (Wiley-Blackwell, 2012); *Mental Health and Human Rights: Vision, Praxis and Courage* edited by Michael Dudley, Derrick Silove and Fran Gale (Oxford University Press, 2012); *Social Injustice and Public Health* (Second Edition) edited by Barry S. Levy and Victor W. Sidel (Oxford University Press, 2013); *The Social Determinants of Mental Health* edited by Michael T. Compton and Ruth S. Shim (American Psychiatric Publishing, 2015).

For a sobering, searing account of Irish psychiatric institutions in the past see Hannah Greally's thinly veiled, compelling and disturbing account of her 19 years in St Loman's Mental Hospital, Mullingar between 1943 and 1962, in *Bird's Nest Soup* (Allen Figgis and Co., 1971). I have previously written about the history of mental health services in Ireland and the social challenges faced by the mentally ill in the past and today in *Hearing Voices: The History of Psychiatry in Ireland* (Irish Academic Press, 2016).

In relation to 'structural violence', see: *Pathologies of Power: Health Human Rights, and the New War on the Poor* by Paul Farmer (University of California Press, 2003); *Partner to the Poor: A Paul Farmer Reader* edited by Haun Saussy (University of California Press, 2010); B.D. Kelly. 'Structural violence and schizophrenia.' *Social Science and Medicine* 2005; 61: 721-30; B.D. Kelly. 'The power gap: Freedom, power and mental illness.' *Social Science and Medicine* 2006; 63: 2118-28.

Endnotes

1   Farmer, P. 'Pathologies of power: Rethinking health and human rights.' *American Journal of Public Health* 1999; 89: 1486-96.

2   For a discussion of these themes, and further references, see: Kelly, B.D. *Mental Illness, Human Rights and the Law* (RCPsych Press, 2016).

3   O'Carroll, A. and O'Reilly. F. 'Health of the homeless in Dublin: Has anything changed in the context of Ireland's economic boom?' *European Journal of Public Health* 2008; 18: 448-53. See also: Holohan, T. 'Health Status, Health Service Utilisation and Barriers to Health Service Utilisation Among the Adult Homeless Population of Dublin.' Dublin: Royal College of Physicians of Ireland, 1997.

4   Cowman F, Whitty P. 'Prevalence of housing needs among inpatients: A 1-year audit of housing needs in the acute mental health unit in Tallaght Hospital.' *Irish Journal of Psychological Medicine* 2016; 33: 159-64.

5   Kennedy, H.G. 'The future of forensic mental health services in Ireland.' *Irish Journal of Psychological Medicine* 2006; 23: 45-6.

6   Penrose, L.S. 'Mental disease and crime: Outlines of a comparative study of European statistics.' *British Journal of Medical Psychology* 1939; 18: 1-15.

7   Kelly, B.D. 'Penrose's Law in Ireland: An ecological analysis of psychiatric inpatients and prisoners.' *Irish Medical Journal* 2007; 100: 373-4.

8   O'Neill, C., Sinclair, H., Kelly, A. and Kennedy, H. 'Interaction of forensic and general psychiatric services in Ireland: Learning the

lessons or repeating the mistakes?' *Irish Journal of Psychological Medicine* 2002; 19, 2:48-54.

9 H. Kennedy. 'Prisons now a dumping ground for mentally ill young men'. *The Irish Times*, 18 May 2016.

10 Flynn, D., Smith, D., Quirke, L., Monks, S.G. and Kennedy, H.G. 'Ultra high risk of psychosis on committal to a young offender prison: An unrecognised opportunity for early intervention'. *BMC Psychiatry* 2012; 12: 100.

11 I am very grateful to Dr Shari McDaid, Director, Mental Health Reform, for this information.

12 This material is adapted from, and full references to relevant studies are available in: Kelly B.D. 'Voting and mental illness: The silent constituency'. *Irish Journal of Psychological Medicine* 2014; 31: 225-7. doi:10.1017/ipm.2014.52. ©, College of Psychiatrists of Ireland, published by Cambridge University Press, reprinted with permission.

13 Bullenkamp, J. and Voges, B. 'Voting preferences of outpatients with chronic mental illness in Germany'. *Psychiatric Services* 2004; 55: 1440–2.

14 Melamed, Y., Shamir, E., Solomon, Z. and Elizur, A. 'Hospitalised mentally ill patients in Israel vote for the first time'. *Israeli Journal of Psychiatry and Related Sciences* 1997; 34: 69–72.

15 Valentine, M.B. and Turner, T. 'Political awareness of psychiatric patients'. *Canadian Medical Association Journal* 1989; 140: 498.

16 Melamed, Y., Doron, A., Finkel, B., Kurs, R., Behrbalk, P., Noam, S., Gelkopf, M. and Bleich, A. 'Israeli psychiatric inpatients go to the polls'. *Journal of Nervous and Mental Disease* 2007; 195: 705–8.

17 Humphreys, M. and Chiswick, D. 'Getting psychiatric patients to the polls in the 1992 general election'. *Psychiatric Bulletin* 1993; 17: 18–19.

18 Siddique, A. and Lee, A. 'A survey of voting practices in an acute psychiatric unit'. *Irish Journal of Psychological Medicine* 2014; 31: 229-31.

19 H. Kennedy. 'The general election campaign'. *The Irish Times*, 23 May 2007.

20 Melamed, Y., Donsky, L., Oyffe, I., Noam, A., Levy, G. and Gelkopf, M. 'Voting of hospitalized and ambulatory patients with mental disorders in parliamentary elections'. *Israel Journal of Psychiatry and Related Sciences* 2013; 50: 13–16.

21 Appelbaum, P.S., Bonnie, R.J. and Karlawish, J.H. 'The capacity to vote of persons with Alzheimer's disease'. *American Journal of Psychiatry* 2005; 162: 2094-100; Raad, R., Karlawish, J. and Appelbaum, P.S. 'The capacity to vote of persons with serious mental illness'. *Psychiatric Services* 2009; 60: 624-8.

22 Nash, M. 'Voting as a means of social inclusion for people with a mental illness'. *Journal of Psychiatric and Mental Health Nursing* 2002; 9: 697-703.

23 http://www.samaritans.org/your-community/samaritans-ireland-scotland-and-wales/samaritans-ireland/media-guidelines-ireland

Chapter 16

HAPPINESS AND WELL-BEING IN IRELAND

Happiness matters to everyone.

While this might seem like an obvious statement, it is only in recent decades that public policymakers and researchers have started to take happiness seriously. And while happiness is important at all times, it is probably especially important in Ireland today, as we emerge from a period of economic turbulence and austerity into a different national and European landscape, full of change and possibility.

Recent years have seen a veritable deluge of self-help books, guided recordings and DIY manuals devoted to the meaning of happiness, ways to attain fulfilment and strategies to stay happy forever. There have been lengthy volumes about the economics of happiness, the psychology of satisfaction and theories underlying the new 'politics of happiness' which has taken root in many countries around the world.

The recent revival of interest in the politics of happiness finds its roots in the distant Kingdom of Bhutan, a tiny, mountainous country in south Asia, with a population of fewer than one million. Up until the 1970s, Bhutan's chief point of distinction was that it possessed one of the smallest economies in the world, based primarily on forestry and agriculture. Economic progress, as measured by traditional measures such as Gross Domestic Product (GDP), was minimal.

In 1972, Jigme Singye Wanchuk, the new king of Bhutan, attracted international attention by deciding that 'Gross National Happiness', instead of GDP, was the measure by which national progress in Bhutan would be measured henceforth. Gross National Happiness quickly became a key element in the country's economic and social planning.

In Bhutan, Gross National Happiness had four key pillars: (1) good governance and democracy; (2) stable and equitable socio-economic development; (3) environmental protection; and (4) preservation of culture. The emphasis on good governance and democratisation led the king to relinquish many of his traditional powers and introduce an elected assembly and council of ministers. Interestingly, the king's push toward democracy occurred *without* the active support of many Bhutanese people, who did not oppose democracy *per se*, but were generally happy with the rule of the king and saw little need for change.

Nonetheless, Bhutan's emphasis on happiness found strong support in various other countries around the world which are now placing greater emphasis on happiness, well-being and life satisfaction when planning public policy. This is a sensible move: people value happiness above most other things in life, including wealth. Happiness matters to everyone.

Of course, happiness itself may prove elusive, so – very pragmatically – people also value the *pursuit* of happiness as a useful interim measure. As long ago as June 1776, the Virginia Declaration of Rights outlined 'certain inherent rights' of the individual which included 'the enjoyment of life and liberty, with the means of acquiring and possessing property, and pursuing and obtaining happiness and safety'. The importance of the pursuit of happiness was soon declared 'self-evident' in the US Declaration of Independence that July:

> We hold these truths to be self-evident, that all men are created equal, that they are endowed by their Creator with

certain unalienable Rights, that among these are Life, Liberty and the pursuit of Happiness.

The Pursuit of Happiness

Over two centuries after the US Declaration of Independence, the right to pursue happiness remains central to ideas of human freedom and fulfilment. The practical importance of happiness is underpinned even further by clear evidence that happiness is associated with better future health, higher earnings and longer life. These findings emphasise not only the importance of happiness for the individual, but also for politicians and policymakers, the need to identify and understand predictors of happiness in order to guide 'happiness-oriented' public policy.

Certain countries have already taken steps to increase emphasis on well-being and happiness in public policy. In February 2008, Nicholas Sarkozy, President of the French Republic, indicated that he was 'unsatisfied with the present state of statistical information about the economy and society' and sought 'to identify the limits of GDP as an indicator of economic performance and social progress' and 'consider what additional information might be required for the production of more relevant indicators of social progress'.[1]

As a result, President Sarkozy established a Commission on the Measurement of Economic Performance and Social Progress in order to re-focus public policy on happiness and well-being:

> The commonly used statistics may not be capturing some phenomena, which have an increasing impact on the well-being of citizens. For example, traffic jams may increase GDP as a result of the increased use of gasoline, but obviously not the quality of life...emphasising well-being is important because there appears to be an increasing gap between the information contained in aggregate GDP data and what counts for common people's well-being.

The Commission duly made a range of recommendations for an improved approach to evaluating economic performance and social progress. The Commission placed a strong emphasis on measuring 'objective and subjective dimensions of well-being', social inequality and environmental sustainability. Critically, the Commission emphasised 'political voice and governance', as well as the role of public services, in shaping 'life satisfaction'.

A similar initiative was commenced in the UK, placing increased emphasis on happiness and well-being. In 2010, the UK's National Statistics Measuring National Well-being Programme was launched. As part of this programme, the Office for National Statistics published an 'initial investigation into subjective well-being' in 2011, reflecting the fact that 'individual or subjective well-being, that is, people's own assessment of their own well-being, was also thought to be important for measuring national well-being'.[2]

But given this renewal of enthusiasm for well-being and happiness in public policy, is there any actual evidence about how to pursue this matter effectively, and how to achieve these goals? Do we know what factors or activities promote well-being and happiness, and what factors hinder them? Is there a systematic, scientific evidence base to guide us here? Is it even possible to study happiness scientifically or is the very idea simply absurd?

Can Happiness Be Studied Systematically?

For most people, happiness is an intensely personal matter and the things that make one person happy may differ greatly from those that make the next person happy. Moreover, happiness can vary dramatically from moment to moment in response to circumstances and events. In the face of such seemingly insurmountable challenges and uncertainty, has anyone developed a reliable and meaningful way to measure happiness to facilitate the study of happiness across populations, countries and eras, and to guide public policy and individual behaviour?

While happiness has been the subject of intense philosophical and literary speculation since the start of recorded history, it is only since the mid-twentieth century that this interest was translated into the systematic, scientific study of the social and psychological correlates of happiness. An initial question arises immediately, however: what *is* happiness?

Most definitions consistently link happiness with feelings of pleasure and contentment. But even so, there are still myriad contrasting definitions dating from ancient times to the modern era. And many would argue that it is simply impossible to say what happiness *is* in words: you can only feel it. To confuse matters even further, it seems that popular conceptions of happiness have changed considerably over time.

Nonetheless, it is now relatively clear that there are two main conceptualisations of happiness: hedonic and eudaimonic. Hedonic happiness refers to feeling pleasure in the moment: riding a roller-coaster, tasting a fresh croissant, cycling down a hill. Eudaimonic happiness refers to a sense of fulfilment in life: knowing you have a job, valuing the presence of family and friends, feeling satisfied that your lifestyle is generally conducive to good long-term health.

Clearly, both conceptualisations of happiness are entirely valid and are closely linked with each other: I feel hedonic happiness when I am enjoying a very expensive holiday abroad this year (even though it means I cannot afford any holiday next year), but I experience eudaimonic well-being (or longer-term fulfilment) when I budget carefully and enjoy a moderately-priced holiday this year with the promise of another moderately-priced holiday next year. It's all a matter of perspective, and most people achieve a dynamic balance between these two conceptualisations of happiness in their lives. Hedonic considerations are mostly related to happiness in the moment; eudaimonic ones are linked with long-term well-being and sustainable life satisfaction.

While much research interest in recent years has focussed on hedonic happiness (that is, feeling pleasure), it is clear that both the hedonic and eudaimonic approaches offer useful and subtly different perspectives for policymakers and politicians. For example, unemployment is associated with substantially reduced life satisfaction but with less change in hedonic happiness.

In order to cut though these complex and overlapping concerns, most useful recent research has focussed very simply and directly on *how the individual feels* as a measure of subjective happiness, incorporating elements of both hedonic happiness and life satisfaction, but with a probable emphasis on hedonic happiness. When surveys use this simple, direct approach, they receive extremely high response rates, indicating that simple, direct questions about happiness make most sense to people being surveyed.

With this in mind, this book includes, among other material, some recent analyses of data from the European Social Survey (ESS), which assesses happiness by asking tens of thousands of people the following question: 'Taking all things together, how happy would you say you are?' (where 0 means 'extremely unhappy' and 10 means 'extremely happy').[3] This question shows good research validity and reliability.

So, what does this kind of research show, if anything?

Findings from Happiness Research

The research literature about happiness is now quite vast, and many studies contradict each other on various specific points. Overall, however, certain trends have finally emerged consistently.[4] First, it is now clear that happiness varies significantly with age, with the youngest and oldest people experiencing greatest happiness. For many, the low point occurs in the early to mid-40s, when professional and personal life can be at their most intense. This U-shaped distribution of happiness across the life-course has been reported in the US, Europe, Latin America and Asia in over 70 developing and developed nations.

What about gender? Who rates themselves as happier – women or men? These relationships are fascinating and have changed substantially over the past four decades. Studies from the US in the early 1970s showed that women were more likely than men to report being 'very happy', but in the 1980s the difference between genders began to diminish. By the start of the twenty-first century the self-rated happiness of women was equal to, or even less than, that of men. Thus, while most objective measures indicate the lives of women improved during the latter half of the twentieth century, measures of subjective well-being indicate that women's happiness declined both absolutely and relative to that of men.

So, while in the past women traditionally rated themselves as happier than men rated themselves, happiness ratings have now converged towards the midpoint between the genders. In fact, men might now rate themselves slightly happier than women rate themselves – a startling turnabout over the past few decades.

The role of health in relation to happiness is relatively clearer and more constant: good health is, quite simply, the largest single predictor of happiness. Mental health is especially important, but so is maintaining good general health and having a reasonable and healthy lifestyle. Happiness is also associated with having a low-conflict upbringing, living in a stable community and holding clear personal values (including religion). Happiness increases following the birth of a child but this boost may only last for a couple of years.

Happiness decreases if you are unemployed (that is, searching unsuccessfully for work), and a 10 per cent increase in national unemployment rate makes everyone unhappy, regardless of whether or not they are employed. This is an especially important point for policymakers: unemployment is uniquely corrosive of happiness at individual and societal levels.

Happiness increases with income up to a certain point, but there is little incremental increase beyond that point. In other words, when income is sufficient to ensure basic needs are met, and a certain amount of discretionary income is available, additional income has diminishing returns in terms of happiness. This makes sense: earning a million euro when you have just €1 in the bank will make you much happier than earning a million euro when you already have one hundred million euro in the bank. Relative income also matters: a majority of people think it's more important to earn more than their neighbour earns, rather than increase the absolute amount that they earn themselves.

All of these factors taken together, however, appear to explain less than 25 per cent of the variability in happiness between people. Other factors must be at play to explain the other 75 per cent of the differences in self-rated happiness from person to person. But what are these other factors?

In recent years, it has become apparent that the genes we inherit from our parents play a significant role in shaping well-being and happiness. Each person has a unique genetic make-up which is like a blueprint for how the body works and responds to different environments. We inherit these genes from our parents but they can be altered through random changes, and some can be activated or deactivated by circumstances and events throughout life.

It can be difficult to study the effects of genes on something like happiness or well-being. Nonetheless, there have been studies of monozygotic twins (for example, identical twins) who share all the same genes, and dizygotic twins (non-identical) who do not share all the same genes (they are like regular siblings). It turns out that, even when twins are reared apart from each other, levels of happiness are much more alike in monozygotic twins compared to dizygotic twins. This suggests that there is a degree of genetic pre-programming towards or away from happiness, but that external circumstances matter too. The precise biological mechanisms involved in this are entirely mysterious, but it is now estimated that genes account for 40 to 50 per cent of individual variations in happiness.

This, then, leaves just 25 per cent of the variance in happiness between individuals unexplained. Do we have any hints about this? Other conclusions from recent research suggest that happiness and well-being are variously linked with a range of other factors, including belonging to a network of happy people, having good family relationships, maintaining high community trust, and experiencing satisfaction with democracy. There are also differences between countries, with Denmark generally reporting the highest self-rated happiness of any European country. What about Ireland?

Happiness in Ireland since 2000

As Irish people, we have traditionally rated ourselves as being very happy, happier than most other countries in the world (but not, interestingly, Denmark). The past decade, however, saw real challenges to this position, as Ireland entered an economic recession in 2008, followed by a period of austerity. But in 2009, just as Ireland's economic woes were deepening, the National Economic and Social Council (NESC) published a timely, insightful report about the importance of well-being at such a juncture, titled *Well-being Matters: A Social Report for Ireland.*

From a policy perspective, the NESC report was the most inclusive, systematic consideration of well-being in Ireland to date. NESC used a notably broad definition of well-being:

> Well-being in this report is understood as a positive physical, social and mental state. It requires that basic needs are met, that individuals have a sense of purpose, that they feel able to achieve important goals, to participate in society and to live lives they value and have reason to value. Well-being is enhanced by conditions that include financial and personal security, meaningful and rewarding work, supportive personal relationships, strong and inclusive communities, good health, a healthy and attractive environment, and values of democracy and social justice. [5]

Following detailed consideration of individual and social factors associated with well-being, NESC concluded that 'the way we state some of our high level goals could be modified' to include 'sustainable growth', 'sustainable communities', 'a more egalitarian society' and 'responsive, flexible, person-centred and tailored publicly funded services'. The report also concluded that 'having a level of income to meet basic needs matters' and the 'fundamental elements which contribute to long-term well-being include participation in meaningful activity, along with affectionate and caring relationships, a secure, safe and attractive environment, good social relations, and good health.'

NESC suggested the use of a 'well-being test' based on the 'developmental perspective' outlined in the report, as well as three immediate policy priorities:

- The need to address *unemployment* through diverse and intensive activation measures;
- The *provision of financial supports, including pension reform*; and
- The *transformation of institutions and improved accountability.*

This all makes excellent sense, especially the emphasis on addressing unemployment, which affects happiness both broadly and deeply. The NESC priorities were even more urgent owing to the recession:

Well-being is affected by economic upturns and downturns. A shock to one domain of our well-being may have an impact on another domain. For example, loss of a job and income can affect our relationships and health. These impacts can affect people in different ways depending on their circumstances. Depending on how we, as individuals and as a society, deal with these adversities can make a major difference to our longer term well-being. Some of the factors identified which can make a difference include using our capabilities, having a sense of purpose, engagement in meaningful activity, the support of family and friends, having trust in our institutions and having a sense of hope.

NESC's emphasis on well-being was insightful and timely. But what actually happened to happiness in Ireland from 2008 onwards? Research based on ESS data, analysed by our research teams at Trinity College Dublin and, previously, University College Dublin, demonstrate key trends over this period. The question central to these analyses was the ESS happiness question already mentioned above: 'Taking all things together, how happy would you say you are?' (where 0 means 'extremely unhappy' and 10 means 'extremely happy').

In 2005, these data showed that mean self-rated happiness in Ireland was 7.9 (out of 10), but by 2007 this decreased to 7.7. By 2009 it had diminished further, to 7.5.[6] The decline continued until 2012, when mean happiness bottomed out at 6.8, as the effects of the recession were felt most widely.[7] By 2014, however, as the recovery took hold, mean happiness recovered significantly to 7.2, in line with Ireland's improved economic position.[8] By 2016, Ireland was ranked nineteenth happiest country in the world out of 157 countries in the *World Happiness Report* compiled by the Sustainable Development Solutions Network.[9] This was a remarkable recovery by any standards, and indicates the resilience of both Ireland and its people, and our innate tendency towards happiness.

How to Be Happy

So what does any of this mean? What can we do, as individuals, in order to be happy? And what can the government do to create conditions for happiness and well-being to flourish in society?

For individuals, some of the findings from happiness research are immediately useful. Others are a little less obviously helpful, but can still make a contribution. Turning to the helpful findings first, it is clear that maintaining good health is centrally important not just for one's physical well-being but also for mental health, happiness and well-being. This is easily the most important route to happiness: stay healthy.

It is also important to have a level of income sufficient to cover basic needs and live with dignity: this is something that must continue to inform national social policy. It is also important to remember two key research findings about income: (a) ever-increasing income has diminishing returns in terms of happiness, so there's little point focussing solely on ever-greater wealth; and (b) we have an utterly self-defeating tendency to compare our incomes with those of other people, to the point of pathology: a majority of us think it's more important to earn more than our neighbour than it is to increase the absolute amount that we earn; that is, we would prefer to have less money ourselves if that somehow meant staying ahead of our neighbour. This is entirely in keeping with human nature but it does not help with happiness. In fact, it reflects a much broader point about the path to happiness which, from a psychological perspective, might well be summed up in just five words: Stop comparing yourself to others. This may be an impossible task, but it is important to try.

What else can we do? Happiness increases if we devote attention to maintaining a stable community, holding clear values (including religious values), linking with happy people (and being a happy element in your own network of family and friends), and supporting the development of strong democratic values: voting, participating in political debate, and staying actively involved in community and social life.

Turning to the research findings that are not immediately, obviously helpful in guiding us towards happiness, many of these findings still provide important material for reflection and – when needed – consolation. Take age, for example. The happiness low point for many people is mid-life, during their 40s. This is often a time when financial, family and other demands are at their most pressing. The U-shape of the happiness curve provides real reason for hope here: later life holds the promise of an increase in happiness, with possibly more potential than at any other time in life. This underpins the need to pay close attention to our physical and mental health, in order to ensure that we are still alive by the time later life rolls around and in sufficiently good health to exploit the unique opportunities for fulfilment that it presents.

As regards gender, it is interesting that recent decades saw self-rated happiness diminish in women and increase in men; this requires further research, especially in relation to how increased equality has been operationalised and how can this be improved for the benefit of both women and men. Further work is also needed on the relationship between genetic inheritance and happiness. This association likely reflects a complex series of relationships between specific genetic factors and physical or psychological characteristics which predispose towards happiness in specific external circumstances. There is much work to be done on this topic.

Finally, it is important to think about these factors associated with happiness in trans-generational terms too. For example, the research is clear that a low-conflict upbringing is associated with happiness in later life. While an adult cannot change the upbringing that they experienced as a child, it is entirely possible for the adult to ensure that their children enjoy a low-conflict upbringing and thus increased chances of happiness. This point is especially important for parents who are experiencing difficulties in their relationship: if such parents decide to stay together 'for the sake of the children', it is essential that conflict is brought to an immediate and lasting end. Exposing children to conflict does not by any means extinguish all possibility of happiness in later life, but it does make it a whole lot harder. And it denies the child an equal possibility of the happiness that all human beings naturally seek to achieve and enjoy.

Can the Government Make You Happy?

Those are all the individual-level factors that can and should shape our behavior in the direction of greater, lasting happiness. Most of this advice is not new, and one can argue that happiness research was not required in order to generate many of these recommendations. But happiness research has added new weight and emphasis to many of them, and provided additional reasons to pursue them, that is, staying healthy, becoming more involved in communities, paying greater attention to mental health and well-being in day-to-day life, and not just when something goes wrong.

Can the government help with these tasks too? It most certainly can – and should.

First, the government has a unique role to play in addressing unemployment, one of the greatest causes of unhappiness in all countries, including Ireland. This matters to everyone, employed and unemployed alike, and the happiness research provides strong evidence that efforts to reduce unemployment are probably the single most important steps government can take to increase population well-being in the short, medium and long term.

Second, there is good evidence that happiness is strongly related to public trust in governmental institutions, including European institutions. The more confidence people have in government, the happier they are. Globally, increases in democracy *precede* increases in happiness. So, democracy matters deeply, and this places responsibilities on all stakeholders. Representative democracy works best when our elected representatives behave in a responsible fashion, and participatory democracy works best when everyone gets involved: voting, supporting, protesting and staying engaged.

Third, government has a unique role in promoting happiness and well-being at community level owing to the relationship between happiness and 'social capital'. Trusting, co-operating communities have increased happiness, reduced crime and lower rates of suicide. Focusing public policy on increasing this kind of 'social capital' at community level will not only enhance cohesion, reduce crime and deepen trust, it will also increase happiness. This can involve deepening participatory democracy, devolving decision-making to local forums, or protecting public services that deliver inestimable value *at community level*: community Gardaí, public health nurses, and functioning, properly staffed public libraries.

Fourth, happiness is strongly related to mental health and there is a unique role for government in supporting and expanding relevant services for all. In addition to focusing on mental illness services, however, it is useful for governments to focus on mental health and, more specifically, the concept of 'mental capital'. Mental capital came to particular prominence in 2008 owing to the Foresight Mental Capital and Wellbeing Project, a UK Government initiative aimed at achieving 'the best possible mental development and mental wellbeing for everyone in the UK in the future':

> A key message is that if we are to prosper and thrive in our changing society and in an increasingly interconnected and competitive world, both our mental and material resources will be vital. Encouraging and enabling everyone to realise their potential throughout their lives will be crucial for our future prosperity and wellbeing.[10]

Against this background, the Foresight Project developed 'a vision for the opportunities and challenges facing the UK over the next 20 years and beyond, and the implications for everyone's mental capital and mental wellbeing', and 'what we all need to do to meet the challenges ahead, so that everyone can realise their potential and flourish in the future'. One of the key concepts in this work is 'mental capital', which is defined in broad terms:

> This encompasses a person's cognitive and emotional resources. It includes their cognitive ability, how flexible and efficient they are at learning, and their 'emotional intelligence', such as their social skills and resilience in the face of stress. It therefore conditions how well an individual is able to contribute effectively to society, and also to experience a high personal quality of life. The idea of 'capital' naturally sparks association with ideas of financial capital and it is both challenging and natural to think of the mind in this way.

The idea of 'mental capital' is holistic, ambitious and pragmatic. It reflects a need to expand our thinking beyond mental illness and psychological problems to the broader themes of mental wellness, resilience and resourcefulness – all of which are reflected in the idea of 'mental capital'. On this basis, government could usefully devote greater attention to this concept, as well as systematically increasing trust in democratic institutions, enhancing social capital in communities and protecting mental health services – all of which will further deepen happiness.

It is clearly now necessary to pay both increased governmental attention and increased individual attention to happiness; the former to create the broad context for happiness and well-being to flourish, and the latter to actually attain happiness for the individual. In Ireland, our long history of high self-rated happiness, our robust social stability throughout economic turbulence and austerity, ongoing positive economic trends, and the guidance provided by the growing happiness literature, all combine to make the prospects for continued happiness in Ireland extremely bright.

In addition, of course, many of the steps taken in order to increase happiness are likely to yield additional benefits along the way. Examples include playing sports, attending public events, reading, listening to music, knitting, meditating, practising mindfulness, composing poetry or just sitting quietly (a favourite of mine). Becoming utterly absorbed in activities such as these is an important part of being a fully realised, happy human being.

Many such activities are undertaken, and choices made, without the *express* intent of increasing happiness. But they will still, in the words of American philosopher Henry David Thoreau (1817-62), quietly open the door to happiness in a profound and lasting way:

> Happiness is like a butterfly: the more you chase it, the more it will elude you, but if you turn your attention to other things, it will come and sit softly on your shoulder.

Useful Resources

Several books provide very useful guides to individual happiness well-being: *Protecting Mental Health* by Keith Gaynor (Veritas Publications, 2015); *The U Turn: A Guide to Happiness* by Conor Farren (Orpen Press, 2013); *Flourishing: How to Achieve a Deeper Sense of Well-Being, Meaning and Purpose – Even When Facing Adversity* by Maureen Gaffney (Penguin Ireland, 2011).

Barbara Ehrenreich provides a smart, alternative view of the positive thinking movement in *Smile or Die: How Positive Thinking Fooled America and the World* (Granta, 2009). Richard Layard provides an excellent overview of the scientific literature on happiness in *Happiness: Lessons from a New Science* (Second Edition) by Richard Layard (Penguin, 2011). For a guide to well-being in later life in Ireland, see *Ageing and Caring: A Guide for Later Life* by Des O'Neill, (Orpen Press, 2013).

Malcolm MacLachlan and Karen Hand examine the 'prospects for psychological prosperity in Ireland' in *Happy Nation?* (The Liffey Press, 2013) and Derek Bok provides a broad political perspective in *The Politics of Happiness: What Government Can Learn from the New Research on Well-Being* (Princeton University Press, 2010).

In relation to 'mental capital', there is an excellent (large) volume titled *Mental Capital and Well-Being* edited by Cary L. Cooper, John Field, Usha Goswami, Rachel Jenkins and Barbara J. Sahakian ('Foresight', Government Office for Science/Wiley-Blackwell, 2010). This book comprises a series of reviews by leading international scientists on specific topics related to mental capital and well-being. Various sections deal with 'mental capital and wellbeing through life', 'learning through life', 'mental health and ill-health', 'wellbeing and work', 'learning difficulties' and, finally, 'cross-cutting reviews' which provide valuable overviews of various over-arching aspects of the field.

Further information on the UK government's Foresight Mental Capital and Wellbeing Project is available at: https://www.gov.uk/

government/publications/mental-capital-and-wellbeing-making-
the-most-of-ourselves-in-the-21st-century

The National Economic and Social Council (NESC) was established in 1973 and further information about 'Well-being Matters: A Social Report for Ireland' and NESC's other work is available on its website, www.nesc.ie.

Endnotes

1   Stiglitz, J.E., Sen, A. and Fitoussi, J-P. Report by the Commission on the Measurement of Economic Performance and Social Progress. 2009.

2   Office for National Statistics. Initial investigation into Subjective Wellbeing from the Opinions Survey. Newport: Office for National Statistics, 2011.

3   The European Social Survey (ESS) is an academically driven cross-national survey conducted every two years across Europe since 2001 (www.europeansocialsurvey.org). Data are free to download and use, subject to certain conditions. See also: Jowell, R., Central Coordinating Team, European Social Survey 2006/2007: Technical Report. London: Centre for Comparative Social Surveys, City University, 2007.

4   Many of the research findings in this section are summarised, with original source references, in Kelly, B.D. '"Happiness-deficit disorder"? Prevention is better than cure'. *The Psychiatrist* 2011; 35: 41-5; Doherty, A.M. and Kelly, B.D. 'Social and psychological correlates of happiness in seventeen European countries: Analysis of data from the European Social Survey'. *Irish Journal of Psychological Medicine* 2010; 27: 130-4; Kelly, B.D. *Hearing Voices: The History of Psychiatry in Ireland.* Dublin: Irish Academic Press, 2016.

5   National Economic and Social Council. *Well-being Matters: A Social Report for Ireland.* Dublin: National Economic and Social Council/Government Publications Office, 2009.

6 Doherty, A.M. and Kelly, B.D. 'When Irish eyes are smiling: Income and happiness in Ireland, 2003-2009'. *Irish Journal of Medical Science* 2013; 182: 113-9.

7 Kelly, B.D. and Doherty, A.M. 'Impact of recent economic problems on mental health in Ireland'. *International Psychiatry* 2013; 10: 6-8.

8 Kelly, B.D. *Hearing Voices: The History of Psychiatry in Ireland.* Dublin: Irish Academic Press, 2016 (Chapter 8).

9 Helliwell, J., Layard, R. and Sachs, J. (eds.), *World Happiness Report 2016*, Update (Volume 1). New York: Sustainable Development Solutions Network, 2016.

10 Foresight Mental Capital and Wellbeing Project. Final Project Report – Executive Summary. London: The Government Office for Science, 2008.

Chapter 17

Dignity, Mental Illness and Human Rights

This book has covered a broad variety of topics, ranging from depression to happiness, from how to access mental health services to the precise workings of Ireland's new mental capacity legislation. I hope some of these discussions are helpful.

One of the common themes running through all of the preceding chapters is the idea that people with mental illness, mental disorder or psychological problems (or whatever phrase makes most sense to you) are entitled to support, understanding, mental health services, social services and all the assistance needed in order to get through the difficulties that they and their families currently face. But most of all, they need to be accorded the dignity that is their entitlement as human beings, and which is so often denied to them by a society that is commonly inhospitable to those with psychological problems – and that still systematically excludes those with enduring mental illness from full participation in civic and social life (Chapter 15).

With this in mind, the 2015 'Report of the Expert Group on the Review of the Mental Health Act 2001' proposed that 'dignity' should be one of the 'guiding principles' of Ireland's mental health legislation, with 'a presumption that the patient is the person best placed to determine what promotes/compromises his or her own dignity'.[1] Dignity is a central concept in human rights and there is no human right that is unconnected with dignity.[2] This closing chapter examines the idea of dignity in some detail in the context of mental illness, and concludes that dignity is central to all human rights and to all well-being. Maintaining and enhancing human dignity should lie at the heart of every aspect of mental healthcare.

Human Rights

A right is an entitlement, something that one may legally or morally claim. The term 'human rights' refers specifically to rights which a human being possesses by virtue of the fact that they are human. Human rights recognise extraordinarily special, basic human interests and do not need to be earned or granted; they are the birth-right of all human beings simply because they are human beings.

In the early twenty-first century, the term 'human rights' is most commonly understood by reference to statements of human rights dating from the mid-1900s, including, most notably, the Universal Declaration of Human Rights adopted by the UN General Assembly in 1948. Other relevant statements include the UN Principles for the Protection of Persons with Mental Illness and the Improvement of Mental Health Care (1991) and the UN Convention on the Rights of Persons with Disabilities (CRPD) (Chapter 13). From a legal perspective, however, most weight is accorded to the European Convention on Human Rights of the Council of Europe (1950) which is incorporated into national law in Ireland through the European Convention on Human Rights Act 2003 and in England through the Human Rights Act 1998.

In Ireland, the Mental Health Act 2001 addresses certain human rights issues in relation to individuals with mental disorder, chiefly related to involuntary treatment and assuring standards. Notwithstanding the challenges that the legislation presents to mental health services, there is significant agreement that it improves protection of the right to liberty among individuals with mental disorder and increases Ireland's adherence to international human rights standards in areas of traditional concern in mental health care, especially involuntary admission and treatment.

It is important, however, to emphasise that rights-based approaches to any matter, including mental healthcare, occur in specific social and political contexts. For example, the legal observance of many civil rights requires relatively ready access to an independent court system. Mental health legislation helps meet this requirement by ensuring access to mental health tribunals, free legal representation and advocacy. In Ireland, the 2001 Act makes specific provisions for free legal aid, mental health tribunals and court appeals.

More globally, however, these kinds of measures presume the existence of an independent court system and the availability of public resources to fund legal representation and advocacy. On this basis, while human rights themselves may be 'universal', the effectiveness of human rights-based approaches to specific issues, such as mental healthcare, relies on a set of assumptions which not all societies meet, that is, the existence of an independent court system, clear legislative provisions relating to mental disorder, certain standards of democratic governance and the (related) likelihood that human rights concerns will inform systemic change.

Many of these requirements reflect other human rights, emphasising the indivisibility of all human rights. The necessity for an independent court system, for example, is underlined in the European Convention on Human Rights which states that:

> Everyone who is deprived of his liberty by arrest or detention shall be entitled to take proceedings by which the lawfulness of his detention shall be decided speedily by a court and his release ordered if the detention is not lawful.

On this basis, the rights that mental health legislation may seek to protect (for example, right to liberty) are inextricably linked with other rights (for example, right to access a court system or tribunal).

The situation is rendered more complex in countries where a rights-based approach to mental health care might not rest easily with certain societal practices and cultural beliefs, especially countries with different economic, professional and cultural contexts than the economically advantaged countries in which human rights discourse is most prevalent (for example, England, Ireland, US). This emphasises the importance of human rights as *one element* within a broader approach to social justice, combined with political activism and social advocacy, *all* of which are vital in working towards social justice for the mentally ill.

The Centrality of Dignity

Against this background, the idea of dignity is central to ideas of rights and social justice. In the context of mental healthcare, dignity is important to *all* individuals with mental disorder and not just the minority who experience involuntary detention and treatment. Indeed, for the majority of patients who engage voluntarily with primary care or mental health services, the key issue is not loss of dignity through violation of rights by mental health professionals or the state, but access to services.[3] Globally, the WHO advises that a majority of people with mental disorders in many countries do not have access to the treatments they need.[4] The issue for most, then, is not protection from over-exuberant psychiatric care, but simple access to basic services. An approach to service planning which recognises human dignity as a key value permits a nuanced response to this situation, aiming to achieve optimal observance of rights, including the right to a basic level of care consistent with human dignity *and* the right to liberty.

There may, however, be additional complexity in mental health settings, especially if the individual temporarily lacks the insight and/or mental capacity to exercise their own rights or promote their own dignity in certain important respects. For example, an individual with psychosis, who is untreated, homeless, and singing aloud or undressing on the street is, by most objective standards, in an undignified position, but the individual might not perceive this indignity subjectively, owing to the effects of illness. An individual without such a mental disorder in a similar position is more likely to perceive their situation differently, experience subjective indignity and take corrective action.

This situation and dilemma highlight the fundamental conceptualisations of dignity outlined by Deryck Beyleveld and Roger Brownsword in 2001.[5] Their idea of 'dignity as empowerment' focuses on dignity as advancing the individual's autonomy in a direct fashion, but they also recognise that dignity can reflect an *objective* value reaching beyond the individual such that, if an individual inadvertently violates this value, human dignity is compromised irrespective of whether or not the individual has knowingly agreed to perform the act in question. Therefore, if the individual with severe mental disorder lacks sufficient insight into their situation, they may violate this shared, objective idea of dignity, possibly resulting in arrest (at worst) or involuntary treatment under mental health legislation owing to treatable mental disorder and/or risk of harm.

This objective aspect of dignity is especially important among individuals who (usually temporarily) lack the insight and/or mental capacity to cultivate subjective dignity or recognise its loss, to varying extents.[6] Critically, these individuals, always and forever, still possess intrinsic human dignity by virtue of the simple fact that they are human. In such circumstances, there is a powerful moral and, ideally, legal duty to protect and restore their dignity by having ultimate regard for the dignity, rights and welfare of the individual when making decisions relating to them, including decisions about mental health care.

To a certain extent, the Mental Health Act 2001 imposes such a duty on mental health services and the Gardaí in relation to individuals with mental disorder, although it is limited by the fact that the over-arching principle of the legislation is 'best interests' rather than dignity itself. As a result, the recommendation by the 'Expert Group on the Review of the Mental Health Act 2001' that 'dignity' should be one of the 'guiding principles' of the 2001 Act is a good idea: it is sensible, empowering and pragmatic.

It is possible, of course, that objective conceptualisations of dignity could be interpreted inappropriately in certain circumstances. This points to a broader problem with legislation-based solutions to problems experienced by individuals with mental disorders who have reduced insight into their own mental state and, occasionally, into the maintenance or loss of their own dignity. The key issue here is that the rule of law takes as its subject the fully rational, self-determining person and generally lacks a sufficiently nuanced approach to people with diminished rationality, reduced mental capacity (Chapter 14), or limited insight for specific periods of time.

This issue is especially complex in Ireland owing to the emphasis that the Constitution places on welfare-based concerns for the vulnerable.[7] Consistent with this, the Supreme Court has made it explicit that the Court should approach certain medical matters 'from the standpoint of a prudent, good and loving parent'.[8] The High Court made a similar point in the context of the Mental Health Act 2001:

> In my opinion having regard to the nature and purpose of the Act of 2001 as expressed in its preamble and indeed throughout its provisions, it is appropriate that it is regarded in the same way as the Mental Treatment Act of 1945, as of a paternal character, clearly intended for the care and custody of persons suffering from mental disorder.[9]

The Supreme Court agrees that interpretation of the 2001 Act 'must be informed by the overall scheme and paternalistic intent of the legislation',[10] as exemplified by the 2001 Act's requirement that the 'best interests of the person shall be the principal consideration with due regard being given to the interests of other persons who may be at risk of serious harm if the decision is not made'. The High Court has stated that this section 'infuses the entire of the legislation with an interpretative purpose'.[11]

Overall, the courts' explicit paternalism in its interpretation of the Mental Health Act 2001 may, on the one hand, represent a disproportionately disempowering approach to mental health law, at least in certain cases.[12] But it also, on the other, very clearly reflects the Irish state's undeniable constitutional obligation to protect the vulnerable.[13] In England, the tendency towards paternalism is less pronounced overall and is generally attributable to public safety concerns rather than a stated obligation to protect the vulnerable.

Some of these concerns may be resolved, at least in part, by mental capacity legislation which assumes a nuanced approach to mental capacity, facilitates careful evaluation of the individual's capacity to make specific decisions, and offers supported decision-making procedures. In Ireland, the Assisted Decision-Making (Capacity) Act 2015 offers a real opportunity to achieve these goals (Chapter 14). Even in England, however, which has revised both its capacity and mental health legislation relatively recently, there is still evidence of significant difficulty integrating the concepts of human rights and dignity with legitimate and necessary welfare-based concerns, in a reasonable and empowering fashion. So how can these concerns be balanced?

Rights, Dignity and Welfare

The difficulty with balancing and integrating rights, dignity and welfare-based concerns relating to the mentally ill is apparent throughout the recent and current processes of legal reform in Ireland and England. Any proposed solution that is based solely in mental health or capacity legislation will, however, invariably be subject to the intrinsic limitations of legal approaches to such problems, that is, requirements for an independent court system, financial resources to access courts and certain standards of democratic governance.

In addition, developing ever more detailed mental health or capacity legislation has the distinct demerit of expanding the remit and complexity of such legislation,[14] and potentially reinforcing the discriminatory assumption that individuals with mental illness or impaired capacity are sufficiently dangerous as to require elaborate legislation in order to maintain public safety.

A further complexity associated with exclusively legal solutions to dilemmas relating to mental disorder or impaired mental capacity stems from the fact that not all human needs are best met through dedicated legal assurances of specific rights. Indeed, a great majority of human needs are not claimed as rights at all but fulfilled by mechanisms other than legally based human rights claims, for example, by means of exchange, political (as opposed to judicial) allocation of public resources, family networks, charity, etc.[15]

This fact is reflected, at least in part, by a strictly rights-based analysis of mental health legislation in Ireland and England which showed that recent revisions of mental health legislation in both jurisdictions have resulted in stronger protections of certain civil rights of the mentally ill (for example, right to liberty) and that the greatest remaining deficit relates to protection of social and economic rights through mental health legislation.[16] This supports the idea that mental health *legislation* is best suited to the protection of so-called 'negative rights' (for example, prohibitions on torture and degrading treatment) rather than so-called 'positive rights' (for example, right to access services).

In other words, while constitutional rights and dedicated mental health legislation can and should guarantee basic rights, and ensure that the rights and needs of vulnerable persons and the underprivileged are not neglected by the political process, these are not necessarily the only or even the best mechanisms for fulfilling positive rights to, and needs for, healthcare, housing, social protection, etc. The most important governmental interventions in these areas are based not on enforcing direct laws but on implementing sustainable policies, creating accountable institutions to meet collective needs and, when indicated, direct provision of goods and services.

Thus, an emphasis on human rights and needs may be usefully complemented by an emphasis on human nature, that is, a combination of shared observations about the state of being human including, for example, the existence of an individual sense of human dignity. This underscores the importance that Martha Nussbaum attaches to *human capabilities*,[17] a concept which was notably absent from the processes of legislative reform in Ireland and England in recent years. This is a real pity because creating circumstances in which people can exercise their capabilities is central to the restoration and maintenance of dignity, especially in mental healthcare.

David Seedhouse and Ann Gallagher (2002) place capabilities at the very centre of their definition of dignity, arguing that an individual has dignity if they are in a set of circumstances that permit them to exercise their capabilities.[18] As a result, promoting dignity among individuals with mental disorders would involve the individual, supported if necessary by health and social services, improving their capabilities and/or improving circumstances with a view to greater exercise of their own capabilities and thus enhancement of dignity. From the point of view of mental health service providers, improving capabilities might involve judicious use of psychiatric treatments which enhance capabilities (for example, psychological therapies, medication) and various measures to improve circumstances, which might involve providing services and care in proactively dignified, empowering settings, and actively promoting social integration and political empowerment of people with mental disorder (Chapter 15).

Values in Legislation and Policy

Broader recognition of these kinds of values, especially dignity and capabilities, in Ireland's mental health legislation would not only advance protection of human rights through mental health legislation and help realise the 'general principles' of the CRPD, but also acknowledge the intrinsically complex, multi-faceted nature of mental healthcare and decision-making in relation to mental disorder. On this basis, the recommendation by the 'Expert Group on the Review of the Mental Health Act 2001' that 'dignity' should be one of the 'guiding principles' of the 2001 Act is important. It is also vital that, as proposed, there is a clear 'presumption that the patient is the person best placed to determine what promotes/ compromises his or her own dignity'. This balances autonomy with the need for care, recognising both subjective and objective aspects to dignity.

'Dignity' would be especially useful as an *overarching* principle owing to its clear interpretation in situations in which the individual has full insight and capacity (for example, if I am elderly and decline an indwelling catheter which I see as undignified, that is entirely my choice to make) *and* situations in which the individual's insight and/or mental capacity might be impaired. In the latter situation, it might be necessary, for a period of time, to rely on objective or shared conceptualisations of dignity which might, of course, be disputed, but which (a) could be guided by the interpretative guidelines similar to the 'guiding principles' of the Assisted Decision-Making (Capacity) Act 2015, with a strong emphasis on the 'will and preferences' of the person (Chapter 14); and (b) are less disputable that certain other proposed concepts, and for which a significant literature exists to guide and assist with interpretation (see above).

Incorporating dignity into Irish mental health legislation in this assertive fashion would also significantly advance the principles of the CRPD, the explicit purpose of which is 'to promote, protect and ensure the full and equal enjoyment of all human rights and fundamental freedoms by all persons with disabilities, and to promote respect for their inherent dignity'. In more practical terms, it would mean that practitioners, mental health tribunals and courts would have to consider explicitly the effects of their decisions on the dignity of patients, weighing up the indignity of untreated mental illness against the dignity-related implications of involuntary treatment. It would also create an imperative that treatment be offered in a fashion that explicitly prioritises dignity, an approach which would be best advanced through the provision of effective, efficient treatment in a respectful and dignified fashion.

On this basis, there is a compelling argument for dignity to become the *overarching* principle of mental health legislation in Ireland and elsewhere. Even if this occurs, however, it would still be a mistake to rely exclusively on legislation to promote the dignity and protect the rights of individuals with mental disorders. The history of Irish mental health services over the past five decades provides an excellent example of the importance of *non-legislative* factors in transforming public mental health services. Between 1945 and 2006, when the Mental Health Act 2001 was implemented in full, mental health legislation did not change significantly in Ireland. Nonetheless, between 1963 and 2003, the number of psychiatric inpatients decreased by an astonishing 81.5 per cent (from 19,801 to 3,658).[19]

This reform was a result of changes in mental health policy and attitudes of Irish society in general, rather than changes in mental health legislation. While this level of change raises unresolved issues about the right to treatment, and there are undoubtedly substantial problems with levels of mental disorder in prisons (Chapter 15) and elsewhere (Chapter 12), it remains the case that while the psychiatric inpatient population declined by 16,143 between 1963 and 2003, the prison population rose by just 16.4 per cent of this number (2,642).

These trends provide compelling evidence of the unique power of mental health and social policy (rather than law) to increase the liberty enjoyed by the mentally ill. Today, Ireland's involuntary admission rate is toward the lower end of rates across European countries and is less than half of that in England (Chapter 13). In addition, Ireland's mental health legislation now meets the vast majority of international human rights standards in relation to involuntary detention and treatment. As a result, while there is always room for improvement with legislation, it is neither practical nor realistic to expect mental health legislation alone to protect and promote the broader rights of individuals with mental disorder, especially social and economic rights.

There is also, in the specific context of mental health, particular need for a broad-based, collaborative approach to human rights and dignity, involving mental health service users, families and carers, mental health service providers, social services, health and policy planners, Gardaí, voluntary groups and legal practitioners. The actions of all of these stake-holders impact directly on the dignity and rights of people with mental disorders, so it is now timely that dignity would become the overarching principle in Irish mental health legislation – and that this principle is carried well beyond mental health services, tribunals and courtrooms into the broader arenas of health and social policy, and throughout society in general.

As a country, we have done far too little to include the mentally ill in society, for far, far too long. There are solutions to hand, and many are outlined in the various chapters of this book.

It is time to fix this.

Useful Resources

There are many available resources relating to the central themes of this chapter, in the context of Ireland and elsewhere, including: *Dignity, Mental Health and Human Rights: Coercion and the Law* by Brendan D. Kelly (Routledge, 2015); *Creating Capabilities: The Human Development Approach* by Martha C. Nussbaum (Harvard University Press, 2011); *Human Rights and Their Limits* by Wiktor Osiatyński (Cambridge University Press, 2009); Seedhouse, D. and Gallagher, A. 'Clinical ethics: Undignifying institutions'. *Journal of Medical Ethics* 2002; 28: 368-72.

In 2011, TASC, a 'think-tank for action on social change' (www. tasc.ie), published a report on 'Eliminating Health Inequalities – A Matter of Life and Death' by Sara Burke and Sinéad Pentony (TASC, 2011), which considers mental health at various points. Further information on mental health is available on the website of the Institute of Public Health in Ireland, www.publichealth.ie.

Endnotes

1   Expert Group on the Review of the Mental Health Act 2001. Report of the Expert Group on the Review of the Mental Health Act 2001. Dublin: Department of Health, 2015 (p.15; see also Chapter 13 of the present book).

2   Material in this chapter is drawn from (and full references to relevant studies, papers and reports are available in): Kelly, B.D. 'Dignity, human rights and the limits of mental health legislation'. *Irish Journal of Psychological Medicine* 2014; 31: 75-81. doi:10.1017/ipm.2014.22. ©, College of Psychiatrists of Ireland 2014, published by Cambridge University Press. Reprinted with permission.

3   Petrila, J. 'Rights-based legalism and the limits of mental health law'. In: *Rethinking Rights-Based Mental Health Laws*. McSherry, B. and Weller, P. (eds.). Oxford: Hart Publishing, 2010 (pp. 357-78).

4   http://www.who.int/mental_health/mhgap/en/

5   Beyleveld, D. and Brownsword, R. (2001). *Human Dignity in Bioethics and Biolaw*. Oxford: Oxford University Press, 2001.

6   Feldman, D. *Civil Liberties and Human Rights in England and Wales* (Second Edition). Oxford: Oxford University Press, 2002.

7   Whelan, D. *Mental Health: Law and Practice*. Dublin: Round Hall, 2009.

8   Re A Ward of Court (Withholding Medical Treatment) (No. 2) [1996] 2 IR, [1995] 2 ILRM 40; p. 99.

9   *M.R. v Cathy Byrne, administrator, and Dr Fidelma Flynn, clinical director, Sligo Mental Health Services, Ballytivnan, Co. Sligo* [2007] IEHC 73; p. 14.

10 *E.H. v St. Vincent's Hospital and Ors* [2009] IESC 46; p. 12.

11 *T. O'D. v Harry Kennedy and Others* [2007] IEHC 129; p. 21.

12 Craven, C. 'Signs of paternalist approach to the mentally ill persist'. *The Irish Times*, 27 July 2009.

13 Kennedy, H. "Libertarian" groupthink not helping mentally ill'. *The Irish Times*, 12 September 2012.

14 Bowen, P. *Blackstone's Guide to the Mental Health Act* 2007. Oxford: Oxford University Press, 2007.

15 Osiatyński, W. *Human Rights and Their Limits*. Cambridge: Cambridge University Press, 2009.

16 Kelly, B.D. 'Mental health legislation and human rights in England, Wales and the Republic of Ireland'. *International Journal of Law and Psychiatry* 2011; 34: 439-54.

17 Nussbaum, M.C. 'Human functioning and social justice: In defence of Aristotelian essentialism'. *Political Theory* 1992; 20: 202-46; Nussbaum, M.C. *Women and Human Development: The Capabilities Approach*. Cambridge: Cambridge University Press, 2000; Nussbaum, M.C. *Creating Capabilities: The Human Development Approach*. Cambridge, MA: Harvard University Press, 2011.

18 Seedhouse, D. and Gallagher, A. 'Clinical ethics: Undignifying institutions'. *Journal of Medical Ethics* 2002; 28: 368-72.

19 Kelly, B.D. 'Penrose's Law in Ireland: An ecological analysis of psychiatric inpatients and prisoners'. *Irish Medical Journal* 2007; 100: 373-4; Kelly, B.D. *Hearing Voices: The History of Psychiatry in Ireland*. Dublin: Irish Academic Press, 2016.

INDEX